Author Bio

Michael R Mundy, spiritual name Taran Nam Singh, is an Australian author and spiritual mentor. This former business executive, pastor, school principal, and Dale Carnegie Instructor has spent most of his adult life exploring the commonalities of all the major religions in the world. He believes that there are universal truths in all that are compatible with each other. The most important of these being that a Divine Life Force known by different names in different religions does exist, and desires for us all a life of peace on earth and of goodwill to all mankind. That above all else, peace and love is our common calling.

Lila
The Shepherd
and The Wolf

Also by Michael R. Mundy
The Love Connection
I Will Always Love You
The Camping Conundrum

Lila
The Shepherd and The Wolf

*A story of love, lust, lies,
and loss of spiritual innocence.*

MICHAEL R MUNDY

National Library of Australia Cataloguing-in-Publication
Creator: Mundy, Michael R., author.
Title: Lila the shepherd and the wolf : a story of love, lust, lies, and loss of spiritual innocence / Michael R Mundy ; Laila Savolainen (cover design).
ISBN: 9780987622808 (paperback)
Subjects: Spiritual warfare--Fiction. Good and evil--Fiction.
Other Creators/Contributors: Savolainen, Laila Kristina, 1967-

Publishing Consultants
Design: Pickawoowoo Publishing Group
Lightning Source | Ingram (USA/UK/EUROPE/AUS)

Acknowledgement

—To my friends Trevor, Perry, Pierre, Maggie and Gerry, thank you for all of your suggestions.

To my proofreader Denise Baxter, your skill and sound advice is always so very much appreciated. Thank you for your tireless work. You are the best.

To my daughter Julianna Sexton, a precious gift to my life.

" *The present moment and everything it brings to our doorstep is all we ever really have, for yesterday is history and tomorrow is a mystery. Find the goodness in the present moment, embrace the opportunities in it for righteous outcomes and align each stage of the course of all things to the ever-loving source of all things. Do this and a peace filled conclusion to every life event is guaranteed.*

– Michael R Mundy

Lila
The Divine
Playground

PROLOGUE

In the writings of the ancient seers of India, when referencing this world we human beings inhabit, the word often used was *Lila*, which when translated into English meant the Divine Playground, or the Playground of a Divine God.

They utilized this word when they spoke of the day in day out functional aspect of the universe: how things happen, why certain things happen, and the measure of spiritual oversight and Divine intervention that is involved in these events.

Not necessarily all events, but certain ones that occur as part of the changing life experiences of human beings where incidents transpire that are seemingly outside of one's own personal influence and control, and where circumstances appear that bring a specific person into one's life at the appropriate time.

The wise men taught that a Divine life force or a supernatural energy force that most people commonly refer to as God, uses the world of form and of people at specific moments in time to co-create with human beings righteous and peace filled outcomes in various situations. They believed that when people ask, "well where was God when all this happened?" they could confidently assure them: "God was there all the time, God was working through someone, you just didn't see it, believe it, or understand it."

Their conviction was that the ultimate goal of God's more often than not unrecognized participation in the affairs of mankind is to bring peace to a situation or to regain peace lost from any situation. They were adamant that this earth and everything in it was created in peace, and that the people who inhabit this earth, regardless of race or religion, are all called by their creator God to live a life of peace.

Early Christian writers aligned themselves with this Hindu philosophical and spiritual teaching with Biblical text confirming that above all else our creator has called us to peace, teaching also that a Divine Being facilitates peaceful outcomes working through the omnipotent, omnipresent and omniscient qualities of its own spiritual presence.

However the wise seers of ancient times spoke of more than this. They likened each game being played out in this Divine Playground as being like a jigsaw. In that where a situation of conflict or disconnect exists, specific people are chosen by God as pieces, and placed into the puzzle at the right time to bring about reconnection, reconciliation, and a resolution to the conflict and separation: thus creating a picture of perfect peace.

They believed that when Divine Goodness gets involved in world affairs, the entity of evil that brought about the disconnection between people is vanquished. Whether it be a disconnect between an individual and an individual, between a household and a household or between a nation and a nation, they were assured in their minds that the completion of each jigsaw would evidence the success of the prevailing power of goodness over evil.

They further taught that all of us in our earthly walk will be selected, perhaps many times, to be pieces in a puzzle, part of a game, and that our actions and involvement play a significant and absolutely vital part in the successful righteous outcome of each game. We are all conscripted creative co-workers with a Divine Life Force in the propagation of peace on earth and all participants will be rewarded: for blessed are the peacemakers.

They spoke of this universe as a plaything for Divinity's pleasure and purpose alone, and were certain above all else that human beings are intentionally and sometimes unknowingly stakeholders, chosen by this Divine energy force to be a co-contributor in whatever game God desires them to be involved in.

Now most human beings at some stage in their life will mentally seek out further understanding of why they have been put here on this earth. Questions sometime arise when people either contemplate their current life situation, particularly if it seems boring and meaningless, or think about their own personal life trajectory over a period of time, which may have given them a sense of failure.

"What reason if any is the higher purpose for my being here?"

"Is this all there is to life?"

"I get up, I go to work, and I come home."

"I then eat, and I sleep to enable me to have enough strength to do the same thing the next day."

"Is this what my life was meant to be about?"

"To work hard, to make a good living so that I can enjoy more things along the way and then get to die more comfortably…and that's it."

This type of mental ruminating will lead some individuals to act out their lives as a type of sporting challenge: a tenuous competitive struggle for the ball against what seems like insurmountable opposition, trying to get possession of that one elusive ball in the competition, the ball called happiness. Is there anything more?

The seers of ancient India believed that there was more, much more, hence the concept of Lila. They pointed back to the beginning of time, a time of darkness upon the earth, when the only thing that existed was a Divine energy force, omniscient, omnipotent, and omnipresent: knowing everything, all-powerful, and present in all places at the same time. However it was a life force that was quietly bored in its own existence, for even though it had all and was all it hungered for the pleasure that could be obtained from the successful completion of a new creative experience.

They told of a force that having acknowledged the darkness and emptiness surrounding itself began creating things of form. A world that was once void and in darkness was creatively populated with light, with objects of material matter, and with a multitude of evident life forms that became known as nature: plants and animals.

But then, still feeling a measure of personal aloneness the energy force decided to create a different type of form: form it could communicate with directly, have companionship with and co-create with, which resulted in the manifestation of an interesting and peculiar set of inhabitants on the earth called homosapiens.

These homosapiens or human beings were an entirely different object of form, created in God's spiritual image, but not physically eternal, and like all other form subject to Divinity's own earthly Law of Impermanence. They were beings that were distinguishable from every other life form in that they possessed a Soul, a receptacle for Divine communication, had superior mental development, emotional capabilities, power of articulate speech, and upright stance. They were beings that could be easily used as co-creators in the ongoing manifestation of activity in this the Divine Playground.

Historical records tell us that similar Lila type teachings also pervaded the early Christian culture. Ancient manuscripts would tell us that God created all things, created human beings in his own eternal image, and that everything was created for God's own pleasure.

So we have two major religions, Hinduism and Christianity, supposedly at opposite ends of the spiritual and societal spectrum, both purporting that life is a series of Divine games: pleasure games continuously directed by this force that watches intently as each human being either struggles against or cooperates with the various moves being brought into play by it.

In commenting about this, the famed philosopher and psychologist William James wrote that by opening ourselves to Divine influence in these games of life, our destiny, and our true purpose for being here will be fulfilled. He was convinced that the universe and those parts of it which our personal being constitute takes a turn genuinely for the better or for the worse as each one of us fulfills or evades God's demands.

However whilst ancient writings told how from the one life force everything physical and emotional was formed, they also taught that along with this every spiritual polar opposite similarly appeared to create the competition and to enhance the game. Thus was revealed what you might call the devil in the detail, with evil forces, entities, choosing through self-will to participate in each game. Now you really had a competition for peace and happiness. It became primarily a spiritual warfare in the heavens being played out as a physical and emotional warfare here on earth.

These were Spirit forces, originally created to be the servants of Goodness, who of their own volition chose to rebel against Divine Goodness and embrace the character qualities of their leader Lucifer, the qualities of evil. Sometimes known as fallen angels, they promoted self-realization and self-determination for all human beings, or secular humanism, as it became known, rather than the natural unfolding of a human being's destiny through co-operation with and allegiance to the supreme creator.

They emerged with the sole intent of getting possession of the ball and producing an illusionary happiness in people's lives and a false sense of peace mostly based on material things rather than spiritual things. In doing so their main goal was to hinder the righteous outcome of each game, thus stifling any true peace that comes out of connection and co-operation between human beings and Divinity: the peace that passes all understanding.

So now in every game we find a host of spiritual forces influencing and sometimes totally controlling people's behaviours and actions, as human beings born with a free will discover they have freedom of choice: freedom to choose to respond to the promptings of goodness or of evil, of righteousness or unrighteousness, of rightness or wrongness, or as Biblical text expresses it, to choose life or death.

There would be no excuses however for choosing unrighteousness.

For spiritual records would also evidence that an understanding of the difference between right and wrong, righteousness and unrighteousness, had been imprinted in the hearts of all men and women, and communicated to every individual intuitively in every situation through the voice of conscience as it became known, residing in the Soul.

And so it happened that evil spiritual forces were activated in this warfare striving against angelic warriors for the cooperation and allegiance of all human beings. When the Angel of Courage motivated someone to press on the Spirit of Fear and Doubt came to dissuade him or her and when the Angel of Compassion impacted on an individual or a group's behaviour, so the Spirit of Indifference rose up in others to balance its positive effect.

As the Angel of Truth expressed itself in situations so the Spirit of Lies and the Spirit of Deception came to stifle the message. The Spirit of Hatred infiltrated into ideological discussion to try to extinguish the Angel of Love.

With the arrival of the Angel of Wisdom came the Spirit of Folly to suppress it, and when the Angel of Knowledge appeared to proclaim truth and understanding, the Spirit of Ignorance rose up to contain it.

A galaxy of competitive warring emotional energy forces, angels and demons, all polar opposites, came into play in each game. They were spiritual forces sent forth from a battle station in heavenly places having allegiance either to their fellow angelic warriors of Christ and the characteristics of Goodness or to the spiritual forces of Lucifer and the characteristics of evil.

⸺⸺

So what is this struggle that we call life all about?
It is simply this, that in this Divine Playground we call the universe, in Lila, the eternal life force of Goodness encourages individual participants in specific circumstances to make the righteous and ethical

choice: to choose to do what is right, to choose to do the righteous thing.

To choose in all of life's situations to embrace and live out our own inbuilt Divine characteristics, our own Divine Nature, one of integrity and righteousness, and in doing so come to the realization of our own personal destiny and the fulfillment of the primary Divine purpose for our being here on earth: to be an instrument of peace.

In every Divine game there are human players and there are two polar opposite spiritual players: angelic beings and evil entities. Human participants will choose either to align themselves with Goodness or conversely choose not to co-operate with Goodness and allow evil to triumph: a principle best summed up by the British statesman Edmund Burke, who many years ago said that all that is necessary for the triumph of evil is for good men to do nothing.

The wise men of old knew and understood that mankind is primarily involved in a spiritual warfare which translates on earth into the physical war we see broadcast daily on our televisions. We wrestle not against flesh and blood they said, but against the rulers of wickedness in high places.

So don't sweat the small stuff…life is just a multitude of spiritual games in one big Divine Playground. The present moment and everything it brings to our doorstep is all we ever really have, for yesterday is history and tomorrow is a mystery.

Find the goodness in the present moment, embrace the opportunities in it for righteous outcomes and align each stage of the course of all things to the ever-loving source of all things. Do this and a peace filled conclusion to every life event is guaranteed.

Every human being will be chosen to participate in one or more spiritual war games, maybe momentous maybe minor, as his or her life journey progresses. Every person will become a player in the games that occur daily in Lila.

Embrace your opportunity to co-create with Divinity righteous outcomes in every difficulty you encounter in life and in doing so become the instrument of peace you were called to be and a practical expression of the angels cry, peace on earth and goodwill to all mankind.

The Game Players

The Two Entities	Goodness and Evil
The Shepherd	Michael Winton
The Wolf	Garret Sloan
The Wife	Bettina Sloan
The Friend	Cherie Goldway
The Minder	Thorpey Goldway
The Schoolteacher	Archie Vernados
The English Hippies	Jeff and Janet Gibbons
The Gypsy Neighbours	Daniel and Zelda Westwood
The Beekeepers	Bernie and Helga Eagleton
The Realtor	Patty Patel
The Specialist	Dr Unwin Nicholls
The G.P.	Dr Margie Morrison
The G.P.'s Sister	Dr Francis Morrison
The Former Model	Capricia Rossi
The Bookstore Manager	Colleen Jones
The Tourist Park Owners	George and Jenny Purcell
The Daughter	Kelly Purcell
The Senior Minister	Rev Terry Channing
The Reverend	William Hawkesbury
The Restaurant Owner	Morty Mortensen
The Donors	Ian and Evelyn Robinson

Contents

Michael Winton

ONE

The word loss is an interesting word, short and succinct in itself, but long chronographically and expansive emotionally in its practical outworking. Most people define loss differently according to their own particular personal life experience with it. Michael Winton in thinking back on his own encounter with loss would describe it as having someone leave or be taken away from you, and of being left with strong feelings of grief when that special someone had gone from your life forever.

Archie too had her own personal understanding of loss, and whilst it was of similar definition to his and comparably tinged with the same emotions of sadness, regret and grief, hers was significantly far more poetic. She had shared it with him on a few occasions, the final time being on that emotional last night they were together.

Her words had come from the romantic writings of the poet William Wordsworth from an ode he had written in 1888 as he reflected on his younger days. In that lyrical poem, in one simple but beautiful verse, he had described the time of the relationship, the person involved, the loss itself, and his process of dealing with that loss.

The time of the relationship had been portrayed as the hour of splendor in the grass and of glory in the flower. The person and the loss were described as the radiance and brightness taken forever from his sight. And how he had dealt with that loss was expressed as a process of gaining strength to go on by remembering the wonderful memories of that time.

Archie had shared the writer's beautiful poetic words with Michael for the final time as they sat together sipping wine on the balcony of his hilltop beachside apartment, late on that Saturday evening in July 1973. That was the last time he saw her.

September 1994.

It was nearing late afternoon on a Friday in September as Michael wound his car window down. The onset of dusk was imminent and the fresh fragrance of the spring's seasonal new growth could be smelt periodically in the air. Moving shadows were beginning to form across the landscape signalling the impending approach of day's end.

As his car slowly wound its way along the highway that snaked through the rolling hills and deep valleys of the countryside, he reflected on a time in his life, some twenty five years prior, when he had caught his first glimpse of this environmental masterpiece.

Visually it was a stunningly beautiful region: long green stretches of lush farming land, with mile after mile of undulating emerald knolls and dales bordered to the east by the stunning aqua blue waters of the Pacific Ocean. A region sparsely dotted with sprawling farmhouse properties that to the naked eye as one drove past were recognizable only as black specks, tiny dots midst the mass of greenery in the valleys far below the road.

But not only was the area visually spectacular it was also a thriving prosperous part of the local economy as well. The soil was richly fertile and as such it was ideal for crop farming, as well as the growing of fodder to support a burgeoning sheep and dairy cattle industry. Notwithstanding this, the abundance of marine life in the surrounding sea had over the decades since first settlement spawned a bustling fishing and trawling industry, which complemented the huge variety of agricultural opportunities in the district.

Almost reverently and with no pre-thought Michael slowed his car down, pulling it over to the side of the highway, deliberately positioning its park so as to give himself maximum viewing space of the scattered cloud shadowed valleys below.

Michael had been a meditator for many years. He loved walking along deserted beaches as the sun rose, and sitting in the late afternoons watching that same sun morph back into the darkness of the night. He enjoyed taking time out to meditate whilst strolling through bushland enjoying the beauty of nature. He was aware of the immediate benefits of meditative mindfulness on the physical body and on the mind. He knew that just to sit and meditate on this view, even for a short time, would substantially refresh him.

Something startled him and he turned his head to the left. An unexpected movement accompanied by a rustling sound had suddenly interrupted his anticipated reverie. It seemed to be emanating from the dry undergrowth just beyond the fence line, about 25 metres from where he was parked. Curiosity getting the better of him and moving slowly and quietly he stepped out of the car. His eyes simultaneously searched beyond the small grassy knoll across from him, trying to ascertain what this movement and noise might have been.

Without warning a small head appeared from the bush and looked around, almost nervously, investigating its surroundings. Its stiff legged posture gave an indication that it was in full alert mode for anything or anyone that would interfere with its present moment situation or perhaps its intended course of action.

Michael was puzzled. What was it? It was a wolf like animal he thought, or maybe even a wild dog or a large dingo cross. It had thick grey streaked hair with faded cream tips, and stood about sixty centimetres high. He had remembered reading once that a wolf has a bulky coat consisting of two layers. The undercoat was usually grey, regardless of the colour of the outer coat, with the outer coat made up of tough guard hairs to repel the water and dirt.

Couldn't be a wolf he thought. Can't remember a wolf ever being sighted around here. But then again, this did look like a wolf.

He moved slowly closer. The animal was standing silent, erect and tall, with an arrogant bodily manner. Its ears were upright and forward as if intently listening, with the hackles on its outer coat bristling slightly in what Michael saw as a stance of mistrust. It was in control of the moment and its intention was set. Nothing would take that power away from it no matter what the cost.

It remained in this position for only a few minutes and then suddenly in the next instant, perhaps sensing Michael's presence, as quickly as it had appeared, it was gone. It swiftly disappeared back into the undergrowth to continue its undertaking, whatever that might be.

Maybe it was on a mission to cause harm to one of those innocent looking sheep quietly grazing in the late afternoon shadows below Michael thought. He wasn't really sure. But the one thing he did know was that something about this situation wasn't quite right. This animal, which appeared on the scene seemingly out of nowhere, had the look, attitude, and the mannerism of a predator.

Heading back to the car he slumped back into the comfortableness of the car seat, resting his neck on the headrest support and closing his eyes. Thoughts of his youth, recollections of his mother Rose, and reflections on his early childhood flashed across his mind as they had habitually done so over the years whenever he had shut his eyes to rest. There were always so many unanswered questions.

As his thinking began free flowing into a smorgasbord of memories, he recalled that in growing up he had lived constantly with the feeling that there was something not quite right in the family he was born into. It was a feeling that continued as he passed through his teenage years into early adulthood, but as a young man he was never able to ascertain what caused this ongoing mental disquiet.

All he knew was that the joy and excitement that came with personal success was always short lived, and sometimes ended up clothed in an overcoat of emptiness. He would feel that something in his life, perhaps his true purpose for being here on earth, just seemed to be reluctant in its unfolding.

He thought about his mother Rose, now in her twilight years, 88 years of age, and how life would not have been easy for her having the responsibility of raising eight children. But the Rose he remembered never seemed to display, neither in attitude nor in word, any of the inner anxiousness or uncertainty that she must certainly have been feeling as dramas involving her growing children surfaced daily on her doorstep.

As a loving mother she always went about her time diligently, patiently dealing with the traumas and tantrums that continually arose, as five boys and three girls under the same roof interacted and argued their way into adulthood.

Rose's only respite came on Sunday mornings when she would put on her best dress and hat and walk by herself the short distance to the local Baptist church, gradually distancing herself from the chatter of the older children bickering and debating as to who was to be in charge in her absence.

The minister at the church, the Reverend Gray A. Parker was of a grandfatherly type, an elderly white haired well dressed dapper man, with a kind and gentle nature. Michael recalled the Reverend's monthly visits to their family home for afternoon tea with Rose; a cup of tea, an orange slice biscuit and a chat. It was during these times, as they came home from school, that Rose would quickly relegate the siblings to the backyard to play. She wanted her privacy for whatever reason.

But he also remembered the occasional times when on arriving home from school and walking down the hallway beside the sitting room, he would see his mother wiping tears from her eyes with her handkerchief, as the minister with his hand on her shoulder quietly prayed. He had always wondered why she was crying, and over the years was plagued with feelings of regret that he had not asked her about this whilst she was still in full control of her memory and all her mental faculties.

Rose Winton was a Godly woman. Her ancestors before her and

their descendants were all hard working country folk with farming backgrounds. Her grandparents had emigrated from Britain before the Great War. She was born in 1906 and raised in a dairy farming and gold mining district in a town named Boxborough in the country's north.

It was a time when the nearest emerging city to Boxborough, and a sure place to source farm supplies, was a full dawn to dusk, dusty, dirty, horse and wagon ride for two hundred kilometres on unsealed roads. Her family was at the time considered both affluent and influential in the township, owning considerable pastoral interests as well as the local hotel. Her older brother Arthur worked in the Shire Council and had leverage in local government activity.

Rose was the only daughter of her mother May, but unfortunately for Rose May gave more attention to and took more pride in the achievements of her three brothers, in particular her brother Arthur. Any of Rose's accomplishments just didn't seem to be worthy of family discussion in May's eyes or so it seemed.

This attitude over time fostered seeds of rebellion in Rose, which eventually sprouted, seeing her whilst in her early twenties falling pregnant, and against her mother's wishes, marrying a British immigrant of questionable means, one William Winton. Rose had met William Winton at the local Saturday night country barn dance.

William was a whiskey drinking, cigarette smoking man with a reputation for being a philanderer: a man who her ofttimes critical mother was quick to express was a person of dubious character and one who carried with him what she described as his own particular clandestine family history. But she never shared what she knew.

Rose had married him to avoid the scandal that always surrounded pregnant young single women in the day. It would be six months after their shotgun wedding as they were called in those times that she gave birth to her first child, a daughter Maggie May. Maggie May was the sister that Michael never really knew because prior to his birth when she was just a tender twelve years of age, Rose and Maggie boarded the train heading from the city to Boxborough and Rose returned alone.

Maggie May had been taken to her grandparents' home in the country to live with them and be raised by them, and none of her siblings in the years to come were ever told why. It was another unresolved issue and unanswered question for Michael.

Michael would see Maggie May occasionally over the years when in her adulthood she would periodically call in to the family home in the city. He remembered his oldest sister as being very pretty and extremely kind natured. She would always bring sweets for he and his sister Elizabeth on these infrequent visits. However he would discover even more about her on an occasional school holiday excursion to his grandmother's house.

After Maggie started work as a nursing sister and had moved out of her grandmother May's home, personal items of her childhood had sat motionless, gathering dust, locked in a time warp in various corners of the lounge room in Boxborough for many many years. You see Grandmother May was a hoarder; she never threw anything out including Maggie's stuff.

A piano accordion Maggie had played as a teenager, photos including those of her at her debutante ball, a 3D viewer of the day, a Martha doll, and Maggie's first record player. Michael discovered them all tucked away in boxes in the dark atmosphere of a lounge room that was seemingly never used by the residents and certainly deemed off limits during the grandchildren's holiday visits.

As a young boy Michael would use the absence of his grandmother from the home having gone to the local store, to snoop around, trying to gain further understanding about his sister and about his family history. It would be during one of those voyages of discovery that Michael found something that fascinated him more than anything else. It was a vinyl long play record, tucked away in a box of piano sheet music and gathering dust in a cobwebbed corner of the lounge room beside the sofa.

As he slowly removed the record from its cover and looked at the circular label in its centre, he was fascinated to see that it read RCA Victor, The Tennessee Waltz, written by Pee Wee King, sung by Maggie May Winton. He had known that Maggie May was gifted at playing the piano accordion, but was not aware what a beautiful singer she was too and that she had made a record. He wished he had known her better.

He reflected on the circumstances of his own birth and his relationship with his mother. He recalled how in his formative years in many sibling arguments his mother would take his side; perhaps he rationalized because he was the youngest. This would then subject him to the taunts of his older siblings crying out pet…pet.

It would be during one of those times on a Sunday morning when he was around eight years of age that his mother, seeing him distressed with the teasing, had sat him on her knee on the verandah and explained to him the story surrounding his birth.

She was forty-two years of age when she fell pregnant with Michael and was advised by her doctor to have the pregnancy terminated. In those days it was considered dangerous to both the mother and child for a woman over forty years of age to give birth.

On the day before she was due to visit the clinic for the termination she started to have second thoughts and so sought out advice from the Reverend Gray A. Parker. He advised her to follow her heart, calling it that little voice inside her head silently speaking to her. He had confirmed to Rose what she had already been thinking, and so she followed her heart and continued the pregnancy.

She had named him Michael after the angel Michael, one of the seven archangels in the Bible, the only one who is named in the Bible, and the one recognized as the conqueror of Satan. She knew that the name Michael meant gift from God.

Michael had never forgotten that as she finished telling him this she kissed him on the forehead and said, "that's why I love you Mikey, best in the world. You were meant to be here for a reason." It was a phrase he would hear repeated from his mother many times on his journey from childhood and through his teenage years: "I love you Mikey… best in the world."

As he sat quietly looking at the view, reminiscing, he thought about how his upbringing had been so vastly different from Rose's and in a way probably so much more fun. Whilst her after school activities involved helping with the milking and various other farm chores, his was as far away from work as possible.

He had grown up in the city and lived there all his formative years into early adulthood. Raised in suburbia as it was called, the family lived in a sprawling wooden house with a huge fully enclosed louvre windowed verandah, and a corrugated iron roof that created a wonderful feeling of cosiness when the heavy rain beat down on it during the summer storm season.

There were a couple of dozen houses opposite each other in the street where he lived, each bordered on all sides by painted wooden paling or wire fences that reached to no more than shoulder height, fostering friendly neighbourly communication. Everyone was always ready to lean over the fence and have a chat if they spotted their neighbour hosing the garden.

Bordering the back boundary of their home was a creek, or brook as it was called, which the neighbourhood boys visited regularly in search of tadpoles. The property had a huge backyard featuring a giant mango tree supporting a makeshift cubby house in the centre, and on the side a swing with an old car tyre attached: both constructed by a couple of the siblings during the boredom of the latter part of their Christmas school holiday break.

The rest of the yard was dotted with a variety of different types of fruit trees and a watermelon patch, the favourite at Christmastime. At the rear of all of this was a chicken coop or chook house as it was called: a purple flowered vine covered enclosure with a makeshift wire fence surrounding it, tucked away in the back corner of the yard, contributing solely to the family's weekly supply of eggs. The chickens themselves all held a not to be eaten under any circumstance status.

The house was owned by Rose's brother Arthur, a man who had become very adept at snapping up bargain priced properties when they came on the market, not only in his hometown but also in the city due to inside information he was able to garner from his contacts in the State Lands Department.

After purchasing this property, and as a result of his mother May's insistence, Arthur had rented the house to Rose and her family in what could only be described as a generous arrangement: no contract and a very small, monthly financial consideration. Michael's grandmother had no faith in Rose's husband William to be able to provide financially for the growing family in a consistent manner. To Michael's mind in looking back she was right.

William was a man of inconsistent behaviour and of strange contradictions. He had passed away when Michael was ten years of age, and amongst Michael's memories of him gleaned from his own mental archives, there were none that indicated a close active father son relationship, as one would normally expect.

There was no involvement or interest from him in any everyday activities like school homework or school sporting events. Rather the extreme opposite. Michael could not recall any meaningful conversations they ever had and could not remember any demonstration of affection occurring between the two of them.

The only physical contact that took place between them was when as a little boy Michael's chore was to sit under the dining table and clean his father's shoes each morning as William sat eating his breakfast and reading the newspaper. The only social contact was the occasional visit to the factory he owned on a Sunday afternoon with his sister Elizabeth.

Years later as an adult when asked the question as to how he had felt on the morning of his father's passing, him being only ten years of age, Michael could only describe the feeling as one of nothingness, with a sort of quiet relief. Although he did remember in the years shortly after William's passing having feelings of isolation when his mates at primary school would talk about their own fathers.

At the time he wasn't sure why he felt that way, why he felt the nothingness on the morning of his father's passing. But years later he would come to believe that perhaps the quiet relief he felt was subconsciously related to the many secrets about William's character that remained frustratingly unanswered, before and after his passing.

The few memories that Michael did have of William Winton were of him being a distant man with his activities in his work and his family history shrouded in a curious type of secrecy and mystery. The story was that he had emigrated from Britain by boat as a sixteen year old and on arrival in the country found work as a farm labourer. But his family history was always a closed book save for a faded photograph supposedly of his mother and brother that was produced by Rose whenever the subject of William Winton's family was raised by any of the siblings.

By occupation he described himself as an Industrial Chemist but carried with him no printed evidence of his academic achievements. It was believed that he held several jobs in his lifetime, however during the time of Michael's childhood William was self-employed, jointly owning a small non-descript company named Industrial Chemicals, his partner being a largely proportioned, arrogant natured, bad tempered doctor named Herbert Aloysius Nothling.

Michael recalled that William and Dr Nothling rented a small factory warehouse about thirty minutes drive from the family home. It was here that they produced and packaged what was purported to be a new easy to apply revolutionary product that William had invented, and whose research Dr Nothling had financed.

The product was to be used for repairing corrosive rust holes in cars, household saucepans and frypans, or any other iron or steel object. It was a thick liquid solution that when applied to a metal product for repair purposes immediately hardened. They had named this product plastic steel.

Their partnership was a fragile one laced with secrecy and mistrust and Michael remembered the time it finally fractured. He was home from school on the day and had witnessed Dr Nothling, who to him as a child seemed a large and scary man, storming up the front stairs of their house in William's absence.

He had violently pushed the front double doors at the top of the steps open, and in an angry and threatening manner demanded of Rose the written formula for plastic steel that William had kept hidden from him all the time of their business association. Michael couldn't remember whether Rose had given it to him, but he thought not.

However it was the factory itself that became for Michael over the years the source of some of his most puzzling and unanswered memories of his father. He recalled visiting the factory at various times with his closest sibling his sister Elizabeth who was eighteen months older than he. He remembered a middle-aged lady who lived by herself in a house next door to it. His father would pop in and visit her on occasions whilst he and his sister were left to amuse themselves on the factory floor.

He could recollect as a seven year old he and Elizabeth being taken by their father to the factory on the occasional Sunday afternoon. It would be at these times that his father would lift him up to sit on what he remembered as a huge high factory work bench that he was unable to get down from without help. He would then be given the job of placing labels on the cans of plastic steel.

He recalled that Elizabeth would then be allocated the task of tidying his father's office at the far end of the warehouse. Michael was always glad when his father and Elizabeth emerged from the office as it meant he would be lifted down off the workbench, as both the plastic steel and the glue from the labels had a strong uncomfortable chemical smell about them.

It also meant that he and Elizabeth would be able to play 'I spy' during the drive home in the back of the Vauxhall Ute. "I spy…with my little eye…something beginning with?"

Sitting in the peacefulness quietly thinking, he acknowledged in his mind that regardless of any dysfunction in the family due to his father's distant behaviour, it was solely due to his mother Rose that his overall suburban life was one of perceived safety and of wonderful memories.

He had grown up under her guidance cultivating a love of adventure and romance. He was self-fed by his insatiable appetite to read books and to see movies: particularly those that had a hero and a villain as the two main characters, and of course the love interest of the hero as the other main character. These were the genre, the type of movies and books that he loved visiting.

At school Michael would be seen pushing his way to the front of the class queue lined up at the school library door for the students monthly selection of a library book. He knew he had to be one of the first in line to ensure he got his choice of the limited supply of The Famous Five or The Secret Seven adventure series of books by the famous author of the day Enid Blyton.

He marvelled at the works of authors such as Charles Dickens and Jane Austen, all of which were filled with the type of main characters he loved, once again the hero, the villain, and of course the woman who was the love of the hero's life. At eleven years of age after visiting the local cinema and seeing the movie A Tale of Two Cities based on a book by Charles Dickens, he raced home and pleaded with his mother to buy him the book.

When she did he read it three times, even memorizing passages such as greater love has no man than this that a man lay down his life for his friends. He loved the excitement, the adventure, and he loved the themes of love, loss, sadness and eventual triumph embedded in the story of this type of movie or book.

But apart from that there were so many personal activities that appeared to make the family home and his first sixteen years growing up in it seem a time of joyous spontaneity and normality. There was the ritual game of backyard cricket each afternoon after school, alternated with visits to the creek out the back with his mate Ronnie to catch tadpoles and put them in a jar.

With the approach of spring and the warmer weather the neighbourhood girls could be seen sitting on the grass covered footpath, threading the stems of clover flowers to see who was able to make the longest clover flower necklace. Simultaneously the neighbourhood boys busied themselves swapping comics with each other as they sat on the front steps of the house.

Then there were the occasional times when Michael's successful bartering of comics would be interrupted by the voice of his mother calling out for him to come and get a cake to deliver to Mrs Stanton who lived up the hill not far past the Baptist Church. But Michael didn't mind being separated from his comic swapping mates. He liked Mrs Stanton.

Nell Stanton was a good friend and confidante of Rose, who Rose had met at the Baptist Church Women's Guild they both attended, and it was always Michael's job to deliver the tea towel wrapped fruit cake to her after Rose's monthly bake up. She was a kindly lady and on one of Michael's trips to her house when he was around eight years of age she had given him a gift, his first spiritual book.

It was a small book that he carried with him all those years as he grew into adulthood and he read it often: a small black leather covered New Testament with a handwritten inscription on the inside cover, "trust in the Lord with all thine heart and lean not to thine own understanding, in all thy ways acknowledge him and he shall direct your paths." And she had signed it, your friend Nell Stanton.

Weekends would see bike races up and down the street outside their house, much to the delight of the family dog Ricky who could always be seen excitedly joining in the fun, crouching down and yapping and biting at passing car tyres, ambushing unwary motorists as they drove by. And of course he had never forgotten the annual ritual every November 5th called Guy Fawkes Night, which was by coincidence his sister Elizabeth's birthday. Also known as Bonfire or Cracker Night it contributed immensely to his happy childhood memories. Guy Fawkes Night was an annual English tradition hundreds of years old, which was also celebrated in other British Colonies.

The historical basis for the night came from events that occurred in London in 1605. It was when a man named Guy Fawkes, a member of a group known as the Gunpowder Plotters, was arrested while guarding a pile of explosives that the plotters had placed beneath the Parliament House in London in an attempt to blow it up and kill King James 1.

In celebrating the fact that King James had survived the attempt on his life, the citizens of London lit bonfires around the city. Months later an Act of Parliament was introduced called the Observance of the 5th November Act which enforced an annual public day of thanksgiving for the plot's failure.

This then grew over the centuries to a suburban social celebration. Bonfires were built months ahead at local parks, and then lit up on the night, whilst families gathered in their backyards to set off a huge variety of firecrackers, which were readily available for purchase at the local corner store.

But for Michael and his neighbourhood mates, the highlight of the evening would be when under cover of darkness and the noisy sound of firecrackers, armed with pocketfuls of three-penny bungers as they were called, they would sneak off to neighbouring houses in surrounding streets. The intent was to blow the lids off as many tin letterboxes as they could and then disappear giggling into the darkness.

He recollected that in his emerging teenage years he was a loner of types and enjoyed his own company. From the age of eight years Saturday afternoons would see him walk half a mile to the local picture theatre for the afternoon matinee viewing. Arriving early he could be seen standing outside the front of the theatre alongside four or five like-minded pre-pubescent boys, all lined up one hour early so as to be first in line at the ticket box when the doors of the theatre opened.

There was of course an entrepreneurial strategy behind them arriving early. As soon as the doors were opened the first half dozen in the queue would buy their ticket, race inside, crouch down, and peer under each row of seats to ascertain where patrons from the previous evening session had abandoned their empty coke bottles.

Scooping up as many bottles as they could carry they would rush to the kiosk for the three-penny refund per bottle and use the proceeds to buy themselves refreshments for the viewing, which for Michael were more often than not a container of candied popcorn and a packet of Wrigley's juicy fruit chewing gum.

The boys had discovered that there was only a small window of opportunity between when the theatre manager opened the doors, gave the lady in the ticket booth some help with the initial rush, and then proceeded himself into the theatre to keep an eye on things. They had to be fleet of foot and determined in heart to scoop up as many bottles as they could before the keeper of order, the theatre manager, swooped on the would be scavengers and with a stern warning confiscated their booty.

But it was not just about the booty. Michael grew up loving the finery of his local picture theatre. The luxurious heavy red velvet curtains covering the screen gave the theatre an aura of majesty, causing people to hush their voices as they entered. Visually these curtains seemed to him to be almost in a way demanding that people be on their best behaviour.

And of course there were those stately uniformed men and women who not only escorted you to your seats, but spent the rest of their time keeping their eyes out for miscreants attempting to sneak in without paying. They were the self-appointed guardians of behaviour who were quick to shine their torch and 'shhh' folks who talked during the movie.

More than this though they seemed to get some sort of righteous pleasure out of focussing this ever-present long handled flashlight on the large proportion of teenagers ensconced in the brown canvas seats at the front of the theatre. It was of course done in an attempt to catch some poor pimpled highly hormone charged teenage boy attempting to explore the lips of his female companion at a particular time when the glow of the screen was illuminating the theatre the least. These were innocent times.

Michael grew to love this weekly event with the movies themselves impacting intensely on the formation of his cultural and musical likes and dislikes and the growth and direction of his spiritual life and his sense of adventure. The movies of the fifties and early sixties were a smorgasbord of creativity and excitement, with musicals like Guys and Dolls, Oklahoma, and of course Elvis in Blue Hawaii, and adventure movies like High Noon, Ben-Hur, and Gunfight at The OK Corral, where the good guys always won in the end.

Saturday afternoons had become for Michael a wonderful escape from the present and an imaginative glimpse of a world that he could grow up into where goodness would always eventually triumph over evil. However it was a movie that he saw shortly after his father passed that had a significant impact on him: a movie that he later came to realize was pivotal in defining his destiny. It was an exciting but at the end deeply sad movie titled A Man Called Peter.

The movie told the true story of a humble Scotsman, Peter Marshall, who attributed a narrow brush with death to divine intervention. Because of this he immigrated to the United States, studied for the Christian ministry, became a successful preacher and author, and grew to national renown when he became the youngest man to ever be appointed as Chaplain of the U.S. Senate. He had then died at the age of 46 years having fulfilled what he saw as his divine destiny.

The timing of the movie was only a few weeks before Michael's eleventh birthday and he remembered talking about the movie with his mother on his return from the theatre. It was only natural then that shortly before his birthday, when Rose asked Michael what he would like for his present as she did with all the siblings, he told her he would like a book written by a woman named Catherine Marshall. It was a book titled A Man Called Peter.

He recalled that this movie was the catalyst which saw him some four years later, at the age of 14 years, with his mother's blessing, walk to the nearest tram stop, board a tramcar, and head off to the city showground where, along with thousands of others, he attended a meeting conducted by the world famous Baptist evangelist Billy Graham during his first visit to the country.

His mother liked the fact that he was heading off to the meeting on his own and of his own volition. She had always fostered any kind of spiritual activity in the children, but since she did not get much response from the older siblings, her concentration was always firmly on Michael and Elizabeth. During their pre-teen years Sunday morning would see Rose fastidiously bundle off a bow-tied Mikey and a pretty frilly-frocked Elizabeth to the Baptist Church for their weekly Sunday School class.

It was at the end of Dr Graham's sermon as the choir sang the hymn Just As I Am, and as Billy Graham asked the question that he had become famous for at the end of each of his meetings, "Will you come, will you come?" that Michael had leapt up from his seat in the grandstand and walked the 100 metres to the preacher's platform in the centre of the arena.

As Peter Marshall's own spiritual journey was initiated after a narrow brush with death, Michael would later wonder whether this, his first spiritual experience, was borne out of his subconscious contemplation on his own brush with death prior to his birth, as told to him when he sat on his mother Rose's knee that rainy Sunday morning.

—∞—

The loud sound of a trucker's horn warning motorists of its descent around a tricky bend in the road near where Michael was parked jolted him out of his childhood reverie. He realized it was time to get moving and to continue his journey. He thought back to the wolf-like animal he had witnessed in the undergrowth some twenty minutes prior. That old saying 'a wolf in sheep's clothing' crept silently into his mind as he drove off.

He was now thinking of people and incidents all long since passed that had occurred in this region all those years ago. It had been a special time for Michael, when all the pieces of his life seemed to be falling almost without effort into place. He had a good job, many like-minded friends, and his long held spiritual hopes and hippie lifestyle dreams were all starting to come together.

A comparison between that time and what he had just witnessed with the wolf like animal caused him to consider those years for a moment, the good and the bad of them, all now firmly locked away in his memory bank. Those memories also involved a wolf, but it was a wolf of the human kind. His name was Garret Sloan, an itinerant Pentecostal tent preacher, a man in his early fifties, a charismatic man: a man who on first impression convinced most people that he possessed the character traits of a spiritual man, a true shepherd of the congregational flock so to speak.

He appeared selfless, compassionate, and kind, with a caring attitude and a genuine interest in the spiritual and emotional well being of those around him. However it was only after a set period of time and a series of events that the truth of Garret's inner nature came to be revealed, a truth totally opposite to his outward behaviour. Garret Sloan was a man with the outward mannerisms of a shepherd, but with the dark predatory inner nature of a wolf.

He was a person who would outwardly feign God dependence but in truth was totally self-reliant: a man who was very deft in uncovering as much information as possible about a person's life, and once discerning their vulnerabilities, cunningly exploiting them for his own personal benefit: a man with a spirit of evil lurking in every shadow he cast and in every secret deed he undertook. The real Garret Sloan was not a shepherd, but a wolf in shepherd's clothing.

It was a beautiful blue-skied balmy late afternoon in spring and Michael was on an expedition to the past: a mission overflowing with thoughts of a life long since gone, and filled with memories of love and betrayal, of courage and cowardice, and of goodness triumphing over evil. He was working his way back to the beautiful village of Springfield and would soon be there.

As his car slowly curled its way around the final set of hills reaching the last outlook, the township came into sight in the valley below. Here it was again, seemingly ageless, gently snuggled down in its lush surrounds, lovingly embraced in a blanket of eternal greenery as if in a deep sleep. On its eastern outer perimeter sat Lighthouse Bay, the small riverside fishing village and port that complemented Springfield, flattening out as it stretched forward to the beautiful blue waters of the ocean.

It was around twenty-five years previously that Michael had first experienced this view, his first trip to the village, and the question as to why he was returning now all these years later quietly intrigued him.

Was he seeking some sort of emotional or spiritual closure on those series of events in his life that had so very much shaped his ongoing destiny? Was it just a moment of madness, hoping to turn back the hands of time, to once again embrace and for a moment relive those wonderful memories of the way life was in those days? Was he trying to reconnect with a romantic ghost from the past? Or was it perhaps all three?

He glanced out his side window at the sign...Springfield 2 miles... speed limit 35 miles per hour. He drove past the Gothic Cathedral on the outskirts, past the giant pink donut in the rest area where a few excited children were getting their photos taken, and then finally into the township. He would go to the old picture theatre, the auditorium first he thought.

Michael parked his car a short distance from the theatre and walked slowly down towards it. He stood for a moment across the road opposite it and looked over, reflecting on all the hard work that had gone into its restoration all those years back.

The outside looked neglected now, sadly in need of maintenance, with the paintwork on the outer awning faded almost into oblivion as the creeping death called rust had sought to extinguish all evidence of it. The signage showing the church name on the huge facade was still visible, albeit just, and the once bright steel cables, stretching out proudly holding the awning in its state of suspension over the years, were now all covered in the dust and grime of the years passed.

The fire escape stairwell converted to a covered stairwell at the side of the building, that at the time had given access to the clinic of Dr Unwin Nicholls upstairs, was obviously no longer used. A huge iron gate, a length of chain and a padlock had been added since Michael had last climbed it on one of his many bi-monthly visits to see Unwin. If buildings could die this one was giving off the appearance of a slowly rotting corpse.

Michael remembered the neglected appearance of the building when he had visited it for his first meeting with Dr Nicholls in December 1969 as part of his role as manager of the District Farmer's Co-Operative.

In its heyday it was the only picture theatre in the town and was typical in design of the theatres of the 30's. Its original look was nothing short of grand: tall and imposing on the outside, marble floored entrance at the front where the ticket boxes and kiosk were positioned, with the inside possessing the old-fashioned elegance of its era. It was like the theatres of his childhood.

But in 1958 it had closed as an operating picture theatre giving way to progress in the form of a new cinema, constructed from modern building materials, which had opened down the road in opposition to it. The owner had been unable to compete with the clout of the corporate theatre groups and had subsequently shut the business down.

When Michael had first sighted it eleven years after its closure whilst visiting Dr Nicholls, its grandeur as the original picture theatre in the township was almost unrecognizable. The outer awning and huge facade had been painted over with black paint and a large lettered very amateurish sign had been placed across its front that read, The Markets.

He remembered that the original marble floor entrance had been covered over with a type of heavy-duty straw matting affixed to the marble with glue in an almost desecratory manner. Sticky taped posters advertising individual local events, mainly of the nightclub variety, were spasmodically positioned in an untidy way across the dust covered sliding glass doors at the street entrance to the building.

The inside walls and ceiling had been painted black and the theatre was furnished with fifty or more trestle table tops, obviously for the weekend markets, each separated by black curtaining. It was a dark place, dark in looks and in atmosphere, with cobwebs crowding every available corner where the tall walls met the ornate but heavily peeling plaster ceiling.

Destiny dared to differ however on what the townspeople over time had seen as a fait de complis, in that the theatre would remain in its present state of disrepair probably until a developer tore it down. That wasn't fate's intention.

It was in July 1971 when Michael and Dr Nicholls had stood across the road from the theatre in the same spot where Michael was now standing. It was the morning of its auction and with excitement and a sense of anticipation they had discussed its possibilities. It was the day when at 11 a.m. Michael had raised his hand in a successful bid for its purchase, not really knowing where all the money for the purchase would come from.

Within six months its deteriorating condition went into a state of remission as the builders, carpenters, painters, electricians, and a host of volunteer labourers, all members of the commune gathered together to commence restorative work. The historic building that had been neglected and discarded for so long was soon renewed and turned into a meeting place, a crèche, a bookshop and a place of worship for a group of believers who fate and destiny had magically brought together.

It was now September 1994 and Michael was once again standing across the road where some twenty-four years prior he and Unwin Nicholls had stood. However on this day, his thoughts were not of excitement and anticipation as they were back then, but rather thoughts of disappointment tinged with a type of sadness.

He walked slowly across the road and stood silently beside the now rusted and disused stairwell that once led upstairs to the medical clinic. There was a cold breeze blowing bringing with it a slight chill to the surrounding air. The glass doors to the foyer of the building were partially open and he could hear several voices coming from the inside. He glanced through the entrance expectantly. It looked cold and dark with an obvious electricity cost saving exercise happening, as there was only one dim light on.

Pretending to be a curious observer Michael entered the doors to find two males and two females sitting on chairs appearing to be having a meeting. The women had the appearance in dress of old fashioned dowdy Pentecostal women from another era and Michael was soon to find out that one of them was. His entry was greeted with suspicious glances giving him the impression that strangers were not welcome.

He thought he recognized one of the ladies but wasn't sure. Those looking at him all emanated an attitude of secrecy in their mannerisms. He reasoned in his mind that perhaps this was because, even subconsciously, they might still be hiding from the darkness of their own history. But he also felt the powerful presence of the Spirit of Distrust amongst the small group. It was still alive and active in this place after its original entrance into the game in the month of July 1973.

He looked around. The foyer, which once contained a thriving exciting looking bookstore, had a couple of bookstands with a few sad looking dust covered books on them giving an overall appearance of a business gone broke. A solid black curtain now separated the foyer from the main hall, obviously so that no outsider or those passing by could look in. The auditorium that had once appeared so bright, open and welcoming from the main street had now become secretive and closeted.

He glanced sideways to the copper and wood dedication plaque on the entrance wall that had been lovingly placed in memory of Evelyn

Robinson. It was now tarnished through age and neglect: mostly neglect he thought. The beautiful inscription and rose emblem that could easily be restored with some Brasso and a polishing cloth was now barely readable.

Michael pretended to browse the bookshelves and then looked across at this strange group of suspicious people watchers who had not taken their eyes off him since he had entered the building.

"Hi…how are you…I used to worship here…can I have a look beyond the curtain into the auditorium?" he queried.

He was given tacit approval by one of the women; one would describe it as a sullen nod with a motioning hand gesture to accompany it. He turned and casually walked towards the curtain and noticed out of the corner of his eye one of the males taking a photo of him as another male and a woman followed him in. Finding himself beyond the curtain he stopped and paused to have a look around.

The woman who had silently motioned him inside left her chair, slowly shuffled up to him, stared him in the face and with a bitter and contemptuous tone in her voice said, "I remember you."

She then turned and walked off.

Michael smiled at her and the others, and with a thank you he turned around and left the building. He had walked into the foyer with a sense of anticipation and walked out of the foyer with a sense of resignation. The beautiful spirit that once permeated every aspect of this auditorium's functioning was now nowhere to be seen. The Spirit of Light had left the building.

The first part of this mission into the past has been completed he thought as he slowly walked the short distance to his car, and it was now time to move on to the second and in his mind the most important component. A visit to where it had all begun, to the property where the commune had with all positivity and with all certainty speedily come into existence.

—⦿—

As he rounded the last bend in the road leading uphill just outside the township he turned into the side road, once dirt, but now kerbed with a beautiful wide bitumen covering that flowed down to the centre of the property.

He glanced to the right paddock, to the place where around two acres of thriving crops had been lovingly planted and nurtured by Janet and Jeffrey, Kelly, Daniel and their team of helpers. The crops had long since gone. After falling into a state of neglect, what the wild goats had not eaten had over time been buried beneath an avalanche of weeds and undergrowth.

Halfway down the dead end road he turned a curve, glanced to the left and it happened in an instant, as if magically, the schoolhouse came into view. It looked different now, more modern perhaps. There were some new buildings. But somehow it still retained the beauty and the old-fashioned appearance that it had possessed when the commune had first discovered it.

It was rundown then, disused, hidden away in the bush, but Michael and a group of his closest friends could see the potential in it. So after purchasing it for a pittance and dissecting it, they had moved it to their communal property, where together over a period of time it had been lovingly and painstakingly restored to its former glory.

Michael slowed his car, pulled over and parked to get a better view. He was gazing down in deep thought at the picturesque schoolhouse nestled about fifty metres below him in a grove of trees when he caught an unexpected glimpse of her. She was seated on a bench positioned on the school verandah talking intently to two young teenage girls.

She looked different now and yet somehow still looked the same. Time had silvered her thick long black wavy hair but her timeless inner beauty was still being reflected in her gestures and overall outward demeanour as she engaged in conversation with the two students.

Over the years his memory of her outer appearance had dimmed slightly, but he had never forgotten those mannerisms, particularly the smile, the wholesomeness, the warmth and the laughter that was forever framed in her face: the face of this girl, this schoolteacher, this Argiroula Vernados, or as she was affectionately known to her family and friends…Archie.

His hand reached for the car door handle as he impulsively considered just stepping out, walking down the path to the school verandah, hugging her, and holding her in his arms once again. But the words from one of his favourite songs of the seventies that had been playing on a compact disc on the drive down suddenly flashed across his mind. There will be another song for me for I will sing it, there will be another dream for me, and someone will bring it.

Michael hesitated in that instant and slowly drew his hand away from the door handle. He thought he saw her stop talking in that moment and glance upwards staring in his direction for a few seconds. It had happened quickly and he wondered if he had imagined it. He hoped he hadn't. He hoped she had sensed his presence.

He sat quietly wondering about the last twenty years of her life and how it had turned out for her. He had heard in correspondence recently from his dear friend Janet Gibbons in London that Archie had never married and appeared to have devoted her life to the school and the little children. Janet and Archie had kept in touch over the years, particularly on birthdays and at Christmastime.

Perhaps he thought Archie had in part fulfilled her teenage imaginings that she had shared with him on their first night together. As a young girl after seeing Audrey Hepburn in the movie The Nun's Story she had told her mother she would grow up to be a nun. Then years later as a teenager after seeing Julie Andrews in The Sound of Music movie she had told her mother she wanted to work with children when she grew up.

Maybe in some way, Michael thought, as he stared down at her and remembered Janet Gibbons comments in the letter, Archie may very well have fulfilled a combination of both childhood imaginings.

He leaned back in the car seat and thought about the year of their first meeting. It was 1969 and the last year of the fabulous sixties. It was the year of Woodstock, and the dawning of the Age of Aquarius. It was a time when the message of love, joy, and peace was being articulated from the hearts and minds of all hippies and from the mouths of many who were merely hippies at heart. Christmas Day was only a few weeks away, and the world was fast approaching a whole new decade, the fantastic seventies.

It was also the beginning of the most impacting decade of Michael's life, and he had just turned 27 years of age. Yet now to him, at the end of today's drive it seemed quite surreal. Had all that time passed so quickly? Was it that long ago since he had made the many monthly pilgrimages down the highway from the city to this place? But he knew it was long ago: it was a very long time ago.

It was a journey Michael felt compelled to undertake one weekend each month for a period of around 12 months. It began after a sudden change in his existing employment contract in the township had seen him temporarily returned to a position just north of the capital city. Almost robotically on the last Friday afternoon at the end of each month he would mentally prepare himself for the trip to Springfield in excited anticipation.

Springfield was a time weary but seemingly timeless village, nestled in the valley of a beautiful district on the East Coast and a town that to the outsider had minimal claims to fame. This was contrary to the opinion of most of its residents who believed that they had at least three. Firstly there was a huge old Gothic style church on the outskirts of the town that was the scene of one of the two Sunday markets in the district and used as a community hall during the week.

Secondly there was a giant pink plaster donut situated in a rest area on the outskirts of town. You see in 1990 after the release of a new television series in the United States, an imaginative local government councillor had used taxpayers' money to erect a huge, non-edible giant pink doughnut on the approach into town. His idea was to publicize a non-formal sister city association with a well-known town in the USA named Springfield, the home of the Simpson family. The donut was ugly but cute, and the children of visiting tourists loved to stop and get their photo taken pretending to take a bite out of it.

And lastly their third claim to fame was the lighthouse. The lighthouse had been built on the opposite side of the river mouth to the township and stood on a grassy rocky headland on top of a precipitous cliff with a sheer drop of around fifty metres. It had been constructed in 1899 from a vision that a local politician had of seeing Springfield become a port for the trade of produce grown in the coastal districts of the area, which at that time included timber as well as agricultural products.

The government nautical surveyor in this district at the time had felt that the river mouth had a small and dangerous entrance that needed to be rectified if the port was to be developed as a distribution hub in the area. He had subsequently set about drawing up a plan not only for the construction of the lighthouse but extensive ongoing work on the river mouth and the port facilities.

Half a century later the lighthouse had become part of the ongoing focus on tourism in the area. An enterprising retired trawler fisherman had set up an hourly ferry service transporting visitors across the river for a tour of the facility and a photo opportunity with the numerous wild goats that had taken up grazing residence on the rocky outcrops.

Michael had lived, worked, and built a life amongst the people of Springfield for approximately two years until a sudden non-negotiable temporary transfer initiated by his employer had taken him from this district back to the city, where as he described it, he had to exchange the passion of a peculiar like-minded bunch of people for a type of entrenched apathy about life amongst many of the city folk.

Due to his strong and binding ties to the community, it was generously written into his contract that he be given a three day weekend break at the end of each month to enable him to travel down to Springfield to fulfill his commitments there should he so desire.

However whilst there was an absolute measure of truth in this, for Michael personally the higher reality was that he had established an emotional and spiritual bond with a group of like-minded people. These were people who shared his vision of a communal spiritual type of lifestyle, and it was primarily these bonds of friendship that kept drawing him back to visit the village and catch up on the progress of the commune, weekend after weekend and month after month.

It was in Springfield that Michael felt his life purpose was truthfully unfolding when around 10 p.m. on the last Friday of each month he would slowly wind his car half a kilometre up the dirt tree lined driveway to the beautifully restored farmhouse cottage of Jeffrey and Janet Gibbons: a peaceful location where only two things interrupted the silence of the night. The occasional screeching of a masked owl, and the non-stop chirping of the male bush crickets setting about their nocturnal task of trying to attract the female crickets that were present: or as Jeffrey Gibbons would jokingly put it, "dem crickets singing their song of love."

To Michael every single thing about the four-hour drive would be worth it. For on arrival at his destination it was here that once again he would be lovingly embraced and welcomed by his dearest of friends, the Gibbons, to begin not only his weekend spiritual adventure with his friends, but his three-day emotional adventure with Archie also.

I think we've always got to be open to the fact that certain people cross our path in life for a reason. People use the phrase, 'well it was fate that brought us together', and fate of course is regarded as some unknown power of a spiritual kind that predetermines a particular event.

– Michael Winton

The Gibbons

TWO

"I'm not sure dear. I hope this thing they have got involved in won't interfere with our plans for Jeffrey to eventually take over the business. I spoke to Tom Williams the other night. He seems okay with it. Said they are just exploring the adventurous sides of their nature and that once it was out of their system they would be back."

Jim and Valerie Gibbons were sitting sipping tea in the courtyard of their cottage discussing Jeff and Janet's decision to stay a while in Australia.

The Gibbons, or the Gibbos as he affectionately called them, Jeff Gibbons and Janet Williams, were generous of heart and of belongings and lovingly obliging to Michael on his weekend visits once a month. They had become over time his dearest friends and their home had become his weekend accommodation every time he visited the village.

But the friendship was not just an emotional attachment that had formed because of compatible personalities. The three all felt and had discussed many times that it went much deeper. They had agreed that this bonding was of the spiritual kind first and the emotional kind second: a joining of three souls, a sort of 'meant to be' friendship, as if they had all been brought together to fulfill some specific spiritual purpose, the unfolding of some Divine plan.

Jeff was a builder by trade, a man with a great wit, an amateur musician and an avid reader, with a copious collection of books, some new, but mostly second hand. In particular books of a historical, philosophical, or spiritual genre.

It was common to see Jeff reach for a book in his collection regularly, perhaps half way through a late evening discussion the three were having, to add additional information to the topic they had been debating from those he called the experts. In doing this he would always preface his movement with the words, 'let's see what the experts have to say', expressed in a slow drawn out drawl, sometimes showing a hint of sarcastic inflection in its tone.

Jeffrey Gibbons would readily admit that he did not suffer fools gladly. He had his own personal and sometimes differing viewpoints than those that were common in the day on many subjects, and did not necessarily see all these writers as experts: it had simply become a turn of phrase for him.

Some of these nightly discussions had stayed in Michael's mind over the years more than others. He remembered a particular night when the three of them were knee deep in a conversation about how certain people meet in life and why particular people are brought together.

Suddenly to the announcement of "I know but let's see what the experts have to say," Jeff had reached across for a book that was sitting close at hand on the bookshelf.

The book looked almost as old and worn as the comfy recliner armchair from which he would espouse his personal philosophy on life late into the night. By its appearance, faded cover, torn binding, it obviously had been purchased second hand, and Michael's thoughts were confirmed as with a flurry it was introduced by Jeff as a book he had picked up at the Gothic Church Sunday Markets and contained a chronological history of the ancient religion of Hinduism in India.

After quickly scanning the index Jeff had selected a page and, prefixed with a slight pause as he breathed in, had explained that the chapter was about Sanskrit, the ancient Indo-European language of India. He then referred to a particular word in use in the Sanskrit language called Lila that the ancient seers of India used to describe what they saw as the Divine Game of life, with its true meaning being Divine Play or the Play of Creation.

It spoke of how the wise men believed that certain human beings and certain human experiences are appropriated and used in Divinely controlled games in the Divine Playground.

"We are all pieces in Jehovah's jigsaw," Jeffrey had said as he put the book down, "being fitted together to complete the picture of what God is trying to create or fulfill."

Now since both Michael's and the Gibbons' family backgrounds were of the Christian faith, to ward off any potential skepticism Jeff was quick to point out that this ancient Hindu teaching correlated exactly with teachings in the Bible.

"What do you reckon Mickey?"

"What's that?"

"Well you've read the Bible how many times now is it...ten?" Jeff enquired grinning.

"No...not quite, the Old Testament twice and the New Testament around five times."

"Oh yes...and the Koran once," Michael continued smiling.

"And the Bhagavad Gita...once."

"And did I mention the Tao Te Ching...once," he said cheekily.

"Yeah alright...alright," Jeff quipped, "smarty pants...spiritual guru."

"So what do you reckon about it?" continued Jeff, trying to ignore Michael's flippancy even though he knew it to be true. He had read all those books.

"About what...the cookies and hot chocolate?"

"Nice...very warming."

"About what I just said doofus," Jeff replied laughing.

"Oh right...yes...okay I'll be serious but only for a moment. It's too late at night to be too serious."

Michael continued.

"Well from my understanding of the Bible I believe that God has called us to connect to all of humanity by leading loving righteous peace filled lives, and to that end, God and spiritual forces influence our behaviour to bring about those things."

"I think that a Divine life force that people refer to as God gets involved in the affairs of mankind through us. But the results happen only as we co-operate with the Divine promptings. You know the intuitive part of our being…that still small voice in our head."

"I believe God looks for people who will fit into his plans and if those chosen won't align themselves with his purpose he will try again to find someone else for the task at hand."

"So if that's the case, then yes, it is a sort of a game isn't it?" returned Jeff.

"I guess it is," replied Michael.

"Yes…I like that Michael," returned Janet, "I like that."

"It sort of takes the pressure off things doesn't it?" she continued.

"What do you mean Janny?"

"I mean the problem that we think is such a massive problem, well it's only a part of a game, don't worry about the outcome, just do what you can and do the right thing."

"It does Janny…it does take the pressure off things."

"Perhaps that is the reason we all got to meet Michael…perhaps it was our destiny…we might together be part of a particular game…what do you think?"

"You could be right Janny."

"I think we've always got to be open to the fact that certain people cross our path in life for a reason. People use that phrase, well it was fate that brought us together, and fate of course is regarded as some unknown power of a spiritual kind that predetermines a particular event."

"I remember reading a quote of sorts somewhere, can't remember exactly how it went. But it was saying that we should accept the things to which fate binds us and love the people who fate brings into our lives with all our heart for they are part of our life purpose."

Michael remembered thinking out loud as he drove back to the city that same weekend.

"Could this be what this particular friendship with the Gibbons is all about?"

"Is this why I have this compulsion to drive for four hours on a Friday night once a month?"

"Am I co-operating and involved in a particular present or upcoming Divine Game, or in one of Jehovah's jigsaws as Jeff had so cleverly put it?"

"Maybe so he reasoned. Maybe so."

No matter how late it was when Michael arrived at the Gibbons' home nestled in the hills that surrounded the village, his arrival was always greeted with heartfelt hugs, homemade ginger cookies and hot chocolate. The hot chocolate was sipped slowly as they sat crossed legged on the soft sheepskin rug directly in front of the glowing but dying embers of the wood fireplace and talked late into the evening. Winter nights were especially cosy.

The home was a small but compact cottage, with verandah surrounds, tucked away almost magically in a shady tree grove midst an undulating expanse of lush green farming country. Originally a tired run down old farmhouse cottage, well over 100 years old, it had been purchased some six months after their arrival in the village with the help of funds from Janet's trust account generously released by her father Tom.

Over a couple of years, it had been painstakingly but lovingly renovated by Jeff and Janet, with intermittent help on weekends from their friends and from Jeff's father on holiday visits from England.

Not forgetting the constant availability during heavy lifting times of support from some of the Gibbons' alternate lifestyle neighbours and friends living in the bush surrounds. In particular their closest neighbours Daniel and Zelda Westwood, another pair of Woodstock graduates who rented a place quite close to the Gibbons, and Bernie and Helga Eagleton, a couple of travelling beekeepers who lived nearby.

Both Bernie and Helga were hard working people. If you asked Bernie he would tell you that he couldn't remember the last time they had taken a weekend off. For most of their adult life they had chased the blossoms with their truck and trailer full of beehives and had now set up their base in the district.

Daniel and Zelda were on the other hand what you would describe as a hippie gypsy type couple. Daniel looked and acted like a hippie and Zelda looked and acted like a gypsy. They both used Daniel's surname Westwood, pretending to be a married couple although they were not. Zelda had a beautiful wit. If the subject came up amongst close friends as to how long they had been married, Zelda would simply reply, "we're not," and then go on to explain.

"We came to this arrangement in Woodstock and then just decided to keep it going."

"It was my idea to do it because every time I did a belly dance I would find a dozen guys wanting to hit on me. They found my dancing so fabulously alluring."

"Which by the way," she would grin, "I sooo totally understand... but it became awkward at times."

Zelda was an attractive girl, thick long black hair, tanned, with a Mediterranean type of skin tone. She dressed like a gypsy, wore lots of beaded necklaces and open toed sandals, which revealed toenails painted with bright red polish, and of course she could perform an amazing belly dance.

As for Daniel he dressed like a hippie and believed he had a gift in the form of visions and dreams that came as messages from God for specific people, to either edify them or to admonish them. This would eventually be proven to be right. Daniel would describe some of the visions he had as prophetic warnings of things to come, likening himself to the prophets of old, bringing specific corrective messages about someone's behaviour to that person from God.

He was an electrician by trade, played the mouth organ beautifully, and was a wonderful help to Jeff and Janet in their home renovation process. He would often say that his gift was accurately recorded in the Bible with the verse, "in the last days your young men will see visions and your old men will dream dreams," which was correct.

Michael liked the openness and honesty of Daniel and the wit and dry sense of humour of Zelda. To anyone who was curious about her obvious skill in belly dancing Zelda would say that it was part of her gypsy heritage, which was quite true: although she had learnt a few new moves at a belly dancing class she took in her early teens.

In terms of her family history her ancestors were actually from a culture of travelling gypsies known as Sintians, who came into Germany out of the Romani people of Central Europe. The tribes had migrated to Germany in the late 15th Century and converted to Christianity even though they were generally accused of being beggars and thieves. The art of belly dancing had been carried down through generations of her family.

Zelda had a wonderful wit. She was overjoyed in September 1971 when the singer Cher released her hit song Gypsies Tramps and Thieves, and was quick to use the lyrics of the song to everyone's delight when she would wittily answer the all too often question she was asked: "how did you come to take up belly dancing?" She would reply with a melodious twang in her voice.

"Well I was born in the wagon of a travellin' show and my mama used to dance for the money they'd throw."

For this reason Jeff would often affectionately refer to Zelda as his little Hoochie Coochie, the term used for a sexually provocative belly dance, and would also speak of Daniel as his good friend Danny the Dream Catcher.

A young couple in their early twenties Daniel and Zelda had met Jeff and Janet at the Woodstock Festival in August 1969. Both couples were camped alongside each other, amongst the hundreds of thousands of others in the rain soaked muddy fields, as Jimi Hendrix took the stage to perform as the last act of the Aquarius explosion. A bond was formed and as a result of this friendship they had extended their Woodstock adventure joining Jeff and Janet in their travels. Over time both couples had become good mates.

Bernie and Helga Eagleton were from a totally opposite side of the cultural and social spectrum. Both in their early fifties they, along with their two teenage girls and trailer load of beehives, had originally come to the district in pursuit of the flowering Leatherwood blossoms for the four months of their annual blooming. They had fallen in love with the area, purchased an old farmhouse in the hills, and set up their base long before the slow infiltration of the hippie culture into the region had begun.

The location itself was perfect for their nomadic working lifestyle. It enabled Bernie to leave his hives on his property for some months of the year and easily shift them by truck to other areas in the region when the gum, clover or blackberry blooms came into season.

Bernie or Bernie the Beekeeper as Jeffrey called him was an interesting man. He gave the appearance of always being dressed and ready for work, his stock standard dress being dungarees, the bib-and-brace overalls of the day, made of denim with riveted pockets similar to those seen on jeans, and a well-worn flannelette check shirt which was always the perfect accessory.

In the warmer months of summer Bernie could be seen walking around with no shirt at all but still always in the bib-and-brace overalls, even at social functions. Although he would, out of courtesy to his hosts, introduce a white short sleeved polo shirt and paisley tie into the outfit at dress up occasions such as weddings and funerals.

A likeable, kindly man, Bernie suffered from a nervous tic on the left hand side of his face: consequently his vocal interactions were always preceded with a few seconds of stutter. But as Jeff Gibbons jokingly described him on many occasions, he was a beautiful man who would give you the bib off his front and the braces off his back if you needed them.

Not only was he an experienced beekeeper Bernie was also a man who could build anything and who could fix anything mechanical that was broken, without having had any experience or training. Tinkering with engines of all sorts was his favourite way of relaxing. He was what you would call an engine whisperer who could encourage with his hands and positive self-talk any tired and cantankerous old engine back to its full functioning glory.

The Gibbons on the other hand were an evolving hippie couple: that would be the simplest way to describe them.

Originally from London, Jeff was born into a lower middle class family in the mid-forties. Both his father, and his father before him were builders, working in their home construction business for around 80 years. Three generations of the Gibbons family had lived in their suburban London cottage for a century or more and all the male family members of whom Jeff was the youngest of three were carpenters by trade.

It was a generally accepted fact, though not often discussed, that Jeff would eventually follow in his father's and his brother's footsteps; being that once his education had been completed he would do his carpentry and joinery apprenticeship whilst employed in the family business. However as it subsequently turned out the dance of Jeffrey's destiny differed from his parents' expectations. Fate had other ideas for him.

Janet came from a different social status. She was upper class, but somehow different from her peers in that she lacked the pretentious attitude normally associated with this particular section of society in London in the day. She and her twin sister Judith had been born into a high-income family. They were hereditary landowners with a hereditary peerage, and a hereditary trust fund for the twins that came with it.

Brought up in her early years by a nanny, schooled at home by a private tutor, it was as Janet was approaching her teenage years that her parents made what in those days was regarded as a most momentous decision, one that would change the course of not only her life but also the destinies of both her and Jeff forever in a dramatic way.

It was in 1962 when a spokesperson at Buckingham Palace made, what was for some people, a life influencing and life-changing announcement. The press communication was a startling reversal to the normal Royal protocol observed in the formal education process of those of Royal birth. It was proclaimed that Queen Elizabeth and her husband Prince Phillip, rather than continue with the private schooling and education of their son Prince Charles, would instead be enrolling him in a public school situated on the shores of the Moray Firth in Scotland.

With this earth shattering announcement came a rush to keep up with the Jones's, or in this case to keep up with the Royals. In London, a craze quickly developed amongst upper class families, with high school ready children, to forgo the ease and accessibility of the class cultured private schools in favour of sending their children to public schools, to enable them to mix with the masses no matter what their race or social status.

This was quite an extraordinary shift in the social conditioning of the day relative to educational matters, and so it was that the twins Janet and Judith became a by-product of this proclamation as their progressive parents made their future schooling choice for them.

It followed then that on the first day of her new secondary school experience Janet was given a seat at an aged wooden oak school desk beside another first day student, one from a suburb socially poles apart from hers and whose reason for being there was totally different from hers: being that this student had been enrolled here not to keep up with the Royals, but because it was the same public school his father and his father's father had attended. The young man's name was Jeffrey Gibbons.

Jeffrey and Janet met in class on the first day of high school and as fate on behalf of 'Lila' dictated the deal, in time they fell in love and became inseparable teenage sweethearts. Jeff would later jokingly say that it was Janet's sense of non-adventure and his non-conformity to the status quo that had brought them together, and which had kept them together during the rest of their school years. But their families saw it differently.

Even after they had both graduated from high school, upon Janet embarking on a three year Veterinary Science course at the local university and Jeff commencing his three year builder's apprenticeship in the family business, they were still always inseparable. Janet would spend her weekends passing bricks to Jeffrey on a building site and Jeff would spend his weeknights passing books to Janet and encouraging her in her study times.

The word swimmingly is an old English word meaning smooth uninterrupted progress, and was the word most often used in reply when family friends or relatives asked both Jeff and Janet's parents about the progress of Jeff and Janet's romance. Both families were very happy about the relationship. For them it was going swimmingly.

Jeff's mother had felt that Janet's outgoing personality had succeeded in bringing her mentally cocooned son out of his slightly introverted nature that always found him with his head buried in a book when his neighbourhood pals were out kicking the soccer ball in the backyard.

Whilst Mr Williams was of the opinion that the quietness, calmness, and the 'think before you act' part of Jeff's character was ideally suited to balance the impulsive and sometimes 'out there' decision making processes of his daughter. A balance of character qualities and personality traits was his idea of a pre-requisite for a successful relationship.

It was with this mindset that on the evening of July 7th 1969 at a gathering of both families for some celebratory drinks to announce the couple's engagement, and as a sign of his blessing Tom Williams, Janet's father, made a magnanimous gesture. On that evening six months to the day of Janet's successful graduation as a Veterinary Scientist he presented the couple with two British Airway return plane tickets to New York.

Tom Williams had gifted Jeff and Janet a holiday that would change the ongoing lifestyle of them both in a most adventurous and unexpected way. They stepped off the plane in New York on 1st August 1969, just two weeks prior to the start of the history making music festival billed internationally as the Aquarian Explosion: a three-day moment in time that society would come to describe later as the definitive nexus for the larger counter culture generation.

Jeff and Janet were on their way to Woodstock, four days of love, peace and music and for many some naked bathing in the local lake, held on a 600-acre dairy farm in the Catskills near the hamlet of White Lake in the town of Bethel New York. It was a pivotal moment in the world of countercultures and a pivotal moment in popular music history, which saw 32 live music acts perform before an open-air crowd of 400,000 people a musical fusion of rock and folk, of blues-rock, folk rock, hard rock, and psychedelic rock.

It was at a time approaching the end of a decade when there were wars and rumours of wars, when hippies around the world were burning their draft cards protesting the inhumanity of the Vietnam War, and when singer songwriter Barry McGuire was in his hit song telling everyone the reasons why the world should believe that it was on the eve of its own destruction.

It was rainy and wet, the ground was muddy, and the fields were covered with an intertwining of bodies some still awake and some still asleep as Jimi Hendrix and his band came on stage at 8.30 a.m. on the Monday morning to perform the final act of the festival. Jeffrey Gibbons poked Danny in the ribs.

"Wake up Danny boy, wake up, it's Jimi Hendrix, the final act," Jeffrey shouted as he turned to his newly found buddy Daniel Westwood, asleep with his girlfriend Zelda on the ground beside he and Janet, "last act Danny…last act."

It would be around six months later that Michael Winton would have his first encounter with this lovable rebirthed hippie couple and their gentle German gypsy travelling companions. Jeffrey, Janet, Daniel and Zelda after journeying halfway around the world with Tom Williams' blessing had decided to extend their adventure and stop off to see a little of Australia on their way back home. It was an encounter that would impact on all their lives for decades to come.

"His eyes followed her down the pathway until she had reached her front door. She turned and waved and then disappeared inside. There was something about this girl that was starting to fascinate him. She just seemed so naturally lovely."*

The First Encounter

THREE

⸺ ⊷⊶⊷ ⸺

"**I** can't believe you would say that Jeffrey Gibbons...that's so disrespectful. I believe he truly is a man of God."

"Mags as I've said to you before. You have a perfect right to have your opinion and I have a perfect right to have mine. It just so happens in relation to this topic our opinions are complete polar opposites."

Jeffrey Gibbons and Margie Morrison were having one of their oft repeated discussions about the spiritual relevance of Garret Sloan as they stood at the entrance to the showgrounds with their friends waiting for Michael Winton to arrive.

⸺ ⊷⊶⊷ ⸺

December 1969.

"Please God...please please God...take me away from this financial nightmare and bring something nice into my life," Michael muttered frustratingly as he sat hunched over the pile of paperwork on his desk. His wish was quickly and unexpectedly answered with a soft but confident knock on his office door.

"Hi...I'm Archie...well really Argiroula, Argiroula Vernados, but everyone calls me Archie...you must be Michael."

"I'm a friend of the Purcell family, you know our extra friendly tourist trailer park people."

Her introductory greeting echoed through the confines of his small office in a happy and almost melodic tone. He had been deeply engrossed in a review of the trading statements of the business, witnessing what he had described silently to himself as an accounting nightmare, when her words had startled him out of his concentration.

Only a few days earlier he had arrived in this picturesque agricultural and sheep farming township and port to take up his role as the Manager of the District Farmers Co-Operative, or the DFC as it was more commonly known. Regarded in the accounting community as a young marketing and financial management guru, Michael had been appointed to his current role to investigate and fix serious trading and profit deficiencies in the co-operative's business.

The successful operation of the DFC was pivotal to the livelihoods of all the local growers and producers in the district. It was the life-blood of the town and a lifeline for the profitable marketing and sale of their produce. The philosophy of local business was, "if the DFC is in trouble, the town is in trouble."

"I heard you're staying in one of the Purcell's cabins at the park," his unexpected visitor continued, as she sat down on the chair directly across from his desk, and leaned forward as if in expectation of an immediate yes I am answer.

Slowly almost casually Michael lifted his head and shoulders from their concentrated and crouched position. He glanced up and across at this curious and questioning visitor who had felt confident and comfortable enough to, after only a couple of knocks and without invitation, take up residence albeit temporarily in the corner of his office.

She was an extremely attractive young woman probably in her early to mid twenties he ascertained at first glance, medium height and of slim build: a brunette, her long black slightly wavy hair surrounding a soft pale complexion, with sparkling emerald eyes that glistened like raindrops on rose petals after the rain. All these features encompassing what he felt was a most beautiful if not slightly mischievous smile that seemed to be permanently etched upon her face as she talked.

The musicality of her speaking voice evoked memories for Michael from his childhood: those lazy hazy Saturday afternoons, when the beautiful music and carefree lyrics of Doris Day would waft through the family home as his mother Rose sat on the verandah and played her favourite record album, The Greatest Hits of Doris Day.

Archie had this melodic conversational tone as if she was singing every sentence, with a joyous soft sounding laughing intonation in her every word. In a moment she had made him feel relaxed.

"Hi Archie…yes I'm Michael," he said, as he stood up and extended his hand of greeting to her.

She was of European origin he guessed, and spoke beautifully, almost posh, Audrey Hepburn sounding you could say, with what seemed like a slight Greek accent. With the looks of a young Elizabeth Taylor, the melodic sound of Doris Day and the voice tone of Audrey Hepburn, this unexpected visitor definitely had a movie star quality about her Michael thought.

She was dressed in a long hippie style paisley chiffon printed dress of the day, looking soft and feminine, and her appearance and attitude seemed to for a magical moment dissipate the dreary atmosphere of his mundane office environment.

"Pleased to meet you Michael, cool," she replied, as she took his outstretched hand in hers and gently shook it.

She spoke with softness and a sincerity that he had not found in any of his previous introductory encounters in this town, for this was a township that seemed to have an initial questioning suspicion of any strangers that took up residence here. She spoke in a way that convinced Michael that she really was pleased to meet him and not just being polite.

"I'm sorry to interrupt your work," she continued, "but there's a small group of us from our local church fellowship heading off to the showground at Lighthouse Bay this Friday night for the Christmas Carols By Candlelight."

"Jen Purcell at the Tourist Park mentioned that you had asked for a brochure on church services in town, and they suggested that you being new in town might like to go with us, you know to the Carols, with some people around your age."

Slightly taken aback by this impromptu invitation and in the moment not really giving it any thought, Michael paused for a second and then quickly accepted the offer.

"Sure…ah yes…that would be nice…thank you," he abruptly blurted out.

"So it's Friday night is it?"

"Sure is."

"Great…so where are you meeting and what time…I'll be there?"

Archie too was surprised at his quick response but also pleased.

"That's cool Michael."

"There will probably be about six of us and we're meeting at the entrance to the showground near the kiosk, at about 7 o'clock," she replied, showing her look of surprise whilst being excited that he had so readily accepted her invitation.

"You'll see a big Coke sign lit up on top of the kiosk."

The conversation became stilted for a moment as Michael got over his sudden acceptance and Archie got over the fact that he had so quickly accepted.

"That's great…so are you settling in okay Michael?" she queried, as she slowly stood up to go, much to Michael's disappointment.

"Yes…not too bad…a lot to do…next big challenge is to find a home. I don't like living out of a suitcase."

"That shouldn't be too hard hopefully," replied Archie, "being a tourist spot, plenty of holiday places that will take semi-permanent bookings…good luck."

"I'd better go and leave you to your work."

"I knew you would be busy being your first week here but thought I would pop in while I was downtown. Friday nights are not good nights to be by yourself, particularly if you are far from home."

"Great...no thank you...a night of caroling suits me fine," Michael replied with a slightly manufactured tone of enthusiasm, whilst pondering on her statement about Friday nights and half thinking about the work he had ahead of him for the rest of the week.

"Cool...that's great, see you then," she quipped, and with those final parting words she floated down the stairs and was gone: she vanished as quickly as a butterfly in a spring garden of daisies.

Michael sat for a moment with his gaze silently staring at the doorway she had so briskly flittered through.

"What was that?" he questioned in his mind trying to see a valid reason for him so readily accepting this invitation from a perfect stranger.

Was it the Carols he was interested in? Was it the Friday night syndrome and perhaps the thought of meeting people and making some new friends in town? Or was it simply that the opportunity of spending some more time with this delightful young woman was an invitation too good to refuse?

Yes...that was it, he thought, that was it...all three.

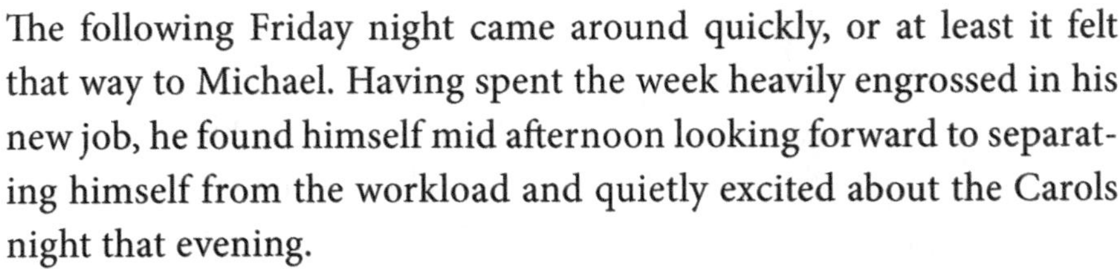

The following Friday night came around quickly, or at least it felt that way to Michael. Having spent the week heavily engrossed in his new job, he found himself mid afternoon looking forward to separating himself from the workload and quietly excited about the Carols night that evening.

It was 5.30 p.m. as he slowly and methodically cleared his disturbingly cluttered desk, turned out the light, paused, looked around, locked the door, and quietly sauntered to his car in the car park. He turned the ignition on, and with a blast of sound signifying a radio volume control previously left on high, the words and music of Frankie Valli and the Four Seasons exploded into his eardrums. "Oh what a night...late September back in 63."

A great song he thought as he quickly reached for the volume control to turn it down. But the song had given him a heightened sense of anticipation for the evening ahead, his first Friday night in this town.

It was 6 p.m. as he turned off the highway into the Tourist Park entrance knowing that he had just one hour to prepare himself for his second encounter with Archie, and a night of Carol singing. He was starting to feel excited.

"Oh come all ye faithful…joyful and triumphant…oh come ye oh come ye…to Bethlehem." The sound of the local church choir warming up rang out nostalgically and beautifully; it was resonating through his ears as he casually strolled the ten-minute walk from the tourist park to the showground. This music was in stark contrast to his earlier encounter with the Four Seasons he thought.

The sound of Christmas Carols had always evoked a warm spine tingling type of experience with him and this time was no exception. He was aware of feelings, melancholy feelings that created a temporary state of peacefulness, a feeling that all was right with the world, even if for a lot of people it wasn't.

Michael would not have labelled himself a religious person, but he did possess specific beliefs courtesy of the example set by his devout Baptist mother, and from spiritual insights and understandings he had acquired through many years of study and searching.

It was fast approaching 7.15 as he walked along the cobblestone footpath, quickly glanced at his watch and slightly speeded up his pace. That's a bit slack of me he thought, she did say around 7 ish. I can't be late for the first date of sorts.

As he neared the gate to the entrance of the showground his gaze searching ahead, Michael spotted the illuminated Coke sign that Archie had mentioned. His eyes were simultaneously drawn to what was below it, the shadow of Archie's slender figure and shoulder length hair softly silhouetted by the reflection of the light on the side of the kiosk wall.

It appeared the group had positioned themselves so as not to miss his approach, which he found very welcoming. Looks like I am the last to arrive he thought to himself, feeling slightly conspicuous. His eyes fell upon Archie. Looking radiant in a pretty yellow cotton dress she was laughingly engrossed in conversation with a group of what looked like about six other people.

Archie spotted Michael first and with a beautiful smile and a melodious hello came forward to greet him.

"Sorry I'm a little late," he muttered, slightly embarrassed for the time of his arrival and for what he self-consciously thought might seem to others as a touch of tardiness.

Archie gently put him at ease.

"That's alright Michael, it's not a problem. I'm so glad you were able to make it, it's so good to see you again," she voiced as she leaned forward to greet him.

She gently placed her arms around his shoulders and gave him a gentle and tender up close squeeze hug.

"Bless you Michael, come and meet the gang."

Michael quietly mumbled a reply of "and bless you too," as he turned in the direction of the group who were all standing back watching and smiling. Archie swung around and walked the short distance to the group with Michael following. With her voice moving up a couple of octaves, she cheerily announced to the waiting throng:

"Everyone this is Michael from the Co-Op who I told you about. He's staying at the Purcell's Tourist Park."

"Michael this is everyone," she quipped, and continued with the introductions.

"This is Judy who flats with me. She's another out of work schoolteacher. We both graduated together this year."

"This is Daniel who works at my dad's furniture store when he hasn't got any jobs on as an electrician which is his trade, and this is Zelda his partner."

"And this is Kelly."

Her introduction was interrupted as Michael interjected "yes I know you…Kelly…front desk Tourist Park."

"You were there helping Jenny and George."

"Busted" replied Kelly, "that's my mum and dad. They own the park."

"Speaking of mums and dads," Kelly continued, "Arch is your mum and dad here tonight?"

"Yes they are here, somewhere."

"Everyone keep your heads down," Archie continued, "and my brother Peter and his girlfriend are here too."

"If Mum spots us we will all end up back home eating Baklava biscuits and drinking Greek coffee."

Everyone laughed as Archie kept going.

"For those of you who are not aware of my homeland's customs our traditional Greek Christmas activity officially starts tomorrow, December 6th and goes until January 6th…you know the song…on the twelve days of Christmas my true love gave to me."

"Well for Mum it's the thirty days of Christmas and starts tonight. She will be raring to go and spread some Christmas joy, so coffee and biscuits tonight with us would be a good head start for her."

"Keep your heads down."

Archie continued.

"Okay back to our intros."

"Kelly is our funny funky and a little flirtatious but friendly tourist greeter."

"Yeah right," replied Kelly, "busted again."

She leaned over, put her hand up to Archie's ear and whispered.

They both immediately burst out laughing.

"Well," said Jeff, "aren't you going to share it?"

"Secret girl's business, Jeffrey, secret girl's business."

"More like a naughty girl's business," returned Archie.

"Okay…moving on…these two hippies are Jeff and Janet."

Jeff extended his hand to Michael and Janet smiled.

"They live on acreage about 10 miles out of town with some others. A sort of a like minded community you could call it I suppose," she said as she grinned and winked at Jeff.

"Age of Aquarius types you know."

"Daniel and Zelda are their nearest neighbours."

"Jeff builds houses, Janet works at the Animal Shelter, well works there but in my opinion she should be running it. You know, she's a vet and a very kind one at that."

"Thank you Archie, you are very good at introductions and are too kind…and sooo correct," returned Janet.

They both laughed.

"Jeff and Janet, they well you know, grow their own produce on their acreage," she grinned again.

"Not sure what you call them, self-sufficient beings perhaps."

"I call them very small crop farmers," quipped Judy with a mischievous smile and a wink, only to receive a gentle elbow nudge from Jeff.

"Yeah right," chirped in Margie, "and not all the farmer's crops are legal enough to be taken to market."

Jeffrey scowled, "not true."

"Well timed," continued Archie, "and last but by no means least this is Margie. She's a doctor and our go to girl if you get a sniffle."

"Yes right," returned Margie extending her hand, "nice to meet you Michael. I'm a sniffle specialist."

"Do you work at the hospital Margie?"

"No I have my own G.P. practice Michael, my own small and relatively new G.P. practice."

"I share office and clinic space with the town's might I say prestigious specialist in gynecology and obstetrics Dr Unwin Nicholls."

"Now there's an interesting man," she added.

"Right…great…that's a coincidence," returned Michael, "I have arranged an appointment with him the week after next. He's one of the D.F.C's very important clients so I have been informed."

"Yes he has other business interests apart from his medical practice," replied Margie.

"So gang, this is Michael, and Michael, this is gang," continued Archie, receiving a rousing handclap from the group.

"If you are sick, if your dog is sick, if you need holiday accommodation or even want a house built with lights installed, or if you just need to brush up on your A B C, then we here are your go to gang," chimed in Zelda.

Everyone including Michael chuckled.

"So how did you guys all meet?" he queried when his curiosity about this mixed group of personalities and professions got the better of him.

"Archie and I met at Teachers College," Judy replied, "but all of us met through the Young Adults group at our Anglican Church."

"We all attend the Anglican Church on Sundays and the young adults group during the week but we're not all Anglicans. Jeff and Janet of course are, being Londoners."

"And Kell's family is Presbyterian background, Scottish you know, ahh young Kelly Purcell," chimed in Jeffrey.

"Yep but they reckon the Presos and the Methos will eventually join up...sorry Methodists," quipped Kelly, "so then I'm not sure what we'll be."

"Although her mum is leaning towards a switch to the Pentecostals, that right Kell?" Archie commented.

Kelly nodded.

"Yep...the happy clappers."

Jeffrey chuckled and Kelly continued.

"Yes she likes all the spiritual gifts they practice, you know, prophesying and things."

"Your mum is very precious," continued Archie.

"I'm a Greek Orthodox but that type of church is in short supply in this area. Like real short supply, as there isn't any."

"Judy and Margie are from the Assemblies of God faith originally, you know Pentecostals, and Dan and Zelda, Dan what are you guys?"

"Look…we are both travelling Gypsy Orthodox Michael," returned Daniel in a serious formal tone, much to the amusement of the others.

"What religion are you Michael?" queried Archie.

"Well I'm Baptist from my upbringing. My mother was a regular Baptist church attendee and I went to the Baptist Sunday School as a child, and I've had some experience with the Assemblies of God church."

"When I was up in the north of the state, my next-door neighbour, an Italian man, Luca, Luca Rossi, was a pastor at the big Citiville Assembly of God church in town, or the AOG as it is called. He convinced me to go along to their Sunday service and have a look."

"So I started going to their evening services, and since I love studying the workings of different religious groups I ended up enrolling in their Bible College to study part time and graduated with a diploma after three years of hard slogging."

"I've since delved into many other religions, particularly eastern ones you know like Buddhism and Hinduism, and have found a lot of good things in all of them."

"So I guess you could say I'm multi-faithed."

"But you're an Assemblies of God Pastor are you Michael because of your studies?" Margie curiously queried.

"No not officially, but I am able to be ordained as a Pastor of the AOG church if ever I want to."

"Do you think you might one day?" replied Margie, inquisitively.

"Maybe," replied Michael, "wait and see hey."

"Perhaps my different views on the world of religion and religious groups might not be easily accommodated by the AOG hierarchy."

"Right," said Archie, "well anyway we're all of different faiths, but the Anglican church, well it's the liveliest most musical church in town so that's why we go there."

"Yep" replied Jeffrey, "except when Elmer Gantry rides into town, now that's a really lively church service."

"Wasn't there a movie about an American evangelist called Elmer

Gantry some years back?" queried Michael.

"Yes," continued Jeffrey, "well this one's name isn't really Elmer Gantry. We nicknamed him that after the evangelist in that movie. It came out about eight years ago, Elmer Gantry. You know with Burt Lancaster."

"Yes…I remember that," returned Michael.

"Who gave him that nickname Jeffrey?" queried Margie with a look and tone of exasperation.

"Okay let's try that again. I nicknamed him Elmer Gantry."

Jeffrey grinned and winked at Michael.

"You see Michael Elmer Gantry in the movie was a conman evangelist selling religion in tent meetings to small town America in the 20's I think it was."

Michael realized that Jeffrey was looking for a reaction out of Margie. It was obvious that this wasn't the first time they had conducted a debate about this evangelist.

"Yes" interjected Margie, with a slightly indignant tone in her voice, "but this one isn't a con man."

"He's a Pentecostal preacher Michael who visits here around four times a year with his travelling big top tent. His name is Garret Sloan and boy does he put on a show. Great music and singing."

"And speaking in tongues, and casting out demons, and fake prophecies and dubious healings," interjected Jeff.

"How do you know they're fake Jeffrey?" Margie retorted with a slight hint of exasperation.

"Well," Jeffrey paused putting his finger to his lips in thought, "perhaps not all fake…it's hard for an Anglican to tell, healings in our church services are a very rare occurrence."

Margie cut short her discourse with Jeffrey and turned her attention to Michael.

"Anyway" she continued, "the Reverend Sloan has been very helpful in sorting out some personal issues I had when I first arrived in town, and my mum and dad love him. They help out at his meetings when he visits their town."

"My folks live about two hours south of here at a place called Gratton Michael, but are moving up here probably around November next year with my brother Ron. He graduates this year with a science degree."

"They're leaving my sister Francis on her lonesome for twelve months until she graduates and moves up here to start a practice with me hopefully in early 72."

"When Garret Sloan visits for a crusade in Gratton he will stay for a few nights at mum and dad's place so they have got to know him well. They like him."

"Have you ever had any experience with the Pentecostal religion Michael?" Margie enquired, "oh of course you have, you mentioned your Bible studies up north."

"Yes, and recently back home in the city. Before I moved down here I was attending the big independent AOG church," he replied. "It's called Christian City Church. I went along quite regularly and got a little involved. Pretty different from my Baptist church heritage."

Jeffrey, unable to help himself as he listened to what he thought was some kind of legitimate recognition of the spiritual relevance of Garret Sloan by Margie, looked across at her and immediately burst into his own version of a well-known 18th century English nursery rhyme he had learnt as a child called Sing A Song Of Sixpence. But it was his version not the original.

"The king was in his counting house counting out his money; his slaves were in the kitchen eating bread and honey."

Daniel grinned. You're a stirrer Jeffrey he thought.

Michael found out later that night from Daniel this was apparently in reference to a rumour that from the huge amount of money collected at the tent meetings of Garret Sloan, very little if any payment was given to his team of assistants. As well as this there was also a story circulating that Garret Sloan had rented a small office in the main street that Jeff referred to as Father Hubbard's cupboard where the cash collected from the king's crusades is counted. But no one knew if this was true.

"Don't be mean," Margie quipped, when Jeff had finished his rhyme, "that's not Christian."

"Neither methinks is he," Jeff quickly retorted.

"Now children," interjected Archie, in an attempt to terminate any further discussion about the Reverend Sloan, "it's Christmas, let's all be nice."

"Michael have you heard the joke about the Irish priest and the devil?" Jeff continued.

"Don't think I have."

It was obvious Daniel had. He was grinning before Jeffrey had even started.

"An Irish priest Father Murphy walks into a bar and sitting on a stool at the bar in his red tights and holding a red pitchfork was the devil. The devil had obviously had too much whiskey and was sobbing uncontrollably."

"So Father Murphy orders a drink and sits down beside the devil in an attempt to console him."

"He puts his arm around the devil's shoulder and leans towards him and says, "aw poor Mr Devil, what's wrong Mr Devil?"

"It's them Pentecostal preachers father," the devil said.

"What is it about those Pentecostal preachers that upsets you so much my son?"

"Father," the devil said, "they keep picking on me all the time. Sure I know I get up to mischief a lot but they keep blaming me for things I never even got a chance to do. I mean it's very hurtful."

Several chuckles could be heard from all except Margie.

"Jeffrey," returned Archie, in what sounded like a schoolteacher's tone of voice in dealing with a disruptive child, "that's enough about Pentecostals too."

"It's Christmas…peace on earth and goodwill to all."

"Has everybody got their song sheet?"

Michael liked the good-humoured teasing. He quietly enjoyed this spontaneous display of friendship and rapport. It was obvious that they were a close-knit group regardless of religious backgrounds. This is nice he thought as he joined in the fun of the moment: it's Christmas and I like it. Tongue in cheek banter with my newly found fraternal, a new town, it's a good way to spend a Friday night.

The evening continued with no more mention of Garret Sloan. Michael was mesmerized by the beautiful melodic voice of Archie as she sang the Carols. There was friendly banter, bottles of Coke and Panda Potato Chips. But for Michael best of all was this opportunity for him to exchange a predictably lonely Friday night in a new town for a night of fun, laughter and companionship with what seemed to be turning out to be a group of like-minded people.

"Oh what a night," perhaps not in the same way that the Four Seasons were conveying when they sang those lyrics, but unbeknown to Michael, this Friday night was in itself positioning him at the start of a journey where his spiritual destiny and personal purpose for the next few years would slowly begin to unfold.

The Carols had finished, the kiosk was closing up, and people had started to move on as Jeff turned to Janet.

"Suppose it's time to go babe?"

"Yes gang it's time for us to go," she replied.

"Michael I live just up the road from here, would you like to be a gentleman and escort me home safely? It's on your way to the trailer park," chimed in Archie as the group were saying their farewells and having their goodbye hugs.

"Jude is going for coffee with Kelly."

"Sure…no problem."

It was a beautiful clear-skied starry night with a soft cool breeze gently blowing. The smell of the sea in the air and the distant sound of the waves crashing over the river bar entrance accompanied the two as they slowly walked the fifteen minutes to Archie's front gate, quietly engaged in conversation of various sorts.

"Thank you for coming along tonight Michael, it was a great night," Archie turned and softly said as they arrived at her home and began exchanging goodbyes.

"I hope you had fun?"

"I did…it was great."

He leaned across in front of her, lifted the latch on her wire front gate and slowly opened it for her.

"A nice cosy looking cottage," commented Michael.

"Yes" returned Archie, "it has three bedrooms, so there is myself, Judy, and another girl from my dad's business sharing the costs."

"Mum didn't like it when I moved out of home about twelve months ago. She's Greek, which when translated means very protective. But she's got used to it."

"Thank you Michael," she said as she leaned forward and gave him a gentle but warm hug goodnight softly whispering as she did so, "bless you…it was fun."

"It sure was Archie," he replied, "and thanks for inviting me," he continued whilst still savouring her perfume and once again being mesmerized by her sparkling emerald eyes and the lilt in her voice.

"Would you like to catch up for a coffee during the week?"

"I would Michael, I really would like that," she replied. "I'll give you a call at the Co-Op when I look at my work roster. I'm balancing three jobs."

"Okay, sounds great, nite," said Michael.

His eyes followed her down the pathway until she had reached her front door. She turned and waved and then disappeared inside. There was something about this girl that was starting to fascinate him. She just seemed so naturally lovely.

Michael breathed in deeply the crisp salty air of the night and headed down the road to the trailer park. I wonder where this thing is going were his thoughts as he slowly and pensively walked the remaining distance to his cabin. Not sure he thought.

But there was one thing Michael was sure of as the evening and his big week finally came to an end and he flopped down wearily on his bed. There was one thing that he was most definite about in his thinking. He really did want this thing to go somewhere.

66 "Hope I didn't get you up, but a beautiful day to be up," came the greeting as Patty gestured upwards towards the clear blue sky. "You wouldn't be dead for quids on a day like this," he continued in his upbeat salesmanship like manner.

Patty Patel

Graham 'Patty' Patel

FOUR

⸻ ∞ ⸻

"**I**t's all about who you know, who you can influence, and what subsequent financial benefit the business can get out of it and what you yourself personally can get out of it."

Patty Patel was in his car driving and considering his philosophy of life. The same life philosophy that had caused him to arise early and head off down to Lighthouse Bay to do a friend a favour, when he had previously arranged to have a Saturday morning at the golf course.

⸻ ∞ ⸻

"Always doin' favours for someone…always doin' favours for someone…someone's always callin' in a favour," Patty muttered softly as he shuffled his way to Michael's cabin.

Michael sat bolt upright in his cabin bed, startled. He was sweating. He was aware that he had been having that same dream again. It was a dream or more so a nightmare that had reoccurred on and off for the last fifteen years of his life, ever since he was a young boy, and a dream that had puzzled him for the same amount of time.

In his early teenage years when he had shared the dream with his mother she had dismissed it saying, "Mikey you used to sleep walk quite often as a little boy, so you were probably dreaming about something imaginary. Don't worry about it sweetheart." But he did wonder about it.

In the dream he was about seven years of age and sleeping in a small room beside the kitchen in the family home. It was a family of eight siblings and whilst the boys each shared a room, the two girls had separate rooms of their own. Everyone in the house was asleep. He found himself awakened by the sound of loud voices, in particular that of his mother. She is angrily yelling out the words, "if you touch her again I'll kill you."

Frightened by what he is hearing he climbs out of bed and seeing a light on in the kitchen he fearfully rounds the corner only to see the eldest brother in the family, already in his twenties and quite tall and imposing, looking slightly drunk and standing facing off with his mother who is holding an empty tea cup.

His mother's nightly ritual was to have a cup of tea in the quiet of the evening before she retired, and what looked like the total contents of the cup, the tea and the tea leaves, were all running down the shirt and trousers of his eldest brother.

His mother, startled to see young Michael standing there looking frightened and rubbing his eyes, immediately leads him back to his bed, tucks him in and with a gentle kiss on the forehead says, "go back to sleep Mikey, you were having a bad dream."

But over the years Michael had sensed that it wasn't just a bad dream he was reliving in these reoccurring nightmares. Something sinister had happened in the family home on that night and that same something sinister had over the years been covered up by his mother Rose from him and from the rest of the siblings.

So here it was again, probably two years since the last one, but nevertheless the same dream that always ended with him awaking startled and puzzled. However this time the loud voice and noise in the dream seemed to be corresponding with a real life loud voice outside his cabin door. Michael immediately threw both legs over the side of the bed and onto the floor in one choreographed movement.

He had been suddenly awakened from a deep sleep. It was Saturday morning, no work today, and his highly anticipated sleep in was being interrupted by the sound of a loud, continuous, almost authoritative knocking on his cabin door, accompanied by a rather gruff sounding male voice enquiring, "Michael…are you in there…Michael are you in there?"

For a brief moment he thought that he might have imagined it, after all he was coming out of a dream state, until the reality of it was confirmed with a repeat occurrence of the knock. Michael automatically glanced at his bedside clock. Hmm 7 a.m., a little early for a visitor he thought, then again perhaps not. This is farming country and farmers are early risers.

"Just a minute, coming," he called out as he scrambled into his tracksuit pants hopping on one leg and almost tripping over as he hurried to put them on. He opened the door and was immediately greeted by a portly man, a short portly man, probably in his early forties he thought.

He was dressed in a dark, slightly crumpled suit, wearing a loosely knotted out of fashion wide paisley tie: a tie that looked as if it had been having a long term relationship with some late night television dinners, since the paisley patterns were in some places obscured by small unwelcome intruders of the gravy type.

"Graham Patel," the visitor announced confidently in a gravelly monotone voice as he stretched out his hand to shake Michael's.

"Hope I didn't get you up, but a beautiful day to be up," came the greeting as Patty gestured upwards towards the clear blue sky.

"You wouldn't be dead for quids on a day like this," he continued in his upbeat salesmanship like manner.

He noticed the puzzled look on Michael's face.

"From Patel's Real Estate in the main street" he continued.

Michael stretched out his hand to greet his unexpected visitor.

"Michael Winton," he replied, trying to sound professional and businesslike even though he felt disheveled.

"Yea...I know," Graham replied almost casually, "nice ta meet you."

"I heard you were in town and might be looking for a place to rent. I'm a friend of the Purcells here and they thought I might be able to help you."

"Well...yes...I am looking for a place," Michael blurted out surprised at this spontaneous offer of help.

"Any particular part of town...you know...here or in Springfield?"

"Well somewhere near the river or the beach would be nice," Michael continued, remembering that Archie had spoken about the holiday rentals.

"If there's anything available that is, and perhaps with a view."

Graham paused for a few seconds rubbing his chin in thought.

"I might have something Mikey…yes I might."

"Great…would appreciate your help Graham."

"It's Patty," he interjected, "you know, Patel…everyone calls me Patty, Patty Patel."

"The river or beach eh…view eh…right…let me think."

It didn't take long.

"Yeah…I think I might have just the place for you."

"Do you like old?"

"I mean it's not ancient but it's older and renovated."

"It has got the odd possum in the ceiling at times, but they can be good company, like having a pet you don't have to feed, but it's cosy ya know, and great views and it's fully furnished. Just need to buy yourself some linen."

"I think you'll like it, the view always sells it."

"Wanna have a gander this afternoon?"

"I could pick you up at about 2 o'clock," he continued all in one breath.

"Sounds good to me," Michael replied, quietly feeling excited about the prospect of getting into his own place so quickly.

"Great…done," said Patty as he reached into his coat pocket, pulled out an oversized check handkerchief and with a flurry loudly blew his nose, creating a sound Michael later likened to a child playing their first note at their trombone lesson.

"Excuse me," he mumbled, "think I'm picking up a cold."

"Okay…I'll pick you up at 2," he continued, and with a quick firm handshake, this Danny De Vito lookalike wheeled around and strutted back towards his car whilst giving another glimpse of his ambidextrous character. He blew his nose again, wrote something in his small notebook and opened his car door all in one beautifully synchronized movement.

Michael slowly closed the cabin door, sauntered back to his bed, and fell back onto it with a sigh, silently contemplating the events of the last five minutes and quietly drifting into thoughts about the happenings of the last week. In only a few moments he had quickly fallen back asleep.

It was a beautiful blue-skied late Sunday afternoon. Soft pure white clouds like giant cotton wool balls floated silently and gently across the sky, at the same time casting shadows on the sparkling misty blue waters of the ocean below. The sun was commencing its journey into rest as Michael leaned back stretching his body into the comfortable canvas of the old squatter's chair on the balcony of his newly rented residence, courtesy of Patty Patel.

There was the same fresh crispness in the salty seaside air and the predominant sound of silence present in his surroundings as there was on the previous Friday night during his walk home with Archie, and it caused him to think of her.

The afternoon seemed unusually still and peaceful save for the intermittent sound of trawler engines as one by one they chugged and honked their way to the river mouth, once more venturing out into the open seas for their evening fishing mission.

Michael had the perfect view of them from his balcony, and the sight and sounds of these fisher folk in their boats heading off to work had a distinct melancholy about them. He thought about the different lifestyle they led from his. As the tourists and resident onlookers were winding down for the day the fishermen were winding up for the evening.

His reverie was soon interrupted by the sound of his phone ringing. Thinking it was a work issue Michael reluctantly peeled himself out of the chair and headed inside to answer the call.

"Hello…Michael speaking."

"Mikey," came the gravelly sounding voice on the line.

"Patty here," he just as abruptly continued.

"Just thought I'd give you a buzz to see ya settled in okay."

Then in what Michael thought later was the briefest phone conversation he had ever had, with the echo of his own reply, "settled in good thanks Patty" still flowing down the line came the reply.

"Good…great…glad I could help mate…must catch up for a drink…av a good week…see ya."

An all in one breath explosion of dialogue from his newly found realtor friend Patty Patel, and then he was gone.

Michael casually glanced around at the kitchen clock amazed at how loud its ticking sounded in the quiet of the approaching evening. He looked at the time, almost 6 p.m. After pouring a wine he wandered back to his balcony chair and continued his solitary reverie. Darkness was slowly descending as he sat sipping his second glass of red.

After being introduced to this haven on Saturday afternoon by Patty Patel and told he could move in immediately, he had quickly decided to rent it. For even though it was an old weatherboard building it exuded a special kind of cosiness, and the views were unsurpassed.

Now with the gentle navigation lights of the trawlers reflecting on the river surface as they slowly wended their way out to the sea, accompanied by the melancholy chugging noise of the boat engines and the synchronized sound of each ship's horn, he quietly realized what a wonderful decision he had made, impulsive as it was.

His thoughts drifted back to his encounter with Archie and her friends only two nights before. It seemed such a perfect forty-eight hours he mused. He was feeling as though he was entering a special stage of his life, new beginnings, with this new job he had undertaken, meeting Archie, and being able to find this most comfortable little hideaway.

Was this part of some broader plan he pondered? Wait and see Michael, and just enjoy what each moment brings he thought, as he lifted the last sip of wine to his mouth.

Yes…just wait and see.

"When you see a child being born you sometimes feel that there's a power greater than us that gives rise to that kind of miracle."

Dr Unwin Nicholls

Dr Unwin Nicholls

FIVE

"What if I'm all wrong about this. What if Sloan is all wrong about this too. What if the books are all wrong about this. He hasn't got much to lose, but I have my reputation to consider in getting involved in something like this. I could lose everything."

Dr Unwin Nicholls was in his car driving the short distance from his home to his clinic. He was thinking about his conversation on the phone with Garret Sloan the previous evening and his upcoming meeting with Michael Winton that morning.

Michael parked his car, stepped out, looked across the road, and stopped suddenly, surprised at what he saw. Have I got the right address he asked himself? This doesn't look like a medical clinic. It looks more like an old picture theatre. It was. The large building resembling a cinema had the unusual name The Markets emblazoned in metre deep letters across its front awning.

He walked over to the building and pressed his face against the front glass sliding door trying to get a glimpse inside. The exterior size, height, and style of the building along with its wide front entrance had given Michael the impression that in its heyday the building had probably been the town's original picture theatre.

"Must be a weekend market only," he mumbled to himself, "no sign of people here today."

He looked at the street number positioned above the sliding doors. It is the right address he thought. He glanced sideways, noticed a stairwell at the far end of the building with what looked like a couple of business signs at its entrance, and casually strolled down to see what they said.

On the side wall of the stairwell at the street level were two plaques: one stating Dr Unwin Nicholls Gynecologist and Obstetrician, and underneath it one reading Dr Margaret Morrison General Practitioner. On the opposite wall was a singular plaque that read G.S. Enterprises Pty. Ltd.

"An unusual location for a medical clinic," Michael mused as he slowly headed up the side stairs in anticipation of his meeting with this renowned specialist, Dr Unwin Nicholls.

He reached the top of the stairwell and was greeted by two single glass doors. The door on the left was signed G.S. Enterprises and the one on the right Springfield Medical Services. Michael instinctively cupped his two hands against his face to look inside the glass door on the left. He saw it was empty of any furniture or anybody but noticed a few boxes tucked away in the corner of the front office. There was the distinct smell of freshly laid carpet coming through the closed door.

He was more bemused however, when he opened the glass-panelled door to the clinic and stepped inside the clinic's waiting room. Whilst it was quite large in size, more than a normal waiting room, it was not the size of the room that caused him to be taken aback the most, rather the most unusual décor that greeted him.

The walls had been covered in brightly coloured velvet textured wallpaper with a Union Jack pattern, the national flag of Great Britain, and the floor was carpeted with a plush shag pile carpet, a brilliant shade of royal blue, presumably to match in with the colours of the Union Jack.

Dotted around the room were eight round white café style tables with stylish white seats and bright red round seating cushions. In one corner of the room was a modern coffee and tea making facility with cups and saucers, and alongside this an ample supply of plated up biscuits, with a highly visible sign above them stating "not to be eaten if client is having a procedure today."

The only wall that was not adorned with Union Jack wallpaper ran the full length of the room on the left side. It was a curtained wall that seemed to traverse the entire width of the building. The curtain itself was magnificent, floor to ceiling, made of deep dark red velvet material. It was of the type that would be seen on stage in the olden day picture theatres hanging in front of the cinema screen.

He ascertained in an instant that the clinic was located in what was known as the Dress Circle of the original picture theatre, and that behind that curtain would be a view of the downstairs ground floor level of the theatre.

Several people, ladies and babies, all presumably patients of the doctor were seated at different tables, sipping their teas and coffee, eating their biscuits and socializing, obviously waiting for their appointments. They all, almost in unison, turned their heads and glanced curiously towards Michael as he entered the clinic.

There was soft background music playing: violins and flute. It was a classical piece, and reminded him of something you might hear as a tourist walking through some noteworthy European cathedral. It was calming. The whole theme of the room seemed very British, but then again he thought, according to his research so was Dr Nicholls, very British.

The receptionist greeted Michael warmly and after confirming him in her appointment book ushered him down a narrow hallway past three or four procedure rooms.

"Doctor won't be long. He's carrying out a procedure and asked that I make you comfortable in his consulting room. He shouldn't be too much longer."

On reaching the room she opened the door, ushered him in with the standard friendly "take a seat Michael, doctor won't be long," as if he was a patient, and then just as promptly left, quietly almost reverently closing the door behind her as she went.

Michael glanced around and was once again greeted with a display of the unexpected. But whilst his waiting room experience caused him a little amusement, this experience quietly intrigued him. It was the most unusual doctor's consulting room he had ever entered, not that he had been in many.

A huge polished ornamental oak desk sat almost proudly at the back of the office accompanied by a tall black leather upholstered chair. There was a bulky maroon coloured Chesterfield leather lounge positioned against the wall on the right side of the room, whilst on the opposite wall was what could only be described as a blanketed wall of books, old and new, stretching from floor to ceiling, encased in a mahogany timber polished bookcase.

Nestled inch deep in the plush chocolate coloured shag pile carpet in the centre of the room were two single high backed leather recliner chairs on either side of a large round silver metal low set coffee table. The coffee table was emblazoned with what looked like dozens of different types of hieroglyphs of the ancient Egyptian or Greek style, he wasn't sure which. But they were certainly pictorial symbols telling what seemed to be some sort of religious or spiritual story.

As he walked towards the seating Michael glanced sideways at the array of books he was passing and stood to pause for a while. Outside of a library he had never seen such a display with so much variety, certainly not in a personal collection.

From medical books to books on history and wars, and even a collection of Shakespearian novels congregated in one block. There were biographies of well-known religious and political leaders, as well as a proliferation of news publications, some very old in appearance and some looking very new.

As he sat down and settled into the comfortableness of the leather recliner his eyes set upon another small group of books, about six or eight that were sitting in the centre of the coffee table. The books were bordered at each end with two ornate wooden bookends containing a carved image of what appeared to resemble a goat's head or perhaps a symbol of some other animal.

But it wasn't the unusual bookends that most gripped his attention, it was the titles of the books they held in place: A New World Order, The World Bank, The Illuminati, 666 The Mark Of The Beast, Nostradamus, and a few other books written by a well known doomsday author of the day, Pastor Barry Rumsey Smith. Michael had read one of his books and knew what the pastor's passion was: it was end time theories.

Michael's sense of curiosity and intrigue was interrupted with the sudden opening of the door as the doctor entered with outstretched hand.

"Michael is it?"

"Unwin Nicholls."

"Good Morning."

"Sorry to keep you waiting…how are you?"

Michael stood.

"Good Morning Dr Nicholls…very nice to meet you," he returned as he stretched out his hand in greeting.

"Please…call me Unwin."

He was different in appearance from what Michael had imagined after researching his business credentials and commercial interests a week earlier. As well as being the only specialist doctor in obstetrics and gynecology in the area, Unwin was the owner of a number of agistment properties for cattle grazing and had a diversity of other business interests, including a guava farm and a macadamia nut plantation.

"Well," Michael continued, "Unwin, I finally get to put a face to a phone conversation."

"Yes …it's good."

"Please…have a seat again," Unwin replied as he gestured for Michael to sit.

"I've arranged for reception to bring us some tea and biscuits." "Do you drink tea or would you like coffee Michael?"

"Tea will be fine."

"Great…shouldn't be long."

Much discussion followed, including Unwin's reasons for wanting to meet with Michael and Michael's reasons for wanting to meet with him. Most of the conversation was initiated by Dr Nicholls and centred around his thoughts on how they both could benefit by having a close working relationship and regular contact.

When Michael had set up the appointment after talking to Unwin's receptionist, for some unknown reason he had pictured the doctor being tall, and having a sort of cowboy commanding presence, a John Wayne type; a kind of hard-hitting successful businessman.

He was also aware that Dr Nicholls had been Oxford educated, and had imagined in his mind perhaps a slight clash of cultures with himself being of the public school variety and Unwin being a product of a prestigious overseas school, a toff of sorts. Michael had done his research accurately or so he thought.

But to his absolute surprise Dr Nicholls was nothing as he had imagined, neither in looks, nor in nature, nor in attitude. Unwin was warm and quite personable, short in stature, silver haired and gently spoken, nothing at all like the researched man, the imposing man who Michael had neatly catalogued in his mind.

After about thirty minutes the doctor glanced at his watch and rose to his feet.

"Michael I have an hour or so to spare."

"Would you like to take a drive to my closest property. It's actually also my home base and I can show you around and we can talk further?"

"Do you have the time to spare?"

Michael stood up.

"Sure…sounds good to me," he replied.

Unwin paused at reception on the way out, issued some instructions, smiled and said hello to a few of the patients seated in the waiting room, and then led Michael to the door and down the stairwell to the street, only to round the corner and run head first into Patty Patel.

"Doc…Mikey," came the sound of Patty's gravelly voice.

"Patty," came a reply in unison from both Unwin and Michael.

"Settled in Mikey?"

"Yes thanks."

"Great…gotta rush…my office is here next door to the Doc's if you need anything."

"Thanks Patty."

"Yeah no problem…good to see ya Mikey…catch ya Doc."

"Good to see you too Patty," replied Michael.

"He's always in a hurry our Patty," commented Unwin, "always looking for his next dollar."

"My car's just around the corner."

"If you like we will take it and I'll drop you back afterwards so you don't get lost," continued Unwin.

"Sounds good to me…thanks."

It would only be a short drive, around fifteen minutes, to Unwin's large property tucked away in the hills above the township, but Michael saw this as an opportunity to satisfy his curiosity a little further.

"I couldn't help but notice you have an interesting collection of books Unwin," he said, in an attempt to engage him in conversation and to get to know him a little better.

"A lot of books and books about end times on your coffee table…you like reading about spiritual things?"

"Yes I do love books."

"I'm interested in all kinds of subjects including end times."

"You know the beginning of the world and of creation and the end of the world and of this earth as we know it, and all the theories that go with it."

"I like delving into other spiritual writings too, not just end times."

"I figure it must be because my occupation as a gynecologist deals with creation, you know."

"When you see a child being born you sometimes feel that there's a power greater than us that gives rise to that kind of miracle, and that there must be another side to life, a spiritual side."

"Right...yes...I understand that," replied Michael.

Unwin calmly questioned.

"You ever think much about the spiritual side of life Michael, have you had any spiritual experiences?"

"Yes I do Unwin and actually yes I have had some experience."

Michael felt quite comfortable in sharing with Unwin his conversion experience from his youth and how that now as an adult he felt that the mainstream church services seemed to be too ritualistic, and lacking in real life changing substance. He shared with Unwin that it was this thinking that had led him to explore the writings of a smorgasbord of other religious cultures apart from Christianity.

"So I guess you wouldn't have had a chance to attend any of the Reverend Garret Sloan's meetings in the district?" the doctor queried.

"Oh of course you wouldn't, you've only been here a few weeks."

"Now there's a man of substance and power," continued Unwin.

"No I haven't Unwin, but I have heard about him and am looking forward to going along to one of his meetings when he is next in town."

Unwin paused as if carefully phrasing his next question.

"Michael can I ask you a question?"

"Sure."

"If someone was really searching, wanting to add some practical spiritual component to their lives and they came to you and asked what road they should take...what would you tell them...you know based on your experience?"

"Like would you just say well find a church that suits you and start going to the Sunday services?"

"No I don't think I would say just that."

Michael paused in the moment and reflected. He knew that Unwin was in fact asking the question for himself.

"Unwin I think firstly I would say that they need to bring it back to the starting point and ask themselves the question, do I believe in God or don't I?"

"When I say believe in God, I also mean believe in the things of God that people of limited spiritual knowledge speak about, such as heaven's reward and hell's punishment and a belief in a spiritual world."

"If the answer is I don't: I don't believe in God, and I don't believe in the afterlife, then there is really no need to go any further. Because if you're searching to add some sort of spiritual component to your life, that has to be a measure of belief in something beyond ourselves as being real."

"Think about it."

"If you don't believe there is a God nor a heaven nor a hell then you can choose whatever philosophy of life you want. You know kill or be killed or give and it shall be given unto you, whatever good or bad life philosophy you are drawn to."

"Because if you think there is no God, and with that comes the no heaven and no hell belief, then to you nothing's lost with what lifestyle philosophy you choose, because it doesn't matter."

"You live, you die, and that's it."

"You are choosing to dictate the terms of your life experience here on earth and the outcomes in the afterlife which you believe are none, and in doing so are accepting responsibility for the outcome if you are wrong."

"Of course if you take that path and it turns out to be wrong then you chose the course so there is no one to blame but yourself."

"I mean I hear people say things like, well I don't believe in God, I'm not into all this religious stuff. I mean that kind of fixed lifestyle choice can be a bit risky."

"My answer to that is well I don't believe in a lot of that religious stuff too, but I do believe there is a Divine Being who has a plan for this earth and all who are in it, and I'd like to know as much about it as I can."

"True...I see that."

"So that's the first thing to sort, and if we decide yes I believe in God then comes our responsibility to ourselves to follow through."

"You know if we say yes, I believe there is a God, or a universal life force that created all things and sustains all things, then is that all we should do, you know just accept it?"

"Or should we try to find out how this whole God thing all works."

"Is that what you did Michael?"

"Yes I did."

"I came across a bible verse many years ago that said, study to show thyself approved unto God."

"You see God knows we don't understand it all…but God wants us to know more, to grow in understanding."

"Unwin some people who say yes I believe in God settle for thinking of that God only as an old white haired man dressed in robes, sitting outside the gates of some place paved with gold called heaven, waiting to tick you off the entry list when you arrive after you die."

"Along with this they align that thinking with the polar spiritual opposite. They think of the devil as a skinny little man with horns, dressed in red tights, carrying a pitchfork, and sitting outside the gates of a huge furnace also waiting to tick you off his list."

"But it's all they know because that's all the understanding they have ever been given in their formative years."

"You remember when our mums would say when we were children…if you're naughty God will punish you…well I know mine did occasionally."

"So is formed from childhood for some people a singular spiritual or religious goal in life."

"What's that Michael?"

"To try to be a good person so as to go to heaven when they die and not to hell."

"Is that a bad thing?" Unwin queried.

"No not if it motivates them to be a good person in life but it limits them."

"In what way?"

"Well I think if we limit our understanding of a spiritual life to just the heaven versus hell thing that seems to me to be an entire waste of a belief."

"What do you mean?"

"Well by limiting your understanding you've drawn the short straw… it's risky."

"You know, you get to the gates of heaven thinking all's good. St Peter looks at his list, says sorry mate your name's not here try one floor down, you might be on that list."

"You know…head south."

Unwin threw his head back and laughed.

Michael continued.

"So you think, oh bugger, why didn't someone tell me I'd got it wrong: that there was more to it than just a white haired old man up north and a skinny man in red tights down south and a heaven and hell theory and me trying to be as good as I could while I was alive."

"I mean I thought I was doing so well."

Unwin laughed again, "interesting."

"So you're saying Michael that we should try and find out as much as we can about this whole thing called the spiritual life and its workings while we are still here."

"Yes…that's right…it's too late after we're gone…but only based on the premise that you actually believe in the first place that there is a God, that God does exist."

"If you don't believe…then enquire of yourself why you don't…and there is usually a deep personal reason for atheistic type thinking…and if that doesn't rationally change your mind then live your life as you think right…give it your best shot as they say."

"You ask the average person on the street do they believe in God and most people will adamantly say of course I do."

"Then Unwin if you ask them what are they doing about it you will probably find that most are doing absolutely nothing…except perhaps trying to lead a good life."

"Some might be going to church at Easter and Christmas or be regular attendees at the annual Christmas Carols night but that will be about it."

"Most people spend every ounce of energy while they are alive trying to create a heavenly life on earth and put in no effort with regards to a future life in the heavenlies after they pass."

"Our earthly life is temporal but our afterlife is eternal."

"To me it's insane to have a belief of such mammoth proportions…you know we are talking about the complete afterlife experience here…and yet some people are just living in hope that one day they'll go to heaven."

"So how did you study to find out how the spiritual life works Michael, you mean by reading books?"

"Yes, that's helpful of course, but remember some books whilst written with the best intention don't necessarily reveal God's intention, more so what a particular author thought about God's intention."

"You mean books like the Bible too?"

"Yes the Bible too."

"I mean look, if we want to get as close as possible to the truth about God and God's purpose the ancient unadulterated spiritual books like the Bible will get us closer to the truth more so than Joe Blogs personal interpretation."

"But I mean even in terms of the Bible a lot of important books were left out."

"Do you know how our current Bible came about Unwin?"

"No I don't."

Michael continued.

"The Bible is known as a canon, which is a collection of spiritual texts. When the New Testament canon was originally put together by the church leaders of the day, a lot of the books that are in the current New Testament like Hebrews, and James and Jude and Revelation were not included."

"Then gradually over two to three hundred years of disputes amongst

Catholic leaders as to what texts should be included, the Bishop of Alexandria in the year 367 signed off on what would become the final New Testament. So you could say that what God wanted us to know about everything spiritual all came back to the opinion of one Catholic bishop, old Athanasius the Bishop of Alexandria."

"I personally find it a bit daunting that on one man's opinion due to the church politics of the day certain books were left out: The Gospel of Thomas, The Essene Gospel of John, 1 Clement, Shepherd and Earnest, and others. They're known as the Lost Gospels."

"But you know whether it be the Bible for the Christians in the world, the Koran for the Muslims, the Bhagavad Gita for the Hindus, or the Tipitaka for the Buddhists, it's by exploring the teachings in these books we come to our own conclusions about God and God's purpose."

"Some people will only stick with what they know, particularly some Pentecostal Christians. You know to some of them if it's not of the Bible it's of the devil, which is really the heaven or hell theory in practice once again."

"Unwin if you were a Pentecostal minister and said to one of your congregation in a counselling session that the less they respond to negative people the more they will have God's peace in their life, they would take it as a word from God."

"But if you followed it up with...that's a quote from the Buddha's teachings, well they would stutter and splutter and think you were possessed by a demonic spirit of Buddha that needed the laying on of hands to be cast out."

"You know...loose him...in the name of Jesus," Michael bellowed with a loud voice, "spirit of Buddha come out of him."

Unwin laughed.

"True...true."

"Unwin, Gautama Buddha received far more wisdom from God to teach people about the spiritual life than did a combination of all the Pentecostal ministers alive."

"He was in communion with God before Jesus was born."

"So what do you think Michael?"

"You mean about the different religious teachings?"

"Yes."

"I think there are Divine truths in all of them and there are many points of agreement in all of them, but we can never forget they were all put on paper or papyrus by flawed men and women like us who were also searching."

"But here's the good part Unwin…I can tell you this one thing that is common to all of them, this one thing for sure."

"What's that?"

"They all speak of and believe in a supreme being…God."

"They all believe in God, even if they all have different names for God."

"So that's a start."

Unwin threw his head back and laughed.

"Right."

"But look, in simple terms, my thoughts."

"If you say you believe in God just quietly enquire further. Read, meditate, talk to the God you believe in, perhaps attend a church you feel comfortable in, and listen to your heart, you know, that little voice in your head. And of course above all, love all, and do good to all and seek peace."

"Anyway Unwin I hope that didn't sound too complicated?"

"No it didn't Michael, it didn't."

"Quite the contrary."

"Thanks Michael I like that."

"Thank you for your insights…we must talk more."

"Here we are, we've arrived."

The property was a magnificent piece of land tucked away in seclusion high in the hills surrounding the township.

"Nice and private Unwin."

"Like my privacy," quipped Unwin.

"Nearest neighbour is a good two hundred metres downhill."

The house was exactly as Michael expected it would be, belonging to a man of Unwin's profession and business assets: large and low set, sprawling, its driveway lined with large spreading Jacaranda trees, some with their umbrella of beautiful purple bell like flowers almost fully closed due to the onset of summer.

"Let's grab a coffee while I show you about," suggested Unwin, "come inside."

"The kids are at school and my wife Marie will be out doing some charity work with one of those women's groups you know."

"Sure."

Michael and Unwin entered the house through the front door that led straight into the lounge room.

"How many children do you have Unwin?"

"Two boys and two girls."

Inside the house the surroundings could only be described as opulent. The home was not the standard layout of the day. It was obviously architecturally designed with a beautiful central sunken lounge area tastefully decorated, the furniture colours themselves complementing a large fireplace constructed of stacked rustic stone tiles stretching from floor to ceiling. Close by in the room were two baby grand black Yamaha Pianos.

Unwin had noticed a slight sense of bewilderment on Michael's face as his eyes settled upon the two of them, and was quick to comment, "got two for the price of one at a factory clearance…looking for a church I can donate one to…sort of have one in mind…we'll see."

Nothing more was said.

"Coffee or tea?"

"Coffee this time thanks."

Dr Nicholls entered the kitchen area located at the far end of the large open plan room with Michael closely following. It was a classic design with the main wall of storage cupboards built in a semi-circle facing onto a huge circular marble topped bench obviously used for food preparation.

Built into the middle of the wall of cupboards was what Michael recognized as a black wood-fired oven. They were a type of cooking oven that did not need gas or electricity but could be heated merely by burning wood in a chamber. Food is then cooked in the same heated chamber after the fire and coals have been swept out.

"Love the wood-fired oven Unwin," Michael said as he watched him reach into the cupboard for the cups and coffee.

"You don't see many of those around."

"Yes…thanks…I like it…it's great for pizzas and if you are really adventurous for baking bread."

"Don't need gas or electricity."

"All you need is a ready chopped stockpile of wood, and of course the ingredients."

"Black or white?" he queried.

"With or without?"

"White with one," replied Michael.

"There you go…bring your coffee and I'll show you outside."

At the rear of the home was a beautiful manicured looking lawn covering several hectares. Positioned amongst this were eight corrals, each surrounded with a wood and stranded cable fence painted white. To the bottom at about a distance of fifty metres was a huge outdoor tin panelled storage shed of barn type construction.

Alongside the barn Michael observed what was the biggest non-commercial water storage tank that he had even seen. It had obvious underground connections to gather the rainwater run-off from the house with pipes visibly protruding into it at ground level as well as a large round open topped mesh roof covering to gather rainwater directly.

One corral housed some Australorp type chickens: a chicken breed of Australian origin developed as a utility breed with a focus on egg laying, another had two beautiful riding ponies, the property of his two teenage children as Unwin was quick to share, and the third corral housed three Jersey cows. Vegetable gardens occupied pride of place in all the other corrals.

"Almost a self-sustainable living environment," Michael commented as he and Unwin leaned on the fence overlooking the scene below.

"You've got the milk and the eggs for the protein and the veggies for the fiber."

"You're not taking those end times theories too seriously are you?" Michael joked.

Unwin laughed and quickly side stepped Michael's end times comment.

"Right…a self-sustainable living environment…never thought of it that way, it is Michael…it is."

"Come let's walk down to the shed. I'll show you something interesting."

"You would have studied ancient farming methods and history as part of your Agricultural Science degree wouldn't you?"

"Yes…I did."

"Well then you'll be really interested in this."

The huge high ceilinged barn like shed was locked as Unwin reached for his car key ring that held the key to the padlock on the large door. He swung one side of the huge double doors outwards to allow entry. It would be as they idled their way through the shed that Michael saw what he would some years later come to realize were the final pictures that caused all his latent suspicions to fall into place.

On the left hand side of the barn there were dozens of tied up bales of grain. The reason for them being there was described by Unwin in a slightly flippant comment saying, "that's my little Triticale stockpile…you never know where your next meal is coming from."

Beside them in a corner were a rather large stockpile of chopped firewood and three bicycles.

"You know what Triticale is Michael I presume?"

"Yes I do," replied Michael, but Unwin still went on to explain.

"It's a grain that is a hybrid of wheat and rye, disease and environment tolerant, has long life, mostly grown for fodder, but is also used in some breakfast cereals. It's human tolerant, so readily digestible."

"Good healthy fodder for my cows and my kids," he laughed.

"Patty has got a few milkers too, so I share it with him."

Tucked in a dark corner at the back end of the stockpile was a tall weird looking contraption with a large bladed wheel. It looked like a picture Michael had seen once of a non-electric mechanical machine coming out of England's transition to new manufacturing processes in the 18th century: known as the Industrial Revolution.

"Here's what I said you'd be interested in."

"It's sometimes called a flour miller he went on. It's a machine for grinding a variety of grains."

"Wow…it's amazing."

"Yes I've read about these…how does it work?"

"I believe it's water powered?"

"Well it is water and generator powered," continued Unwin, "although you could adapt it to be powered simply by wind or livestock if you had no water or power."

"Water is pumped using a generator through the sluice gate and it flows under the wheel to make it turn. This then activates those two other gear wheels."

"You've got your bottom bed of stones which are fixed and your top stone which rotates to crush the grain."

"The grain is fed through those bins at the top there…and falls down to the millstones below. The milled grain is collected as it emerges through grooves in the runner stone."

"Take the flour to the kitchen and you can bake your own bread," he continued grinning.

Unwin laughed, "and if the power is out you can bake it in your wood fired oven."

Michael laughed.

"So Michael like it?"

"Love it."

"It's fascinating Unwin, fascinating."

"I have a bee farmer friend who is handy with his hands…he built it."

"Your bee farmer friend is a very clever man."

"He is Michael…that he is."

"Just thought you might like to see that."

Unwin sat down on one of the bales of grain as Michael circled the gristmill checking it out. Unwin sighed, paused and looked like he wanted to chat further. It was obvious to Michael that Unwin had a lot of unanswered questions in his mind, particularly about the spiritual life.

"Michael, Margie tells me you have done a lot of study of the Bible over time."

"Yes I guess I have."

"Okay can I ask you a question?"

"Sure."

"If you could sum up what the Christian life or the spiritual life is all about, then how would you describe it Michael?"

Michael sensed what he had thought earlier when he had first entered Unwin's office, that this man had an almost unquenchable desire to understand the things of the spiritual world.

"I guess I see it as a warfare, Unwin."

"I am a firm believer in the Bible verse that talks about the Christian life as a warfare."

"But not a warfare that we see constantly where different religions or different denominations fight with each other over what teaching is right and what teaching is wrong, or what doctrine is right and what doctrine is wrong."

"It's a spiritual warfare by two opposing forces aimed at capturing the thoughts and subsequent allegiance of every individual on this earth."

"The heaven versus hell theory?" queried Unwin.

"Sort of but without a white haired old man and a skinny man in red tights."

"It's a warfare of polar emotional and attitudinal opposites supported and fed by polar spirit opposites."

"What do you mean Michael?"

"You know the emotion of love versus hate, the attitude of pride versus humility, the emotion of happiness versus sadness, the attitude of compassion versus indifference, kindness versus selfishness, courage versus fear etcetera."

"Unwin this is the warfare that you and I are confronted with every day."

"I believe there is a spirit with the same name that feeds these emotions and attitudes in our thought life, and is strengthened in return by our behaviours according to whatever emotion or attitude we have aligned ourselves with."

"Which then perpetuates the cycle whether it be of rightness or wrongness, of morality or immorality."

"Can you give me an example of that?"

"Sure and I'll try and keep it simple."

"Let's look at the Spirit of Lust. The Spirit of Lust feeds you lustful thoughts. You either reject them or entertain them and if you entertain them for long enough it begins to influence your behaviour."

"Your behaviour then embraces immoral activity which then strengthens the influence of that entity, the Spirit of Lust in your life."

"The Pentecostals refer to it as being possessed, but I also think a lot of Pentecostals really don't understand the process or the difference between an obsession one might have and the state of possession."

"Does that make sense?"

"Pretty much."

Michael continued.

"Everyone knows that proverb, as a man thinketh in his heart, so is he. The word heart in that proverb means mind, and the true meaning is, as a man continually thinketh in his mind so is he."

"So as a person continually thinks in their mind a particular emotional thought, that emotional attitude will flow over into their physical body and their behaviour and actions will mirror that particular emotion."

"Our behaviour is the physical outlet for our dominant mental thought pattern and or our dominant emotional state."

"Think fearful thoughts all the time and you will become a worrier, a fearful person in your behaviour which then accentuates the involvement of the Spirit of Fear, you know spiritual forces."

"Do you remember that television series called The Untouchables? It finished around six years ago I think."

"I do Michael…one of my favourites…Eliot Ness and his team of federal agents versus the Chicago mobsters."

"That's right…I liked it too…it had a goodness versus evil theme to it."

"Do you remember the crime bosses always had an enforcer…one who made sure the bosses' evil plans were carried out?"

"I do Michael…Frank Nitti…I remember he was Al Capone's enforcer."

Michael laughed.

"Good memory."

"Yes…I loved that show."

"Okay…that's what these spiritual entities or demons as the Pentecostals call them are…I prefer to call them life forces…they are the enforcers of Lucifer's will: enforce…an entity that forces."

"Yes…I see that Michael."

"Thank you for that Michael…thank you."

"So you see this life on earth as just one continuous spiritual warfare?"

"I do Unwin…I do…being played out here on earth…and we are told that in the Bible. We wrestle not against flesh and blood but against wickedness in heavenly places."

Having finished their coffee and their walk around they both headed back to the house.

"Well I had better be getting back Michael…you know patients to see…a quick tour is a good tour."

"Sure…and thanks Unwin…thanks for showing me around."

They drove the short distance back to the surgery.

Unwin had gone quiet for a moment at the start of the drive and then glanced across at Michael.

"Michael can I ask you one last question?"

"Sure Unwin."

"I know you've been involved in the Assemblies of God Church which has Pentecostal beliefs…you know they believe in the supernatural… demonic possession and the casting out of demons."

"Sure."

"You mentioned when we were talking in the barn that Pentecostals believe in demon possession but most could not explain how the process works."

"That's right I did."

"Okay…this is something that has puzzled me for a while too…how do these evil spirits get into a person's life?"

"I mean how do people get possessed…as the Pentecostals call it…in the first place?"

"That's a good question Unwin."

"Probably the first premise you have to accept is that there is a supernatural world…a world of operational spirits or entities as they are known…you know God and the Devil…goodness and evil in spirit form."

"A lot of people have trouble with this. They will believe in the supernatural aspect of God the Holy Spirit. You know the Bible does say God is Spirit, it doesn't say God is an old white haired man, and they believe in Casper the friendly ghost…because well of course he's friendly…but whoa…don't take it any further than that…you see people get scared at the thought of evil spirits."

"Okay let's try and keep it simple but here is what I believe about how people get possessed."

"We spoke a little about this before Unwin but it bears repeating."

"In all human beings the emotional energy that transforms or changes people's behaviour arises at the point where the mind meets the body, where our thoughts start to dictate our emotional state and our emotional state influences our bodily actions."

"Our emotional energy is our body's reaction to our mind's dominant thought pattern. If our thoughts are constantly angry, our emotional energy will be one of anger."

"You hear people say it quite often, I don't know I just feel angry all the time."

"That's an emotional state…anger is an emotion."

"This then triggers our bodies to respond angrily in some way, we will act out that angry emotion we are feeling in some way. You know most probably we will get into arguments with others and we will be disagreeable quite often. People will say we are a cranky person."

"That's the lower end of the emotional scale."

"But that's not demonic possession that's just an emotional obsession."

"However if you emotionally obsess long and hard enough about something you build up that dominant energy force to a point where you open yourself up to demonic influences because entities are an energy life force that feed on like emotional energy."

"Human beings emotions are a fuel source for entities."

"You become possessed by a Spirit of Anger."

"So that's when what should have been a disagreement only or a minor argument between two people coming out of angry emotions can be elevated to a behavioural act of violence."

"It's where an emotional obsession graduates to a physical possession. Like entity is attracted to a like energy and they both subsequently feed and energize each other."

"It's in the Bible…where it talks about the fact that everywhere Jesus went he found people possessed and cast the demons out of them…he took the people back from the devil's control."

"How did Jesus know they were possessed? Well apart from his intuitive gift, their emotional behaviour and actions were a good indicator from the start."

"When through continual particular emotional obsession you allow the same spiritual energy force to come in, then you become possessed, and it takes a stronger more powerful spiritual force to get it out."

"Will power just can't quite do it."

"Thus endeth the lesson Unwin."

"Yes I see that…thanks Michael…thank you."

"Okay Michael, well here we are… it was great to see you and get to know you."

"We'll organize a regular get together…perhaps bi-monthly if that suits you?"

"Sure."

"Hey…just had a thought," Unwin continued.

"I've got a group of my investors getting together on Saturday to have a look at their holdings in my nut and guava farms."

"Be good for you to see how it is all coming along. Is your diary free?"

"Could pick you up if you like."

"Sure, I'm free, sounds great," returned Michael.

"What time?"

"Say 8 ish outside the surgery."

"Good…great," replied Michael.

They shook hands and Unwin disappeared quickly back up the stairwell.

Michael put his key in his car door and was about to open it.

"Michael…how are you?" came the cheery greeting from behind as he was opening his door.

He quickly turned in the direction of the voice.

"Margie…Hi…I'm good…yes good…just been up to Dr Nicholls' place."

"How did it go?"

"Good."

"He's very easy to talk to. It was much more relaxed than I thought it would be."

"Sort of personal, not all big business."

"Yes…he's like that…he has a nice place."

"Been there?"

"Yes I have."

"Did he let you into his secret man cave…you know his shed?" queried Margie.

"Yes he did."

"Well Michael you have done yourself proud…he is a very private person. That means he likes you."

She leaned over and gentled touched the left side of his face just below his ear with her finger.

Margie grimaced slightly.

"Looks like you have a little mole there, it would be wise to get that looked at."

"Give the clinic a ring to make an appointment and I'll check it out for you."

"Okay…thanks, I will."

"Well," she continued, "gotta go…on my lunch break…is the gang still meeting at your place Wednesday fortnight?"

"Sure are."

"Okay Michael…see you then…bye," she said as she scuttled up the stairwell.

Margie suddenly stopped halfway up the stairs.

Michael in the moment thought she must have forgotten something. But she merely turned around and called out loudly as she did.

"Hey Michael…I won't see you before then, so Merry Christmas for next Thursday."

"And a Merry Christmas to you Margie," he replied smiling whilst opening his car door and climbing in. She seemed nice he thought. It will be good to get to know her more in their next group get together.

It had been during Michael's first post Carols coffee hook up with Archie that Archie had raised the subject of a regular get together since they had all got on so well at the Carols night. Archie had suggested that they could meet at each other's homes on a rotational basis on a Wednesday night every fortnight or so for fun and fellowship. She had then done the liaison with all the others and for the initial gathering all except Judy would be available to attend.

"How about if I can organize it that we have the first one at your place Michael," she had suggested.

"It could double as a house warming party without the presents," she had joked as they sat drinking coffee on the day.

"Sounds good."

"The only admission prerequisites are to bring a happy attitude, your musical instrument if you play one and your own beverage of choice, wine or soft drink."

"The host which in this first instance is you Michael provide the venue only," she had quipped, "the rest of us will supply the drinks, nibblies and snacks."

It had been a busy week for Michael. He paused before starting his car to drive off and thought about the events of the last hour or so.

Unwin Nicholls was an interesting and personable man he thought, but there was something about their time together that niggled Michael slightly and he wasn't quite sure what it was. Perhaps he thought it wasn't what he saw and heard from Unwin Nicholls during their time together: it was what he saw and didn't hear.

He was evasive in some parts of their conversation and in his manner of delivery. It had mentally alerted Michael to the fact that with

Unwin Nicholls what you saw was not necessarily what you really got, that there was a lot more going on in Dr Nicholls' head than he was prepared to reveal at that moment.

Michael thought for a few minutes more.

Yes…his seemingly unquenchable thirst for a greater understanding of spiritual things, the particular genre of his coffee table book collection, his sustainable living environment with his grain crusher and his triticale stockpile, his tendency to blush and evade entertaining any discussion where the words end times were mentioned. There was more going on with Unwin Nicholls than was being revealed.

He put the car into gear and slowly drove off…anyway he thought… that was then and this is now…only two days to go and it's Saturday and I get to see Archie for coffee again. Now that's something even better to think about. End time conspiracy theories can wait.

> *"Michael can I ask your opinion on something?"*

"Sure."

"I'm twenty one years old, still a virgin, and my mother wants me to date and eventually marry only boys of my own Greek nationality. Do you think that's right?"

Archie Vernados

Argiroula 'Archie' Vernados

SIX

—◦◦◦—

"I'm sorry I can't come around and help you mama. I've arranged to go paddleboating with Michael Winton. I know what you're thinking mama, is he Greek. No he's not, but I'm sure if you got to know him you would really like him."

Archie was in deep discussion with her mother at the Plaka Pastry and Café, after meeting up with her to request extra work hours for her best friend Kelly.

—◦◦◦—

It had been two weeks since Michael and Archie had got together for their first coffee date. Now it was only a few days out from Christmas Eve and they were meeting for their second one. Archie had suggested they catch up at the local bakery cafe half way down the tourist strip alongside the river in the fishing village of Lighthouse Bay. The Plaka Pastry and Café as it was called.

It had been a hectic time for Michael getting settled into his new role and his new living quarters, catching up with the financials of the business, meeting some of his clients, and all this interspersed with a couple of drives back to the city to give updates to his employer.

Archie had been busy too. Since there were no permanent positions available as a teacher in the local school, she worked at three different part time jobs: two days a week in her father's furniture and electrical store business, two days in the family bakery, and some occasional tutoring on any other free days.

In the constant bustle of each day, the memory of her walk home with Michael after the Carols night had floated across Archie's mind frequently, including all the naturalness and niceness surrounding their conversation. She found herself excited in anticipation of getting to know him better and looked forward to catching up with him again for their second coffee date.

Whilst she had mulled over in her mind many times most of that night's conversation, she had particularly thought a lot about an incident that had happened at the start of their walk home. She had felt it reflected strongly on the character of this man, Michael Winton. It occurred as they were coming out of the park gate.

Michael was positioned on her left nearest the houses and shop fronts. In an instant he had immediately done a skip step, ducked behind her, and crossed over to her right side so that he was positioned nearest the gutter side of the footpath.

When Archie had queried him as to why he had done this, he went on to explain that his mother had taught each boy in the family from an early age that it was customary when walking with a lady for men to walk on the roadside of the footpath: that it was the correct etiquette.

Michael had shared that in his grandmother's day, the olden days as he called them, when couples were out walking, they were often accompanied by passing horses leaving deposits on the roadside, or horse drawn carriages which had a tendency to swerve off the road and splash filthy water or worse still horse manure onto the kerb. So the man's role was to protect his strolling lady friend from unidentified flying objects as Michael had humorously put it.

She had laughed when he expressed it that way. But to her it was more than just a story about the customs of a previous generation. She felt it showed in Michael a beautiful old-fashioned attitude to relationships that seemed to be missing in the society of the day. She liked that, and she liked Michael. She felt safe with him. There seemed to be a kindness but at the same time a gentle strength in his character.

She had always preferred spending time with male friends who exuded these kinds of protective qualities, even more so if the male who had them was not aware of it, and not aware of how special it was to most women. But so far in her dating life she had found the number of available men like this were few and far between.

But there were other things on the night. Like the way he just automatically leaned across and opened the front gate for her to walk through when they arrived at her cottage. Then when she had put her key into the front door and had glanced back over her shoulder to the gate, fully expecting to see Michael walking off down the road, she found him still standing there watching her. She realized that he was waiting for her to safely enter her house before he left.

She had appreciated this gesture and had given him a goodnight wave as she turned, and he had returned it. She liked that.

However Archie was always subconsciously aware in her daydreaming times that there was a problem to any thought of a long-term relationship with Michael: not a problem from her point of view but rather from somebody else's. She had seen it happen before. The dilemma was that even though Archie knew her mother would surely like Michael, it would not be enough. Liking a suitor was not the first priority for a traditionalist Greek mother in determining who might be a good life partner for her daughter.

From her mother's point of view, the starting point of any potential long term relationship with her daughter had always been and would always be that the male beau should without exception be of her own Greek culture by birth.

The Vernados family was what you might call the traditional Greek family. Her father Makis, her mother Aurelia, Archie and her brother Peter were a close-knit family. Originally from the Plaka district in Athens, they had operated a bakery there that had been in the family for more than three generations. It was however in 1951 at the time when Archie was around three years of age that the family had made the momentous decision to sell the family business and to emigrate to Australia.

This was a time of significant activity in the era of Australia's post war economic and social development and Makis had been fortunate in obtaining employment in a massive hydroelectricity and irrigation complex that had commenced two years before in the southeast of the country. It was called the Snowy Mountains scheme.

It was a massive post war engineered construction project consisting of sixteen major dams, seven power stations, a pumping station, and two hundred and twenty five tunnels, pipelines and aqueducts and was expected to take at least twenty years to complete. It had commenced in 1949 and the scheme was noticeable in its immigrant and mostly European workforce. Makis had applied and been successful in becoming a part of that workforce.

His employment in this work environment over a period of twelve years would see him eventually save enough money to purchase the furniture and electrical retail business he now operated with his family in Springfield, as well as opening a bakery style café. The shop was positioned in the perfect location, right beside the beautiful blue river flowing alongside the tourist stretch of Lighthouse Bay. It had been set up and was now being managed by his wife Aurelia.

Aurelia had brought a slice of her mother country into play when she designed, outfitted and subsequently opened her new establishment. It was a bakery with an exterior that had a settled relaxed loveliness of appearance, with the interior possessing an elegant old-fashioned casualness of décor and furnishings.

On the outside it was a business look that would have fitted quite comfortably amongst the whitewashed shops and restaurants along the seaside promenade of Mykonos back home in the Greek Islands, with the interior retail and dining area of the cafe being equally as tasteful and delightful in appearance.

Refrigerated glass fronted cabinets were heavily laden with sweet pastries and biscuits that were traditionally of Greek origin:

Baklava cigars, Kataifi Muffins, Finikias, Cream Kataifi all cleverly lined up, deliciously tempting, and eagerly awaiting patronage by an unsuspecting tourist who happened to stumble in merely looking for a coffee with a view as the sign out the front had said.

It was here at The Plaka Pastry and Cafe that Archie had suggested she and Michael get together for their second coffee date on that Saturday morning.

Aurelia, Archie's mother, was a dyed in the wool traditionalist, a proud likeable Greek woman who carried with her into her new life in the lucky country, as she often called it, generations of longheld Greek customs and values.

In traditional Greek society there is an emphasis on family unity. To Aurelia everything that happened within the family unit, every decision made and action taken by all members must always be underpinned by and focussed on maintaining that unity. However for some Greek children who had grown up in a non-Greek culture in another country this kind of attitude could be socially suffocating.

Not only this, in a traditional Greek family everything was collectivist. Family resources were communal. Everybody in the family contributed and everyone received back both financially and socially. In Aurelia's mind, the collective basis of her family's operation meant that her whole family either gained or suffered from the repercussions of any member's individual behaviour with a special focus always towards the behaviour of the daughter.

For Aurelia, as in all Greek families, her concentration was centred on her husband first, their unmarried children second, and lastly herself. Aurelia's main focus in life was to provide the next generation of Vernados families with economic security, not only through their own personal endeavours but also through the correct choice of a life partner for both her children. For Archie this would predominantly be through an arranged marriage with a Greek male, as was the custom for female siblings.

To assist her in her mission Aurelia had a little book of behavioural quotes that she would refer to often as she instructed her children in moral values and reinforced traditional Greek customs. She had purchased the small book in the early years of her marriage after it had caught her attention as it sat amongst a pile of clearance books on a table at the local market.

Her noticing it had nothing to do with the quality of its content but rather because of the title boldly printed on its front cover: Famous Sayings and Quotes of Marcus Aurelius. For her husband's name was Makis, albeit spelt differently, and her name was Aurelia, almost the same as Aurelius, perhaps the plural of Aurelia she had reasoned when her eyes first fell upon it.

She had kept this book for years, read it often, and subsequently brought it with her to her new country, where the book had over time become for her the ethical behaviour instruction manual and guide for herself and her growing family.

Archie, ever conscious of her mother's watchful and sometimes overbearing parental eye around her, when arranging the meeting place with Michael, had picked a specific day and time when she knew her friend Kelly would be manning the bakery. Her mother Aurelia would always take Saturday mornings off to attend to her home duties.

⸺⸙⸺

Michael hadn't been down this end of the tourist strip before and was enjoying the gentle warmth of the sun on his face as he strolled towards The Plaka Pastry and Cafe for his 10 a.m. catch up with Archie.

"Hey Kelly…this is a surprise…I didn't know you were so multi-skilled," Michael blurted out as he entered the bakery, upon sighting Kelly Purcell, apron on, standing behind the counter handing a customer her change.

"Hey, what can I say," replied Kelly cheerily, "sooo multi-talented, give me a counter and I can work it."

"And not only that."

"Can I show a tourist where their room for the night is?"

"Yes I can."

"Can I change their linen for them?"

"Yes I can."

"And can I come down here and knock up a few pastries and coffees for their breakfast after telling them that the best place to eat in town is here?"

"Yes I can," she and Michael both chanted in unison.

Michael liked Kelly. She had a similar wit to his.

"Arch is out there in the cosy corner on the balcony," she said gesturing towards the door without looking.

"I'll be out in a sec with the menu, and don't worry we've got it covered, it's her mum's half day off."

"Right…thanks," replied Michael, slightly puzzled by the last part of her statement.

The location of the bakery and the layout of it were superb in his eyes: not a large place, just an adequate size, it was perfectly positioned halfway down the main street of the Lighthouse Bay Village tourist area.

Lighthouse Bay, whilst being the port of the township of Springfield, had become over time a thriving little village in its own right, with a retail tourist hub complementing the fishing and trawling activities of the bay. The village had seen considerable growth in tourism over the years, supported by the availability of reasonably priced accommodation at the large tourist park owned by the Purcell family, Kelly's parents.

However any proposal for the establishment of a new retail shop in the main tourist strip fell under strict appearance covenants demanded by the local authority as it sought to preserve the original old-fashioned village atmosphere of the precinct. Aurelia's cafe had strictly complied with these covenants.

Originally an old small fibro cottage, obviously someone's residence in a time long since past, and tucked in between two other established outlets, both formerly housing, it had been lovingly restored by contractors under strict instructions from Aurelia.

Its condition when Aurelia first sighted it had varied depending on what wall you were looking at. It had noticeably undergone several attempts at being renovated by a variety of homeowners since its original construction in the late 1890's. Parts of the building were obviously structurally fragile with not much preparation having gone into numerous attempts over time to repaint it. Colours were to be seen coming through a variety of other colours in areas where the paint had begun flaking.

But with the removal of a few interior walls, the sanding and staining of the original floorboards, a professional repaint of both the interior and exterior, and the restoration of the original colonial lace style wrought iron facade at the front, the building was transformed. In addition, after trailing through the facade blossoming pink bougainvillea flowers surfacing from huge concrete pots spaced along the front footpath, the exterior of the bakery had ended up with a kind of old fashioned fairytale look about it.

Then after adding a large covered balcony seating area at the back of the building overlooking the moored fishing boats on the river, and outfitting it all with white imitation lace styled wrought iron chairs with matching café tables, the Vernados family had a business look of which they could all be proud.

Archie was sitting in the cosy corner of the outdoor verandah as the locals called it, just as Kelly had said: a shaded, lattice surrounded corner, covered in climbing red bougainvillea flowers closest to the water's edge. She was positioned with her back to Michael as he approached. Her head was down in concentration mode, firmly engrossed in the book she was reading.

"What are you reading?"

Archie jumped, startled, and looked up.

"Oh Michael," she said, slightly surprised at the sound of his voice, "sorry I was far away."

"No I'm sorry I gave you a fright."

"Don't be sorry I was in another place…it happens sometimes whenever I find a book that really interests me."

She stood up and squeeze hugged him and he squeeze hugged her back.

"Wow…has it only been a fortnight…it seems like ages, please…sit here?" she said as she patted the chair beside hers and gestured Michael to sit.

"Thanks…sorry I'm a little late…been out and about with Dr Nicholls and a group of his investors. He was giving them an update on his guava and nut farms and thought I would provide some support for him in terms of current and future marketing opportunities so he invited me along."

"How did it go?"

"Good…yes good…I like Unwin, he's very down to earth…although I think he might be a bit of a closet end times theorist you know."

"Really…I don't know much about him…I've never met him."

"Yes…I think he is."

"What makes you think that Michael?"

"Well apart from all the books about end times that he has in his office and the fact that his whole personal living environment is basically self-sufficient, you could say it's just a gut feel."

Archie threw her head back and laughed.

"Yes…why look for evidence when you've got a gut feel…but if you've got both well that's even better."

"True…but he certainly is searching for an understanding of spiritual things…he asks a lot of questions."

"I'm sure you answered them perfectly Michael."

"Well I hope so…I hope I was of some help to him…I wouldn't like to see him go down the path of those doomsday cults that are springing up."

Archie looked as radiant and lovely in her ankle length yellow coloured flowing cotton dress as she did the first time he had seen her. Her long black hair cascaded down, finishing a few inches over the shoulder straps of her dress and resting on a strap and pearl choker necklace. Along with this the soft pale skin of her neck gave her a beautiful old-fashioned look of elegance that fitted in well with the stylishness of the café décor.

"You look lovely."

"Thank you Michael…and if I might say so do you."

Michael grinned.

"Right…do I…thank you."

"I mean it. The early morning crisp farm air puts a rosy glow in your cheeks."

Michael grinned and glanced down towards the book she was reading.

"So…a book girl…what type of books do you like to read?" he queried.

"Well I like all kinds of books I guess…but I tend to lean more towards those stories truth or fiction that have a hero in them, you know… someone that saves the day…the good guy winning against the bad guy."

"Nice…so do I."

"Is that book one of those?"

"Yes I guess it is…I've only just started reading it."

"What's the name of it?"

Archie bookmarked her page, closed it, and flipped over to the back cover.

"The book title is The Cross and The Switchblade and it's a true story about the life of a man named Dr David Wilkinson. It's a type of autobiography I guess, but with a variety of characters in it that turns it into an adventure."

"What's it about?"

"It's the story of a young Pentecostal pastor who risks his own personal safety to go and work amongst the street gangs of New York."

"It's a good story, it really got me hooked from the first page."

"Margie Morrison loaned it to me."

"If you like I can check with Margie when I am finished if she would mind if I loan it to you?"

"I would have to check since I noticed on the inside cover she has hand written 'Please return to Margie Morrison'. I'd say like most of us she's loaned out books before and never got them back."

"Yes…I know the feeling."

"Great…thanks…yes I'd like to read it."

"Do you like books Michael?"

"Yes I do…love reading…I'm what you might call a collector as well as a reader, quite a collector."

"Some of them that I've carried around for years I haven't read yet, but I know I will eventually."

"I try to buy on instinct, and sometimes I can buy a book and then find it means nothing to me at the time of purchase but something to me a long time after I bought it."

"What kind do you like?"

"Well I'm a bit like you actually."

"I like stories that have a hero that wins in the end."

"I used to love Phantom comics when I was young and loved cowboy movies. I would always be the Sheriff when we kids in our neighbourhood would play cowboys and Indians. Nobody could get that Sheriff's badge off me."

"But I also love reading spiritual books of all kinds. You know ones like that one you have or teaching books about the spiritual life."

"Like the Bible?"

"Yes…but not only the Bible…spiritual books of other religions like the Bhagavad Gita of the Hindu religion or the writings of the Buddha."

"Even just teaching books written by spiritual people."

"Have you read the Bible?"

"Yes I have."

"All the way through?"

"Yes…all the way through."

"Old Testament only once, but the New Testament quite a few times."

"Coincidentally the first novel I ever owned which was a present given to me by my mother was in a lot of ways in the same genre as the book you are reading. It was a true story titled A Man Called Peter."

Archie grinned.

"I know a man called Peter."

Michael was surprised.

"Do you…have you read it?"

"No…a man called Peter…he's my brother."

"Very clever Ms Vernados."

"Michael I could just imagine you as the law abiding Sheriff going after the baddies."

"Yes…pin a star on my chest and I'm your man."

"Hey saw Kelly in there, that was a surprise," he continued, "I didn't realize she worked here as well as the Tourist Park."

"She said she would be out in a minute with the menu. She said something funny…about it's all good your mother isn't working today."

"Oh trust her," Archie replied laughing.

"Let me explain."

"My mum owns this place and Kelly knows my mum is always keen on knowing who I am out with, particularly if it is a male. It's a Greek thing."

"But that's okay…her saying that to you I mean…and speaking of the angel, here she comes with the menus."

"Hey you two lovebirds…ready to order some of my delicious faire?"

Michael blushed.

"Ooh Mikey…did I notice a little rosy pink in the cheekie weekies?" Kelly mischievously giggled.

"Here are your menus guys."

"Now while you're pondering yours Michael I need to talk to Arch, secret girl's business," she continued.

"Arch doesn't have to read the menu, she co-wrote it."

Grabbing Archie's arm Kelly ushered her to the other side of the balcony where she then proceeded to cup her hand against Archie's ear and whisper something. Michael looked across. They were both grinning. They looked like good mates. Archie immediately said something back to her and as Kelly cupped her hand again and replied Archie let out a loud laugh. Then with an audible reply as she walked back to the table of, "I'll see what I can do," she resumed her seat whilst Kelly went back to her duties.

"Onya Arch" Kelly called out as she scurried back inside.

"She's outrageous but a beautiful soul," commented Archie.

Seeing the curious look on Michael's face she continued.

"She's so funny."

"I'll tell you what she said if you promise you won't say anything to anybody. She wouldn't mind me telling you though, she likes you."

"Of course…I won't say anything."

"Well she asked me could I put in a good word for her with mum so she could get more hours. She said I'm saving up."

"When I asked what she was saving up for… she said…a boob job."

Archie giggled out loud again.

"Can you believe it?"

"She's serious you know."

Michael felt his face slightly flush again.

"I'm sure she is."

"Michael do you remember on the Carols night when I was introducing you to everyone and I introduced Kell and I think I said funny and a little flirtatious?"

"Yes I do…and you used the word funky too."

"Right…yes…and then she had leaned over and whispered in my ear something that made me laugh?"

"I do," replied Michael, "she described it then to Jeffrey as secret girl's business."

"That's right…she did."

"You've got a good memory Michael."

"Well the words she whispered in my ear were."

"Yea right Arch…funny, funky, flirtatious, and here's another 'f' word if you're seriously into them, flat chested."

"That's why I laughed at the time…she has always had this thing about how girls with bigger boobs are more attractive to some of the male species."

"She's funny and sometimes scandalous in what she says but she's my best friend. I love her to death."

Archie picked up her menu and was looking at it as she spoke.

"So what do you reckon Michael?"

"Well I like the look of the Baklava biscuits and probably a cappuccino would suit."

Archie laughed.

"Noooo…not the menu…what do you reckon about boobs?"

"Come on…be honest…what do you reckon Michael?"

"Are men more attracted to girls with bigger boobs?"

"Well…there's a tricky question for you," Michael replied as he gathered his thoughts.

"Look I can't speak for all the men in this lovely little village but for myself I am more attracted to what is positioned physically in every female just behind the breast…which is the heart or soul of the person," he replied.

"Oh…and I love emerald coloured eyes," he continued with a smirk, his chin resting on his interlocked hands as he glanced up from his menu and stared intently across at her eyes.

"Yes a beautiful heart and sparkling emerald eyes…it's a perfect turn on. Now that's what attracts this man."

Archie smiled, blushed and thought to herself "he's done it again… he just melted me."

"Okay you smooth talker, I believe you," she returned.

There was a moment's pause in the conversation.

Archie still feeling slightly flushed in the face quickly changed the subject away from herself and quipped, "right…two Baklavas and two cappuccinos coming up."

"You'll love the Baklava Michael if you like sweet things."

"I do," he grinned staring at her.

"You're being naughty again Michael."

"Okay I'll cease and desist…for the moment…yes the Baklavas they just looked so delicious in the photo."

"What are they?"

"They are a Mediterranean dessert, originally from Turkey I think but super popular in Greece. They are layers of paper thin dough with a filling of honey and ground nuts. Really nice."

"As a part of my involvement in our family Christmas food cook up my Mum always allocates the Baklava biscuit cook up to me. She has this set number of them that must be baked regardless of how many we have left over, and there are always quite a few dozen left over."

"So expect there to be some freebies to give out to my friends after Christmas Day."

"You'll like them I'm sure."

"Okay…good timing, here comes Kell for the order."

Kelly took their order and with a chirpy "thank you…back soon love-birds," she skipped off back inside the bakery.

Archie grinned and turned to Michael.

"She really is Michael…she really is."

"What…outrageous?"

"No she really is serious about getting a new set of boobs."

They both laughed out loud.

"Good on her," Michael quipped, "good on her."

An hour and a half of conversation had quickly passed when the early lunchtime patrons started to slowly drift into the cafe and out onto the balcony.

"Want to walk down to the Bay Michael. I have to come back here later to see mum so I need to hang around. You said your place is up on the hill, you could point it out to me?"

"Sure…sounds good."

It was a beautiful sunny day and the ever-familiar fish fragrance and salty smell was present in the air as they strolled along the cobble-paved walkway beside the river. The location of Michael's new place of residence was quite unique. Situated high on the hill it overlooked the river, the river mouth and the surf beach. Along with this there was a perfect view of the large artificial lagoon or lake as it was known, built right beside the historic Bay Hotel, about 50 metres distance below his unit.

The lagoon was a noisy energetic area. With the recent installation of canoe and paddleboat hire facilities, the reasonably shallow waters of the enclosed swimming area had become a favourite spot for tourists staying at the nearby Tourist Park to take their children on the hot summer days.

Michael's apartment was originally a two-storey home that the owners had subsequently renovated into the two apartments it had now become. The top floor apartment that Michael rented had the advantage of being fronted by a huge outdoor balcony with a vista of views. The refurbishment had been tastefully and thoughtfully carried out, for in addition to the balcony being added, the highlight of the interior was a brick fireplace made out of heavy slate rock tiles that had been built into the far end corner of the lounge room.

"There it is," Michael said, pointing upwards as he and Archie stood looking up from the shore of the lagoon below, "easy to spot, the only one with a balcony."

"Wow," she uttered, "what great views you must have."

"Yes I do, and the balcony is a great place for a late afternoon relaxation session with a wine and some good music."

"I bet it is…it looks fabulous."

"Hey I've got an idea," continued Archie.

"How about I come back here later this afternoon. We could hire one of those double canoes and have a paddle around and perhaps you could show me inside your unit afterwards."

"You up for it Michael?"

"Absolutely...for sure...yes I am...let's do that."

"Okay great, so I've got to go see my mum at the bakery about Kelly's request for extra hours, she comes in just after lunch, so I'll meet you back here say around 4 o'clock."

"Great."

"We'll meet here at the canoe hire sign."

"Sounds good...see you then."

Michael watched as Archie headed off over the small arched bridge that led back to the tourist strip. He was starting to enjoy these coffee hook ups with Archie, albeit this was only the second one. But he was starting to feel that he would certainly be ready and available for the next one.

It was 3.45 in the afternoon, and the sun was partially hidden behind an increasing amount of dark cloud as Michael wended his way down the road in his board shorts and tee shirt to the lagoon for his meeting with Archie.

Storm clouds were starting to gather. He could see Archie from the distance as he rounded the corner into the hotel car park. She was sitting on the beach waiting for him beside the For Hire sign. She had changed into a pair of shorts and a blouse, presumably to be comfortable in the canoe, and stood up brushing the sand from her shorts as Michael arrived.

"Hey...I thought I was going to be early but you beat me," he called out on approaching.

"Yes, I brought my car this time as this morning I only had to walk back to the bakery to see mum...you know...Kelly's extra hours...but since I will be heading home after this it's a bit too far to walk."

"It'll be safe in the car park here if we leave it and walk up to your place later."

"So what do you reckon?" Archie said as she gestured towards the gathering storm clouds.

"Well I'm up for it," replied Michael, "but perhaps we might go for the paddleboat rather than the canoe."

"Good idea," Archie responded.

It was a wise choice. They had not long ventured out, and were at the far side of the lake about fifty metres from the hire area engrossed in conversation, when they felt the first heavy drops of rain begin to fall.

Michael glanced upwards.

"Perhaps we had better head back to shore Archie, I think it's about to pour down."

And it did, first one drop, then a few drops, and then very quickly the heavens opened up.

"Captain," Archie cried out laughing, "Captain…methinks we are about to be scuttled…what orders have you?"

"First mate," cried Michael, "first mate, my orders are methinks you need to pedal harder to get the captain safely to shore."

They both laughed.

The rain was now bucketing down.

Archie unable to stop laughing began to pedal hard but not too hard: she was enjoying the fun of it. She had always loved the feeling of rain on her body and leaned back in the moment to feel it beating down upon her face.

The air temperature had dropped quickly and the rain had a cold almost icy feel to it, but it was still refreshing. She tilted her head back as they pedalled and ran her hand through her hair to remove it from her face. It all felt exhilarating. A rain cloud burst directly above them and they felt the stinging sensation of the raindrops on their face, arms and legs with more intensity.

Archie leaned into Michael laughingly enjoying the fun as they frantically pedalled their way to shore. She was aware that it wouldn't be long before the front of her blouse would be totally soaked. She knew that this would create a see through look from her blouse to her black lacy bra and for some reason she knew she didn't care.

It happened as she thought, and happened quickly. She could sense her nipples firming with the coldness of the moment. She began wondering if when they reached the shore Michael would notice this and she secretly hoped that he would, whilst all the time she kept pedalling.

Michael loved the fact that they were both still giggling as they reached the shore. He thought that perhaps they were enjoying their paddleboat adventure with the rain beating down more than they would have without it. The spontaneity of the unplanned moment was fun and exciting, and when they finally reached the shore they were both soaked through.

As the boat scraped the sandy bottom of the shoreline Michael quickly jumped out, much to Archie's delight, with a cry of "the captain's got this one me first mate." Then in a sort of gallant way with his voice sounding like some kind of Scottish pirate he followed up with, "stay seated lassie while I beach this jolly clipper," at which time he went behind the paddleboat eventually pushing it closer to the shore and onto the sand.

With a flourish of his arm and a bow to Archie, Michael reached out for her hand to help her off the boat and as he did so her rain drenched body stumbled directly into his arms. She looked incredibly beautiful to him as she stood there in front of him, her hands on his arms and steadying herself. She was still laughing. Her rain soaked white blouse was clinging to her body giving a revealing display of her nipples hardened by the cold rain pushing outward through the thin lace lining of her bra cup.

Archie made no attempt to hide her body, and as for Michael well he tried not to show that he had noticed. But it was hard not to like what he was seeing. He laughed and talked to her in a gentlemanly way as he helped her out of the boat. Archie had seen him stop for a second and stare at her rain soaked body in her now see through clothes, and it had made her tingle even more than the cold. She knew that he had looked at her breasts and she liked it.

"Have you got a change of clothes?" he queried.

"Yes I've got another pair of shorts in my bag, but not another blouse."

"Guess I was only expecting our bottom halves to get wet."

Michael immediately took charge of the moment.

"Okay it's still raining…how about we walk up to my place and dry out…I am sure I have a spare shirt for you."

"Great…hope it stops raining, I'd love to see the view from the balcony too."

The rain was continuing to fall but gradually easing as he took her hand and they commenced the uphill walk to his apartment. The warmth and firmness of his hand midst the coldness of the rain made Archie tingle yet again. They laughed and excitedly relived in conversation the previous fifteen minutes as they casually strolled up the roadway, the rain still beating down upon their faces. They were enjoying the moment and there was no need to hurry. They had agreed that they couldn't get any wetter than they already were.

———∞———

The entrance to Michael's unit was from an easement at the rear of the building. They paused in the small alcove near the door and supported each other as separately they both removed their sneakers. Michael opened the door and ushered Archie in.

"Welcome to my humble home."

"Wow…nice Michael," she said as her eyes fell upon the fireplace in the corner."

"We'll get dry and changed and I'll take you on a tour if you like, which will probably only take around thirty seconds as it's not a very big unit."

"Great."

Michael went straight to the linen closet and retrieved two bath towels and after handing one to Archie and drying his head a little he went to his bedroom returning with a checked long sleeve flannelette shirt for her.

"Here first mate," he said doing a poor impression of a pirate's voice and passing it to her, "this will keep you warm."

"Oh yes almost forgot," he said returning to his normal voice as he reached into a kitchen cupboard, "and here's a plastic bag for your wet clothes."

"You can use the bedroom over there and I'll use the bathroom if you like," he said gesturing towards his bedroom.

She thanked Michael with a smile and headed towards the bedroom. Archie liked how organized Michael was. She noticed out of the corner of her eye as she turned to go to the bedroom that Michael's eyes had followed her walk, and she silently hoped it was because he had wanted to take one more glance at her rain soaked body.

She entered the room and closed the door, took her spare pair of shorts out of her carry bag and laid them on the bed alongside the shirt Michael had given her. She glanced around the room for a moment looking at her surroundings. The room was sparsely but tastefully furnished. There was a purple and pink patchwork doona covering the king size grey coloured iron bed in the centre of the room with two matching side tables beside it. Each of the side tables had a small lamp with a lampshade of a silvery chrome colour.

On looking more closely she could see there was a pattern outline on the outside of each lampshade. It consisted of the outlines of dozens of roses almost looking like they had been sketched on to the shade. The inside of the shade had what looked like a coating of a red plastic type of material. Archie thought they looked pretty.

Positioned centrally above the headboard of the bed was a large canvas print. It was the well-known picture of the actors Humphrey Bogart and Ingrid Bergman gazing into each other's eyes from the award-winning movie of the 1940's Casablanca. It too was a combination of light grey and white colourings complementing all the other colours in the room. Romantic she pondered.

Tucked away in one corner of the room was a white framed standing Cheval mirror, a full-length mirror mounted so that it could be swiveled on a frame. All the furniture pieces seemed to complement each other. He's good at colour co-ordination she thought.

Archie dried herself down and then slowly began to remove her clothes until she was standing naked. She glanced at her body for a moment in the mirror before she began drying herself off. Her thoughts drifted to the fact that here she was standing totally naked in the bedroom of a man she had only known for a few weeks, and right beside the bed where that man slept. But not only that, the same man was right outside her door in another room taking his clothes off too. She felt those tingles again.

After drying herself off Archie quickly dressed and then bundled her blouse, shorts, panties and bra into the plastic bag that Michael had given her. She was glad she had brought the spare shorts and panties. All I'm missing now is a bra she thought.

She was also glad that Michael had given her a shirt of a heavier material so her braless state would not be as obvious. She wondered whether in his respectful considerate way he had deliberately done this. She thought he might have. She went to her bag, retrieved her hair brush and her favourite miniature perfume spray bottle, walked to the mirror, towelled her hair again to dry it a little more and then brushed the knots out of it.

After two spays of perfume on either side of her neck and on her wrist she checked herself out in the full-length mirror. She cupped her hands under her breasts and gave them a little bounce to assure herself in her mind that the shirt she was wearing had given her sufficient thickness of cover to camouflage any movement brought about by her braless state. Then she opened the door and left the room.

Michael was already in the lounge room bending over in front of the fireplace adding a couple of logs and some kindling. He turned and looked up when he heard the bedroom door open.

"Hey Archie…everything okay…the bathroom is free if you need to use it…I like the shirt…it looks better on you than me."

"Thank you and yes I will use the bathroom."

"Would you like a glass of red to warm you up?" Michael questioned as she headed to the bathroom.

"That would be nice Michael…yes…but only a half glass for me… wine tends to make me a bit sleepy…gotta drive."

"Yes thank you for the shirt…it's great…a couple more inches longer and I could use it for a dress," she laughed.

Michael went to the kitchen and poured the wine. He liked the thought of her wearing his shirt. It felt sort of intimate to him that her bare breasts were gently rubbing against the inside of his shirt.

Archie came out of the bathroom.

"I love the furnishings in your bedroom Michael…everything matches."

"And I love the little lamps."

"Did you turn one on?" he queried.

"No I didn't."

"Come I'll show you."

Michael took her hand and led the way back into the bedroom. She tingled in the moment knowing that five minutes earlier she had been standing there naked.

"Watch what happens when I turn them on."

He turned one and then the two lamps on and the lampshades immediately lit up to reveal dozens of small red roses on the outside of the shades.

Archie gasped.

"Oh that's beautiful Michael."

"Isn't it?"

"The red colour of the plastic liner on the inside of the shade reflects the bulb light onto the rose etchings on the outside. I found them in an antique store in the city."

"They're beautiful Michael…just beautiful."

"Yes they are…I just thought they were so unique when I saw them."

They returned to the lounge room and Michael turned into the kitchen area.

"A cosy fire…a nice red wine…and a big soft couch…it's a nice way to relax on a Saturday night."

"Yes…and some nice music," Archie commented, "is that your record collection over there?"

"Yes it is. I've had that collection a long time, and it has travelled with me many many miles over many many years."

"I was reading recently that in the next few years or so records will be a thing of the past as these new tape cassettes will flood the market and change the whole way we listen to music. You know along with portable cassette players you can take your music collection anywhere."

"And the article said they will eventually install them, I think they called them cassette decks, in cars. So the new cars will have a radio and a cassette player."

"Wow Michael, isn't technology moving fast?"

"Then all of these records of yours will become collectors items," Archie continued as she walked across to the sideboard where Michael had four stacks of long play records, each stack at least ten or twelve records high.

Michael brought Archie the half glass of wine and sat it on the sideboard beside her as she stood there curiously browsing through each pile of records. He took his own glass, placed it on the coffee table, and then flopped back onto the sofa, his body sinking quickly and comfortably into its soft surrounds.

He raised his glass.

"Cheers Archie…here's to paddleboats."

"Cheers Michael…yes…and to the beautiful rain that brought us here."

Archie gasped in surprise.

"Wow Michael…you really have a great collection here, a few pop ones but lots of folk music. I love folk music."

"Hmm…not only do we have similar tastes in books but now I find in music also," she continued.

"Nana Mouskouri, Joan Baez, John Denver, some great ones here," she said as she raised her glass to her mouth for another sip.

"Cheers again…this is nice…thank you."

"Nana Mouskouri is my mum's favourite singer. I think though it might only be because she's Greek. She comes from Crete which is about 11 hours drive from Athens where I was born."

"Hey this is different."

"Which one is it?"

"The Greatest Hits of Doris Day," Archie replied.

"Yes," Michael's voice softened, "it belongs to my mother Rose. She would play it often when we were kids. She can't use it now she's in the nursing home. It's my share of her future will she said. She gave it to me early when I moved out of home. She knew I loved it."

"Hmm," mused Archie as she stood there reading the back cover of the record jacket.

"This song was written when I was five and it says here that it was used in the Alfred Hitchcock movie The Man Who Knew Too Much starring Doris Day and James Stewart."

"Oh…yes…I know it…I just love this song Que Sera Sera, whatever will be will be."

Archie continued browsing the song list on the back cover of the Doris Day record.

"I love this song Michael."

"What's that?"

Archie sang the one line take me back to the Black Hills.

"Oh yes…The Black Hills Of Dakota…one of my favourites too. She sang it in the movie Calamity Jane that I saw as a young boy."

Archie continued.

"She makes it sound sooo romantic when she calls it the beautiful Indian country."

"Perhaps we could go there together one day Michael, wouldn't that be great?"

"It would Archie…it would…it is on my bucket list."

"That might be part of our destiny Michael," she continued.

"But I love Que Sera Sera."

"Speaking of mums Michael my mum has a little book of quotations, written I don't know when, around a thousand years ago I think by a Roman Emperor, and she is always quoting to us what she calls little words of wisdom from it. It is written in Greek and she brought it with her when we emigrated. Some of them she knows off by heart."

"Like the one she uses whenever she catches my brother or myself complaining about anything."

"She will say Argiroula…accept what comes to you woven in the pattern of your destiny, for what could more aptly suit your needs."

"I know it off by heart because she has quoted it so much over the years."

"And it is sort of like que sera sera isn't it?"

"Do you believe that Michael?"

"About the destiny?"

"Yes…I mean like we should just go with the flow…whatever will be will be…that it's part of our destiny?"

"Yes…I guess I do."

"I have a less eloquent saying Archie that I've used for many years. It says…what is…is."

"It means accept and co-operate with the present moment, with what has been brought to you. Don't fight what has already happened and wish to change it back, because you can't turn back time, and if you try to, all it brings is stress and unhappiness."

"It works for me."

"I kind of relate it to the verse in the Bible that says, all things work together for good to them who love God and are called according to his purpose."

"It does Michael."

Archie glanced sideways.

"Hey is that your guitar over there?"

"Yes of course it is, it must be," she answered herself, "it's here isn't it."

Archie didn't wait for his reply but walked over to the corner of the lounge room where the guitar was leaning.

"Do you play Michael?"

"Yes…but with difficulty. I don't practice enough."

"One of my brothers teaches guitar and when I was young he taught me some chords and then for a while I had some classical guitar lessons from a Spanish man who lived about an hour's walk from our home. But I got tired of the walk and didn't practice enough as he so eloquently told me, so I eventually gave up taking lessons."

Archie picked up the guitar and sat down on the stool beside it facing Michael. She plucked a few strings, turned a few of the tuning knobs and looked thoughtfully upwards whilst intermittently doing a couple of strums and humming.

"Now let me see, I think it's C, G, D, and D…no D7."

She started strumming slowly at first as she sorted out the right chords and then got into the rhythm. Within a moment she had lifted her voice and sang the first four lines of the song's chorus. Que sera sera, whatever will be will be, the futures not ours to see, que sera, sera. She sang it about four times, staring directly at Michael and smiling as she did so and to Michael it was a magical moment. Then just as quickly she put the guitar down, walked back to the record collection, and started browsing again.

"That was beautiful Archie, your voice I mean, and I didn't know you played guitar."

"Yes…and piano…and the flute."

"My mum says that music soothes the soul. I think that could be another saying from her little book of quotes. She had both my brother and I taught from an early age."

"Sounds like my mum," replied Michael.

"When I was around eleven my second eldest brother Geoff who was still living at home bought a second hand piano so that my sister and I could take piano lessons."

"Once a week we would walk up the road with our music books under our arms to the home of a very old Irish woman named Kath Maloney. Well she seemed very old to a young boy."

"She was a concert pianist when she was younger. However in her later years her hands became riddled with rheumatoid arthritis. It caused all the joints of her fingers to be stretched and swollen."

"Oh that's sad Michael."

"I guess so."

"But wow, even though her hands were all twisted and misshapen she still managed to bounce out a song. I did learn to read music though which was good for me now because I muck around a little with the ukulele."

"That was nice of your brother to buy the piano Michael."

"Yes…it was…he was a good person…he passed away about five years ago. He was living at home and one night he went to the refrigerator to get a glass of milk and just collapsed and died."

"Oh Michael…that is so sad."

"I suppose he wasn't married since he was living at home?"

"No…he had an on and off girlfriend. Lyn was her name. Lyn Stanton. I used to deliver cakes occasionally to her mother, cakes that mum had baked. Mum and her mother were good friends."

"She was a beautiful looking girl…looked like the actress Ingrid Bergman…you know the Casablanca print in the bedroom…he met her at the Baptist Church."

"But he was pretty engrossed personally, you know studying medicine for six years and then starting up his own practice and it just didn't work out. Not really sure why."

"I think studying medicine stressed him out. I remember we shared a bedroom and he had his study desk in the corner of the room with all these huge medical books stacked on it."

"And he would have a little desk lamp on so as not to keep me awake as he would study late into the night."

"Occasionally I would wake up and see him hovered over his books and he would be pulling lightly at his front hairline, you know," Michael gestured, "just above his forehead, like this."

"He was in the last year of his six year course and over the twelve months he went bald on the top front of his head, you know, from pulling at his hair."

"So I think he was stressed with his final exams coming up and perhaps this affected his relationship with Lyn...not sure."

"She seemed a lovely girl though...her mother Nell gave me my first New Testament Bible. I used to deliver cakes from my mother to her. Oh I already said that didn't I. She was a nice lady."

"That's just so sad...not sad that you had to deliver the cakes," she laughed, "I mean about your brother."

"It is Archie," Michael replied, "but que sera sera...what is...is, I suppose."

"Actually he loved music too. He tried to teach himself on the piano he had bought. I would come home from school and he would be practicing Chopsticks. Did you do the chopsticks thing Archie?"

"Yes I did Michael...I think any kid who ever came across a piano did Chopsticks," Archie laughed.

"I remember his favourite song was Turn Turn Turn by The Byrds. It came out shortly before he died."

"Do you remember," Michael hummed the words of the first line, "to everything...turn turn turn...there is a season...turn turn turn."

Archie finished it for him.

"I do remember it Michael…and a time for every purpose under heaven."

"That's it."

"Well I didn't know it at the time but discovered later when I was reading the Bible that the words of the song, apart from turn turn turn, are from the Book of Ecclesiastes in the Old Testament," continued Michael.

"The song was written by Pete Seeger who wrote a lot of songs for Peter Paul and Mary. Geoff actually bought the long play record. It is in the pile there. It has another hit of The Byrds on it too that I love, Mr Tambourine Man. It was written by Bob Dylan."

"Yes…here it is here Michael…wow…I suppose you think of him when you play it?"

"I don't play it much…but anytime I hear Turn Turn Turn, you know, on the radio, I do think of him."

"He was a good person."

"How many brothers and sisters do you have Michael?" Archie queried as she continued browsing through his record collection.

"Four brothers and three sisters."

"What do they all do Michael?" she continued in her attempt to get to know him better.

"Well I remember as a little child Mum saying once that all she ever wanted was for one of the boys to be a doctor and one a minister."

"She didn't care which of the boys it was."

"Well she got her wish," he continued.

"Let's see…brothers."

"I'm the youngest, the oldest is in real estate, and working downwards age wise there was Geoff the doctor, the next one is studying to be an Anglican Minister, and the next down is a music teacher, a guitar teacher to be exact."

"With the girls the oldest Maggie May is a Nursing Sister, and the next down age wise a beautician, and the youngest girl Elizabeth works in the office of a department store."

"Maggie May has the music gene. She played the piano accordion in her youth and when she was in her late teens made a recording of The Tennessee Waltz, you know Patti Pages's big hit."

"Yes I do…I just love that song."

"Wow Michael…that's a great mixture of professions," she continued.

"Yeah…I guess so."

"Are your family close Michael?" she queried.

"No Archie…well not everyone…but that's a story for another day."

"And what about you Archie?"

"I mean I know what your family do, but you, did you always want to be a teacher?"

"You mean an unemployed teacher Michael?" she laughed.

"Yes, I suppose so, although I think my choice of a profession came out of which particular movie was out at the time."

"How's that?"

"Well I'm not sure if I mentioned it but since I was about eleven years of age every year my birthday comes around my mum always takes me to the city to buy some clothes followed by a movie."

"The first movie I ever saw with her on these trips was around 1959 when I was about eleven and it was called The Nun's Story. It had Audrey Hepburn in it. She was beautiful."

"It was the story of a young woman who struggles with what she sees as her calling to be a Nun."

"So after I saw that movie I told mum I wanted to be a nun."

"Then I changed my mind when my mum took me to see The Sound of Music on my sixteenth birthday."

"From then on I wanted to be a teacher or a governess or something working with children."

"Soooo here I am…a teacher…now all I need is a teaching job."

Michael laughed, "right...well I'm sure you'll get one, who could resist employing you?"

"Thank you Michael...thank you...you are lovely to me."

Archie took a sip of her wine, continued browsing and then paused suddenly. With an excited voice she yelled out "yes yes...this is definitely my favourite record...would you leave this to me in your will...please please Michael?"

Michael chuckled, he found her so delightful.

"Which one is that?"

"It's Peter, Paul and Mary singing the works of Bob Dylan."

"Cool" she gasped, as she worked her way down the list of songs, "look at these."

"He is the best songwriter ever."

"Don't Think Twice It's Alright, Mr. Tambourine Man, The Times They Are A Changing, Just Like A Woman, It Ain't Me Babe, Blowing In The Wind."

"Wow...this is soooo good."

"He's certainly up there with the best."

"So Michael what about you, do you have a favourite composer. You know if you had to choose who would you nominate to be your favourite song writer?"

"I think if I had to choose out of my top five which includes Dylan by the way I would say it would have to be Stravinsky."

"Stravinsky" repeated Archie with a surprised look.

"Yup," replied Michael, "Igor Stravinsky, he composed some wonderful songs."

"You're kidding Michael, aren't you? Tell me you're kidding. I mean I know he was a gifted composer but."

"Yes Archie, he was a gifted composer...and yes I am kidding."

"Michael...you're naughty," cried Archie as she moved over quickly to him and playfully punched him in the shoulder.

She walked back to the record collection.

"So…favourite composer…truthfully?"

"Okay…it's a toss between Bob Dylan and Jimmy Webb."

"Oh Michael…I love Jimmy Webb's songs."

"Last year when his song MacArthur Park was released…you know, sung by Richard Harris, after I heard it on the radio, I was lined up outside the record store to get a copy before the store even opened."

"I say lined up but I was the only one in the line. I thought they might run out of the singles, so I arrived early."

"So out of the two…your favourite, if you had to decide?"

Michael took a sip of his wine.

"Okay, if I had to decide, I would say out of the two it would be Jimmy Webb."

"When I worked up north last year before I was appointed down here I used to like to get out of the office at lunchtime, so I would drive down to the waters edge, sit in my car, watch the small waves rolling in, listen to the car radio and eat my lunch."

"It was refreshing."

"You could guarantee that at some stage in my thirty minutes there that MacArthur Park would be played on the radio. People either loved it or hated it. I happened to love it."

"Me too…so what other songs has Jimmy Webb written?" queried Archie.

"Quite a few…and they have become hits for a lot of singers."

"Somewhere in that bundle you'll find an album by Glen Campbell…got it early this year…he's one of my favourite Country singers."

"There's quite a few Jimmy Webb songs on it that he sings…you know, By The Time I Get To Phoenix, Galveston, Wichita Linesman, Didn't We."

Archie gasped with surprise.

"That's the song on the other side of my Richard Harris MacArthur Park record Michael."

"What song's that?"

"Didn't We."

Archie walked over to Michael looked him straight in the eyes and hummed and half sang the words, this time we almost made the pieces fit…didn't we boy.

Michael loved the melodic tone of her voice. To him it was a gift.

He grinned back at her.

"Yes I love that song too Archie."

"When I was driving up to the city the other week I heard a new recording of it by Frank Sinatra, it sounded good."

"Jimmy Webb also wrote that song by The Fifth Dimension…Up Up and Away."

Archie chimed in, "in my beautiful my beautiful balloon."

"Yes I like that too."

Archie walked back to the records took another sip of her wine as she continued reading the back cover of the Peter Paul and Mary album. She turned and looked at Michael, paused for a moment and then spoke.

"Michael," she said in a subdued serious tone of voice but with a slightly mischievous look on her face, "can I ask you a serious question?"

"Sure," he replied.

She lowered her glass still staring at Michael lazing back on the couch and continuing the serious tone she said, "how many roads must a man walk down before you call him a man?"

Michael threw his head back, laughed out loud and immediately replied. "The answer my friend is blowin' in the wind, the answer is blowin' in the wind."

"Good answer Michael…you are very wise."

"Play it if you want, the player is just over there on the small table," Michael gestured.

Archie put the record on and turned the volume down just enough so that it would not interfere with their conversation. As the fire crackled she picked up her glass of wine, walked over to Michael and sat down beside him positioning herself so close to him that the sides of their legs and thighs touched. The atmosphere felt relaxed and intimate for them both.

"Thank you for a beautiful day," she whispered as she turned her face towards him, "cheers for the third time."

"You're welcome," he replied, "and thank you."

"Charlie" he said.

"Pardon" she replied.

"It's Charlie by Revlon. That's the perfume you are wearing."

"It's my favourite."

Archie grinned.

"I thought you had called me Charlie instead of Archie."

"You're amazing Michael. I can't believe that you just guessed my perfume."

"It's beautiful Archie, I love it and it suits you."

"Yes…I use it sparingly as it is so expensive."

"My mum bought me my first bottle when we were in the city for my last birthday."

"She said Archie…we're gonna hava to getta you some perfume. Coco Chanel said a woman who doesn't weara da perfume has no future," continued Archie imitating her mother's voice.

"She said Archie…in da Greek culture it is da good omen for marriage and having da children. Inna your ya-ya's day they would boil da rose petals and violets to maka dere owna perfume."

"What's ya ya?" Michael smiled.

"Itsa your grandmother," Archie replied.

Michael laughed.

He enjoyed listening to Archie sharing about her Greek heritage and particularly imitating her mother's accent. The few times they spent together over the previous few weeks had generated a growing closeness between the two. Archie was feeling that every moment spent with Michael and the more she learned about him increased her sense of trust in him.

She leaned across to the other sofa, grabbed the throw over blanket that was lying there and tucked it around both their legs. Michael placed his right arm across the back of the sofa gently resting his hand on Archie's shoulder. She liked this physical closeness.

"Michael can I ask your opinion on something?"

"Sure…anything."

"I'm twenty one years old, still a virgin, and my mother wants me to date and eventually marry only boys of my own Greek nationality."

"Do you think that's right?"

Michael was only slightly taken aback. He was starting to realize more and more that this type of questioning and openness was a beautiful part of Archie's nature.

"Okay…right," said Michael, slightly amused by her honesty, particularly the virgin part.

"So you want me to comment on the virgin and the marriage part but not the age?" he quipped.

"Everything please."

He grinned.

"You know," she continued, "sometimes I feel like some of my personal life at this age is not normal compared to my friends. You know, look at Kelly. She's nineteen and she's done it."

"I mean she's not promiscuous at all. She just broke up with her boyfriend of three years, and when she told me about the break up she said that she wished she hadn't been doing…you know…it…with him."

"I mean…why would she say that?"

"Why would she wish she hadn't done it?"

"Okay," Michael paused, "so you'd like my opinion," he continued as he took a deep sip of his wine and gathered his thoughts.

"Yes I would Michael, you're a few years older and wiser than us, what do you think?"

"More than a few years Archie…perhaps four or five…now let me think."

Michael paused, and then slowly turned his head sideways towards her. He spoke with softness and gentleness in his voice. He had suddenly felt very protective of this lovely young woman who was sharing her innocence and her intimate thoughts with him. But it was not just this; it was also the fact that she was seemingly valuing his opinion on these very personal matters.

"Archie firstly I think that there is no shame and nothing wrong with you being a virgin at your age."

"Sexual contact in your teens can sometimes complicate things."

"What do you mean Michael…did it complicate things for you?" Archie quietly questioned.

He paused and breathed in slowly.

"Well yes it has or should I say did when I was in my teens."

He sensed that Archie wanted to enquire further about his teens but she didn't, and he was glad that she hadn't. There were things that had happened and he knew he wasn't ready to share them with her just yet, and so he continued.

"Well when I say sex in your teens can complicate things I don't just mean complicate things for you alone."

"I mean sometimes the consequences can affect a lot more people than yourself and I think more young people need to be conscious of that. I know I wasn't when I was in my impulsive teens."

"Say in a simple way in regards to yourself."

"If you were having sex with someone you hardly knew and your mum in whatever way found out, how do you think that would affect your relationship with her?"

"Get you," Archie replied, "it would really complicate things."

"She probably wouldn't trust me again."

"That's right…so when Kelly said she wished that she hadn't…you know…done it…she was obviously suffering some sort of regret or ramifications from her experience."

"I have a saying that came out of my own life experience that I try to remind myself quite often…complications and consequences never travel alone…they always bring others along for the ride."

"Nowadays it helps me to think first rather than act on impulse."

"Archie the other thing I think most of us as teenagers don't understand is that there is a difference between love and lust."

"I mean both are natural but most people, particularly teenagers, confuse the two. In our pre adulthood it is due to youth and immaturity and at the same time an explosion of hormones that accompanies our teenage boy girl relationships."

"At other times perhaps as an adult it is due to one member or even both of them in the relationship exploiting the other for their own physical needs."

"I remember someone once saying to me that having sex as a teenager can complicate things and having no sex in a marriage can complicate things…so you lose either way, which was quite a clever way of putting it even if not entirely accurate."

"But for whatever reason…teenage sex particularly if it comes out of peer pressure can and does complicate things. Teenagers think…well everyone else is doing it I had better catch up."

"Archie I don't want to sound like a prude believe me I'm not…but I really believe that sex without true love and commitment is just lust gratifying itself."

"But sex that eventuates out of a true love relationship is really that true love of the heart giving itself to the other person in a total act of commitment physically and emotionally."

"I guess you could say that sex for the sake of sex comes out of lust in the mind and making love comes out of love in the heart wanting to complete the connection."

"We all have moments of lust when we feel an attraction to a member of the opposite sex. We all get aroused. It's part of our physiological makeup. It's natural and normal and might I say quite nice."

"I remember Doris Day sang about it in the movie called Annie Get Your Gun. She described it as doin' what comes naturally. Natural things happen. Arousal is natural."

"So we all get sexual tingles. There is no harm in that. I like them. The harm sometimes follows and can come out of us gratifying ourselves outside of the right circumstances for both. You know regardless of the emotional repercussions on the other person."

"I think men are more guilty of pushing the sexual act on their partner than women."

"I might be wrong Archie but from my experience I believe particularly in young first time relationships that when a young couple have sex many teenage girls interpret it as an 'I love you' act, whilst many boys see it as a conquest."

"It's an emotional thing with most girls but a physical thing with most boys."

"Polar opposites of thought."

"You're right Michael."

"Well anyway…that's my thoughts…I hope I didn't make that sound too complicated Archie?"

"You didn't Michael…no you didn't…I like that…and I love your thoughts…thank you."

"On the contrary," she continued, "you have a way of making things so much clearer."

"Thanks…and as for your mum and her beliefs about who you should marry," he continued, "I know it seems unfair, but she obviously as part of her Greek cultural heritage and traditional value system believes it is what is best for you."

"My advice Archie, for what it is worth, is wait until you fall in love… wait until you find that special person, then if he is not Greek, deal with the issues of his nationality in that very moment. You know, enjoy the present moment, and don't worry about tomorrow today. Que sera sera."

"Wow…thank you Michael, thank you soooo much…whatever will be will be."

"Yes…that's right."

Archie clasped his hand.

"Hey…you'll like this Michael."

"In the Greek family tradition, when the daughter reaches her teens the mother will sit her down and give her you know the sex education talk. Well I think its tradition cause it happened to me and to one of my cousins."

"Guess how long it takes Michael?"

"Ah…too long?"

"No" Archie replied, "about three minutes with no questions or audience participation."

Michael laughed out loud, "really, what did she say?"

"Well…mine went something like this."

My mum came into the lounge room and said, "Argiroula…we needa to talk…come…sit down here beside me…we needa to talk about important women things."

"So I sat down beside her and she said."

"Argiroula…you are goin' to be a startin' high school this year…and you are going to meet Australian boys…and you know what that means?"

"So I humoured her and said, no mama what does it mean?"

"She said, Argiroula they willa want to ask you out, you know, on da date, and you know what dat means?"

"I was grinning inwardly but didn't show it cause for her this was a serious talk, so I said, no mama what does that mean?"

"She said, Argiroula these boys are growing into young men, and as my mama, your ya-ya used to say, most of them have just signed on to the WHC."

"I couldn't help myself so I said."

"What's the WHC mama?"

"Is that like the YMCA?"

"My goodness Argiroula…no no no no no. It's da wandering hands club."

"You know they will be inquisitive about sex things. So they might want to do things, you know, like explore with their hands."

"Yes mama."

"She said, so remember dis Argiroula. It's a what my mother taught me and her mother taught her."

"You canna let them kiss you and you can letta them touch any part of your body only if it is abova your belly button."

"But you don't letta them touch no part of your body belowa the belly button. That can only happen when you getta married."

"Okay…that's all I wanna say…I've got ta getta your papa's dinner ready."

Archie laughed.

"And that was it Michael."

"That was my sex education Greek parenting style."

Michael laughed.

"So no books or pictures or question time…just that?"

"Yep," Archie replied, "just that."

"Pretty clear ehh," she chuckled.

"Yes…very clear," returned Michael, "very specific I might say…they should introduce that into the school curriculum."

They both laughed out loud.

"I am thinking that perhaps your mum might be pretty strict in her outlook on raising children?" Michael questioned.

"Like she's a woman of old-fashioned values?"

"Yes, I guess she is," replied Archie, "but probably more than that she's of old fashioned Greek family values which can be pretty strict. You know particularly with anything that relates to the evolution of our family. Like who I and my brother Peter should date and who we should eventually marry."

"I love my mum the best, but sometimes we get into serious debate about what's best for me, particularly in my personal life."

"I mean with mum decisions are either good or bad. Choices are either right or wrong. She has non-negotiable codes of conduct especially around family things and sometimes I find it hard to share things with her from my point of view."

"But hey...enough about me and my mum...let's enjoy the music...
que sera sera."

Archie and Michael sat listening to the record for a while both enjoying the coziness of the moment and feeling the warmth of each other's
bodies snuggled into each other. The record finished playing as Archie
glanced down at her wristwatch.

"My goodness where did the time go. Judy will be sending out search
parties for me, or worse still my mum."

Michael slowly eased himself out of the couch.

"Okay, no problem. I'll get you a pair of flip flops to wear home since
your sneakers are all wet."

He held her hand gently as they slowly walked down the hill to her
car tucked away in the hotel car park. The rain had cleared, there was
a crisp fresh feel in the night air and the sky was lit up with an abundance of stars.

"I meant to tell you Michael...I just remembered. I bumped into Margie
when I went back to the bakery at lunchtime...and I told her we were
going canoeing this afternoon...and she said to say hello and to remind
you not to forget to make the appointment...are you sick Michael?"

"No...not at all."

"She spotted a tiny mole on my cheek just below my ear and suggested
I get it looked at. I think she is worried I might disturb it when shaving.
Been shaving for more than ten years now and haven't yet. I thought she
would forget."

"She's like that Michael."

"What do they call it?"

"She's into preventative medicine."

"She's nice. Very caring. She has a younger sister Francis who graduates next year and hopes to move up here so that they can open a
clinic together."

"Yes...I think she mentioned that at the Carols night."

"That will be nice for her...I think she gets lonely for her family at times. But with her parents and her sister Francis's intention to move up here, that should fix all that. They are a pretty close knit family according to Margie."

"Anyway, apart from that when I bumped into her she mentioned that the posters are going up around town saying Garret Sloan's crusade in February has been cancelled and will be rescheduled for late May at a date to be advised. She apparently saw one on the lamppost outside the surgery. Not sure why he cancelled. He normally sticks rigidly to his schedule once he advertises it."

"What do you think?"

"I think no to making an appointment to see her...and have no idea why Sloan cancelled. He may be sick."

"Okay...I won't say anything to Margie about you not wanting an appointment."

"Hey...thank you for walking me to my car Michael," she whispered as she hugged him goodnight. I guess it will be post Christmas before I see you again.

"Yes sadly it will," he sighed as he slowly opened her car door.

"Are you doing much over Christmas?" he enquired.

"Oh yeah...Greek families are known for big Christmas gatherings... and you?"

"Yes...probably head back to the city for a couple of days."

Michael didn't say any more about his Christmas activities. It too would be a discussion for another day.

Standing in the silence of the dimly lit car park ready to say goodbye Archie had a deep sense that something had changed in the last three weeks since she had first met Michael, something personal. She wasn't sure exactly what it was and she couldn't pinpoint the exact time that it had happened, but it had.

Whether it was when she had first met him in his office or whether it was on the Carols night during their walk to her home. Whether it was on their coffee date that morning at the bakery or in the excitement and fun of the paddleboat ride, or whether it was in that special moment whilst sitting with him on the couch in front of the fire when she found herself able to share with a man for the first time in her life her most intimate thoughts, Archie wasn't sure.

All she knew was that something in her life had changed in the last few weeks and had changed forever. She felt different, she felt happier, and she felt alive again.

As they stood in the car park holding each other and not really wanting to say goodnight Archie leaned forward to hug him again.

"Thank you for today and tonight Michael, we really learnt a lot about each other. Isn't it just nice to sit and talk to someone and get to know them?"

"You're right Archie...it was nice."

"You know a lot about music Michael, you know, singers and songwriters."

"I suppose I do."

"You love all kinds of music don't you Michael, even Stravinsky?" she grinned.

"Yes I guess I do."

"You were talking tonight Archie about your mum and her book of quotes. I remember reading once some of the great quotes of Aristotle, you know the Greek philosopher, perhaps one of your ancestors, and there was one about music."

"I remembered it at the time because I was aware how important music had become in my life. He said that when a person hears music of a certain type, you know of a certain passion, their soul becomes imbued with that passion, and I thought at the time, he's right."

"You know the surf music genre as it got into people's heads actually drove them with a passion to explore that kind of culture."

"So it's like beautiful love songs make us sort of hunger after love Michael."

"That's right."

They stopped in that moment and hugged each other, with Michael enjoying the softness of Archie's breasts and the hardness of her nipples pushing through the flannelette shirt as she pressed her body firmly against his. He was enjoying it and sensed that Archie was enjoying it too. When they finally released each other Archie moved to give him a sisterly kiss goodnight on the cheek and as she did her lips gently, softly and lovingly brushed across his and hesitated in the moment. She turned to get into her car and then paused.

"Michael I'll give the shirt and the flip flops back to you next time I see you, and thank you for your wise and kind advice you gave in answer to my questions."

"And not forgetting also thank you for the wine."

They were both stalling.

"And thank you for the wonderful stories about your mum and your Greek heritage."

"I like the way your mum uses quotes by famous people even about perfume."

"What was it…Coco Chanel?"

"A woman who doesn't a wear da perfume hasa no future."

"Your mum sounds like she's quite funny, well to someone who isn't Greek I suppose."

It was obvious that they both didn't want the night to end but knew it must. Archie knew she didn't want to leave and Michael knew he didn't want her to. She stopped, turned around walked back to Michael then impulsively once again hugged him close as she lifted her lips to his ear.

"Thank you Michael" Archie said, "thank you so much for today and this evening, and have a beautiful Christmas Michael Winton…and que sera, sera."

He squeezed her close, gently kissed her on the cheek and looked into her eyes.

"You too Archie...and remember whatever happens in your family gathering on the day...what will be ...will be."

"Merry Christmas Archie Vernados...Merry Christmas."

66 *"Garret Sloan's rhetoric appealed to two totally different ends of the societal spectrum. There were the cashed up people looking for more control and influence in life and the cash strapped people looking for more equality in life. He appealed to both the high brow and the hippie."*

Garret Sloan

SEVEN

"I'm frustrated Michael…I'm frustrated…I'm so damn frustrated." Jeffrey stood up out of his chair and began slowly pacing the verandah of the Gibbons' cottage, as he and Michael were enjoying a hot chocolate and some in depth conversation on the first night of Michael's monthly stopover.

"You sound a little angry mate?"

"I guess I am angry…but I'm more angry at myself than anyone else for not being able to figure out what is really going on."

"I mean I'm even starting to damn well look for hidden meanings in some of his preaching."

"You know what his favourite line is now?"

"No."

"He says, 'well we've all got things in our lives that we're dealing with.' I mean what does he mean by that?"

"He says it all the time."

"You know is it some covert message to someone. Is he trying to justify to someone in the audience who might know a secret or two about him that what he is doing is no different from anyone else, and convince them he's trying to address it?"

"And those little tete a tetes that he, Unwin and Mags always seem to be having after the service over coffee…I mean what's that all about?"

"Does his ego just like being seen hanging out with doctors or is it more than that?"

"I know I shouldn't get angry but it's just so damn frustrating."

"Michael it's like those three are the three left over pieces in a jigsaw puzzle that you just can't seem to find a place for in the picture."

"It's very exasperating."

Garret Sloan was an enigma, a puzzling person. He was an imposing figure but not an attractive looking man: a tall man in his early fifties with a thick head of greasy black hair that looked like it had been dyed and then given an overdose of Brylcreem, a hair styling product for men launched in the late 1920's.

It was a product that achieved much success with a marketing pro-gramme that appealed to the male ego, an entity that was fully functional in the life of Garret Sloan. The ad in its television and radio ditty fea-tured the words Brylcreem the gals will pursue you, if you simply dab a little on your hair. Garret Sloan's ego took it far too seriously: he dabbed a lot more than others, far too much.

But regardless of him being handicapped with thick greasy brush backed style hair, a stomach paunch, an occasional emphysema type cough from years of smoking in his younger years, and of course the ill fitting suit, he still managed to carry himself with confidence as he set about doing what he continually described as, 'the Lord's work...his calling'.

Garret Sloan the man was one of a slowly dying out breed of trav-elling tent revivalist preachers, mostly of Pentecostal origin, but with some Baptists still involved. He was part of the existing Pentecostal church that had been first brought into existence around 1901 by a man named Charles Parham, a Methodist minister. It was at a time when there was a dramatic increase in religious fervour as various Christian groups anticipated and predicted that the end of world was nigh, and that Christ would return to earth soon to judge its inhabitants.

Following on from Parham's work came a series of revivalist meet-ings in 1906 on Azusa Street Los Angeles, which led to a widespread experience of audience participation in a religious phenomenon called 'speaking in tongues'. It was an activity that quickly spread amongst other different denominations around the country and significantly grew the Pentecostal movement.

Pentecostalism had gotten its name from an incident on the day of Pentecost as outlined in the Bible where it describes how the Holy Spirit descended on Jesus' disciples causing them to speak in tongues: to speak a language different from their own birth language. The experience of this happening was known as being 'baptized in the Spirit'.

Compared to the mainstream churches of the day the Pentecostal religion itself was energetic and dynamic but had its specific religious doctrine too. The most important one to them being that a believer as part of their conversion to Christianity must undergo this experience known as the Baptism in the Spirit, which they taught would give them the strength to live a powerful Christian life.

But not only this, they preached that once baptized in the Spirit a person would speak in tongues and be given direct access to the other gifts of the Holy Spirit such as prophecy, discernment, and healing, which was the ability to lay hands on someone and release a direct healing for them from God.

The tent revival meetings with their Pentecostal flair had commenced in the 1920's and continued through the 60's and 70's before eventually dying out in the 80's. This touring type of evangelical entertainment, whilst originally birthed in the United States, had been progressively exported to like-minded English speaking countries.

Most of the tent meetings were held in the rural and regional townships of each country with the evangelization of the city masses being catered for by established church leaders in existing purpose built buildings or churches.

The tent revival meetings had emerged as an ongoing development of what were the old camp meetings of the twenties and thirties which saw religious people in country townships where there was no church, gather together in a farmer's field for their Sunday church services. Here they would sing hymns, and listen to a loud and very vocal transient preacher teach about the Christian life in an effort to 'save souls': the term used for converting a person to Christianity.

The country tent meetings of the forties, mainly led by the Pentecostal churches, were concurrent with but in many ways much broader than a non-pentecostal event that would come to be remembered as The Great Los Angeles Crusade, which occurred in 1949 in the American city of Los Angeles in California.

It was here that a circus tent was erected in a car park with a capacity to seat 6000 people. But because of the huge response to the first meeting the seating was quickly increased to accommodate 9000 people. It was an event that brought the world's attention to an up and coming Baptist evangelist by the name of Billy Graham. It saw him conduct an eight-week crusade and preach to 350,000 people resulting in the conversion to Christianity of some 3000 of them.

Billy Graham was a man who would become a hero to many young Protestant and Pentecostal tent evangelists. The tent meetings that Sloan cut his teeth on as a thirty year old Assemblies of God minister, whilst not being as large in terms of tent size and audience participation as the Billy Graham ones, were much more broader in content and more specific in intention.

They too in terms of the Pentecostal church had their pioneers and heroes, and to Garret Sloan no one more so a hero to him than a Pentecostal revivalist preacher and a friend of Billy Graham in the United States, the Reverend Oliver Robards.

For the uninitiated protestant or catholic who decided to be a first time attendee at one of Robards' tent meetings, perhaps more out of curiosity than anything else, the meeting itself and all that happened it would become a religious eye opener for them. Loud music, singing, hand clapping, shouting, dancing in the spirit, falling down in the spirit, prophesies, salvation calls and long prayer queues for the laying on of healing hands: these Pentecostal healing revivals had it all.

With all the time he had taken to observe the activities of Robards over the years through periodicals, newspapers, and on Robards visit to Australia on tour, no one could do a tent performance imitating him better than the Reverend Garret Sloan. He had successfully mastered the craft.

On outward appearances Garret Sloan was a man that any one of the attendees at his meetings would most likely describe as a religious man. Garret Sloan sold himself as a person devoted to Christian ideals, and one whose work ethic appeared to be of a high standard demonstrating a total dedication to his profession.

It was a commitment evidenced by an intense preaching schedule that he undertook under the auspices of the Christian City Church, an independent church in the state's capital and part of the Charismatic Movement. The senior pastor at the Christian City Church, the Reverend Terry Channing, was a former New Zealand citizen and a minister of much experience.

But for some people, including Jeffrey Gibbons, Garret Sloan from the moment he first saw and heard him was in his mind a fake and a conman with some hidden agenda. If you asked Jeff why he was suspicious of Garret's motives he would not be able to tell you. It was just a gut feel he would say.

Even at the Carols night alongside Archie and her friends, Michael Winton observed that every comment of Jeff's in relation to the Reverend Sloan loudly reverberated with overtones of mistrust. Jeff Gibbons just knew in his gut as he put it that there was something about Garret Sloan that did not ring true.

He believed him to be the proverbial imposter, a man with some sort of ulterior motive, and no manner of discourse amongst the group on that night or opposing argument from an individual, even someone whom Jeff would count as his dearest friend would dissuade him from this belief.

In terms of his activities and attitudes Garret Sloan certainly was not the typical evangelist, but he did demonstrate a lot of the character qualities of other evangelists of the day. He had the gift of the gab, was a superb salesman of Pentecostalism, and a type of independent religious entrepreneur doing his own thing.

He loved seeing his picture adorning posters that were distributed around each town prior to his visit. He liked being seen around people with titles, and loved the chance to have a close up photo taken with them, especially if it was to be published in the local newspaper.

But not only did Sloan like being seen around people with titles he also longed for a title for himself, a title that would give him what he perceived as more credibility in his ongoing career. His out of control ego dreamed of one day having what he saw as a higher religious status, his title being that of Prophet or better still Apostle.

He also had for a long time harboured a desire to have the word Doctor appear in front of his name in newspapers and on posters. He saw this as a way of bringing more recognition and prestige to his undertakings. So in Garret Sloan's perfect world he would be referred to in conversation and in the print media as Dr Garret Sloan, Apostle.

Now whilst many people in the township including some prejudiced leaders of the religious fraternity saw Garret Sloan as an arrogant and self-interested preacher for profit, the opinions of many other townsfolk in Springfield were really quite divided.

There were the loyal parishioners of the established churches who blindly agreed with what their church leaders said about Garret, but there was a second group of people in the township who didn't take on board what they saw as the pre-conceived notions of the priesthood and the malcontent of other ministers, and it was this group of people who supported Sloan at every opportunity.

For Garret Sloan's rhetoric appealed to two totally different ends of the financial and societal spectrum. Firstly there were the cashed up people wanting to align themselves with him whilst looking for positions of personal power and visibility to complement their material success.

And secondly there was the opposite end of the scale. These were the cash strapped people looking for a sense of belonging to compensate for their own perceived lack of material success in life. These people saw Garret Sloan as their best chance of achieving some sort of social equality.

He appealed both to the hippie and the high brow, to the cash upped and the cash strapped, and for the sake of achieving numerical growth in his own personal popularity, Garret Sloan was always ready to accommodate both polarities in his work and more importantly accept their financial contributions to his work.

A lot of his more gullible supporters believed he was a man possessed with a sincere and singular burning desire to see as many souls converted as he could. In a strange way some of these people became like religious groupies following him from town to town, to be a continual part of his hand clapping, praise the Lord shouting, amen agreeing, demon casting out, laying on of hands support group in every meeting.

But Garret Sloan was not as inwardly fervent about saving souls as he outwardly professed. This appearance he gave of having an earnest desire to see as many people as possible convert to Christianity was firmly underwritten by his intense desire to turn as many people away from established religious organizations as possible and bring them into his own fold.

He was obsessed with pushing his converts towards his own particular ideology of the Christian way of life and the Pentecostal brand and, in doing so, building his own religious and financial power base: thus putting him in a position of power and control in the lives and finances of those who had succumbed to his super salesmanship. Sloan's so called spiritual mission was in reality a commercial venture which he propagated and propped up with his very own specific ideological overtures.

Over time Garret Sloan had honed all the necessary strategies and sermon themes that he needed to ensure the success of each and every crusade. He knew how to soften and relax the crowd at the beginning of each meeting, and how to build a sense of fervent excitement with the aid of loud music, singing and hand clapping, led by a perfectly programmed and choreographed choral group.

He understood what were the most successful conversion tactics to be concentrated on in his sermons, most of which involved rhetoric that would meet a predominant and particular pressing emotional or physical need of someone in the audience.

For Garret Sloan had ascertained through countless experiences that, apart from some sightseers, the people who came along to his meetings came along for a specific reason. And that reason always involved having some particular need met in the realm of either a physical healing or an emotional healing. They had a problem and they wanted God through Sloan to fix it.

He had cleverly worked out that in regards to the emotional needs of human beings there were mainly six specific things that people would be looking for help with, and that if he applied his super salesmanship to all these six during a sermon, then at least one of them was sure to hit the bull's-eye with an audience member resulting in their conversion.

They were the six emotional states of mind that weighed commonly on most people which were prone to lead to some sort of a depressive state in a person: fear and worry, grief, guilt, rejection, lack of confidence, and financial problems, and Garret Sloan had a bible verse to address them all.

Sloan had proven to himself, through experience, that by providing the particular medicine to meet that need, by dishing up the appropriate bible references that they wanted or needed they would more often than not be converted to become loyal supporters of his brand. He exploited the message of hope. He was the religious version of the travelling snake oil salesman of the day.

For those visitors who might be physically sick he would proclaim with gusto from the pulpit, "by his stripes you have been healed…only believe…let me pray with you."

For those who might be gripped with worry he would soften his voice and encourage, "consider the lilies of the field they neither toil nor spin…be anxious for nothing but seek ye first the Kingdom of God and all things will be added unto you…only believe…let me pray with you."

For those who might lack confidence or have a poor self-image he would admonish them with, "I can do all things through Christ who strengthens me."

This would be followed up with a thrusting movement of his outstretched arm and finger pointing at a specific individual while crying out with gusto, "you…yes I mean you…you can do all things through Christ who strengthens you…only believe…let me pray with you."

In addition to this as part of his manifesto Sloan had over time steeped his learning and knowledge of the many patriarchal stories in the Old Testament, in particular leaders such as Abraham and Moses. He longed to be seen as a charismatic leader and to become a type of spiritual benevolent fatherly dictator, with his followers deriving pleasure from them being under his control.

In doing so he had come to understand the power one could gain and the authority and influence one could exert over others, particularly women, simply by establishing themselves as a father figure, a shepherd over the flock so to speak.

But as successful as he knew he was at this Garret Sloan wanted more. He was anxious to break away from under the watchful scrutinizing eye of the Reverend Channing, which eventually saw him in a calculated manner turn his ambitions towards a new and growing organization known as the Charismatic Movement.

The Charismatic Movement began to emerge in the early 1960's as some Pentecostal ministers separated themselves from the church hierarchy of religious brands such as the Assemblies of God and started setting up their own independent churches.

Most professional tent revivalists progressively saw a lessening of numbers attending their travelling sideshows as more and more of these Charismatic churches began springing up. They subsequently began looking for opportunities to leave the tent meeting road shows and to set down roots, to establish their own bricks and mortar church building and become a part of this new financially flourishing movement.

Some were prepared to do it from scratch, slowly building their own independent church, whilst the less scrupulous of the bunch began looking for an established church to hijack. They sought ways to establish their own independent church not only to be involved in the popular Charismatic Movement but also to preserve their own religious relevance and their own personal financial future. Garret Sloan was one of these men.

⸺ ⟶⟵ ⸺

The word Charismatic was a name first used by an American Lutheran minister, Harald Bredesen, who had coined the term in 1962 to describe the ever increasing influence that Pentecostalism was having in mainline Protestant denominations. The name Charismatic was derived from the Greek word charismata meaning a divinely conferred power or talent, a spiritual gift.

This growing Charismatic Movement was comprised of an ever-increasing number of independent churches of mixed faiths and backgrounds. They would incorporate into their church services specific elements of the Pentecostal faith, predominantly the flow of what was known in Biblical terminology as the Gifts of The Spirit. Their meetings always included lively loud singing and handclapping, speaking in tongues, prophesying, prayers for healing, and the use of the spiritual gifts, the charismata, as outlined in the Book of Romans and The Book of Corinthians in the Bible.

Around 1969, seeing the progressive decline in attendees at his tent meetings, and knowing he had to do something to preserve his relevance and financial security, Sloan had over time put a plan together in his head for his own personal transition to a bricks and mortar church of his own as part of the Charismatic Movement.

Unbeknown to all except his wife Bettina, Sloan had in February 1970 caught a plane to America on impulse. His purpose was to visit the church of his hero, the transitioned former travelling Pentecostal evangelist Oliver Robards. Sloan, through subscriptions to overseas newspapers and periodicals had closely followed Robards' rising evangelistic and material success and his transition from tent preaching to the Charismatic Movement. He wanted to explore further a new preaching technique he had read that Robards was using.

Robards himself was an interesting man and had an interesting if not in some cases questionable history. After an unsuccessful stint at a Baptist University where he unceremoniously finished his college studies without obtaining a degree, he became involved as a faith healer in the Tent Revivalist phenomena.

He would eventually move from tent preaching to a church, and to televangelism as one of a growing breed of Pentecostal television evangelists. For the sake of enhanced credibility with mainstream religious organizations he would then describe his religion as Methodist Pentecostal and part of the Charismatic Movement.

Now in order for a preacher to grow his church and consequently his own personal wealth, money was needed, and since God can't print money for the preacher personally it had to be migrated from believers. But for believers to give financially they have to be highly motivated and convinced without a doubt of the benefit of giving. Robards had found a way to motivate them. It was through the teaching of what was known in the day as the prosperity doctrine and officially called seed faith.

How did seed faith work?

Seed faith was a teaching loosely based on some Bible verses in the

New Testament commonly known as the parable of the sower, which spoke of the blessings to be obtained when a sower or farmer plants seed in the right place. The entire un-perverted Biblical message in truth referred to the planting of spiritual truths in the hearts of people for them to spiritually prosper not of planting money in church coffers.

The proponents of this heretic doctrine would espouse that if a person sowed, as in gave money or property to the church, to a particular ministry, or to a 'man of God' directly, then God would miraculously give back to that person 30 or 60 or even a hundred times more than they gave.

This teaching of the seed faith doctrine over time saw a lot of church buildings get bigger and a lot of preachers become financially richer, but saw no parishioners get exceedingly wealthy as promised by the proponents. It was in February 1970 that Garret Sloan saw himself on the first floor of this new method of building the church coffers.

Sloan had read about the financial success that had occurred in religious organizations that had promulgated this doctrine and he was eager to see for himself how it was done. It was with this mindset that he had cancelled a crusade in Springfield, boarded the plane and wended his way to America to the church that had become a multi million-dollar religious monolith, the university church of the Reverend Oliver Robards.

It mattered not to Sloan about the stories of financial indulgence and excesses by Oliver Robards in that he owned two homes each valued in excess of a million dollars, had a wardrobe of Brioni thousand dollar suits, and wore diamond rings and solid gold bracelets which he removed from sight when he preached.

Garret Sloan the evangelist had over time, through self-interest and arrogance, drunk in so much of his own phoniness that it was inevitable, a fait de complis he be chosen as an accomplice of evil. His arrogance had taken him to a point where he believed that he had been anointed and that this anointing was a gift from God and could not be taken away. To reassure himself he would continually voice from the pulpit that the gifts of God are without repentance, meaning once given, they can never be taken away.

To give his life a further impression of Christian authenticity at many towns he crusaded in, standing alongside him would be found his most loyal and devoted follower, his wife Bettina. Bettina usually attempted to travel with her husband every second or third trip. She had two children and family responsibilities, so at times she could not be with him.

Whilst as a staunch Pentecostal wife she enjoyed the actual crusade meeting, she got little pleasure and sometimes felt downright uncomfortable when being billeted along with Sloan's other team members in the homes of members of the local denominational churches that were not of the Pentecostal faith.

Bettina was a paradox, a Pentecostal piano playing paradox: overtly the devoted Christian wife of a man of God whilst at the same time covertly being an enabler of that man's weakness of character and lack of integrity.

At every meeting Bettina could be seen seated at the piano whilst gesturing in a conductor like manner with her head and hands to the choir. With an orchestrated glance from Garret as he was about to begin preaching, she would remove herself from her piano stool, walk to the stairs at the corner of the platform with bible in hand, and take a seat at the back of the tent, quietly watching the unfolding proceedings.

Bettina appeared both in dress and attitude to be what one would describe as an old-fashioned die-hard Pentecostal preacher's wife. You could describe her as dowdy but devoted to her role. There was no obvious affection between her and Garret, rather there seemed to be so much emotional tension between them that in her verbal interactions with him her voice always appeared to come across with a tone of bossy sarcasm.

She seemed to have only one close female friend, Cherie, the slightly obese, sullen faced wife of Thorpey Goldway, a short stocky man with a big oblong shaped face and a totally bald head. Thorpey's most noticeable physical characteristic apart from his head was a slight lisp, which along with his rather oversized jaw and large bottom lip gave him the look and sound of an effeminate man. He was a person of limited talent totally fixated on his own sense of importance because he was Sloan's closest male friend.

Cherie and Thorpey also had an indifferent attitude to each other. There were never any visible demonstrations of affection between them, with Cherie very rarely able to bring forth a smile or a kind word to anyone except Bettina. She could simply be described as fat and frumpy with an attitude to match.

Most of the time at the meetings Thorpey would be seen by himself exaggerating his own sense of importance as he walked around barking orders into the air giving the impression of being Garret's minder. But he too had his own egoistic agenda. Thorpey was a minder who it would be discovered later had a hold over Garret that would see him get anything he wanted, and for Thorpey that was primarily to be in on the ground floor of any success that Sloan's activities might engender.

Cherie too seemed to relish this close one on one friendship she had with Bettina. It would be in conversation with Cherie that Bettina would be quick to damn transgressors, especially fallen females as she called them, for not living up to the moral standards that she believed God demanded of all women.

People would speculate once again without evidence that Bettina conducted her oversight of Garret like a woman who had been cheated on by her partner in the past, but had stayed in the marriage for whatever reason. However there was no first hand evidence of this.

Most of those people who succumbed to Garret's conversion tactics and subsequently attended all the ongoing meetings he conducted on his annual ministry schedule had little idea about his personal life or ministry history and most were prepared, regardless of the rumours, to give him the benefit of the doubt.

Some were aware that his home base was in the city about four hours north of Springfield and that he was employed in the administration office of a large independent Assemblies of God church on a casual basis in his downtime from his tent crusades. This in fact was true.

But another fact unknown to his followers was equally as true. Garret Sloan was an ordained minister of the Assemblies of God church, but a minister who was being closely monitored by senior church leaders due to unproven rumours that had circulated for years amongst the parishioners of different churches he had worked in.

The Christian City Church, in ensuring that its brand and the Assemblies of God hierarchy was protected from bad publicity, had in a sense taken Garret Sloan and his ministry activities under their wing, in an attempt to not only hopefully contain any dalliances if the rumours were true, but also to protect their own image and reputation. The responsibility for this covert and at times overt surveillance of Garret Sloan was given to the Senior Minister of the Christian City Church, the Reverend Terry Channing.

Terry Channing was an experienced pastor of many years in the Pentecostal church. Formerly a successful businessman who became an ordained minister of the Assemblies of God church in New Zealand, he had come to Australia along with a few of his fellow ministers to explore what he saw as a new frontier.

Various Pentecostal preachers, mostly from an Assemblies of God church history, began moving to Australia from New Zealand in the 1960's and establishing churches of Pentecostal type theology with links to but operating independently of the mainstream Assemblies of God churches. Their modus operandi was to lease church accommodation in the major cities that could house a congregation of five or six hundred people and begin to promote their independent brand of religion.

Garret Sloan did not like Terry Channing and Terry Channing did not like and did not trust Garret Sloan to behave with integrity. The truth of the matter was that Sloan jealously saw Channing as the epitome of everything he didn't have and so desperately wanted. A man who had become financially successful in his own right before he had entered the ministry, a man of considerable influence, and a minister who was now the head of the largest independent Pentecostal church in the state.

Sloan had convinced himself that Channing was a man who just happened to be in the right place at the right time, and for those reasons and those alone he had become successful. As for Channing he saw Sloan as a self-interested egomaniac, deceptive and deceived, someone who he would describe later as bordering on being a spiritual sociopath, a man totally lacking in integrity and completely unwilling to face up to his own character flaws.

But the real truth was that Garret Sloan was not prepared to adopt the ethical behaviour and high measure of integrity that had seen Terry Channing achieve his current successful status in life. Living a life of integrity was not an acceptable option for Sloan. His ego preferred his own disingenuous lifestyle, the Spirit of Evil kept feeding that ego, and both he and that spirit desired to, through constant co-operation, keep it that way.

It would be this driving force that saw him board the plane in February 1970 and head to America to learn more about what he believed was the key to freeing himself from all his frustrations in living under, as he saw it, the microscopic gaze of the Reverend Terry Channing. Sloan was heading to the University and mega church of the Reverend Oliver Robards, his sole goal being to gain a greater understanding of this new message of seed faith and then bring it back to use in his own, as he believed, ongoing anointed ministry.

However the Spirit of Control had entered the picture and Sloan was to get a bonus. He had unknowingly timed his seed faith visit to the United States to coincide with a one-week series of lectures at the Oliver Robards University by a visiting Pentecostal minister from South America, the Reverend Juan Ortega, a founding member of the Christian Ministry Group.

These were a group of ministers in the Charismatic Movement who were promulgating a new type of operational structure for church congregations named the discipleship or shepherding movement, that Sloan after listening to Juan Ortega would become enamoured with. It involved individual church members being structured into small groups called cells, a cell being a group of up to ten people. Each cell would have a leader appointed to their group and these cell group leaders would be known as shepherds.

Heading up all the cells in a church would be the resident Pastor of the church who would be known as the Chief Shepherd with each shepherd being responsible to the Chief Shepherd for the lifestyle direction and the spiritual and emotional well-being of all members of their cell.

The Discipleship Movement was the perfect vehicle for the activities of the Spirit of Control that was alive and well in Sloan. While he was more of an opportunist than an ideologue he was always prepared to accept any current ideological teaching that would see him fulfill his own personal opportunistic desires. In one short week of lectures he had found Juan Ortega's teaching on discipleship fitted perfectly into those aspirations. All he needed now was a church to effectively implement that operational structure into.

66 *"You know people do talk about me a lot, more than you think. Over the centuries I have become a popular topic of discussion with teachers from a wide variety of philosophical genres, all attempting to come to an understanding of me and what motivates me to do what I do."*

The Spirit of Evil

The Two Entities

EIGHT

$\text{---}\infty\text{---}$

It was the author Oscar Wilde who once stated that he believed he had never really met a wicked person, but then on further contemplation he wondered whether he might have, but perhaps didn't recognize that person as wicked at the time because they looked and spoke just like everyone else. Maybe this is true, for didn't someone once speak of evil as something that lurks in the hearts of men. They didn't say that evil could be seen on the faces of men.

For some people however, evil is not always as repellant as the imaginative illustrated storybooks of our growing years convinced us. To these people evil can be quite attractive and that mindset gives evil the power to make of them not simply victims as in many cases, but active accomplices, allies, and even participants in its soul-destroying schemes. This of course was evidenced in the behaviours of those everyday people who embraced the mindset of Adolf Hitler.

There is one thing however that we can be assured of. No matter how much evil tries, no matter how many people embrace its perverted logic, it can still never match up to the power and might of goodness. For whilst evil may appear to be successfully destructive in its mission for a time, it eventually becomes destructive of itself and implodes within the soul of the perpetrator, its host, as the powers of rightness raise up a standard to oppose its wrongness.

$\text{---}\infty\text{---}$

Hello.

"May I speak with you?"

"Let me introduce myself, for I may be a stranger to you. You may not have spent a lot of time with me thus far in your life, but then again maybe you have, unknowingly. We may have crossed each other's path in a major way or even as is more common, in a seemingly minor way."

"It is conceivable that you have just had some momentary connection with me, unwittingly, through the activities of others or in your personal interactions and involvement with those people who have passed through your life over time."

"Perhaps you may have been a participant in one of my well-planned and precisely orchestrated life events and given me, even unintentionally, unwavering support and assistance in my mission."

"This being the case you could conclude that in achieving a successful outcome in each mission I undertake, whilst I operate through human beings, I also operate independently of them, and certainly not with their best interests in mind. It really is only all about me."

"My catalogue history of intervening and interfering in the affairs of mankind as they universally unfold are extensive numerically and very widespread geographically."

"My singular goal, the end design of all my labour, is always to create a separation. It may be a separation physically, a separation emotionally, a separation spiritually or a separation culturally."

"It can happen between one human being and another, between one family member and another, between a community and itself, or between nation and nation. But rest assured, when I go to work it will happen."

"For me it really doesn't matter who it involves or indeed how many, as long as separation happens, since separating human beings is the primary purpose of every mission I undertake. I am a destroyer of connected human emotional and spiritual relationships. Oneness is not part of my agenda."

"I am sure there would have been many times when you noticed my masterful work influencing and impacting on the lives of certain individuals or groups and probably didn't even realize it was me."

"You observed hurtful things happening, you gave an inner sigh, but just couldn't quite figure out the causal agent and so any capacity or desire to care further was quickly cast aside by you. You became overcome by the influence of one of my cohorts, the Spirit of Indifference."

"These observations may have occurred as you read about my exploits in your local newspaper, or perhaps sat quietly following stories about me on your television or radio news programme, eagerly anticipating the next instalment."

"Yet even though what you were reading, watching or listening to in a way brought a certain amount of revulsion to you, some details of my work subconsciously intrigued you, causing you to raise the same subject matter again later in discussion with family or friends."

"Over the centuries I have been described differently by various writers and commentators, particularly those of the religious or spiritual persuasion, with many saying that I am pure entity. You see an entity is something that exists in itself as a separate being, and does not have a material visible appearance, it has no discernible form: you know like a spirit, or a ghost as you call them. Something that is pure entity is an invisible energy force operating alone and separately from all other things."

"Yes, this is true about me, for I am not visibly obvious to those I work through or work on, but the results of my activities and handiwork are very real and very noticeable."

"I am an isolationist by nature and love creating a feeling of isolation in my victim. That's an intrinsic part of my work. In fact the art of separating people, communities and cultures from each other whilst inflicting as much discomfort and distress as I can is what I am best at."

"So yes, being a pure entity is in fact necessary to enable me to spread my reach as far and as effectively as possible."

"Perhaps to give you a clearer picture about myself, you could liken me to a specific animal in the animal kingdom: can you guess what it is?"

"Of course you can, it's the wolf."

"You see the wolf is regarded by most ethologists, those who study animal behaviour in their natural habitat, as one of the earth's most cowardly and fearful animals."

"Not much of a compliment for me I suppose."

"What is that line in the children's nursery rhyme?"

"Who's afraid of the big bad wolf, the big bad wolf, the big bad wolf," always sung in a slightly contemptuous tone by children."

"Well according to the intonation in that rhyme, nobody is afraid of the big bad wolf, nobody."

"So why would I be likened to a wolf, or indeed be proud enough to liken myself to a wolf, if no one is really afraid of me?"

"I will tell you why."

"It is because of my wolf like character qualities, generally not known about and certainly not very obvious to anyone who is not a trained ethologist."

"Sure a wolf might be cowardly and fearful, but it is also sly and cunning, and as it is well documented, a wolf is one of the most vicious and bloodthirsty of all animals."

"It takes no prisoners."

"It is known to be the only animal that destroys as much prey as possible regardless of hunger and appetite."

"It is smart, it likes to maneuver its prey to a situation of helplessness and a feeling of hopelessness, with nowhere to go and no one to turn to, trapped with no obvious way out. It loves to be in control."

"Hmm, yes, that does sound like me."

"I enjoy it when my prey has seemingly nowhere to turn. Then they are completely under my control and become an ongoing participant in my persistent prosecution of a particular event I have ensnared them in."

"Yes…think of me as a wolf, and if you like sometimes a wolf in sheep's clothing, for deception is one of my other powerful character qualities."

"However enough about my comparative animal characteristics, let's look more closely at me the pure entity."

"You know people do talk about me a lot, more than you think. Over the centuries I have become a popular topic of discussion with teachers and authors from a wide variety of philosophical genres, all attempting to come to an understanding of me and what motivates me to do what I do."

"However more often than not, whilst they have been able to touch on a few of the obvious components of my nature and activity, they have never really come to a complete understanding of the real me, of what inspires me to do what I do, or even how I became active in this role in the first place."

"Today scholars of social behaviour continue to describe me in many different ways: an interventionist, wicked, immoral, without conscience and acknowledge the varying degrees of intensity I possess as I involve myself in the practical lives of specific people both individually and in collective society."

"Yes…collective society. I must say that I do like the collective approach to my work. The more people I can involve in one intervention the more satisfied I am."

"You could call it getting more bang for my buck."

"Some would also say that I am not gender or individual specific, but embrace any prospective ego dominated candidate, someone who has the right qualifications for the job you might say. Others say that I lie in stillness, lurking in the hearts of all men and women, watching and waiting for the ones that show great potential to fulfill my separation agenda."

"Yes…once again… all true."

"But no matter what these scholars espouse when discussing my origin and intent, there are really only two beings in this universe who in total truth know why I do what I do and how I go about selectively choosing my vehicle of operation."

"Those two beings are the Divine Life Force commonly referred to by humans as God, and of course myself."

"So…who am I?"

"What am I?"

"Am I pure entity?"

"Are there any others like me?"

"How did I come to be?"

"What is my history?"

"Let me try and help you understand."

"Yes, look, I am an entity, a pure entity, and there are others like me but I am the first amongst equals."

"We are actually a group of entities working as a team, I guess you could call it a family business."

"We have what you might call a wolf pack mentality with all of us, my siblings and myself, each having a role to play in our own specific area of expertise in the affairs of men and women."

"And yes I am an interventionist in my calling, consequently I never sit still for long. I am always looking for an outlet, and always searching for an opening to fulfill my mission of separation."

"Our family is very patriarchal in type, with me as its head, and with all members being given set tasks according to what I determine is the individual intensity and the level of impact needed in any singular event."

"The better they are at their job the more work they get."

"So who am I? What is our family name?"

"Well even though I and my fellow siblings are known, particularly in some religious organizations by our individual names based on the role each one has, our family name is universal and recognized by all humans no matter what their spiritual persuasion."

"It is the name used to describe us when the everyday news of singular events that we are involved in are broadcast into the living rooms of the world. Love the media. They give me so much publicity, much more than my polar opposite."

"It is the name people use to detail not only our activities but also to describe the character of the people we work through, those who are chosen to host our schemes and fulfill our plan."

"It is the name given to us when long ago we were birthed on our mission into this world to separate the inhabitants of this world religiously, culturally, physically and emotionally."

"Who are we?"

"We are in fact evil, entities of evil, pure evil."

"Who am I and what is my given name?"

"I am the head, the first amongst equals and leading agent of this our family of evil, and I am named Lucifer, the Spirit of Evil."

"Some of you know me as Satan or the Devil, names I find slightly common to be quite honest."

"I am known as Lucifer in the world of spirit, and my deputy, the contact agent within each human being that I work through, is named the Spirit of Ego, which lies dormant within the egoic mind of every human being ready to be activated."

"And who are my spirit siblings, my fellow agents of evil, those I choose most frequently to use when I make entry into the affairs of humankind, and how many of them are there?"

"Well past scholars of my handiwork would say that they number in the area of seven. But I say seven thousand times seven. Nevertheless these academics over the centuries have mistakenly settled on seven and have named their own chosen seven as these: The Spirit of Greed, the Spirit of Envy, the Spirit of Gluttony, the Spirit of Laziness, the Spirit of Anger, the Spirit of Lust and the Spirit of Pride."

"They have even given them a group title, the Seven Deadly Sins."

"Quaint but in terms of the numbers and their chosen seven, not quite correct."

"Sure each one in this group work hard at what they do."

"Look around at how effective the Spirit of Gluttony has been in influencing today's society."

"But who is best to judge the effectiveness of each individual on my team?"

"Yes, me of course, and if asked to name my top most effective life separating and life destroying agents I would offer up these:"

"The Spirit of Discord or Disunity, the Spirit of Fear, the Spirit of Control, the Spirit of Lies and Deceit, and yes I agree with past writers on the other three, the Spirit of Lust, the Spirit of Pride and Arrogance, and the Spirit of Greed and Selfishness."

"However I must reiterate, there are thousands more than these whose name badges are hanging on our Luciferian family tree just waiting to be summoned to their mission."

"Now as with all our interventions, once initiated, they automatically bring entry into our arena of activity, my nemesis, an entity which like myself has also existed since the beginning of time."

"I'm sure you have come across it at times, the Spirit of Goodness."

"This interfering opposing force is in most cases not recognized as a spiritual entity and sometimes referred to by the spiritually bereft component of society as retributive justice, or karma, since it possesses the character qualities of righteousness and the power that comes with it."

"But it is actually the opposing force brought into play as part of a Divine Game in Lila, to prevent my family from being totally victorious in the final wash up no matter how much headway we make."

"It is the reason the phrase 'goodness will always triumph over evil' was coined."

"My family called Evil recognizes the power of our nemesis."

"We continually witness these retributive justice entities, these angelic warriors, running interference in our missions, turning our intrusions into a giant goodness versus evil battle for supremacy."

"It can become a type of David and Goliath situation: a seemingly gladiatorial type of emotional and physical event involving my Goliath, my vehicle of expression, usually a self-interested, self-centred ego driven individual and my nemesis's vehicle of opposition to my work, their David, a righteous type of selfless personality with the well being of others their foremost priority."

"But look, it's not for me to promote the existence or powerfulness of my nemesis, let them explain that for themself."

"The story you have just started to read is about one of my most proudest moments, an intervention I believe that caused maximum damage spiritually and emotionally."

"It involved an area that I love to specialize in."

"The emotional and spiritual lives of individuals and communities that are part of some particular religious group, faith or social culture."

"Enjoy my intervention…I know I did."

⨌

"Hi."

"I am confident that most of you would have crossed paths with me or one of my spiritual siblings at one stage or another in your lifetime thus far."

"You may have witnessed us at work on one of our missions, carrying out some random act, and in doing so I am sure you would have acknowledged that what we did was nice and you may even have commented about the positive effects that we had on someone, materially, emotionally, or even psychologically."

"You perhaps may have been one of those human beings used to carry out one of our missions as we sought to connect in some way with an individual or a group of people."

"You see we specialize in bringing happiness, peace, comfort and a feeling of safeness into a person's life or a group situation."

"Unlike our spiritual opposite whose sole mission is to destroy, to disconnect and separate human beings from each other, our sole goal in this game of life is to maintain existing connections between individuals in society and fix those relationships that are broken."

"We work to prevent disconnections between people, to foster the reconnection of human beings who are separated from each other emotionally or culturally, and to propagate compassion between individual and individual, between community and community and between nation and nation."

"It's what we do."

"We were spoken of in ancient times as those who bring tidings of comfort and joy, and peace on earth with goodwill to all."

"This was actually the proclamation given announcing the birth of our master."

"We are what you might call infiltrators but are interventionist by nature, which sees us as a type of warrior or as some people have more aptly described us, angelic warrior."

"People also see us as a type of retributive justice, avenging angels in the game of life running interference for those people or groups impacted by the activities of the family of evil."

"In some cultures our work and our visitations have been given the interesting name of Karma."

"Our method of operation is always in all ways aligned with integrity and rightness and with what is in the best interest of those we are representing, whether that be an individual's life circumstance or a common collective cause."

"Sadly however, whilst our catalogue of activities in the affairs of humankind are far greater in number and more wide spread geographically than those of our opposing entities, many of our deeds go unnoticed and are unfortunately not reported or publicised with as much fervour as theirs are."

"Only in rare situations do we receive attention in big bold print on the front of a newspaper or as the lead story on the nightly television news."

"Perhaps it's because our work doesn't have any intriguing or unknown aspects to it. It is not open for analysis or interpretation, doesn't encourage ongoing titillating conversation, and rarely would produce divided opinions and judgments."

"Our missions, when accomplished and occasionally publicised, do not provoke the lingering question…why? They are just accepted as being good and right, and are usually more times than not greeted by genuine agreement from a singular observer or with positive concurrence by communities."

"Yes," they will say, "I expected that would happen", or, "well I am pleased that happened," or "well what goes round comes around."

"So who am I?"

"Who are we?"

"What are we?"

"We are all angelic entities and I am the leader."

"I have many siblings that work hard at achieving successful outcomes for me on my chosen mission."

"In ancient spiritual writings, I am named the Angel of Goodness, and work closely with my second lieutenant the Angel of Mercy."

"But my heavenly name is Michael the Archangel."

"As the defender of all things pure and right my actions are the epitome of strength and courage."

"My agents and I intervene in the affairs of humankind protecting people, belongings and reputations."

"I guard against all the effects of fear and fear based entities, and against all the negative energy forces that are behind everything that is unsavoury in the world human beings inhabit."

"Yes our family is all pure entity."

"We are Spirits, the angelic agents of a Supreme Being following human beings wherever they go, watching over them, guarding them, and assisting them in their struggles in life."

"Because of this some people even refer to us as guardian angels."

"My fellow entities and I work by communicating directly with the intuitive mind locked deep within the Soul of all human beings."

"Human beings refer to this as conscience, and some people having listened to our instruction have used the term, a little voice in my head told me."

"That little voice was one of us trying to get your attention."

"This differs from my polar opposite the Spirit of Evil who works solely through the egoic mind."

"It is recorded that an ancient King named David, in writings known as The Psalms, acknowledged that myself Goodness and my lieutenant the Angel of Mercy followed him all the days of his life, guarding him, even when the dark shadow of Evil was closely lurking."

"I Michael the Archangel and my team of angelic warriors have been overseeing the Supreme Being's mission on earth ever since the rising up of the Luciferian family."

"I am both a record keeper and a manager helping human beings to discover the purpose for their lives and guiding them through."

"You see time is of no consequence to me. I'll hang around as long as is necessary. The Angel of Goodness will always triumph over the Spirit of Evil no matter how long it takes."

"People might ask me, "well how many of these angelic warriors are there watching over humankind?"

"I would answer thousands and thousands and tens of thousands. But the ones that seem to be most called upon are the Angels of Unity, of Courage, of Service, of Love, of Truth, of Humility and of Kindness."

"The Angel of Unity to oppose the Spirit of Discord, the Angel of Courage to oppose the Spirit of Fear, the Angel of Service to oppose the Spirit of Control, the Angel of Love to oppose the Spirit of Lust and the Spirit of Hatred, the Angel of Truth to oppose the Lying Spirit and the Spirit of Deception, and the Angel of Kindness to oppose the Spirit of Ill Will and the Spirit of Selfishness."

"What is my role in the game?"

"I choose which of my warriors I send into battle and direct them to the human they are to work through."

"Ancient wise men wrote of me saying "when the enemy, meaning

Evil, shall come in like a flood, the Spirit meaning myself and my angelic warriors shall rise up a standard against him."

"You see a standard is a symbol like a flag in battle raised at a rallying point to lead a charge. Every standard has a bearer, one who raises the flag for the charge. I Michael the Archangel, the Angel of Goodness, am that standard bearer."

"I am he who raises the flag to lead my host of angels into battle. I am the warrior who leads the charge into warfare against the enemy."

"I hope I have explained myself clearly."

"The story you have commenced to read is about one of those battles…a battle of goodness against evil."

"Oh…and by the way, whilst there is always some collateral damage in any battle, it's an inevitable occurrence, always remember this…at the end of every battle I win."

"As he watched the first wave crash past, then quickly recede back into the ocean leaving behind a smothering of different coloured seashells, he thought of the last line of a poem he had written some years before, "for everything that passes... something beautiful remains," and then he began thinking of her...Archie."

The Second Encounter

NINE

"Hi…yes I'm sorry I missed your call, the fellowship group finished late. There was a lot of discussion about it yes, and everyone is pretty excited. So Michael Winton is going to have a meeting with Dr Nicholls about it. Hopefully it will all go well."

It was the evening of the gang's first social get together and Margie Morrison was putting in a late night return call to Garret Sloan.

Wednesday morning one week after Christmas Day had arrived and Michael had started the day with a sense of anticipation knowing that Archie and her friends would be coming to his apartment that evening for their first social get together. He was especially excited that he would be seeing Archie again for the first time since their paddleboat adventure.

Christmas Day had come and just as quickly gone, the day itself for Michael being a time of quiet reflection. He knew that he would spend the time alone, as this was usually the case the first year when he took up residence in a new town because of his work. The company policy regarding transfers was to get the employee settled into their new role in early December during trading downtime and prior to their financial year commencing on January 1st.

Michael didn't mind for he was comfortable with either socializing or solitude, but was aware that his spending Christmas by himself would sound strange to others who thrived on the social aspect of the festive season.

He had been fully aware that he would be spending the day alone when Archie had asked the question as to what he was doing on Christmas Day, but he did not want to get into a discussion about it at the time. He did not want to mess with the mood of the moment.

Past experience had shown him that if he answered honestly and mentioned he would be spending Christmas alone, people would in their kindness be only too quick to offer him a share of their own social or family activities. To Michael this kind of semi-forced imposition on people, most of whom would be complete strangers to him, would be more uncomfortable for him and perhaps them than being alone.

He was never uncomfortable or melancholy and actually enjoyed his own solitude on the day for a change, particularly after an extremely busy settling in period. There had been many social Christmas days in the past and there would be many more in the future. But it was hard to convince others of this. Not only that, Michael had found on previous occasions when he declined someone's offer that it would often leave them puzzled or even slightly offended. Such was their ingrained attitude to the social aspect of Christmas.

So he had decided some years before that for him at times such as this, a new job in a new town, the best thing to do was to say very little when asked the inevitable question: "What are you doing over Christmas?"

Michael liked the downturn in human activity and associated noise in the outdoor world on the day. After the early morning street activity that saw excited children road testing their new bike, scooter, or skateboard had concluded, a peacefulness descended on the deserted streets and beaches as people battened down in their houses for the lunchtime start of the day's social activity. He liked that peacefulness.

For him, on this his first Christmas in Springfield, his day had included walking along the beach in the morning enjoying the solitude, with a visit by ferry to the Lighthouse around mid afternoon. Late afternoon saw him with a glass of red in his hand, stretched out in his squatter's chair on the balcony watching the trawler boats on the river as they slowly chugged their way out to sea.

He marvelled at the disciplined lifestyle of the fisher folk. For them, he thought, 5 p.m. in the afternoon had been the end of Christmas Day 1969. The holiday was over and it was back to work: the fish, their livelihood, were waiting for the rendezvous.

He had enjoyed his Christmas Day and the spacious relaxedness of walking along an almost deserted beach. He knew from past experience that by 11 a.m. most if not all of the early morning beachgoers would have headed back to their homes for the traditional family lunch, and on this Christmas Day he was once again accurate in his prediction.

The beach was almost human free save for one elderly man walking his cute little dog adorned in a red tinsel collar. The man gave Michael a cheery "Merry Christmas" and the dog gave a yap in concurrence as their paths crossed. In terms of life forms on the beach, that was it, one man and a dog, and the occasional jellyfish.

Michael had set out down the road, strolled around the lagoon, and then taken a brisk walk in the sun along the surf beach before diverting onto the rough gravel pathway in the middle of the boulders along the sea wall bordering the river mouth. He had then ambled the short distance to where the river met the ocean, climbed down over the rocks onto a huge boulder and after sitting down, began silently watching the waves crashing endlessly across the bar.

His gaze facing seaward, he stared in an almost mesmerized way at the waves rolling past him gently crashing to the shore on the one side and continuing their journey up the river on the other side. It created not only a deep sense of peacefulness but also a feeling of being close to nothing or no one except nature.

This would also be a time, the one time and one day of the past year that would see him at his most reflective best, time spent totally devoted to self-reflection on the year that was fast coming to an end: where he had been, what he had done, what were the good times, what were the not so good times, and what could he have done better?

As he watched the first wave crash past, then quickly recede back into the ocean leaving behind a smothering of different coloured seashells, he thought of the last line of a poem he had written some years before: "for everything that passes…something beautiful remains," and then he began thinking of her…Archie.

He thought about their time together, when he had felt so comfortable in sharing things with her, things that he had never shared with any other person before. Perhaps he thought upon reflection this might have been because she had been so open and honest in her thoughts with him.

He recalled that his mother had once said to him, "Mikey…be honest in conversation and you will get honesty from those around you, because honesty builds trust and trust is rewarded in return with honesty."

It was a great saying to live one's life by.

But he knew that on that night in some ways he had held back from giving her a true picture of the last twelve years of his life. He wasn't sure why, but he had an idea. Maybe he thought it was because he didn't want this girl he was beginning to care about to think any ill will of him or perhaps judge him.

He thought about how in giving her counsel about her sexual non-experiences he had in a way opened himself up to questions from her about his own sexual experiences as a teenager, and he didn't want to go there. Michael's personal life had always contained the element of privacy in it, for self-preservation purposes mainly, and he was not sure whether he really wanted to venture down that path of a total sharing of everything with Archie just yet.

He thought about his comment to her on the night that sex in your teens can sometimes complicate things, not only for yourself but also quite often for others: those on the periphery of your life such as family and friends. He contemplated the experiences he had not shared with her, and felt glad in a way that she had not questioned him further about the sexual complications of his own teenage years.

It was the late 50's to mid 60's and Michael was a young man who would be described culturally as a surfie. The era was that of the surfing movement which brought forth a generation of young people, a particular breed of their own, whose recreational lifestyle choice was one of sun, sand and surfing. It had started in the 1950's but exploded in the 1960's. Michael lived and grew up as a teenager in those years, owned a surfboard and surfed every weekend.

The surfing culture was one of fashion and lifestyle distinctions surrounding the sport of board riding and surfing. It was one of colourful Hawaiian hibiscus flower printed board shorts for the surfer boys, and itsy bitsy teeny-weeny yellow polka dot bikinis for the surfer girls. Most surfer girls could be described as innocent teenagers who spent their weekends hanging around the beaches, the surf clubs and the surf club dance nights, hoping to meet the bronzed and blond haired stompie wompie boy of their dreams.

The teenage lifestyle of this era consisted of weekends on the beach surfing and sunbaking, and Saturday nights at the local surf club dancing. Midst all of this came their own particular brand of slang terminology and the introduction of a wonderful musical genre that would come to be remembered forever in musical history as surf music.

The song writing and singing genius of bands such as The Beach Boys, Jan and Dean, and The Chantays, had cleverly tapped into this teenage phenomenon and turned it into a lucrative market for those involved in the music industry, even though many of the musos had never surfed at any time in their entire lives.

Songs were written and recorded about waves, big waves such as the Pipeline, about cars, flashy cars such as the little deuce coupe, about the sun and sand in Hawaii, about surfer boys and about surfer girls, and of course about love, particularly first love.

It was in this era of generational revolution and changing behaviours that Michael found himself as a teenager totally immersed. It was a lifestyle of work five days and play for two days. After a full week's work, when the weekend arrived, it was in the car and off to the beach with his mates for two days, surfing during the day and dancing Saturday night at the local surf club.

It was a surfer boy meets surfer girl endless series of situational activities, and it was in the atmosphere of this teenage lifestyle, the surfing, the dancing, the surf music, the surf culture, and the sense of freedom that came with it, that he and the teenage mother of his baby son came to meet.

Michael knew as he sat reflecting by the sea where his comment that sex can complicate things for not only the couple but also for those around them had come from. He knew that those words he said to Archie had come from his own teenage life experience.

In the innocence of his teenage years sex had complicated life for the surfer girlfriend, sex had complicated life for the surfer boyfriend, and sex had complicated things for the families of both. Sadly it had complicated things for the innocent product of that boyfriend girlfriend relationship too, the son he would never see growing up.

As he wandered back towards the Lighthouse Ferry Michael's thoughts turned to how Archie's Christmas Day might be unfolding. He knew it would be different from his but didn't realize how different until she had shared it with him. Archie's Christmas Day had been the polar opposite of his. Culturally they had been worlds apart on the day.

Whilst the traditional Greek pre and post Christmas activities had been modified by Makis and Aurelia over the years to accommodate their new Australian lifestyle, many of the main elements of the Greek style of Christmas celebration surrounding food, family, and friends, were still incorporated into their Christmas Day routines.

For the normal Greek family the festivities of Christmas would commence on St. Nicholas Day December the 6th and finish on what is known as the Feast of the Epiphany, which was January 6th. And whilst the Vernados family did not include every Greek tradition into their own family time, Aurelia had selected individual ones that were important to her in preserving the children's Greek heritage.

The first one was that all the family must attend a night of Carol singing, albeit sometimes separately. Then on the morning of Christmas Eve the children would be seen decorating their father's boat, which was moored down beside the Plaka Pastry and Cafe, with strings of coloured lights. This tradition stemmed in honour of St. Nicholas who is regarded by Greeks not only as the patron saint of the festive season but also the protector of sailors.

On Christmas Eve it was Archie's responsibility to help her mother in the food preparation for the next day. The food menu for Christmas Day could aptly be described as a feast of meats and sweets all traditionally cooked. It was a smorgasbord of foods and cooking processes that as part of Greek tradition had been passed down from generation to generation.

Turkey, roast pork, and a variety of side dishes would head up the main course. Accompanying this would be Christopsomo bread, which was a rich buttery egg bread freshly baked on Christmas Eve, with long ropes of dough shaped in the form of an early Christian cross: hence it was named Christopsomo meaning Christ's Bread.

On Christmas Day Makis would carry out the age-old tradition in which the bread was to be served. He would make the sign of the cross above the loaf of bread, then cut it and give a piece to each person seated at the dining table.

At the family Christmas Eve cook up Aurelia had put Archie in charge of the preparation of the sweets and desserts from a very early age. Whilst there were many recipes to choose from Archie would always go for what she was good at: Galaktoboureko, a custard pastry, lightly lemon scented custard enclosed in layers of thin flaky filo pastry, and Baklavas, thin sheets of filo pastry, sprinkled with nuts, then coiled and baked and dipped in syrup.

After a shortened night of sleep due to some late baking, Christmas morning would see the family drive for two hours to the nearest Greek

Orthodox Church to fulfill what they saw as obligations of their faith, returning late morning to begin the food celebrations. It would be a day of feasting.

Archie's Christmas experience had been a world apart from Michael's, but as Michael thought later after she had shared her day with him, the Greek style was perhaps closer to a celebration of Christ's birth in its individual activity than were the social goings on of most other countries including his.

But Christmas had come and Christmas had gone and now Michael was looking forward to seeing her again. He had missed her and she had missed him, which were the first words she uttered when he opened his apartment door on the night of the first gathering of the group.

⎯⎯⎯⎯⎯ ∞ ⎯⎯⎯⎯⎯

"Hi Michael…I missed you…how was your Christmas?" Archie said juggling two plates of food and her guitar case while simultaneously attempting to hug him.

"It was good…I missed you too," he replied, helping her with the plates.

"Looks like I am the first one here" she continued placing the plates on the dining table.

"That's good…I wanted to be early so I could spend ten minutes with you before the others arrive," she continued as she put her guitar down, turned, then wrapped her arms around his neck and hugged him.

"I brought my guitar 'cause I couldn't fit my piano in the Volkswagen beetle."

Michael laughed, "right."

"I've brought some left over sweets from Christmas too. So much sugar in them they stay fresh for ages, and anyway the gang requested that I bring some."

"Well all except Kelly."

"When I told her I was bringing them her comment was, "aw not those again.""

"Kelly's been spoilt, she gets to taste plenty of free samples at work so these are not a novelty for her."

"Michael the reason I came early is that I wanted to ask you would you like to go to The Heads drive-in theatre on Saturday night?"

"There's a movie on that I saw with my mum in the city a few years ago when she took me there for my 16th birthday. We did some shopping and then went to a movie as is our custom, and even though the movie was sad it was beautiful at the same time. I just loved it."

"It's a love story called Splendor in The Grass."

"Have you seen it?"

"No I haven't."

"It's a beautiful but sad love story. It has Natalie Wood and Warren Beatty in it," she said almost excitedly, "would you like to go with me?"

"I just love it sooo much," she continued before Michael had time to answer.

Michael was enjoying her enjoyment. How could he refuse, not that he intended to.

"It has a beautiful part in it where the narrator quotes the words of William Wordsworth, you know, the poet."

"Yes I do know of him."

"I loved this so much I learned it off by heart."

He says, "what though the radiance which was once so bright, be now forever taken from my sight, though nothing can bring back the hour of splendor in the grass, of glory in the flower, we will grieve not rather find strength in what remains behind."

"Wow Archie...that is beautiful. You must have really loved it to memorize it like that."

"I so did."

"So what do you think Michael...I'll drive?"

"I can borrow one of Dad's furniture trucks, there might be a lounge chair packed on one that we could use to watch the movie. You know just reverse the truck up."

Archie grinned at the surprised and questioning look on Michael's face.

"Just kidding Michael."

They both laughed out loud.

"Sure…would love to go," Michael replied, "and just in case you weren't kidding about the furniture truck how about I drive."

"Okay…that's great…can't wait."

"Hey that rhymes," she returned excitedly at the same time seeming relieved that he had accepted so readily.

Archie had been a little worried whether she might come across as being a bit forward in asking Michael out on a date, part of her strict Greek upbringing being that the man was expected to do the initiating in a potential courtship. But over Christmas she had thought about Michael a lot and had decided to be bold and ask him.

She too, midst all the social activity of Christmas had found time for reflection during the day. She had thought about the openness of their conversation and how comfortable and relaxed she was in his company. She thought about the tingles she had felt when standing naked in his bedroom. But more so she had thought about their shared laughter, particularly on the paddleboat in the rain, and the intimacy of two people sharing a common wit. Yes, it was the laughter she knew she would always remember.

A loud knocking on Michael's door quickly interrupted their conversation.

"Hey the gang's here…I'll let them in," Archie announced as she headed for the door.

And the gang was all there as Michael could remember them from the Carols by Candlelight evening.

"Hey," greeted Archie as she opened the door to be acknowledged in return by a group of giggling chatting people.

"You all come in the one car?"

"Nooo," replied Kelly who was at the front of the pack, having been voted in during the ride as the official doorknocker.

"We're not all that skinny…brought two cars."

"Did you like my knock?" Kelly continued.

Archie looked puzzled.

"Everyone's agreed that for any of our get togethers I will be the official door knocker…I feel quite honored."

"I did stipulate however that I would accept the position only if I didn't end up with the nickname knockers."

"As you are aware Arch I have certain issues with that word."

Everyone laughed.

"Michael you remember all these beautiful people," continued Archie as she ushered them in.

"Kelly, yes of course you remember Kelly, and Jeff and Janet, Margie, and Daniel and Zelda, and this is Shaun, Shaun Cliffe, who wasn't at the Carols night. Shaun is the breakfast show host on our local radio station."

Michael extended his hand, "Hi Shaun…nice to meet you."

"Shaun is also a fabulous drummer and as you can see he's brought a little snare drum."

"Only one in my kit that I could fit in the car," replied Shaun looking around, "nice to meet you Michael, love your place."

"So," continued Archie, "Jeff has his guitar and I have mine, Shaun's got the drum."

"Danny boy did you bring your harmonica?"

"Yup…sure did," replied Daniel as he reached into his pocket.

"And I brought my moves and my tambourine," said Zelda.

"Love those moves my little Hoochie Coochie sister," responded Jeff.

"And," he continued, "I've brought my book of sheet music with lyrics for anyone who might not know the words of the songs written by the best songwriter in the world…drum roll Shaun…Mr Bob Dylan."

"However I'm thinking that this being such an enlightened group of people that the person in question isn't here tonight."

Archie grinned inwardly as she thought about the joke she had shared with Michael, when with a serious look she had asked him a question using the lyrics of Bob Dylan's song Blowing In The Wind.

"Arch…once more you have outdone yourself," interjected Kelly as she walked to the table with her own plate of muffins.

"Yes…once again," continued Kelly, "an oversupply of the world famous Baklava biscuit."

Archie grinned, "just can't help myself, I'm the Baklava babe."

"Wow…look at the view," Jeff exclaimed as he headed towards the glass sliding doors leading to the balcony.

"Look at the river lights, that is so cool. I reckon a change of plans is in order. If it's okay with you Michael I suggest we have all our fortnightly meetings here. And a fireplace, this is so cool…well it's hot actually."

"Everyone agree…yes they do," Jeff continued, without waiting for anyone to reply, "the ayes have it."

Archie smiled as her thoughts went back to the time she had spent with Michael in front of the fireplace.

"No problem with me," replied Michael.

And that's the way it would be for the next six months. Every fortnight a group of like minded people gathering to talk, to joke, to laugh with each other and sometimes about each other, to discuss world events, to discuss spiritual philosophies and beliefs, to share their hopes and dreams, and to sing.

To sing the best of folk music and the best of spiritual music, from Bob Dylan's Blowin' In The Wind, Peter Paul and Mary's Puff The Magic Dragon to Andrae Crouch's I Surrender All, the gang would sing and laugh their way through them all.

———— ✣ ————

It would be around one month after the first meeting however that the subject of communal living came up. It was Jeff who originally raised the subject as he discussed the clusters of hippies that were coming together in his area. But it would be a subject that would always be excitedly embraced by all, inviting enthusiastic discourse and eventually rating permanently on their unwritten talk topic agenda.

They talked about establishing a commune. One that would include their own church or place of worship to reach out to the wider community with a vibrant type of Christian message and charity work to demonstrate the true meaning of the Christian life. It would incorporate a school that would teach Christian values in conjunction with the normal educational curriculum, and would contain an area where small crops could be planted for personal use and also for sale at the local markets to raise funds for the school's needs.

And whilst there would always be a lot of laughter and joking anytime the subject came up, and commenting as to whether they might all be just dreaming, there were also times when the dialogue got into a more serious mode: a type of yes we can do this attitude to the whole conversation.

It would be during these times, usually at the end of the discussion, that the question was inevitably raised as to who should spearhead the project and head it up, who should get things moving, and the finger would always be pointed towards Michael. Jeff, who was always able to make up a rhyme at any time to accentuate the point he was trying to make, would strum a couple of chords on his guitar and end the debate with, "Michael is the man…cause he knows how to plan…cause he's a mannn…ager."

Which usually was a signal for the food to be eaten.

But it would be at their gathering together on the Wednesday evening of May 20th 1970 that during the conversation one member would say something that would set the course for a whole new momentum in the realization of their communal hopes and dreams. It would be straight after Jeff had initiated the subject with his customary introduction of, "hey mister manager how's our plan coming along?" that Margie made her contribution to the discussion.

"Hey…guess what," she interjected.

"I was having my morning tea with Dr Nicholls about a month ago on the Friday. We have morning tea together every Friday just to catch up on how the clinic is going."

"He asked how our fellowship meetings were going. I had told him about them some time ago. I know he is interested in spiritual things so at the time I asked his opinion about our thoughts on setting up our own Christian commune, you know with the church, and school, and charity work. He said that it was feasible and possible."

"Well yesterday he knocked on my office door and asked if we were having our fellowship meeting this week."

"When I said yes we were," he said "well check with your friends and if you are all serious about starting something up regarding a commune let them know that I might be able to point them to just the property they are looking for. It's at least a hundred acres, and if they are really then still interested get Michael Winton to come and see me. I have some ideas."

"Wow," came the unanimous response from the group, with Daniel responding, "are you serious, that's insane?"

"No I am serious," replied Margie, "I think he really wants to get involved."

"Get out of here," replied Kelly, "what do you think Michael?"

"Are you going to talk to him?"

"Sure, that does sound interesting, and for sure I don't have a problem talking to Unwin."

"I'm intrigued by what kind of proposal he has."

"So am I," said Jeffrey, "this sounds cool."

"So are we all in agreement as to where we are heading with this?"

"Show of hands?"

"The hands have it," quipped Jeff.

"Then it's agreed," returned Michael.

"And okay, now that we are agreed, I need to have something to take from us to my meeting with Unwin."

"So we are looking at a school, a meeting hall for church services, crops for the market, and an opportunity for those who want to live on the property…right?"

Michael received a unanimous "right"…and some "correct."

"Just one question," continued Michael.

"If the opportunity became available who would consider actually building a home on the property?"

Everyone went quiet.

"I know I'm not financially able," replied Kelly, "but I bet my mum and dad would consider retiring there. They've been talking for a while now about selling up and retiring. If it was a Pentecostal type service in the church I reckon mum would jump at it. Loves all that Gifts of the Spirit stuff."

"Right," said Michael.

"I might," said Margie "and my mum and dad are looking to move up here in the next twelve months so they might."

Archie was miles away. She was staring at Michael's lips as he spoke and was thinking how much she wanted to kiss him. He always seemed so calm and in control she thought. She thought about that night she had been standing naked in front of his bedroom mirror only a few metres from where she was sitting now. She wondered what the others would think if they had known. She liked the little secret she had.

Kelly had noticed her staring at Michael, smiling.

"Hey Arch what do you think?" Kelly deliberately burst out, startling Archie out of her sensuous reverie.

"Yes, yes, I agree," returned Archie quickly bringing her thoughts back to the moment whilst not really knowing whether someone had asked for her agreement.

Kelly grinned, "me too."

She had been watching Archie staring at Michael for some time from whatever world she was in.

Zelda was confused, "sorry, what are we agreeing to?"

Archie knew what Kelly was up to and quickly changed the subject.

"And Jude and I could teach in the school," continued Archie, wanting to contribute whilst grinning sideways at Kelly.

"You know gratis if we have to until it could pay us."

"And we already have a band going, well sort of a band going, to give us music for the church services," commented Zelda.

"Not forgetting that Michael has been to Bible School so we have a ready made preacher."

"Not sure about ready made," Michael returned.

"And my Dad could count the collection because he's had accountancy training," interjected Kelly.

Everyone laughed.

"Well I can help with any building program," said Jeff, "and Danny boy can do the electrics."

"And I can do first aid when Jeff hits his thumb with a hammer," quipped Margie.

They all laughed again.

Everyone loved the witty dialogue that would flow between Jeff and Margie. They were both strong in their opinions but always enjoyed and accommodated each other's barbs in a genuine spirit of friendship.

"Okay…that's good."

"Gives me something to talk about."

"No problem…I'll give Dr Nicholls a call and arrange a time for a discussion."

"Great," said Archie, "that's exciting."

"Time to call it a night?" said Kelly yawning, "it's a miracle…the biscuits are all gone."

"Oh just one other thing," continued Margie.

"The Garret Sloan crusade that was cancelled in February, it's back on the last week of June."

"Saw the posters going up around town this morning."

"I mentioned it to Unwin and he said that Sloan had to cancel the February one because he was going overseas. Not sure how he knows that."

"But anyway…are we all still going?"

"Sure, sounds good," replied Archie.

"Yes of course," said Jeff, "wouldn't miss it. Looking forward to some light entertainment."

Margie smiled, turned her head, and poked her tongue out at Jeff.

"I love you Mags," he returned.

It was a beautiful starry Saturday night as Archie and Michael strolled hand in hand around the grounds of the drive-in theatre at The Heads. There was a full moon on the night, not white though as one would expect but yellowish with patches of grey streaked across it. It hung at a height that seemed lower than normal as if floating suspended underneath the blanket of stars above it. It was the perfect night Michael thought for what he saw as his first real date with Archie.

The Heads Drive-In Theatre was one of the newer ones in the state, having been fully operational for about five years, and was a favourite spot for families on a Saturday night when young excited pyjama clad children would be bundled into the car and taken to the drive-in for the family night out. A feed and a film.

But as well as being a gathering place for families, due to the proximity of the theatre to the south coast surfing beaches, a plethora of station wagon cars and vans with surfboards on top could always be seen in the early part of the evening reversing into a parking spot so that the rear of the vehicle was facing the big outdoor screen. The ritual for all would be to hook the audio speaker up to a window, turn it on, and then open the tailgate of the wagon or van for group viewing purpose from a sea of mattresses and cushions.

This routine was fully completed when one person was nominated to ensure the speaker was removed from the back passenger window before the car was driven off at the end of the night. Many a speaker had been forcibly removed from its power pole if this process was not strictly observed. That finished, the suntanned teenage occupants would stream across to the kiosk and adjacent dance floor for some pre-movie activities.

This particular drive-in theatre was one of the biggest in the state, having a capacity for six hundred and fifty cars. It had a children's railway line giving free miniature train rides, an outdoor playground for the smaller children, a putt putt green for the older teenagers and adults, badminton facilities and a dance floor, with a resident disc jockey playing the latest pop music usually of the surf music genre. So if you weren't into the movie of the night there was still plenty of other things to do.

There was also a large kiosk facility with an outdoor seating area. This enabled the purchase of food and drinks to be taken back to the vehicle or alternatively eaten while watching the movie at the huge tabled area beside the kiosk.

Archie and Michael sat down on one of the many park style benches surrounding the children's playground. Archie took his hand and leaned her head against his shoulder. There was a kind of magic in the air. The cloudless clear starry night, the sometimes loud chatter of the adults, and the happy sounds of children in their pyjamas laughing and giggling with their new found Saturday night friends as the parents sat back watching, relaxed in the moment.

"Michael, can I ask you a question?"

Michael thought it beautiful that whenever Archie needed to enter into discussion about his opinion on something that was important to her she would always prefix it with, "can I ask you a question." He wondered whether that was part of the classroom teaching scenario whereby a child in a classroom was expected to announce their desire to ask a question with the customary raising of the hand. Or was she just being respectful. The latter he thought.

"Sure," he replied, "you can ask me anything."

Archie looked wistful. She spoke softly and genuinely.

"Michael do you believe in happy ever afters?"

"Not sure what you mean."

"You know…if you try to do what is right and your heart is always right, then even if you get it wrong, everything will work out in the end."

Michael felt his heart melt. He felt so enamoured by the innocence and beautiful simplicity of this girl. He thought in that moment of questioning, this is someone I could fall in love with.

Archie continued, "you know like my favourite television programme as a kid was the Disneyland show, and the theme song says when you wish upon a star your dreams come true."

"So it doesn't say that they will come true only if you do everything right. It says you only have to wish and I guess keep on wishing and believing and then your dreams will come true."

"Wow…that's a beautiful question, and hey I'm not trying to dodge the question I'll get back to that, but would you like a little bit of music trivia."

"Sure."

"You said your favourite song was When You Wish Upon A Star. My favourite song of not so long ago is the Beach Boys recording of the song Surfer Girl. I think it came out about five years ago."

"I love that song too Michael."

"Would you believe that the melody for the song Surfer Girl was taken by Brian Wilson of the Beach Boys from the melody of a version of When You Wish Upon A Star by a group called Dion and The Belmonts.

"Wow…that's almost spooky isn't it?" continued Michael.

"It is," she grinned, "I like that…we have similar tastes in melodies."

Michael laughed.

"Anyway to answer your question."

"I guess my thoughts would be related to a bible verse I love."

"Man looks on the outward appearance but God looks upon the heart."

"And perhaps that could mean that if outwardly you make a mistake God looks upon the integrity of your heart, so the wrong decision accompanied by a pure heart can work its way through to right outcomes as God is the final arbiter of our fate."

"I guess these things are uncharted waters for all of us until we find ourselves in certain situations."

"I like that…thank you Michael."

"Hey and I hope you like this movie, I just love it."

"I'm sure I will. What could anyone not like about a beautiful night like this."

"What's it about again? I remember you said it was a love story and that you saw it on your birthday with your mum."

"Yes," replied Archie, "I don't think mama knew it was so adult when she took me to see it."

"Okay," replied Archie, "here's a quick preview. But I won't tell you the ending."

"It's a story about a couple of high school sweethearts."

"The main roles are played by Natalie Wood and Warren Beatty. Natalie is a teenage girl who is following her mother's advice to resist her desire for sex with her boyfriend."

"Wow…and what does and who does that sound like might you ask?" continued Archie.

"And might I answer my own question."

"It sounds like any normal Greek mother."

"However the mother in this movie isn't Greek."

"Just thinks and acts like a Greek mother."

Michael laughed.

"But it's too complex to explain in detail."

"Right."

"So you'll have to see the movie, which you will shortly."

"I guess it's all about love gained and love lost and all the consequences."

Archie stopped talking and stared into Michael's eyes saying nothing.

"So that's all you're going to tell me?" he said.

"Yes…that's all," she grinned.

"Well that's good Archie, and you haven't spoiled the ending for me, so now I'm really curious."

It happened almost instantaneously after Michael had finished his sentence. Archie's stare converted into movement as she shuffled closer to him on the bench, cupped his face in her hands, pulled his lips towards her in a gentle embrace and kissed him. And Michael kissed her back, gently, not knowing what it meant, not knowing where it would go from there, not caring about anything including those around them, he softly kissed her back.

Back in the car they cuddled in each other's arms throughout the movie and kissed again and again.

"I think I might have to get the book," Michael joked, "due to the amount of the movie I am missing."

"Don't worry, if you keep this up, I'll buy it for you Michael," she grinned.

"Deal."

They both knew in their hearts that something was happening: that this liking could very easily turn into loving. The winds of change had begun blowing wild and free in their lives and they knew that they had only glimpsed a small part of it in that moment.

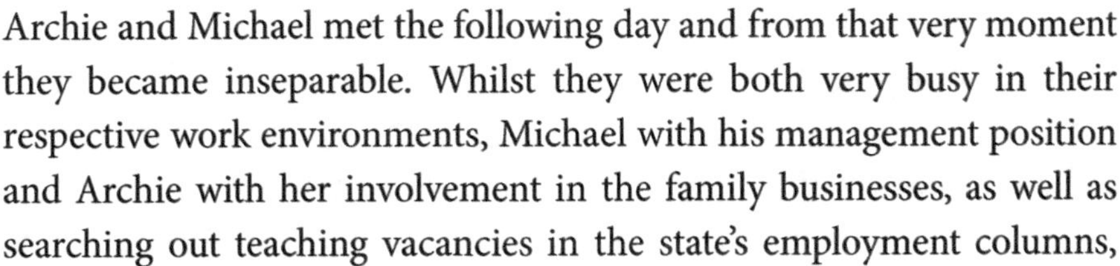

Archie and Michael met the following day and from that very moment they became inseparable. Whilst they were both very busy in their respective work environments, Michael with his management position and Archie with her involvement in the family businesses, as well as searching out teaching vacancies in the state's employment columns, they would try to organize their schedules so that they could spend as much time together as possible.

They still had their friends' fortnightly get together but this didn't allow any alone time for them, so they had worked out a system that would see them every Sunday morning meet at the corner ice cream shop for a quick refreshment before attending the local Anglican church for the morning worship service. But it wasn't just the ice cream shop or attending church together that continued to cement their relationship.

It included the cuddling and kissing in the canvas seats of the local theatre at the Saturday afternoon matinee, the occasional journey to the drive-in theatre at The Heads, days in the sun with bodies brushing against each other in the surf and then lying close together on the beach at Lighthouse Bay sharing their hopes and dreams.

In his alone moments Michael would spend time working out things to do with Archie, including how to paddle a canoe, which they did regularly. And even though it was a lot less exciting than their paddle-boat experience, the best part came immediately afterwards when the romantic magic would come alive.

This was when seated on the balcony with a glass of red wine and a piece of Greek pizza, courtesy of Archie, they would watch the sun slowly setting, they would listen to their favourite music and they would talk about everything, from politics to religion, from families to friend-ships, from hurtful times to happy times.

But for Michael one of the most delightful things that happened between them both in the months following their first drive-in adventure at The Heads occurred on a Friday evening in June on the day of his birthday.

It had been a long day in the office and Michael was looking forward to putting his feet up and chilling out on the balcony. It was dark when he approached the back door entrance to his apartment and as he put the key in the lock his foot brushed against a small flat gift wrapped parcel with a card attached lying on the ground right beside the entrance. He picked it up and knew from its wrapping that some kind person had obviously dropped off a birthday gift for him and he thought, that's nice.

Walking inside he placed his briefcase on the dining table and loosened his tie. He walked to the kitchen, poured himself a glass of wine, strolled back across to the lounge room, flopped back onto the couch and opened the card attached to the parcel.

He read it out loud.

"Sorry I can't be with you as you know because of family stuff. I hope you like this little gift I bought for you. Couldn't get the book I promised, so I bought you the song instead. I know you like all kinds of music including Stravinsky, thanks for the kisses at The Heads, love and happy birthday, Archie xxx."

Michael smiled as he remembered the conversation they had on their first night together when Archie had asked him who his favourite composer was and he had jokingly told her Igor Stravinsky. He picked up the parcel; it felt like a 45 r.p.m. record he thought, and it was.

He opened it slowly and his eyes fell upon the record cover. He smiled. It read, Liberty Music, Splendor In The Grass, written by Jackie DeShannon, sung by Jackie DeShannon.

"Nice he thought…so nice."

"Couldn't get the book so she bought me the song."

He raised his glass and toasted Archie and himself out loud.

"Cheers Archie…thank you."

"Happy Birthday Michael…Happy Birthday."

"And I'm standin' there ya know, just shootin' the breeze, and then all of a sudden this bikie storms out past me, ya know, and mate it was obvious he had a gutful of grog, and he was as cross as a frog in a sock."

Morty Mortensen

Lunch at Morty's

TEN

The word commune comes from the French word communia, which speaks of a large gathering of people sharing a common life: a physical place set up intentionally by a group of people with the intention of living together and establishing a community of like-minded others: a place whereby those living in that community all have common interests, values and beliefs, mostly centred around family and religion.

If ever any group had the necessary attributes to form a successful commune based on communia then Michael, Archie and their friends were that group.

Hippie communes had started to become popular in the sixties and had been progressively growing in number in the hills surrounding the village of Springfield. These were communes of a slightly different kind in that they embraced more of a socialistic attitude in their operation, which included, in addition to the basics of communia, a system of the sharing of income and assets, the mutual sharing of one's material goods.

And even though some in the fellowship group held hippie type attitudes to life, in the vein of the song lyrics that say, come on people now smile on your brother, everybody get together try to love one another, they had not crossed over to hippie commune socialistic type thinking.

Rather they had discussed and agreed many times that their proposed commune, whilst aiming at a level of self-sufficiency such as having their own school and their own church, would definitely not operate under the charter of the mutual sharing of all their worldly goods. It would instead operate under the banner of kindness and generosity in voluntarily helping their brother or sister who may be in need materially.

Their basic desire was to have operational components in the commune that fostered mutual trust, mutual friendships, and a sense of community in all their attitudes to each other and their interactions with each other.

It would be in the week after his drive-in date with Archie that Michael got together with Dr Nicholls to discuss what Margie had described as Unwin's desire to get involved in establishing the communal living project.

<hr>

When Michael had phoned to arrange the appointment, Unwin had suggested that they meet for lunch at Mortensen's Lebanese Restaurant directly around the corner from his clinic. Morty's as it was called, was run by a friendly knockabout type of guy named Johnny Mortensen, commonly known as Morty who had not one ounce of Lebanese blood in him. He was a true blue Aussie.

Prior to opening the restaurant Morty had been a chef on an outback cattle station just south of Wagadilla, and was very used to the fickleness and sometime experimental and changeable nature of people's palates. It would be the latter that had caused him to as he put it "have a go at the Lebo stuff."

Morty was also a storyteller and most of his stories centred around his career as a chef, or a cook with a hat as he often described himself.

"Bugger me mate…you wouldn't dare serve up some dollop of dung to those rough and tumble jackeroos when they came to the station canteen for a beer and a good feed after a hard day in the dust and heat," he would be heard to say as he recounted his time in the outback with a customer. "They not only wanted a good size feed mate, they wanted it to taste good too."

When asked why he had opened a Lebanese Restaurant and not a normal Aussie one since his cooking background as a chef in the outback was of the genre of steak, bacon and eggs Morty had been heard to say with a grin, "well mate if they want that they can get it at home off the missus and besides I wanted a more classy type of clientele than those buggers outback."

Followed up by:

"Naw…not true…mate I went out with this Lebo sheila for a year before I went outback and boy could her mother cook some good tucker."

"Well we broke up when I found out my Lebo was a Leso. Not that I've got any problem with that cobber. I must 'av got it wrong when she introduced herself. Thought she said I'm a Lebo. So I said that's great. My fault for not listening."

"Anyway I was already a cook in training so I flogged her mum's recipe book and took it to Wagadilla with me when her daughter and I called it quits. Just in case you know. It was like a nest egg for my future. Well neither of us had a quid to our names, not a brass razoo, so that was the best I could get."

No one was sure whether to believe that story or not. Morty had plenty of stories, most of them believable and a lot of them outrageous. You see Morty had one unique talent that very few people can aspire to. He had a particularly good ingrained grasp of the Aussie vernacular and when put together with one of his stories it made for a hilarious time of listening for his captive audience.

"You'll like Morty, Mike," said Unwin as they turned the corner and walked into the restaurant.

"He's very different, very country Aussie, and very sociable."

"But here's a tip."

"Don't ask him too many questions or you'll never get to eat." "He can talk the leg off an iron pot."

It was 11.30 a.m. and Michael and Unwin appeared to be the first of the lunchtime clients.

"Dr Seuss me old cobber," came the loud voice from the open kitchen area at the rear of the restaurant midst the clatter of pots and pans and the chatter of Morty's Chinese cook."

"How goes it me ole medical mate," it continued.

"Be with ya in two pulls on a cow's udder," he called out as he turned to his cook.

"Bung lung…hold the fort."

Unwin waved to Morty and ushered Michael to a table in the corner where they both proceeded to sit down.

He grinned.

"See what I mean Michael," Unwin continued, "he's different, he's country and he's social, and we saw all that in just one greeting."

Michael laughed, "yes I see."

Unwin had a cheeky and mischievous grin on his face.

"He has a marvellous gift of the Aussie vernacular Michael. You watch and I'll show you what I mean. I'll ask him a question and get him started."

"Happy to sit there Doc," Morty continued as he walked up with a bottle of cold water and handed them the menus. "Good cobber," he answered before Unwin had a chance to respond.

"Morty I'd like you to meet Michael, he's the new manager of the co-op. Well not new, he's been here for about four or five months I think isn't it Michael?"

"Sure is, pretty close to five."

"Nice to meet ya Mick," Morty replied wiping his hand on his apron before shaking Michael's hand.

"Any friend of the professor is a friend of mine."

"Now…fellas, care for a nice cold pot of the amber brew, a nice cold beer on this very hot day to help my cash flow, or are ya gonna be pikers and just drink water?"

"You won me Morty with that pitch," replied Unwin.

"What about you Michael, a beer?"

"Sure, sounds good."

Morty scribbled something in his little notebook, presumably the drink order. Michael showed a curious look as to why he was writing it down so as Morty finished he turned to Michael and said with a straight face.

"Gotta write any orders in Hanzi Mick, you know Chinese symbols, my cook and barman is of the Chinese origin. I can't pronounce his name so I call him Bung Lung cause he has a little emphysema from smoking too much for many years."

"Anyway ole Bung Lung he can't read English so I have to write the orders in big Chinese characters."

After he had finished he stared at Michael with a completely straight face, which lasted for about five seconds, until Unwin cracked up laughing.

"He does that to all the first timers in the restaurant Michael."

Michael then buckled over laughing.

Continuing his straight face Morty turned back to Unwin.

"Alright professor now you know the drill so you can help Mickey if he needs it."

"The fancy foreign list of tucker I cook is on the front of the menu and my own list of Aussie specials written in invisible ink is on the back."

He winked at Unwin.

Michael immediately turned his menu over to look at the list of Aussie meals on the back then realized he had been hooked again. It was blank.

"Mickey, Mickey, Mickey me ole mate, fair dinkum, get in the game, you're not listening to the Mortmeister," he said grinning, "it's in invisible ink, you can't read it."

They all laughed.

"The Doc knows what's there, he's been here before."

"It's a few selections, well really only two, of what I cook for those who don't think foreign food is fashionable, and might I say both meals are very tasty. But I don't advertise it, after all it is a Lebanese Restaurant."

"Mate I cut my teeth learning how to cook this couple on a fly blown station at the back of Burke. I still like to cook them occasionally, ya know, to keep my skills up."

"There are two dishes."

"The first one is called Morty's Mighty Mixed Grill, which is a steak, two chops, two eggs, half a tomato and a pile of chips. And I'll throw in the Worcestershire sauce at no extra cost."

Michael was grinning now. He was beginning to see what Unwin had meant when he said this guy is a real character.

"And," he continued, "the second of my delectable but invisible to most customers meals at a similar cost so as not to confuse is called Morty's Humongous Hamburger."

"It's a monster and it has the works. Ya know. The beef pattie, bacon, egg, beetroot, pineapple, tomato, lettuce, onion, and it stands about this high," he continued, gesticulating with his hands that it was at least nine inches deep.

"Just kiddin' ya cobbers, not that high. But it's a good feed, very popular in the outback. Doc has had one before."

"So have a gander at the menu, take ya time, no rush, I'll be back in three minutes with your grog."

Michael could not contain himself anymore as Morty sauntered off; he put his hands to his face and laughed out loud much to the delight of Unwin.

"I told you didn't I, the man is an absolute character."

Unwin was getting into the moment now after seeing how much Michael was amused.

"Hey I'll tell you what I'll do. Because you haven't seen nothing yet until you've heard him tell a story. He will have you in stitches. Talk about the Aussie vernacular Morty is unbelievable."

"When he comes back to take the orders I will try and coax him into a conversation."

"Sounds good."

It would be only a few minutes before Morty returned with the drinks.

"Ready to order boys?"

Unwin ushered to Michael.

"I'll have the mixed grill," replied Michael.

"Yeah good one Mickey, play it safe, some days Bung Lung's cooking is not as good as others. Can't make too many mistakes with the grill."

"And Doc?"

"Same for me thanks Morty."

"Great."

"And how's business?"

"Yeah not bad Doc, just a sec and I'll drop this down to Bung and be back," he said, tearing the order from his order book.

He returned in a minute to answer Unwin's question.

"Yeah it's going pretty good cobber. Ya know Doc takes people a little time to get used to a different foreign type food. You know with the Vietnam war going on people get suspicious of things foreign."

Michael grinned.

"You know you've got your Thai, Chinese and Indian in town, so I opened this trying to attract people who might like something different, a bit more European."

"You know Doc, you've sampled a few of my wares before. Lebo food is a bit different. Lots of whole grains and vegetables, lots of garlic and oil, seafood, more poultry is eaten than red meat, and any red meat is usually lamb or goat."

"But yeah Doc it's going all right, not ready to change the menu yet."

Unwin realized his question hadn't worked so he tried another.

"Getting many in at night, I notice you've extended your hours to a midnight close?"

It was the perfect question and then came the reply.

"Yeah mate getting a lot in after the boozer around the corner packs it up for the night."

"A few yobbos will roll down with a belly full of grog lookin' for some tucker, so things can get a bit agro with them."

"And then you've got the picture theatre closing at nine thirty and particularly on Friday nights you get the mums and dads with the little ankle biters and it makes an interesting mix of clientele, ya know families and half tanked yobbos and things happen ya know."

"Like?"

"Well mate like last Saturday night we were real busy. Like Bung Lung was flat out like a lizard drinking. Really had his arse dragging. So I'm trying to help get a few orders out from the kitchen and all of a sudden, bang."

"And I says to Bung what the flamin' hell was that?"

"Sounds like a bingle."

"So I says to Bung I'll be back in a flash me ole China, and of course Bung Lung is spewin', in Chinese might I add, because he was needin' my help to get the orders out. But I had to go and see in case someone had got banged up."

Michael was trying to hold back a grin.

"Well when I got there, here was this Harley over on its side ya know."

"And I'm standin' there ya know just shootin' the breeze tryin' to figure out what was goin' down and then all of a sudden this bikie storms out past me, and mate it was obvious he'd had a gutful of grog, and he was as cross as a frog in a sock cause it was his bike that had been knocked over."

"And mate I tell you, I kid you not, this bikie was a really big bloke, ya know, built like a brick shithouse, and he was absolutely spewin'. And right on his clacker was his sheila and she was two parts hit too."

Michael was bursting on the inside. He had to let it go soon. Unwin meanwhile was listening intently with an occasional nod and a two word commentary whilst enjoying every minute of it.

"Right...right."

"So I thought lucky I've got Alistair on security tonight. He was out the back feedin' his chops at the time."

"Well mate you would 'av loved to have been there."

"I thought 'av a gander at this...leaning over the Harley was this skinny young bloke who had obviously knocked over the Harley as he was trying to reverse park in, and he was trying to get the Harley back on its feet but it was too heavy for him."

"Mate he just couldn't lift it. He was a tiny little bloke. Honestly he looked like a pipe cleaner with glasses."

"Well the bikie storms over and bellows out hey you little stick figure I'm gonna av your guts for garbage."

"Which was an interesting use of words because I recognized him as one of the local garbos in town. He would occasionally do the restaurant pick up."

"But I digress."

"Well the young bloke was obviously a bit frightened see, and he looks at the bikie's girlfriend for some sign of intervention, ya know, to settle her boyfriend down."

"So then the bikie pokes the pipe cleaner in the chest and accuses him of perving on his sheila."

"Well then some deadbeat from the gathered crowd calls out 'why would he perve on her, she's a dog', and I thought, mate, it's gonna be on in a minute, its gonna get ugly, someone's gonna start bluin."

"So the bikie then walks over to the crowd and says, which one of you drongos called my sheila a dog. C'mon, ya pack uv dingoes, ya wanna av a go?"

"Well of course everyone goes quiet and the bikie says, yea just as I thought, you're all just a bunch of koalas...bloody pack uv galahs."

"Now some of the little ankle biters that were seated with their mums and dads closest to the door started to bawl."

"So people starting looking at me mate...seeing what I was gonna do."

"Cobber I thought I'd better do somethin. The little ankle biters were starting to get a bit frightened with the raised voices."

"So I went back to the kitchen and got Alistair. Ya know he's ex police force so he's been in a few dust ups in his days."

"Tell ya what Doc once they saw that mean looking German bastard and knew he wasn't scared of any of them that quickly made the crowd disperse."

"I mean he loves a fair dinkum blue so I had to keep 'im on a leash though he was champing at the bit to have a go."

"I said bugger off you lot and don't come the raw prawn again outside my restaurant."

"So the crowd backs off, the customers clapped, the bikie settles down, picks up his bike and checks it for damage. No damage. So he goes back in with his missus to finish his tucker."

"And the pipe cleaner who obviously thought he had just had a lucky escape jumps in his car and takes off like a robber's dog."

"I tell you what Doc, Mickey, thank goodness I had Alistair on security that night. Could av got reaaally ugly."

"Yep that German Shepherd dog has been one of my best investments. No one would come within a cooee of havin' a punch up with Alistair there on the job."

"So yeah Doc, gets pretty busy at night."

"Ya meals shouldn't be long. Whoo whoo here we go…more customers. Catch ya later boys, at bill time," he winked and grinned.

Unwin looked across at Michael. Michael was finally able to let the laugh out. He picked up his napkin to wipe the tears from his eyes as Unwin looked on grinning.

"Do you reckon that was a true story Unwin…or was he making it up…man he could get a job as a stand up comedian."

"Well one would believe it was a true story. Yes I'm sure it was. And if it wasn't we will never know. But what did I tell you…he's a national treasure."

"He could write a book on the Aussie vernacular."

"You see all it took was the right question. He loves to tell a story."

"He's a funny man, but a good man too, strong Christian beliefs. He's married with two little boys. Can be very outspoken on what he sees are the government shortcomings in relation to children's education. Yes, he's a good man."

It would not be long before Morty returned, and with a "here you go boys, two mixed grills and a bottle of Worcestershire sauce, bog in," he placed the meals down and left.

"Thanks Morty."

"Let's eat Michael, while it's hot, we'll talk over coffee."

The meals had just been finished as Morty returned with the coffee pot, cups, and a jug of milk, cleared the dishes and left Michael and Unwin to themselves. Unwin picked up the coffee pot, poured, and then reached for the milk jug.

"I seem to remember you take milk Michael, say when."

"When…thanks."

"Okay down to business," continued Unwin.

"Margie had mentioned to me that your fellowship group has been talking for some time about the prospect of forming some sort of commune," he queried, "do you think they are all serious?"

"The reason I'm interested is because some families I know have been considering for some time the possibility of starting up an independent Christian school for their primary school age children."

"Most are a little unhappy with the humanistic type of subject matter that is slowly infiltrating the state curriculum, and now with the talk that religious instruction could be on the chopping block as from next year, some parents are a bit worried where all this is heading."

"One of the families is the Morcums. Don who is a friend of mine, he's a lawyer, has been researching an American based company just founded called Accelerated Christian Education or ACE as it's known."

"ACE has links to the Pentecostal church over there. You know the Assemblies of God type churches."

"Yes…I'm familiar with the Assemblies of God Church."

"Oh of course you are…I remember from our first talk."

"Well the curriculum is government approved but differs from the normal curriculum in that it incorporates a biblically based character building programme and it preferences the teaching of creationism rather than evolution or Darwinism."

"They have checked it out with the State Education authorities and were told as long as it incorporates the state curriculum any non state schools can incorporate their own personal additions to it as they see fit."

"Sounds like they're serious about it Unwin?"

"Well yes they are, they all are. I even bounced the idea off Morty the other week and he said count him in."

"All we need is some property, a schoolhouse, teachers, a lot of volunteers and someone to oversee it."

"The schoolhouse could double as a meeting place for church services for those who want to get involved."

"See there are a lot of people in the district interested in the Pentecostal type of church experience, which is why Garret Sloan gets so much support with his crusades. The closest Assemblies of God church to here is two hours drive and I understand that some of Sloan's converts actually drive every couple of weeks to attend a service."

"Have you had much experience with the AOG church Michael?"

"Yes I have. I attended their Bible School in their church up north, and before I came down here I was attending their big independent church in the city called Christian City Church. Have you heard of it?"

"That's right I think you told me that when we were up at my property."

"Yes I am aware of City Church Michael. That's the one Reverend Terry Channing pastors isn't it?"

"Yes it is."

"He seems like a pretty straight shooter."

"He does."

"You see Michael the ongoing potential is enormous. You could turn it into something like a communal living project. People could live on the property if they were seriously looking at commune type living."

"Down the track we could incorporate medical facilities and even a nursing home. I mean it has endless possibilities if you get the right size property."

"I make it sound so simple Michael don't I?"

"Yes you do, but I like your enthusiasm for it."

"So what about your group Michael…do you think they might be serious about getting involved in something like this?"

"Are they serious?"

"Well yes I think all of them are serious about doing something like that."

"Certain ones more than others have this inner hippie in them that is desperately trying to get out."

Unwin grinned.

"I'm not sure though whether any would set up home together," continued Michael.

"They certainly would be acceptable to the school, church, farmers market type stuff."

"What about you Michael?"

"Sure, I like the concept. I think you would have to be careful how you did it and how it appeared to the rest of the community in Springfield. I mean you know this town. Like most country towns it's a bit parochial."

"But another choice of school, particularly with a Christian based curriculum, probably would be welcomed."

"And a Pentecostal church in town would I imagine be welcomed, particularly in light of the stories I hear about the large number of people from far and wide that Garret Sloan brings in to his tent meetings, which I presume are true."

"They are Michael, they are. I've been to his meetings."

"Well," continued Michael, "I mean a Pentecostal church would be welcomed by those people with a Pentecostal bent, perhaps not necessarily though by the other churches, but that's their problem."

"Me personally Unwin, I love the idea."

"But it would have to be sold well so as not to get the townsfolk offside."

"What do you mean Michael?"

"Well it would have to be sold as a communal living project for a start not as a commune, even if it contained commune type characteristics."

"I mean the concept of a commune gets people talking about cults and in particular religious cults or doomsday cults."

"You say the word commune to someone and they immediately think back to the world headlines of what happened around eight months ago."

"You mean the Sharon Tate murders and Manson?"

"Yes right."

"I mean Charles Manson got together with a motley crew of drop-outs, misfits, cretins and hippies, formed a commune, and preached crazy half-brained prophesies of doom and gloom."

"You know end times stuff, supposedly based on teachings in the Bible."

"Then he and his cohorts high on drugs went down town on a Saturday night to Polanski's home and slaughtered his wife Sharon Tate, her unborn baby and five others."

"It didn't give commune living a good look."

"So we would have to be careful how it was sold to the general public."

"The Manson murders are still fresh in everyone's minds, pretty horrific."

"Sure Michael sure...do you know a bit about cults?"

"Done some study on it Unwin. I'm interested in the psychology of doomsday cults. Why people join them, what's the hook the leaders use. Is it fear, deception, or just the Spirit of Control dictating the terms through a charismatic type of leader?"

"I certainly know some of the early signs that might evidence a group is moving over to the cult status."

"If you wanted to form a successful cult you wouldn't take notes from Manson."

"You see everything Manson did gave most people the impression he had formed a cult and not a commune. You know the secrecy, the isolation of the property."

"There was no openness with him, and so people were quick to judge, and in his case, rightly so."

"I mean it's important not to show any semblance of isolation from the community, but if you're starting up a church, also no exclusive separatism from the religious fraternity."

"Good point Michael…good point."

"Anyway I'm all for the idea of forming an open communal project, so where are we going from here?"

"Got thirty minutes to spare Michael?"

"Sure."

"Okay," said Unwin, a little excited, "let's finish our coffee and I'll take you to something I'd like you to see. My car's outside."

They quickly finished their coffees.

"Garcon…s'il vous plait…l'addition s'il vous plait," Unwin called out with his arm extended to get Morty's attention.

"The bill please."

It would be shortly after the ten minute drive uphill to the north of the town that Unwin turned left onto an unsealed dirt road aptly named Paradise Road.

"Michael…can I ask you a question?"

"Sure."

"I've been thinking about our talk some months ago in the car, you know about attitudes and emotions and what you were saying about life being a warfare of spiritual polar opposites, and of emotional opposites, and I've been wanting to ask you something."

"Go ahead."

"If we recognize that life is a spiritual warfare and we choose rightness as best we can in all situations, what are we expecting to get out of it…just a happier life?"

"I mean I understand the thought of eternal reward that some people have regarding leading a good life and then going to heaven, but what about here and now, what's the outcome of living rightly or righteously?"

"Would you like it in one word Unwin?"

"Sure."

"Well happiness as you said is a part of it…but in one word…peace."

"You mean as in a more relaxed life?"

"No it's not the type of peace that people think of when they exclaim, 'give me some peace', it's more than that."

"The peace of God that is available to us is described in the Bible as an unimaginable peace, a peace that passes all understanding. Not just the old peace and quiet stuff that mothers ask for when the kids are being naughty."

"I have a saying Unwin…peace is not the absence of trouble…it's a supernatural rest in the midst of the enemy."

"Everywhere you read about living the Christian life in the Bible it brings up the subject of peace."

"You know words like, let the peace of Christ rule in your hearts, as members of one body you are called to peace, the fruit of the Spirit is love, joy and peace, make every effort to live in peace with everyone."

"And you know it actually links choosing good over evil with peace where it says for us to turn from evil and do good, seek peace and pursue it."

"Christ was called the Prince of Peace."

"Where it talks in the Bible about the angels appearing and proclaiming the impending birth of Christ it says they cried out peace on earth and goodwill to all men."

"The Christian life on earth is all about having peace in our lives and there's a lot of stressed out Christians without real peace tracking around."

"Lack of peace in some people's lives taken to the extreme will cause them to take their own lives. I mean you don't hear people say, I'm so poor I think I'll kill myself, or I'm so hungry I want to die. No it's I'm so hungry I'll eat anything to survive."

"It's lack of peace that kills people."

"It doesn't mean we don't encounter difficulties…it means we can handle them with calmness and an assuredness of a successful outcome."

"God doesn't want to make the Christian way of life difficult for us, even though a lot of Christians make it difficult for themselves. God just wants us to live in his unimaginable peace or as those of the Hindu faith call it…bliss."

"Thanks Michael…I like that."

Michael gestured back towards the signpost Paradise Road.

"What do you think Unwin, could that be a sign?"

"It's a good thought Michael let's believe that it is."

They were no more than 200 metres down the road when Unwin pulled to the side and parked. He looked at Michael and grinned.

"Well here we are. One hundred acres of available land with an abandoned farmhouse tucked away in the corner."

"You're kidding. So it's up for sale?"

"Yes…sure is, and at a very reasonable price."

"The owner who might I say you have met, picked it up at a bargain price in a foreclosure."

"Serious…who's the owner."

"Patty Patel," Unwin replied grinning.

"You're kidding. Patty?"

"That's right."

"Look if ever there was a person that's disillusioned with the humanistic curriculum of the state schools, it's Patty. He has three children, two girls, one boy."

"If ever there was a person who has a desire to see his children educated in a Bible believing Christian environment there is none more passionate an advocate than Patty."

"Wow…wouldn't have guessed it."

"Let's get out and have a look and see what you think Michael."

Both Unwin and Michael strolled to the barbed wire fence. Unwin lifted his head and breathed in deeply.

"Smell that fresh country air Michael...beautiful."

They were looking at a vast expanse of land, around one hundred acres of lush green farming land obviously selectively cleared but still leaving compartmental types of tree clusters, mostly eucalypts: a fast growing evergreen Australasian tree.

The land gently sloped downwards to the east, and levelled out mid centre to a flattened area shaded by three huge spreading fig trees providing shade for the four or five cattle that Patty had on agistment there. Bordering one side of the flattened out area about 800 metres to the left was a new completely developed housing estate.

"No chance for cult type isolation here," Unwin commented as he gestured across to the rooftops of the estate and then back up to the passing cars on the highway.

"You're not wrong."

Unwin pointed to the sprawling old timber farmhouse, surrounded by wide verandahs, and tucked away in a grove of gum trees in the far lower corner of the property.

"What couldn't you do with that? The use of it is part of the deal."

"It is around 60 acres on this side and 40 odd acres on the other side," continued Unwin gesturing across to the right.

"This road is a dead end easement right down the centre of the property so we won't get any through traffic."

"No complaints from neighbours if the choir sings too loud," he quipped.

"Look at that flattened out area with the magnificent fig trees... couldn't you just see a school tucked away in there?"

What do you think Michael?"

"It is magnificent Unwin...magnificent."

"I love it...absolutely love it."

"So how would we fund the purchase?" Michael queried.

"Let's just say how would we fund the lease, not the purchase," Unwin replied smiling.

"A lease?"

"Yes…Patty has agreed to lease the property to us."

"What we would do is form a company and the company would lease the property from Patty."

"He would get a bond just the same as in a house rental and monthly lease payments from the community which he is willing to defer until the school and church start to bring in earnings."

"Anyone who builds would buy the site sub leasehold."

"Patty would be getting income from this as well as the capital growth in the property since he still owns it. And since it's a church he gets some charitable tax deductions in the process. It's all legal, we've checked it out with Don Morcom, what do you think?"

"I think it's fantastic."

"Patty also knows of an old disused timber school about 10 miles from here that we can cut in half, bring it here and start building."

"I know of five families for a start that will put their children into the school and a friend who specializes in getting Department of Education accreditation."

"What do you reckon Michael…you and your talented group in?"

"I'm sure they would be Unwin."

"We'd like you to be one of the directors and head up the project… got time?"

"Sure…sure I've got time."

Light rain had gently started to fall as Unwin and Michael walked back to the car.

"Better get back, looks like a storm."

"Hey Michael…look there's a rainbow…now that really might be a sign."

They drove back to the clinic and Unwin found a park right outside Morty's.

"Michael I'll get the lawyers to get things started and get back to you with an update and we'll organize a get together."

"I'm sure Patty will be thrilled."

"He was really excited about it when we last spoke."

"So will a lot of people including our restaurateur friend," Unwin commented as he gestured in the direction of Morty's Restaurant.

"Now there's a thought for you Michael."

"What's that?"

"Put Morty in charge of the PTA meetings."

"Morty Mortensen President of the Parents and Teachers Association. It has a nice ring to it."

Michael laughed and replied.

"It does Unwin…it does."

"Can you imagine their monthly meetings?"

"Now they would be flammin' interesting cobber wouldn't they."

"Michael and Archie walked hand in hand to their two cars. Sloan's people had locked down the tent and all the stragglers had gone. It was a beautiful night with the dark sky blanketed by hundreds of stars in between what looked in the moonlight like small clusters of storm clouds gathering. After a night of loud singing, loud music, and loud hand clapping there was now a perfect stillness in the air save for the intermittent chirping of the crickets."

The Evolution of
A Commune

ELEVEN

⸺∽⸺

"Unwin my good friend…God bless you…lovely to see you again. Some good things are starting to come together I hear. It might be time for me to meet this Michael Winton that you've spoken so much about. How about the three of us get together after the service and have a little discussion."

It was the first night of Garret Sloan's week of crusade meetings in Springfield and Unwin Nicholls had ducked backstage to see him before the meeting started.

⸺∽⸺

Less than four weeks had passed when Unwin advised Michael that all the paperwork had been drawn up and ready for signatures. By June's end the contract would be finalized and the newly formed directorship could take possession of the property. Unwin, Michael and Patty had then met at Don Morcom's office three days after the signing to map out the ongoing details of the project.

It had been agreed that they would form a limited liability company, a separate entity from Patty the property owner, shielding Patty from any legal liability. Should the company get into any financial trouble or be declared bankrupt then Patty Patel the property owner would not be personally responsible for the commune's debts.

It was decided that the company would be called Springfield Christian Community Ltd and would be of the registered charity type to maximize any tax breaks. There would be three directors appointed, Dr Unwin Nicholls, Michael Winton, and Don Morcum, the local lawyer.

It had been Don who in a discussion with Unwin over coffee had brought up the subject of the Accelerated Christian Education curriculum that was being successfully used in the States and in a couple of cities in Australia. Don had three children all of Primary School age and had practiced law in Springfield for around fifteen years.

The second last week of June had been a hectic one for Michael. Not only was he busy at his own day job, he had spent much time finalizing a go forward plan for the property with Unwin and Patty. It would be in the midst of this busyness on the Tuesday afternoon that he received the phone call from Archie.

"Hi Michael…I know you've been flat out with the community stuff but just wanted to remind you in case you forgot that we are all going to Garret Sloan's crusade tonight."

Michael had forgotten.

"No…all good…would you like me to walk you there from your place?" replied Michael.

"Sure…that would be nice."

"What time does it start?"

"Seven thirty."

"So I will pick you up at say 6.45."

"That would be great Michael…the rest of the gang are meeting out the front of the grounds at seven."

The crowds had started to file in as Michael and Archie arrived. It was a humid night but it didn't seem to deter the people coming out. There were a huge number of cars already parked on the grassy area beside the arena and a steady stream of lights heading down the main street of Lighthouse Bay from the south towards the showground.

"Michael and Archie, this is my sister Francis. She's up here for a fortnight checking things out," Margie commented during the greetings.

"Remember I mentioned that we are looking at setting up a clinic together."

Michael was always quick to get an understanding of people's personality type. He had made it a habit of doing so as to better understand their behaviours. It might only take a few sentences of conversation and he would be able to quickly get a grasp of the type of personality they were.

He had learned this method of personality analyzing in biblical studies up north where he had completed a study course written by a religious activist and minister named Tim La Haye.

It was a psychological theory suggesting that there are reasons for everything we as human beings do, and that many of the reasons for human behaviour, particularly of the emotional kind can be linked to a person's temperament or personality type.

The theory itself could be traced back to the Greek physician, Hippocrates, known as the father of medicine who created something similar as a diagnostic tool for his work. He believed that every person has genetically inherited behavioural tendencies: DNA combinations passed down through our ancestors, and that there are four fundamental personality types grouped into two categories, extroverted personalities and introverted personalities.

In the extroverted category are the sanguine and choleric personalities, both optimistic and socially outgoing and comfortable in a crowd, and in the introverted category melancholy and phlegmatic types, more shy and reserved, who feel anxious about being singled out in a crowd: each temperament having their own individual characteristics, with the choleric type whilst good in leadership roles being easily open to irritability, the melancholic being analytical and quiet, and the phlegmatic, relaxed and peaceful.

It also suggested that most people had a combination of two temperaments as their total personality type, one primary and one secondary.

Francis was different both in personality and appearance from her sister Margie. They just didn't look like sisters or talk like sisters and were totally different in the way that they expressed themselves. Margie seemed confident and one would ascertain could perhaps be a little abrasive when defending her position, whilst Francis came across as shy and reserved. To Michael Francis was a Phlegmel, a combination of phlegmatic primary and melancholy secondary, and Margie a Sanchol, a combination of Sanguine primary and Choleric secondary.

"Hi Francis…lovely to meet you," replied Michael.

Archie hugged Francis, "so great to have you here."

"Okay gang," said Daniel, "seats front or back."

"Let's go back," said Jeffrey, "I like to get a view of everything that is going on, and anyway the front seats are mostly filled."

It would be Jeffrey who positioned himself in the seat to the left beside Michael. It would be Jeffrey also who quietly whispered a running commentary into Michael's left ear during the course of the service, much to the delight of Archie who was seated beside Michael on the right. Michael had caught her grinning at times after Jeffrey's periodic utterances.

"Michael, see that short, stocky, bald man in the crumpled suit with the vacant look on his face, sitting on that chair to the right of the stage like a security guard."

"That's Thorpey…Thorpey Goldway…he's Sloan's minder."

"He is always close to him. I've been trying to figure out if he has a bulge under his coat, you know near his armpit."

Michael grinned but Jeffrey wasn't finished.

"I have nicknamed him Barry the bald eagle."

"He sort of just sits there staring at the crowd like he's perched ready to attack, notwithstanding that he is totally bald."

Archie grinned and leaned across Michael, "Jeffrey shhh, someone will hear you."

It would be as Sloan came on to the platform from the back of the curtain and as Jeff acknowledged his appearance with the words, "let the show begin, here comes the ringmaster," that Michael caught his first glimpse of Sloan.

But it wasn't his first glimpse he acknowledged in his mind.

Where had he seen him before?

"I know that face," he thought.

The meeting was all Michael expected it would be. He had been to a couple of loud and noisy Pentecostal tent meetings on the north coast and Sloan's meeting didn't disappoint.

There was a lively band, chorus singing with vigorous hand clapping, followed by a slower tempo of music with songs that led into what was known as the worship session. Here people would raise their hands in the air, some would close their eyes and move into a dreamlike state with the intermittent shouts of hallelujah, praise the Lord and lovely Jesus, echoing across the crowd.

Then the collection was received by a group of workers carrying buckets and passing them down each row, followed by Sloan preaching an enthusiastic sermon he knew would impact on the needs of the people and then finishing with a salvation hook, that from Michael's viewpoint was of the true 1940's camp meeting style.

"My friends…you have sung…you have laughed…you have rejoiced… you have felt happy…but what did you come out of the wilderness of your daily grind to see tonight…entertainment. Sure…you have seen that…but I'm hoping you have seen something more. I want you to stop, think, and ask yourself the question. What if tonight was my last night on earth to enjoy myself as I have so far…am I comfortable about going to stand before my maker?"

Sloan continued.

"Let me ask you another question."

"How long is it since you thought about the fact that on any night at any time death may demand your soul?"

"You know it could happen at any time…even tonight after you have left this meeting; and if you believe in heaven and believe in hell…are you completely sure where you will be heading if death demands your soul tonight?"

He paused and slowly glanced around the crowd.

"Not sure?"

"Then let me pray with you and give you that assurance, let me give you that blessed assurance that a heavenly home awaits you. Come and taste the saving power of Christ," and in that moment Sloan turned and nodded to Bettina.

Bettina with her band and choir had quietly re-assembled on the stage as Garret was delivering his hook, and on his nod to her the group immediately burst into song with the well known words of the well known hymn…blessed assurance Jesus is mine, oh what a foretaste of glory divine.

People came forward in their dozens and walked towards the platform. Some because they wanted this taste of salvation and an entry ticket into heaven that he spoke of, and others because they just wanted to be sure that they had it already. Just as they had in Michael's youth at the crusade where Dr Billy Graham said those famous words he always used, "will you come…will you come," the people at Sloan's crusade came forward.

As Sloan's prayer warriors came forward to greet and pray with the approaching converts Michael contemplated in his mind as he watched the proceedings that not a lot had changed in the world of evangelism in the last fifteen years. Some of those evangelists still put on a pretty slick show.

"Well…show's over, anyone for coffee," chirped Jeffrey quickly standing up as the prayer warriors continued to do their thing accompanied by the softened singing of the choir singing the chorus He is Lord.

"We're in," chimed in Zelda, "well we have to be because you're driving Jeffrey."

It would be as the group were milling outside the tent at the close of the meeting that Michael heard a familiar voice behind him.

"Michael…Michael…got a minute?"

It was Unwin breathlessly pursuing Michael.

"Hey Michael…I was just down the front talking to the Reverend Sloan and mentioned you and he said he'd like to meet you…got a minute…won't take long?"

"Sure."

"Archie…you okay to wait…I won't be long?"

"I'll keep her safe for you Michael," Kelly responded grinning.

"Hey…I'll see all you guys later…thank you Jeffrey for the commentary."

Michael walked back into the tent with Unwin.

"Arch my friend," continued Kelly putting her arm around Archie's shoulder…come sit with me on this park bench and we shall discuss life together…in particular your love life since I don't have one."

Ten minutes had passed as Archie and Kelly discussed everybody's love lives, except their own, although Archie knew it was coming. She knew Kelly.

"Sooo Arch," Kelly said with a grin.

"You and Michael are spending a lot of time together, and I caught you midstream of the big stare the other night."

"Yes…I know...and thanks for re-introducing me back into conversation. I think I blushed. I knew you were watching me."

"Yes I was my dear friend…like to keep in touch with what's happening in the dizzy world of relationships around me."

"Not only am I funny, flirtatious, funky, and flat chested, I am also… are you ready for this Arch…it's another 'f' word…well it's more of a sentence with two 'f' words in it."

"I am finely tuned in to any potentially fabulous romances that may be developing."

"You sure are…I saw you out of the corner of my eye, watching me like a hawk."

"I prefer owl Arch, owls are curious creatures; hawks are just plain hungry."

"And yes, right Arch…I was watching you like an owl but it didn't stop you did it?"

"So…are you?" she winked.

"Kelly you're terrible."

"Nooo Archie not that."

"Are you getting serious?"

"I'd like to," replied Archie with a longing tone in her voice, "I'm really attracted to him…but."

"I know…it's the Greek thing again isn't it?"

"It sure is…it's never far from my mind."

"Well all I can do is offer you this advice and it might sound dumb, but just enjoy the moment and see where it goes."

"I know…and thanks for that."

"That's what Michael said when we spoke about it."

"Que sera sera."

"But I'll tell you something Kell…he's a great kisser," Archie grinned.

⸛

"Garret this is Michael…Michael Winton…he's heading up the project I told you about."

Michael immediately felt his mind go into personality assessment mode as Unwin introduced him to Garret Sloan. To him Sloan appeared to be Cholsan having a mixture of both Choleric and Sanguine in his personality but Michael sensed some of that might be manufactured, particularly the outgoing Sanguine component.

He was hard to read. He seemed intent on doing everything right and making a good impression on Michael. He seemed almost too nice. But Michael was prepared to put Jeffrey's convictions aside for the moment and give Garret the benefit of the doubt.

"Nice to meet you Michael," Garret extended his hand.

"You too Garret," returned Michael, "enjoyed the service."

"Thanks," he returned, "we who do the Lord's work can only do our best."

"Unwin has been sharing with me what you guys are intending to do with the communal project…sounds great…would love to come on board and get involved and help in any way I can."

"Certainly will be able to help you guys in getting people there…you know if you are going to add a church fellowship component to it I can certainly help."

Unwin interjected.

"Michael, Garret was just saying how he could pitch his tent on the property for his next crusade in November. He would pay us the same price he is paying for leasing the showground here and it helps him also because it puts him more centrally in town. What do you think?"

"I think it's a great idea."

Michael was conversing but his mind had gone into overtime as to where he had seen Garret before, and it suddenly came to him. It was at the Christian City Church at a Sunday Morning service. The Christian City Church had been recommended to him as a place to attend after he had come back from up north where he had attended the Assemblies of God church.

He would normally attend the night service at the City Church as it was a bit more dynamic and lively but for a reason he could not remember on this occasion he had gone along to a morning service. That's where I know him from he thought to himself. He was preaching at that morning service. What was that line he kept using that started to get monotonous? Yes I remember.

"We've all got things in our life we are dealing with."

"So anyway Michael," Unwin continued, "Garret has offered to drive down from the city the week after next and we can have a meeting to nut things out, you, I and him. You know like the tent location, parking, volunteers, how to channel new converts through our church services."

"Sort of set up a memorandum of arrangement."

"No problem with that," replied Michael, "I look forward to it."

The conversation continued for a few more minutes before Garret concluded it.

"Michael…lovely to meet you, and Unwin good catching up with you again…I'd better get back to it…few other people from the local churches I need to see…we'll catch up with you in three weeks."

"Oh Michael have you got a card…I'll give you a call when I sort my diary."

"Sure…no problem."

Unwin walked outside of the tent with Michael.

"Some progress there Michael, what do you think?"

"Yes…for sure."

"I was trying to think when we were talking of where I had seen him before Unwin and remembered he preached one Sunday morning at the City Church."

"Yes," replied Unwin, "that would be right."

"I understand that he does the occasional preach there and works in the office at other times, but not a lot."

"Patty knows him a bit better than me but said that he and the Pastor there, Terry Channing, don't get on too well. That's why he spends a lot of time on the road with his crusades."

"Not sure how true it all is but Patty is in contact with a lot of people with his business, knows the goss, so he's usually pretty accurate with his information."

"Anyway that won't bother us and it might mean we can utilize him more here to help out. I hear he's thinking of cutting back on his road trips at the end of the year."

"Right…sure…you're right Unwin, it might."

"Here come the guys, bookmark that last sentence about Michael being a good kisser Arch…we'll get back to it."

Archie and Kelly got up to greet them.

"Unwin have you met Archie and Kelly?"

"Know Kelly…well know her folks and know her through them."

He turned to Archie and extended his hand.

"Haven't met Archie but have heard Margie speak of you. She says you are a wonderful musician and play the piano. Well you and my black baby grand could become good friends in the months ahead."

Archie grinned not really knowing what Unwin meant.

"Nice."

"And you young Kelly, good to see you again. Must get down to the Plaka for some of those delicious biscuits of yours."

"So has Michael shared with you the good news?"

Kelly turned, giving Michael a blank look.

"Good news ehh…nooo…you been holding out on us Michael Winton," she said giving him a gentle thump on the arm.

Michael laughed.

"No I've been waiting until we finalized things last week. Will share it with you all at the gathering tomorrow night."

Unwin grinned, "and you're going to love it."

Unwin turned to go…"okay well goodnight all...and nice to meet you Archie. I'm sure we'll be seeing lots of each other in the weeks and months to come."

He grinned, rubbed his hands together and headed to his car.

Kelly immediately wheeled around, jokingly grabbing Michael's arm bending it behind his back.

"I'm sure we'll be seeing lots of each other," she repeated mimicking Unwin and rubbing her hands together.

"You tell us Michael Winton…tell us…tell us right now, otherwise I'll never give you sugar for your coffee ever again."

"What about you Arch…do you know something?"

"Perhaps," Archie laughed, "Kell he'll tell us when he's ready."

Kelly went into acting mode and dropped her lip.

"But Arch you know what I'm like with surprises...I won't get any sleep tonight."

Michael laughed and relented.

"Okay…because you make good coffee I'll give you a teensy bit... enough to keep you going until we all meet tomorrow night."

"Thankyou Michael thankyou Michael thankyou Michael, here you can have your arm back."

"It's a go," he said, "the property...we finalized all the details at the end of last week. That's why I haven't been able to say anything yet."

"You mean our commune...or community...or whatever it is," Kelly spluttered.

"That's right...it's a go."

"But I'll give you all a full update tomorrow night."

Kelly and Archie immediately linked arms and started to jump up and down whilst simultaneously doing a circle and making a squealing sound. Michael grinned. The sight of seeing these two girls giggling, jumping up and down and hugging each other and then hugging him made him feel good and excited about the road ahead for all of them.

He knew that Kelly would sleep well that night. It's nice he thought, things are starting to come together for everyone.

Three weeks had passed since the June crusade of Garret Sloan and it would be mid July when the meeting was held with Dr Nicholls, Michael Winton and Garret Sloan to set out an arrangement for the ongoing involvement of Sloan in the spiritual activities of the commune.

Since it had already been determined that the school would not open until the new year it was decided that the goal would be to have the schoolhouse finished in time for Sloan's first tent crusade on the property in November to enable visitors to have a viewing of the project. Then on the Sunday following his Saturday night tent meeting the schoolhouse come church meeting place would be officially opened by Michael Winton with Garret Sloan conducting the first Sunday service there as the guest speaker.

The next six months progressed quickly as work proceeded on the construction of the schoolhouse and other aspects of the commune. Whilst the inevitable rumours of cults and hippies occasionally surfaced amongst the more parochial members of the community, by maintaining a semblance of openness with the press, Michael was able to dismiss these little nuances of discourse immediately they arose.

Fortunately they usually only occurred around a cup of tea and a biscuit within the conversations of the existing denominational churches as each flock gathered together for fellowship after their Sunday morning church services.

The work force that had originally started out as a group of about six families and a dozen or so single young people, gradually over time turned into a group of fifty to sixty people, all volunteering either their downtime from employment or their recreational time at weekends. Word of the project had filtered down through the community and existing volunteers brought friends of friends along to join in the creative atmosphere and fellowship that existed at every weekend working bee.

When a bulldozer was needed to clear a certain part of the property someone would turn up with a bulldozer. When a tip truck was needed to haul away cleared vegetation or rubbish from the building site a tip truck would miraculously appear. Because of the variety of talent in the group which included builders, painters, electricians, carpenters and volunteer labourers, Michael and Jeffrey were able to allocate duties in an organized way that saw quick progress on the site and costs kept to the minimum.

Patty Patel was able to call in a favour that saw a builder friend of his carve up an old disused schoolhouse and bring it to the property. Here it was reassembled and renovated, had a verandah surround added, as well as a lunchroom on one end and an administration office on the other.

This saw the original building almost double in size. Concertina doors were installed to separate the two classrooms from the lunchroom and the administration office, which enabled them to be opened to have a meeting place of one complete room for the Sunday church services.

But it was not all work and no play. There were always times for picnic lunches, impromptu musical interludes when Archie and Jeffrey would pick up their guitars, fun and friendly banter between the young ones, and quiet cozy together times for Michael and Archie as they sat eating lunch on a checkered blanket underneath the shade of the big fig tree.

"Don't you love this Michael?"

"You know seeing something being born out of nothing," Archie mused.

"I mean all of us co-creating something that will stand for years and years to come."

"I do."

"I think there's a God given desire in all of us to create something… or co-create something," Michael added.

Archie got excited.

"Can't wait for the inside of the classrooms to be completed. I have seen a design of the classroom desk set up. Mr Morcum showed it to me."

"Yes I asked him to since you are going to be the teacher and headmistress."

"Hey Archie, did you hear that?"

"No Michael…what?"

"I can hear it now."

"Good Morning Miss Vernados."

Archie laughed and returned, "Good Morning class."

"Wow…I can't believe it's happening and I loved the different looking classroom set up on the plan. You know an open plan look with the individual cubicle desk areas for the students around the perimeter of the room…it's great."

"Yes…well you know the curriculum is part of the ACE system, Accelerated Christian Education."

"Don Morcum is a whiz."

"He knows everything about it. He has even spoken to their head office to sign up for the licence to use their products and even drove up to the city to spend two days to see a class in action at Calvary Christian School on the north side."

"That is something we will arrange for you and Judy to do too, and perhaps Margie's brother Ron. He graduates this year, Bachelor of Science, and is moving up with the Morrisons next year and has volunteered to help out until he figures out where he is going with his degree."

"You will all probably need a full week though."

"So yes…Don Morcom knows the ins and outs of ACE totally."

"That's great."

Michael saw the excitement on her face. He liked that.

"What did he call them…the students offices…sounds so grown up for little kids doesn't it…I love it," Archie grinned.

"Me too…and the new concept of calling it a learning centre rather than a classroom," replied Michael, "it's great."

"Since we will have mixed grades of children all in the same room, the actual design and location of their desks makes it very workable. And it makes it so easy for the teacher, who is you my love, to move around and focus on each student on a one on one basis as they complete the modules they've been assigned according to their current level of schooling."

"Great teaching concept," replied Archie.

"Did you know Don received two separate anonymous donations of five thousand dollars each to buy school supplies to start off with?"

"You are kidding Michael Winton get outta here…you are kidding."

"No I'm not…would I kid you…don't answer that."

"He said the donor or donors want to remain anonymous but I have a feeling Unwin could be a part of it."

"Wow Michael that is so good."

"So are we looking at November Michael for everything in terms of the building to be ready?"

"We sure are Archie…we sure are."

"But as I mentioned to you at the team meeting, since that is close to the summer break starting, the school won't open until the last week of January '71. That will give you and Judy enough time to fine-tune it. You know, enrolments, school supplies, uniforms, prep work."

"The plan as you know is then to give it six months settling in time to get any wrinkles ironed out and to build up the enrolments. We will then go for Department of Education accreditation which will mean we will be eligible for government funding and that means you teachers will get a decent wage."

"That's great…we'll be ready Michael."

"So far we have seven families committed so that gives us a minimum start up of sixteen students, but I know that number is just going to grow."

"It will Archie…it will."

"So…what do you reckon?"

"Lunch break over?"

"Yes I think it is."

———— ✒ ————

The four months since the property purchase had seemingly flown by so quickly, perhaps it was because of the busyness of things Michael thought, but that too was fine. Archie had spent a lot of time completing enrolments for those families that had indicated their desire to have their children attend, and consulting with uniform manufacturers, at the same time getting her head around the curriculum and the new type of teaching environment.

For Michael it had been an equally busy time having to attend to the responsibilities of his day job, trips to the city for work meetings and with most of his time off spent in attending to matters of the community project.

He had also been contacted in October by a good friend and neighbour from the Assemblies of God church in Citiville, a town in the north of the state where Michael had been stationed with his work for a few years. His friend Luca had asked Michael if he could visit with his sister Capricia Rossi who lived in the city and was going through a messy marriage breakup. Michael had managed to slot in a visit to see her whilst he was in the city for a work meeting and had subsequently spent a lot of time helping her get her affairs in order.

As for Michael and Archie going out on dates it had been limited to sharing picnic baskets at working bees, the occasional rushed coffee and baklava biscuit at the Plaka, and only one further visit to The Heads Drive-In theatre to see a recently released movie named Butch Cassidy and The Sundance Kid.

It was Archie who had suggested it for two reasons. She had remembered Michael sharing with her how he liked playing cowboy games as a child and because Paul Newman was her favourite actor as he was for most women of the day.

Jeff and Janet had also been busy rehearsing their new church band. It had been decided by the gang that Jeff would take charge of it. The meetings had now turned into a monthly get together rather than fortnightly due to the busyness of getting the schoolhouse up and running.

The band consisted of Archie on keyboards, Jeff on guitar, Shaun on drums, Danny on harmonica, Zelda on tambourine and Dr Nicholls' son Mark on saxophone, with Kelly, Janet, Judy and Archie's brother Peter as the choir back up singing group. Many nights had been spent putting together a collection of popular worship songs and as Jeffrey put it in a moment of tension, "this is all there is, there will be no audience requests."

And of course Garret Sloan had conducted his first crusade on the site in early November after having been allocated a large flattened out area big enough to accommodate his tent with plenty of parking space beside it. This had been followed up on the Sunday with the first official church service in the schoolhouse as both sets of concertina doors were folded back to provide a meeting space that accommodated one hundred and twenty seats.

Sloan's week of tent meetings achieved one of the best responses in terms of number of attendees that he had ever had in his ten years of crusading in the district. In conversation with Michael later he would put it down to the new centrality of location which saw him drawing people from both the north and the south of the district.

But whilst accepting Sloan's theory accompanied by his self-aggrandising attitude, Michael was fully aware of an initiative that Archie and Kelly had undertaken which he felt had also contributed to the increase in numbers. They had printed off two hundred leaflets of a photo of the inside and outside of the school, with an invitation for any visitors to the tent meeting to arrive forty five minutes early and have a cup of tea and a free tour of the classroom, and any questions they asked answered, or stay back after Sloan's meeting had concluded for the same.

Then on a Saturday afternoon two weeks prior to the crusade, they had commandeered the services of a group of volunteers to walk around the township of Springfield and Lighthouse Bay, and placed the small poster strategically under every poster of Sloan's that they saw. It worked.

Archie had then contacted the uniform supplier for a rush job on three children's uniforms and two adult ones for herself and Judy with the Springfield Christian School logo on it. Then on the night of the tour she had two girls and one boy sitting at their desks modelling how it all worked, whilst she and Judy conducted small group tours and answered questions. It was magic. It was a spectacular success, seeing fifteen indication of interest forms filled out.

⸎

"Michael...have you got a minute," Archie called out to him as he entered the classroom after the crusade had finished.

"Sure."

"I'd like you to meet Ian."

"Michael this is Ian Robinson...he's a neighbour of the Purcells and he's very interested in what we are doing with the school and the church."

"And not only that," she patted his shoulder, "he's a regular visitor to The Plaka in his downtime."

"Ian this is Michael I was telling you about...Michael Winton."

"Ian," Michael replied, reaching out to shake his hand, "nice to meet you."

Ian Robinson was a short dapper looking man, in his late seventies, silver haired, dressed smartly in cream linen slacks and an orange checked shirt that blended in perfectly with the brown tweed jacket and tan shoes he was wearing.

"Nice to meet you too Michael…and might I say I'm very very impressed," he continued, raising his arm in the air and gesturing around the classroom, "very impressed."

"Thankyou…we've got a great team of committed people volunteering in putting this together."

"Did you attend the tent service tonight Ian?"

"Yes I did Michael…I was seated with George and Jenny Purcell. They had to go home but suggested I might like to take a look at the school while I was here."

"I go along to most of Garret Sloan's meetings when he's in town Michael. Been a firm believer all my life in the power of prayer to change things, no matter who's doing the praying. If there is someone offering prayer I don't have any problem in joining the queue," he chuckled.

Michael grinned. He liked the honesty and gentle but confident attitude of Ian.

"I don't get prayer for myself Michael, I get it for my wife Evie. She hasn't been too well lately."

"I take along one of her handkerchiefs and get those prayer warriors to pray over it. Then I take the handkerchief home and lay it on my Evie's heart. You know Michael in the Book of Acts in the Bible where it says that people would take handkerchiefs and aprons that had touched the skin of the Apostle Paul and place them on the sick and their sicknesses would be cured and evil spirits would leave them."

"That's why I do it. Evie's not well enough to come to the service with me. I always carry a couple of her handkerchiefs with me when I'm out. You know Michael God moves in mysterious ways. You never know when you're going to run into a prayer line," he laughed.

Michael grinned. He liked Ian's positivity.

"Some people think I'm mad when they hear this. Silly old fool they say. But I have to do it Michael. I have to do everything I can for her. She's my sweetheart."

"Well anyway Michael, I'm starting to ramble. I'd better get going. But lovely to meet you and to catch up with this sweet girl," he said gesturing to Archie, "she's a keeper."

Ian kissed Archie on the cheek, shook hands with Michael and walked off, but suddenly stopped and turned.

"Michael is it alright if I bring a couple of Evie's handkerchiefs to your first church service tomorrow night?"

"Of course it is Ian, of course. Make sure you come and see me personally please."

"Thankyou Michael...goodnight, and I have a son in the construction business with plenty of contacts in the building materials world, if I can help you in any way please feel free to contact me."

"Thanks Ian...very kind of you."

Michael turned to Archie.

"So that's Ian Robinson."

"What... do you know him Michael?"

"No...I just know of him."

"Do you remember that day at one of our working bees when I told you about the two separate five thousand dollar donations for school supplies?"

"Yes...I do."

"Well I checked with Don Morcum who they were."

"One donation was from Unwin Nicholls as I thought and the other he said was from a man named Ian Robinson."

Michael turned to Archie standing beside him: her eyes evidenced a welling up of emotion.

"Wow...I didn't know that...wow...that's got me all teary," Archie softly said.

"No wonder he was so interested in the school and asking a lot of questions tonight," Archie continued.

"Even said that he would like to see his grandchildren attending a school like this."

"Wow…five thousand dollars."

"He's just such a beautiful man…I always feel sad for him, but Michael he never feels sad for himself."

"He is a nice man," replied Michael.

"He mentioned that his wife had not been feeling well lately, what's the story with that?"

"He always puts it that way, he always understates the situation Michael."

"Evelyn's dying, she is in the final stages of dementia."

Tears welled up once again in Archie's eyes.

"He still looks after her at home. He gets the Blue Nurses in a couple of times a week to help but is absolutely devoted to looking after her."

"Jenny Purcell told me that once when she had visited Evelyn to pray with her she suggested to Ian that he might consider putting her in a nursing home to take some pressure off himself."

"You know what he said to her?"

"No."

"Something like, take the pressure off me, Evie's the one under pressure. She's scared Jenny and it's my job to keep her safe. I couldn't put her in a place full of strangers. She'd be frightened. She belongs here with me, she's my sweetheart, and maybe one day with God's help she will come back to me."

"Isn't that beautiful?"

Michael could feel tears welling up in his own eyes.

"Whew, Archie, now you're going to make me cry."

Archie pulled out a tissue.

"Don't do that Michael, people will think something has gone wrong with the project."

Michael laughed and Archie continued.

"Okay…enough sad talk…on to other things."

"There's someone else I'd like you to meet."

Archie walked across to the far corner of the classroom where a well dressed lady, a redhead, Michael guessed was in her early forties, was quietly browsing through a module in one of the student's cubicles. It was the second session of the school tours directly after the end of the Garret Sloan crusade, and whilst the curious crowds were not as many as the session held before Sloan's meeting, there was still a sense of busy chatter and excitement in the schoolhouse as Archie and Judy showed the visitors around.

"Michael I'd like you to meet Colleen Jones. Colleen manages the Emmanuel Christian Bookstore downtown."

"Hi Colleen," Michael extended his hand, "bless you, nice to meet you."

"Colleen has two primary school age little ones that attend the Springfield Public School and she's interested in what we intend to do here."

"Nice," returned Michael.

"So Emmanuel is it. Is that part of the Catholic Church in town?"

"Yes Michael but it is ecumenical in its operation, you know, non-denominational, non-sectarian, universal catholic, all-embracing and all inclusive. So our range of product whether that be books or religious paraphernalia caters for pretty well all the churches in town."

"Even the Pentecostals," she laughed.

"So how did you hear about our project?" Michael enquired.

"Well apart from the wonderful job Archie did with her posters around town, basically I heard about it from everyone that has come into the shop over the last few months asking questions. So I thought I had better come along and take a look so that I have all the answers for the more curious and sometimes misguided customers."

Colleen appeared to Michael in her confident mannerisms to be a woman that liked to be in charge and have all the answers at the same time. He wasn't sure what it was that he picked up in her personality but there was definitely something not quite right there. She was he ascertained in her conversing and appearance both extroverted and organized even to the point of carrying a small notebook and pen in hand, obviously to take note of particular things Archie might share with her.

She continued taking charge of the conversation whilst at the same time moving her bodily position away from facing both Archie and Michael, focussing her attention directly on Michael. "Anyway I would not miss any of the Garret Sloan's meetings when he is in town, he is wonderful, so committed and caring," she continued almost in a schoolgirl crush type fashion.

"Certain Catholic churches in the state have started to embrace the Charismatic type meetings in addition to their traditional services because it seems to attract a greater proportion of young people who are born into the Catholic faith along to a church service."

"Even though I'm Catholic I have attended a few of those Catholic Charismatic meetings in the city and just love the Pentecostal way of worship and the flow of the gifts," she continued, "and of course the Reverend Sloan is so anointed. He has prayed for me many times," she continued, almost in a gushing manner.

"Well I'd better go," continued Colleen, "my husband Jim is probably out waiting in the car park. He doesn't come to the crusades, just drops me off and picks me up."

"Thankyou Archie for the tour and nice to meet you too Michael," she continued extending her hand to both. "Pop in to the bookshop if you get time Michael and I'll show you the latest releases."

Archie and Michael watched her disappear out on to the school verandah and walk towards the carpark.

"What do you think Michael?"

"About Colleen."

"Personally or professionally?"

Archie laughed.

"She's full on isn't she?"

"Yes she is…Sloan should use her as his public relations officer."

"Interesting," continued Michael.

"You know I was thinking all during our conversation was she really looking for answers for her customers about the school or was she sniffing around for Father Flanagan?" queried Archie.

"Is that her priest's name?"

"No Michael…don't be naughty. That is the name they usually use in movies that have a Catholic priest don't they? Either that or Father O'Reilly."

"Aye lass…I tink she was sniffin' round for the benefit of Father O'Reilly," came the sound of a male voice doing a poor impersonation of an Irish person.

Jeffrey and Janet Gibbons had come out of the school lunchroom both carrying their cups of coffee just as Colleen was saying her good-byes. Archie swung around.

"Well if it isn't super sleuth," she grinned, "what…not carrying your magnifying glass and where did you put your Sherlock Holmes hat."

"And are you Irish or Scottish…I can't quite tell?"

Jeffrey grinned.

"Just keepin' an eye on tings lass…dat's wot ya pay meee for."

"Jeffrey…we don't pay you," Michael interjected.

"Yer right laddie I forgot."

"So seriously what do you guys think?" continued Archie.

"Okay," replied Jeff, "I can be serious."

"I have been into her bookstore quite a few times, just to browse mind you. As you know I am a book buff but don't like paying full price. On more than one occasion when I have been quietly browsing I have caught Mrs Jones might I respectfully call her, giving me a not so Christian evil eye."

"So what are you thinking?" grinned Michael, "that she wants you or that you are a potential shoplifter?"

"Well maybe both, but not really," returned Jeffrey, "but I'm thinking that the 'lovely to meet you Michael' lady that I just saw saying her goodbyes had a different demeanor from the one I have seen in the bookstore on many occasions when she is dealing with a customer wearing flip flops."

"I think she could be a bit socially prejudiced."

"Seems a little fake to my coffee carrying self and to my super sleuth eye."

"Interesting you say that Jeff...I thought that too," commented Michael. "As soon as Arch introduced me she turned all her conversational attention on me. Like she was trying to impress."

"I didn't notice that," replied Archie.

"That's why you need a super sleuth like Jeffrey around you," retorted Michael.

"Exactly," returned Jeff. "I think it could be because you're a male with a title...well almost a title...you know...Pastor."

"Or perhaps she thinks you're running the show Michael and doesn't really know that Jeffrey is," quipped Archie grinning.

"Good one Arch...very well said but unfortunately not correct," Jeff replied, "neither running nor wanting to run."

"I'm a lover not a fighter and in leadership you've got to do both... you know Michael the Archangel type."

"But seriously."

"A couple of times when I have been browsing and someone from the town clergy brigade walks in, usually a turned around collar gives them away, her whole attitude changes. And might I add I have observed her on one occasion having a close up hush hush conversation with Barry the bald eagle."

"Who?"

"Thorpey...Garret Sloan's minder."

"Oh right...I had forgotten your pet name for him."

"And I think I know what that is about."

"What is it about Jeffrey?" queried Archie.

"It's about accommodation my schoolteacher friend, accommodation."

"What do you mean?"

"Well," Jeff continued taking a sip of his coffee, "reliable sources I have in the world of Christian comings and goings have informed me that when Sloan is in town for a crusade he is actually billeted at the home of one Jim and Colleen Jones."

"And who might I ask Jeffrey is your reliable source?" queried Archie.

"It's the one, the only…Mags Morrison."

"Mags," repeated Archie looking puzzled, "how does she know?"

"Glad you asked."

"Do you remember on the Carols night when Margie and I were having a to and fro about Elmer Gantry aka Garret Sloan that she mentioned he stays at her mum and dad's house in Gratton when he has a crusade there?"

"Yes I remember that," responded Michael.

"Well after you both left I put my Sherlock hat on and asked Mags in casual conversation how that accommodation thing all worked for the visiting crusade team members."

"She explained that it was a billeting system done through the local churches who supported his crusades. Whilst some team members are shifted around Sloan always stays with the same family. So in Gratton he always stays at her mum and dad's home."

"Now being the naturally inquisitive person that I am, I casually said."

"Right…so who does he stay with when he visits Springfield?"

"And my fellow curious friends she said," and he paused, "are you ready for it…drum roll…Jim and Colleen Jones, whose names of course I didn't recognize."

"And so I just as casually as previously asked the question."

"Which church are they with?"

"You're dragging this out in a spectacular manner Jeffrey," Archie interjected.

"Yes I am…be patient…the wait is worth it."

"And she said, not sure what church she's with, think it's Catholic, but Colleen manages the Emmanuel Christian Bookstore downtown."

"So Michael my friend…what do you think?"

"I think locked away Jeffrey…locked away."

"What do you mean Michael…locked away?" queried Archie.

"Jeffrey and I have an arrangement, well it's a sort of a pact."

"If he has any intuitive thoughts about something he can feel free to express it. You know, bounce it off me. I will listen but not judge or agree out of politeness. If he is convinced about it I will not enter into any serious discussion about it or dwell on it unless it is something urgent, just lock it away in my mind for future use if necessary."

"And visa versa if I have intuitive thoughts or a gut feel as we call them."

"Seems to work well for us doesn't it Jeffrey?" No arguments or disagreements, just a sort of well let's keep that at the back of our mind and see what happens."

"Works for me," replied Jeffrey finishing his coffee.

"Right…good."

"Well guys time to call it a night. Michael can you help me lock up?" queried Archie.

"Sure can."

Jeff finished his coffee.

"Okay guys Jeff and Jan are out of here…see you tomorrow, don't forget Arch, 10 a.m. band practice, gotta get it right for tomorrow night."

Jeffrey turned to Michael as he and Janet walked off.

"You too Pastor…remember your leading the worship session."

"I'll be there Sherlock…night guys."

Michael and Archie walked hand in hand to their two cars. Sloan's people had locked down the tent and all the stragglers had gone. It was a beautiful night with the dark sky blanketed by hundreds of stars in between what looked in the moonlight like small clusters of storm clouds gathering. After a night of loud singing, loud music, and loud hand clapping there was now a perfect stillness in the air save for the intermittent chirping of the crickets.

"Can you hear that Michael?" Archie whispered.

"You mean the sounds of the crickets?"

"No the sound of silence."

"I read once Michael that the only way we can recognize or sense silence is through sound, and that the smaller the sound the greater the sense of silence."

"You know like too loud a sound mixed with other sound drowns out the silence but just enough sound like the crickets with no other sound accentuates the silence and the stillness."

"Does that make sense?"

"Sure it does, that's true Arch."

Michael continued.

"I remember when I lived right beside a nature reserve which had a walking track through it. And once you distanced yourself from the highway traffic and all you had was the sound of the odd bird crying out you could almost feel the silence coming over you like a cloud."

"Right Michael, that's what I mean."

"It reminds me of that scripture, be still and know that I am God. Stillness or silence brings a sense of God into our personal space."

"Yes Michael, it's like the universal spirit is revealing its presence."

"Michael do you remember about four years ago when that song The Sound of Silence came out. You know Simon and Garfunkel?"

"Yes I do...I love it."

"Well it sort of stuck with me that silence was referred to as a sound in that song, you know the sound of silence."

"We even say 'listen to the silence,' when silence means the absence of sound so how can we listen to it?"

"Let me think…you're right…perhaps we should be saying feel the stillness."

"Yes Michael."

"Well anyway I loved that song so much I taught myself the guitar chords and memorized the words. And I particularly loved the part of the song that said hear my words that I might teach you, take my arms that I might reach you."

"And it made me think that if we listen in stillness and silence, if we listen to the sound of silence it brings us closer to God. That we can actually hear the voice of God trying to reach us and teach us something."

"That's a beautiful way of putting it Arch…I had never thought about the words of the song like that but you are right, which is probably why that verse from the bible is basically saying if you be still you shall know God."

"Actually I discovered in my studies that that is what the whole practice of meditation is based on incidentally. Getting still, getting silent, getting rid of the mind chatter and listening to the intuitive voice within: God's spirit speaking to our spirit."

"It's funny how a lot of Christians particularly Pentecostals think that the art of meditation is of the devil and yet it is the exact same spiritual discipline that was used by the early Christians, except they called it contemplative prayer."

They had reached their cars. Archie turned around and placed her arms around Michael pulling their bodies together and lovingly staring into his face.

"You know Michael with all these stars out on such a beautiful night I think I'm starting to believe more and more in happy ever afters."

"You mean as in when you wish upon a star your dreams come true?"

"Yes…that's right."

"That's beautiful…well I've got another line from a Disney song for you."

Michael sang, "now it's time to say goodbye to all our company…m.i.c.k.e.y…as you know that's me."

They both laughed.

"I remember that, the theme from the Mickey Mouse Club. I think I told you it was one of my favourite television shows. I used to race home every day after school to watch it."

Archie glanced around back over her shoulder to check for privacy, raised her lips to Michael's and kissed him. It was almost hesitantly at first but then grew with intensity for both of them. They were aware why. The busyness of the last few months in getting the project going, along with both their individual personal work schedules had not allowed a lot of private time together. But it had not dimmed the spark. He felt so good to her and she felt so good to him.

She cradled his face in her hands and began kissing it all over, playfully nibbling on his ears as she did so. Her lips grazed across his neck with her kisses moving upwards across his face and onto his forehead. Together they both breathed in the fragrance of each other's bodies as they pressed tightly against each other.

She had loved it when he had recognized the perfume Charlie that she was wearing on that first night in his apartment, and ever since then whenever she knew they would be spending time together she had always made sure she was wearing some.

Her favourite men's perfume was Aramis. Her brother would wear it when he went out on Saturday nights and she had fallen in love with the fragrance. She had given a bottle of it to Michael as a gift and she noticed he continually wore it whenever he was with her. She liked that. She rested her head on his shoulder, pressed her breasts firmly against him and breathed in deeply the sweet smell of his body. And then it happened.

"Oh darn."

She looked skywards and released her body from Michael's.

"Was that a raindrop I just felt Michael?"

"Yes I believe it was. I think it was actually the third one I have felt."

"Seem familiar Arch?"

"What's that?"

"Remember at the drive in when we were snuggling up and kissing in the car as the theme of the Butch Cassidy movie was playing…you know raindrops keep falling on my head, and you joked, "not on this little brown bear's head. No raindrops gonna interfere with my kissin' tonight."

"I do," Archie laughed.

"Well this could be karma my beautiful little brown bear."

"Amongst all the other feelings I have as I kiss you I am having a feeling that the rain is about to bucket down on our heads."

"You're right," Archie quickly kissed him on the lips hugged him and reached into her purse for her keys, "we'd better go."

"Nite my Michael…so see you at band practice…10 a.m…whoops here it comes…don't get wet…see ya."

Michael scurried off.

"Nite Archie…see you tomorrow…and thanks for doing such a great job tonight."

"You're very welcome…bye," she called out as she hurriedly closed her car door. See you tomorrow too.

66 *"Evelyn Robinson had always admired the writer's philosophy of life which led to her loving the author's books. It was simple. Evelyn Beatrice Hall believed in the innate goodness of humanity. She believed that there is more goodness in the world than there appears to be, but people don't recognize it, because goodness is of its very nature modest and retiring. In most cases it doesn't jump out at you and say, look at me, look at me. Elsie was right. Evelyn loved not only the author's books but the humanity of the author as well."*

The Theatre

TWELVE

"I think we've really got to put Michael Winton in the picture Bill. The work is growing so quickly. He really needs to be told. I mean I don't want to deliberately shatter the spiritual innocence of this group of young people but Michael as the leader of the work has to know what he is up against. Perhaps if we handle it this way."

Terry Channing and William Hawkesbury were in Terry's office discussing Bill's up and coming preaching visit to Springfield.

Ian Robinson really was a beautiful man. Ask anyone who knew him as to how they regarded him and one could always guarantee that the first words to be uttered would be, "he's a beautiful man," followed by an explanation of why they thought this.

Now in his late seventies Ian had in the last five years diversed himself of the considerable assets that he had accumulated in a lifetime in property and stocks, keeping a large proportion of the cash in short term interest bearing investment accounts whilst he slowly searched for some suitable charities to donate some of it to.

He had then, along with his beloved wife Evelyn, downsized from a large sprawling house overlooking Lighthouse Bay, to a purpose built apartment in a new block of units recently constructed by his son Stephen beside the tourist park owned by George and Jenny Purcell.

If you asked anyone who knew Ian closely why they thought he was a beautiful man the answer would inevitably be, "well because of the way he looks after Evelyn, particularly at his age. It's just beautiful what he does for her."

Evelyn too was a dear lady. Ian affectionately referred to her as his Evie. The photos scattered in frames around their apartment of her as a young woman in her twenties had a Rita Hayworth look about them, a movie star appearance. She was beautiful in her youth and early adult years, not only in looks, but if you asked Ian he would tell you in her heart also.

But Evelyn's life had changed suddenly in a random check up visit to her doctor in the spring of 1963 when she was 67 years of age, where tests revealed she was in the early stages of Dementia. Evelyn herself had not noticed any symptoms that would indicate this except for the increasing odd period of forgetfulness which she had just put down to the onset of old age.

Ian with the benefit of hindsight, in conversations with her doctor after the diagnosis, realized that whilst he had been aware of changes in her behaviour over the previous year, like losing the thread of conversations and getting irritable and upset when some of her cooking experiments failed, he too had just put it down to old age.

But over the ensuing six years the disease had traversed her life with a determination that now saw her body and mind showing symptoms that they were embracing the final stages of the illness. In the last few months she had been totally confined to her bed, showed no recognition of family or friends, and needed help with everyday tasks such as eating, washing, bathing, toileting and dressing: all of which Ian had committed to do himself, with help from the Blue Nurses who would visit a couple of times a week providing some relief to his carer's workload.

Ian had accustomed himself to the fact that death was inevitable, but when Evelyn's visitors would get that occasional look of sadness on their faces as they witnessed her deteriorating faculties, there was one thing that Ian would always share with them that gave him some hope for the future.

"You know she still has her sense of touch and hearing and she can still respond to her emotions," he would say.

"I mean that has to be a sign that things could change for the better doesn't it?"

"The doctor told me that it's highly unlikely that she will ever lose her sense of touch, her hearing and the expression of emotion, so that's a positive."

So, holding onto this thread of hope, and aware of Evelyn's passion for reading over the decades of their life together, Ian Robinson had made a pact with himself as her condition deteriorated. If touch and hearing and the ability to feel emotions were the last three faculties of life that his beloved Evie could hold on to, he committed that he would always set aside time each evening before bedtime to read to her from one of her favourite books.

Around 8 o'clock every evening Ian would take a book in hand, read to her, comment on the reading, and when her facial expression indicated tiredness, he would gently stroke and kiss her hand for a few minutes. Occasionally, as he always hoped, he would see a tear slowly roll down her face, which to him meant that somewhere in her heart she knew what he was doing. The tear was just her way of telling him she loved and appreciated him.

Then after she had fallen asleep he would lean over her frail form, softly kiss her on the forehead, and then quietly whisper in her ear, "come back to me my Evie…I love you."

This was one of the reasons why those who knew him well would always describe Ian Robinson as a beautiful man.

The year 1971 was a very full on year for those involved in the commune and the twelve months seemed to fly by quickly, especially for Michael and Archie. Due to the busyness of life Christmas 1970 had come and gone swiftly, or so it seemed, with both of them going through the same routine for Christmas Day as they had done on their first Christmas together in 1969.

Archie had spent the last few weeks prior to Christmas almost full time at the schoolhouse, organizing and tidying up loose bits in preparation for the school opening in late January1971.

Even though the commune had conducted its own Carols night at the schoolhouse, the gang had decided to go to the Carols By Candlelight gathering in the park at Lighthouse Bay as they had the previous year just for the fun of it. Drinks and nibblies at Michael Winton's apartment, purely to celebrate their 12-month friendship with food, laughter, and good old folk music followed.

On the following Saturday the week prior to Christmas Day Archie and Michael had spent a fun afternoon together paddle boating at Lighthouse Bay, followed by a loving evening together as they exchanged Christmas presents.

"Michael I know you love your records so I came across this one in the record store. It was only released last year."

"I hope you like it."

"I'm sure I'll love it."

"It said on the cover that the album was produced by Jimmy Webb, and you said on our first date that he was your favourite songwriter."

"He is," said Michael as he tore open the wrapping.

"Wow...A Tramp Shining, Richard Harris."

Michael turned over the album cover.

"Wow great. It has Macarthur Park and Didn't We on it, and yes produced by Jimmy Webb."

Archie smiled and softly sang..."this time we almost made the pieces fit, didn't we boy."

"I love that song Didn't We Michael. I think I told you that on our first night together."

"You did...and I love it too."

"Thank you Archie...I just love this record."

Michael leaned over and kissed Archie.

"And for you," Michael handed his gift to her.

"Merry Christmas Archie."

"I know what this is," Archie grinned.

"How do you know?"

"By the shape of it."

Archie shook the small parcel close to her ear.

"Ya knowa Michael, a girl who doesn't a weara perfume has a no future."

Michael chuckled.

"I am thinking its Charlie perfume," said Archie chirpily.

"Well you did say you love it but that you only use it sparingly because of the price. Now you can splash it all over."

"Thank you Michael…I love it."

The last week in January 1971 saw the school experience a successful first day with invited guests at the opening including the local mayor and a representative of the State Education Office all giving speeches. As well as this most of the parents in dropping off their children stayed for the official proceedings. And of course there were the curious onlookers mingling with the adults sipping tea and eating biscuits in the post speech celebratory refreshment time.

As well as this members of the local press and television station crowed about, eager to fill up reporting space with an event they thought was new and different and a little less mundane than the normal articles and news bulletins about the activities of the mayor of Springfield.

Student numbers had started at eighteen, all being primary school students, and progressively increased to twenty-four by the beginning of the second term. Archie had taken on the role of senior teacher and headmistress with a determination and an energy driven by a self-acknowledgement that this was her calling: a calling of type that Michael thought hovered somewhere between the one she felt she had received when she saw the Sound of Music movie and the one she believed she received when she had seen The Nun's Story.

She was ably assisted in her calling by back up teachers, Judy and Ron and a rotational team of teacher's aide volunteers, including Janet Gibbons, Zelda and Danny in his downtime from his electrical business and Marie Nicholls in any time she could get away from her home duties and charity work. All the hard work put in by Archie, Judy and their team was rewarded when in July 1971 the school was awarded full accreditation by the Department of Education, which then allowed it to access state government financial funding.

The Morrisons, Margie's parents, and their son Ron had moved from Gratton to Springfield and purchased a house in a new housing estate right alongside the north eastern border of the commune's property, leaving Margie's sister Francis alone in their house in Gratton until she finished her medical degree at the end of the year. Ron had got involved helping Archie in the school.

As well as this Janet and Zelda had established a thriving market garden, a small-scale production of fruits, vegetables and flowers as cash crops. This provided a variety of product, which was sold off each Saturday at The Markets, as they were known, based downtown in the disused Imperial Cinema.

The weekend market activity became a focal point for more socialising by the gang, much laughter being generated as Kelly and Zelda took charge of the sales process using a portable microphone and speaker. With humourous antics including cries of "support the school...come and get your sacred vegetables...they taste heavenly" and "good value...hell the prices are out of this world," they catered to the amusement of all passing by and other members of the commune who would pop in to give support.

The project was also positively supported by several of the restaurants in town, including Morty's, with all proceeds of the sale of products grown in their market garden project being channelled back into the work of the school.

An eldership was established to administer all the practical aspects of the church side of the commune. It was decided at the June directors' meeting that it would consist of the three directors, Michael, Unwin, and Don and that each director would choose another person to make up the six elders which was the standard number of elders for a church in those days.

Michael had selected Jeffrey Gibbons since Jeffrey was the construction manager for the project and he trusted him whilst Unwin had selected Garret Sloan, a decision Jeffrey would later describe to Michael in one of his monthly visits back to Springfield as interesting. Don Morcom had selected George Purcell, Kelly's dad, since George had been put in charge of the church and school finances, having had a bookkeeping and accounting background.

The Sunday night church service had seen a progressive increase in numbers as word of the vibrant evening services enticed more and more of the youth of the town, as well as older members of the community looking for an experience with Pentecostalism; much to the concern of some of the clergy of denominational churches in town who witnessed their congregational count shifting downwards.

What had started out in November 1970 as a congregation of some sixty to eighty people had more than doubled in numbers in six months, to a point where at some of the evening services the attendees could be seen flowing out the schoolhouse doors to standing room only on the school verandah.

Garret and Bettina Sloan were spending more time in the district surrounding Springfield, so in his downtime from tent crusades Garret was rostered on to the Sunday preaching schedule to assist. Michael Winton and Dr Nicholls had been bearing most of the Sunday services workload, save for intermittent preaching visits from one of the pastors from the Christian City Church, the Reverend William Hawkesbury.

William Hawkesbury was a white haired man in his early eighties, semi-retired, and a minister of some fifty years who still loved to preach and to teach from the Bible: his main emphasis of teaching always being the Book of Revelation and his interpretation of the end times' component of it. When old Bill preached it was much to the delight of Dr Nicholls. He would always make sure he had a front row seat when the Reverend Hawkesbury was in town.

William had suffered from Parkinson's disease for some time and had got to a point where he exhibited tremors in his body and a quavering voice that continued for most of his sermon, but it never deterred him in taking up preaching opportunities. Everyone loved him and admired him for his courage in spite of the disease, and people would say that the tremors only accentuated his fire and brimstone exhortations as he spoke of the series of events leading to, as he saw it, the end of the world as we know it, the Apocalypse.

During his bi-monthly visits to Springfield Michael Winton would always insist that William and his wife Ethel be billeted with him in his apartment at Lighthouse Bay. He liked and respected old Bill as he called him and he knew that Bill liked him. He wanted to make sure that this dear dedicated elderly man and his wife were comfortable and looked after, so it became a fixed arrangement that they would always stay with Michael on their bi-monthly visit.

Even though Michael thought some of Bill's thoughts on end times were a little complex and hard for many to understand, Michael always thought of Bill as a man of integrity, and a rich source of spiritual wisdom and church experience. Over time they became good friends. Bill and Ethel would usually arrive for his Sunday engagement on a Saturday afternoon as Bill liked to sit on the balcony and chat with Michael about the things of God, the workings of the Spirit, and the current situation and future of the church as he saw it.

It would be during one of those typical Saturday afternoons, in May 1971, as they sat drinking tea and watching the trawler boats chugging their way out to sea, that old Bill turned to Michael and said.

"Michael I am going to say a few words and nothing more and I'd like you not to ask me any questions about what I say. I know it sounds strange but I have my reasons."

"Are you okay with that?"

"Sure Bill…sure."

"Okay."

"Michael…watch Garret Sloan."

"That's all."

"Watch Garret Sloan…we think he's done things before."

"Okay?"

"That's all I can say at the moment."

"But you do it Michael…watch Garret Sloan."

Michael was surprised but knew that Bill wouldn't have said that unless he thought it was of absolute importance.

"Thanks Bill…I know you have a good reason for saying that, so I will Bill…I will…I'll keep my eye on things."

However it would be in early June 1971 that a most significant event in the evolution of the commune came to pass. Michael was in his office heavily engrossed in paperwork and accounts when the phone rang startling him out of his concentration.

"Michael…Unwin…how are you?"

"Good thanks Unwin."

"Michael I'm here in my office with Patty and we've got something we'd like to talk to you about, are you good if we come down in around thirty minutes?"

"Sure…sure Unwin…I'll put the kettle on…see you in thirty."

Michael leaned back thinking, wondering what this would be about and knowing that it more than likely had something to do with the commune. Unwin had sounded a little excited on the phone Michael thought. This could be something good.

Unwin and Patty walked into Michael's office both grinning like

Cheshire cats. Michael stood up.

"You guys look like the cat that swallowed the cream…what's happening…grab a seat."

Unwin and Patty both sat down…still grinning.

"What's up?"

"Michael," continued Unwin, "you know how we discussed the issue at our eldership meeting of the overcrowding at the Sunday night services?"

"I mean the numbers are growing and we just can't fit any more into the school building."

"Sure…I think we discuss it at most eldership meetings."

"Well," Unwin gestured with a flourish, "Patty Patel has brought us the solution…over to you my friend."

Patty cleared his throat.

"Yeah Mikey…well as you know I have a few friends in the business," he winked at Unwin, knowing Unwin would be thinking that's an understatement, and then looking around almost nervously as if he was concerned someone would be eavesdropping he continued.

"Now Michael this is not public knowledge but the owners of the old Imperial Theatre, you know where Unwin's clinic is, The Markets building," he leaned forward and lowered his voice, "the owners, some private equity group, are going to put it up for auction around mid July, and the scuttlebutt around the traps is that the reserve will probably be set around \$250,000."

"I reckon you guys could pick it up for around two fifty."

"Wow…that's interesting…I can see why you're excited Unwin. That's a bargain on today's downtown values if we could get it for that."

"I think we can Michael…I think we can," Patty replied.

"We'll have to keep it quiet though, you know, the fact that we are interested. You know what it's like. As soon as a vendor finds out a church is interested you can be sure they will jack the reserve price up."

Patty continued.

"Look Michael you've been inside the building when the Markets are on. The reason that the reserve is that low is because they have allowed the current lessee who owns the market licence to turn it into a shit tip. You know all the walls painted black, cobwebs in every corner, don't think it's been cleaned in five years. But from what your team of guys and girls have done up at the school, a good clean, a new paint job, and I reckon it's ready for fit out."

Michael thought for a moment.

"Okay so Unwin are we looking at bank finance? I think we would be starting to become an acceptable risk for a bank with what we have done at the school plus speaking to George Purcell we are starting to get a few funds built up in the kitty from the church services."

"Might be able to go one better Michael," replied Unwin.

"No problem with a bank loan for the full amount, one of my friends in Rotary is a bank manager," interjected Patty.

"Who would have known," Unwin replied grinning.

"That's good we'll need that…but here's something else."

"I was talking to George yesterday as to how the tithes and offerings are going after Patty gave me wind of this. George mentioned that when he was visiting Evelyn Robinson the other day Ian had mentioned that he had a sizeable amount of cash he wanted to give to the community as a legacy from Evelyn, you know in her memory."

"Apparently he is very impressed with the school and in particular Archie, and said that if we were looking at any special projects and could come up with a reasonable proposal to him as to how we would use the money, he was open to making a donation."

"I believe Ian was offering it knowing that we would have to extend the classroom soon. Usually for most Sunday meetings, because of Evelyn, he arrives after the service has started when there is only standing room on the verandah. According to George Ian had said he noticed we are outgrowing the space needed for our Sunday meetings."

"So do we know what kind of dollars he is looking at?" queried Michael.

"Asked George the same question and he believed depending on the need of the project that Ian indicated he might go anywhere up to fifty grand."

"Whew…what other word is there for that news," replied Michael, "whew…fifty grand."

Unwin grinned, "you're right."

He continued.

"So if Ian donates the fifty then we have the deposit covered."

"We will bank finance the rest," he turned to Patty, "with the help of Patty's rotary contact."

"Not forgetting also that my lease payment for the clinic upstairs in the dress circle will pretty much cover the initial repayment of the loan until we build up more funds to pay it out."

Michael continued.

"Okay…this sounds good…now I'm getting excited."

"How about I get in touch with George and he and I go and have a visit with Ian. I try to get to see Evelyn once a month, Ian likes me to pray for her, and so I'm due for a visit anyway. We can have a talk with him after I spend time with her."

"Yes I reckon that's the next step," replied Unwin looking at Patty, "what do you think?"

"You got me Mikey," replied Patty, "that sounds good."

"Any questions boys?" continued Patty.

Unwin got up to leave, "no…all good…got to get back to the clinic… so it's done?"

"Done."

"So Michael when do you think you might see Ian?"

"I'll give George a ring this arvo."

"Okay...let me know how you go will you...I'm getting excited?

Can't you see the sign emblazoned across the front of the theatre, Springfield Christian Church?"

"Just one more thing guys," said Patty as he stood up to leave.

"If it comes off the papers will be all over it. I mean it's the town's original old Imperial Theatre, it has a lot of history and people will be talking."

"So I'm not getting involved with anything to do with the purchase. I would not like this discussion we just had to go public, you know re the reserve price, if you know what I mean…the old insider trading look."

"I'm suggesting Michael that you do the bidding at the auction on behalf of the commune and Unwin you tag along so there's agreement on how high we go."

"But take it from me if you don't have any rogue bidders, and I don't think you will, since my contacts tell me the current owners got knocked back on a redevelopment application, something to do with proposed heritage listing, you'll get it for two fifty."

"You guys okay with that?"

"Sure Patty sure," came the joint reply.

⸺ ∞ ⸺

"Good Morning, and how's our girl today?"

"Not too bad Elsie," Ian replied sounding a little tired.

"A few tears this morning when I fed her some scrambled eggs, but that happens quite often. She's just too tired to do anything I think."

"That's normal Ian, just part of the progression. Don't let it get to you," returned Elsie.

"But I did catch her staring at me for a moment Elsie even though she was cranky, so I think she knows me and knows I'm just trying to help her, I hope so."

"I'm sure you're right Ian," Elsie whispered as she gently laid her hand on his shoulder.

It was normal, as Elsie had said, and was part of the progression of the disease for the patient to get irritable or upset if they failed at something, or to become angry or distressed through frustration. Elsie had seen it many times before in other homes she had visited in her twenty odd years as a Blue Nurse.

Ian Robinson had always been an optimist. People had suggested that this was one of the reasons he had been so successful in business, and he had been the eternal optimist for many years since Evelyn's diagnosis.

But lately he had been conditioning his mind to accept that one day he would lose his beloved Evie and he wanted to make sure that she was not just buried and forgotten after she passed. He wanted to do something that would in the years to come cause people to remember her even for just a moment, and the beautiful kind and generous soul that she was. He had discussed this with George Purcell on a few occasions.

George was unable to attend the meeting but had contacted Ian and arranged an appointment for Michael with him to discuss what they all now called Evelyn's legacy, only giving Ian a little information in that it would be something that could be officially dedicated to Evelyn. He would leave it with Michael to discuss the project and the immediate sensitivities in ensuring no information was leaked.

"Elsie dear could you do me a favour?"

"Sure Ian sure."

"I have a colleague coming around in about fifteen minutes to discuss something with me. It's about a legacy I want Evie to leave. You know Elsie something to remember her by. I don't want people to forget my sweetheart."

"Could you stay for an extra fifteen minutes if I need it. I don't think it will take long but just in case the discussion goes past your visit time?"

"Sure Ian sure…that won't be a problem."

"How about I spend ten minutes reading one of her Stephen G. Tallentyre books, you told me that that's her favourite author and that she loves her attitude to life. I know you read to her at night but would that be okay?"

Stephen G. Tallentyre was Evelyn's favourite author. But the author's name was really a pseudonym. The actual author was Evelyn Beatrice Hall best known for her biography The Life of Voltaire. Evelyn Robinson had always admired the writer's philosophy of life, which led to her loving the author's books. It was simple. Evelyn Beatrice Hall believed in the innate goodness of humanity. She believed that there is more goodness in the world than there appears to be, but people don't recognize it, because goodness is of its very nature modest and retiring. In most cases it doesn't jump out at you and say, look at me, look at me. Elsie was right. Evelyn loved not only the author's books but the humanity of the author as well.

"That would be lovely Elsie…thank you…you are very kind," replied Ian.

⚬⚬⚬

Michael paused, leaning with his hands against the rail of his balcony, taking in an early morning look at the view from his hilltop apartment. He breathed in the fresh salty crispness in the air. It was 8 a.m. There was a low lying mist hovering over the river like a protective umbrella as the trawler boats slowly chugged their way down the river heading home.

He thought about the different lives people lead. About how the working day of those faithful fishermen was almost over and the lives of so many others were just waking up to a new day. He thought about Ian Robinson who he was about to go and visit on the way to his office in Springfield, and about the conversations that had occurred between them since he had first met Ian during the schoolhouse tour last November.

Michael had been very touched by Ian's situation and his dedication to his wife and as the Pastor of the work had decided to visit with Ian and Evelyn at least once a month to give them both some pastoral support. It would be after visiting with Evelyn and the laying on of hands in prayer that Michael would spend time with Ian, having tea and conversation seated at the wrought iron table setting in the outdoor area just outside of Evelyn's bedroom.

It was because of Evelyn's love for roses that Ian had arranged with his son, in the building of the apartment block, the inclusion of a semi-circular enclosed and covered patio area, paved with cobblestones and surrounded by a garden of roses, with a white latticed background, directly outside Evelyn's bedroom.

Over the few years since its construction Ian had on their wedding anniversary every June purchased a new brand of rose and, under Evelyn's watchful eye from her bed, planted it in celebration of the event. He felt she knew what he was doing. It was in this garden setting over a cup of tea in those times of conversation, midst the fragrance of the roses, that Michael got to know the true character of the man Ian Robinson and the strong balanced measure of optimism and wisdom that he possessed.

When people spoke about him the two adjectives that were most commonly used were beautiful and optimistic, but Ian was also a very humble man. He didn't recognize this thing called optimism in himself no matter how much others continually verbalized it. To him this optimism they spoke of was just a natural part of him, built into his DNA, something he had been born with, not a special character quality.

When Evelyn's visitors would commend him on his positive attitude he would humbly put it down to being nothing special, it was just in his genes.

"Got it from my daddy," he would say, "he went through the Great Depression. They were tough times for people all around the world, but he didn't cave. My daddy had a favourite expression that has stayed with me to this day. He would say Ian, when the going gets tough…the tough get going."

Michael recalled as he walked slowly to his car when he too had complimented Ian on his optimism and positive attitude and Ian had said to him:

"Michael my Daddy used to say that there are two things you can do when times get tough. You can just get up and go or you can lie down and die."

And as for his accumulated wealth in his life long career Ian would always put it down to the involvement of two components in his activities, the two g's as he called them, God and good luck.

"Pastor Michael...lovely to see you," came Ian's greeting as he opened the door.

"Evelyn's with Elsie from the Blue Nurses, so I thought we might talk first and pray later. I've made some tea."

"Come through I want to show you something."

Ian led Michael out into the rose garden and over to the far corner.

"Have a look at this...isn't it beautiful?"

"It's the latest rose I've bought for my Evie for our wedding anniversary this month."

"What do you think?"

"I purchased it as a bush in early bloom from the nursery last week."

It was a beautiful rose bush, with sumptuous large flowers of glowing apricot tones on it, all giving off an outstanding fragrance. Each flower was a giant in size, an apricot coloured flower of double full bloom and a shallow saucer like shape with numerous small petals inter-twined within it.

"It's beautiful, I haven't seen one that colour before, what is it called?"

"It is beautiful Michael isn't it?"

"I had to get it for Evie as soon as I saw it."

"It's named after one of the owners of an American company who use natural botanical ingredients in their skin care products. The petals of this one are used in a particular line of rose perfume that they manufacture."

"You might have heard of the company Crabtree and Evelyn?"

"Yes...I have...I've seen their products in stores usually around Christmas time."

"Well this rose is called the Evelyn Rose...isn't that perfect?"

"An Evelyn rose for my Evelyn."

"It is Ian…it's more than perfect."

"Now you know why I bought it Michael."

"Michael you know it's a wonderful world, you can never have too much beauty around you."

Michael stared at the rose for a second and thought about Ian's last words, it's a wonderful world, you can never have too much beauty around you. He thought in the minute of the beautiful song released by Louis Armstrong some two years earlier What A Wonderful World, and reaffirmed in his mind once again as so many others had done, what a wonderful optimist Ian Robinson was.

"Come Michael…let's sit, have some tea, and talk about your proposal."

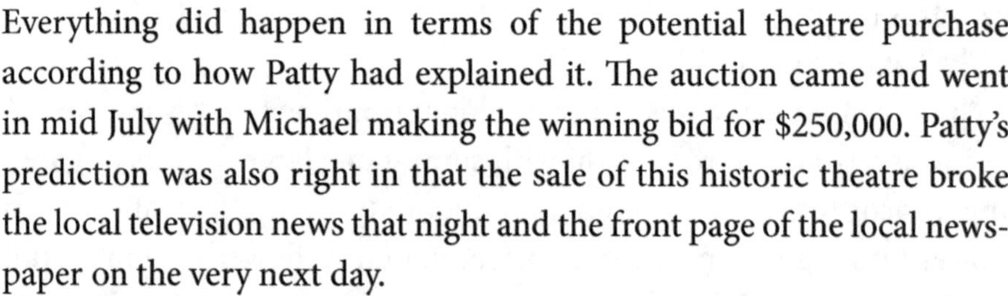

Everything did happen in terms of the potential theatre purchase according to how Patty had explained it. The auction came and went in mid July with Michael making the winning bid for $250,000. Patty's prediction was also right in that the sale of this historic theatre broke the local television news that night and the front page of the local newspaper on the very next day.

The next four weeks waiting for settlement saw Michael and Jeffrey put a plan into place that over the ensuing couple of months would see a team of weekday and weekend volunteers bring the tired and sick building back into a state of remission. A host of selfless workers, some who regularly attended the commune's Sunday services and some just interested friends of theirs, swarmed on the historic old building with an unbridled enthusiasm.

Under Jeffrey Gibbons supervision a myriad of builders, carpenters, painters, electricians, and a host of volunteer labourers male and female, saw the building restored to its former glory.

If scaffolding was needed to fix damaged plaster on the walls someone knew someone who could provide. If a scissor lift was needed to repaint the interior ceiling due to its extreme height someone knew someone who had one. If a telescopic crane was needed to suspend two painters in a basket to paint the exterior facade and hang signage someone knew someone who could deliver.

The interior was recarpeted and the original marble floor entrance lobby that had been covered for years with straw matting glued onto it was cleaned and restored to its original state. A crèche was built and the walls inside adorned with colourful Disney characters hand painted by one of Zelda's talented and gifted hippie neighbours, Rayanne, who painted her perfect cartoon characters merely by referring to some Disney children's picture books.

Included in the enthusiastic group of volunteers was a lone bee farmer, a tinkerer, one Bernie Eagleton, a neighbour of Janet and Jeffrey Gibbons and the man responsible for building the grain-grinding machine housed in Dr Unwin Nicholls' barn.

It would be as Unwin and Michael were walking around outside the back of the building on a Saturday afternoon, as the day's working bee was just wrapping up, that the subject of the non-functioning archaic air-conditioning unit housed in a separate small building at the back of the theatre came up.

"Let's check this out Unwin…we really need some cooling factor in the building during summer and I don't think those huge fans they used at The Markets would do the job if people are in the building for two or three hours on a hot summer Sunday," commented Michael.

As they entered the inside of the fifteen metre square solid cement building they were greeted by a couple of water tanks, a mass of wheels, pulleys, and piping, and a lot of rust and cobwebs.

"You're right we need to do something," replied Unwin, "and if any-one can get this going it will be Bernie Eagleton."

"Bernie the Beekeeper you mean Unwin."

"That's right Michael…it's a job for Bernie the Beekeeper," quipped Unwin doing a rather credible impersonation of Maxwell Smart from the current television series Get Smart.

Michael grinned and Unwin was right.

Bernie the Beekeeper, a man with a good heart and hands, over a few weeks was able to bring to life this huge and archaic air-conditioning unit, a museum piece, one of its kind, which had been sitting unused in a cement building out the back of the theatre for years, and restore it to its former cold air generating glory.

After three months with the final touch ups being completed, a sound and lighting system being installed, deep red carpeting, three hundred blue coloured fold back seats brought in, which only filled half the auditorium, and a carved wooden pulpit courtesy of Bernie Eagleton, the team was almost finished.

Within a couple more weeks after a bookshop at the side of the entrance lobby had been set up, one of Dr Nicholls black baby grand pianos placed on the platform and a small water baptismal tank installed under the elevated stage, the auditorium was ready to open.

The historic building that had been neglected and discarded for so long was renewed and turned into a meeting place, a crèche, a bookshop and a place of worship for a group of believers who fate and destiny had so beautifully and almost magically brought together. Old things had passed away and all things had become new.

On Saturday 6th November the official opening was held. It would be the Reverend Terry Channing who, having been invited by Michael as the official guest speaker, stood in the auditorium entrance alongside many of the township's dignitaries and a crowd of the commune members to unveil the small copper and gold plaque on the entrance wall.

A plaque which simply read:

"Springfield Christian Church. Evelyn Auditorium. Officially opened November 1971. Celebrating the life of Evelyn Robinson. There is always more goodness in the world than there appears to be, because goodness is of its very nature modest and retiring."

At the base of the plaque was a small etching of an Evelyn rose.

It would be approximately four weeks later in the silence of a Saturday evening when, with Michael present, with her family standing heads bowed around her bedside, and with Ian gently stroking her hand, Evelyn Robinson quietly slipped away and commenced her journey home.

It was late afternoon on Christmas Day 1971 when Michael leaned back in his recliner chair on his balcony, took a sip of wine, and thought about the year that had so quickly passed. It had been a relaxing day for him, he had enjoyed it: a measured break from the frenzy of activity that seemed to have dominated his life over the previous twelve months. He thought about all that had happened, the many happy and exciting moments.

There was the school opening, the purchase of the theatre, and the sprucing up of the old farmhouse in the corner of the property ready for its renovation in 1972 as a development centre for girls, to be headed up by Janet Gibbons and Zelda Westwood.

Plus there was the successful approval by the eldership of four applications to build homes on the property, submitted by George and Jenny Purcell, Thorpey and Cherie Goldway, Garret and Bettina Sloan and a retired couple, friends of the Purcells, Dave and Thelma Rogerson.

Not forgetting the odd sad time including the emotional funeral service that was conducted by Michael for Evelyn Robinson, which saw hundreds of coloured balloons float across the skyscape of the property into the heavens above.

Yes, Michael thought as he leaned back, much had happened in a very fast paced 1971 including one of his own personal favourites: the commencement of a once a week thirty-minute radio programme hosted by himself named Morning Has Broken. Radio time that had been brokered for him by Shaun Cliffe, their church drummer, who worked at the district's radio station as their breakfast programme host.

But there was one other thing that was central in Michael's thinking this Christmas afternoon as he reflected on the year past and contemplated the year ahead, the start of his third year in Springfield.

It was a meeting that he had been called to at head office in the city some two weeks earlier when he had been told that he would be pulled out of Springfield for a period of around twelve months to head up a new project in a farming district on the Hinterland Coast about one hour's drive to the north of the capital city.

Whilst being disappointed initially at having to be separated for a while from the commune, Michael was encouraged by the considerate attitude of his employer who was aware of his involvement in the commune or what they described in the meeting as his binding ties to the community.

For this reason it was generously written into his new contract by his boss that he be given a three day weekend break at the end of each month to enable him to travel down to Springfield to fulfill his commitments there should he so desire. The contract was due to start the first week of February 1972.

As he sat quietly on his balcony he thought about the future impacts his separation might have on the commune and how his twelve-month absence from everyday involvement would be handled. He wanted to be sure that it created no disquiet and for this reason he had told no one except Archie, Jeff and Janet.

Michael glanced at his watch. It was nearing 6 p.m. and Jeff and Janet would be arriving soon. He and Jeff had decided to get together in the evening to discuss any processes that needed to be put in place to manage the commune in Michael's absence. It would be Jeffrey then who would verbalize these ideas as his own at the next eldership meeting after Michael had announced his twelve month recall.

Jeffrey had been honest when Michael had shared about the recall with him. He was extremely concerned about the potential for Garret Sloan to exert his influence over the affairs of the commune in Michael's absence. As it would eventually turn out Jeffrey's intuition was right. This particular game in Lila was just about to get serious.

303

66 *"I know I was criticized by a few of the die-hard Pentecostals for using Cat Stevens song Morning Has Broken as my opening theme because of his leaning towards the Muslim religion, but the youngies like it...goodness it's number one on the hit parade charts...it's a beautiful song...it's a song of praise."*

Michael Winton

The Countdown

THIRTEEN

"**K**nock knock…can we come in?" came the friendly female voice through the screen door.

"Guys…sure…of course…come in."

"Hey Jeffrey, and my favourite fiancée of my favourite friend, come in…Merry Christmas."

"Merry Christmas brother," Jeffrey shook Michael's hand and headed straight for the balcony.

"Gonna miss this place…one last look at the view."

"Not half as much as I am," replied Michael.

Janet hugged Michael and kissed him on the cheek.

"And not half as much as we are going to miss you Michael," she said, "Merry Christmas."

Jeffrey turned around and came back inside.

"Yes but think about all the fun we're going to have when Michael turns up late once a month on a Friday night looking for a bed…dog tired after a hard working week and a long drive," Jeffrey grinned.

"So Michael, any chance of getting this apartment again when you come back in 12 months?"

"Don't think so mate, unfortunately. I spoke to Patty the other day and he said he had a couple ready to sign a lease."

"I think he said they move in the week after I go."

"Arch not coming round tonight?" Janet queried.

"No I'm seeing her tomorrow night…she's flat out with her Greek Christmas and getting ready for the new school year…and anyway it suits as I wanted to see you two guys alone just to nut out a few things."

"So, who's for a glass of your red and a final sit on the balcony?"

"I'm in," replied Janet, opening the kitchen cupboard door, I'll get the glasses."

"And I'll pour," replied Jeff reaching for the bottle of red they had brought with them.

<hr>

"I'm going to so miss this view too," Janet said with an almost sad expression as she leant on the balcony rail and gazed out over the river and the glow of the Lighthouse Bay tourist strip in the distance. There was a full moon, a very large full moon it seemed, and it was reflecting on the river sending out sprays of bright silvery lines.

"It's just so beautiful," she continued.

"I'm gonna miss this squatter's chair," replied Jeffrey as he stretched into its canvas surrounds, "it's more beautiful."

Jeffrey loved Michael's chair and had always made a dive to get it first when the group had met each month, on occasions having to deal with a bit of competition from Danny as they jostled each other playfully.

"Do you remember that song Michael," Janet sang the first line of the song By the Light of the Silvery Moon, "that's what this view reminds me of."

Michael sat back in his chair and took a sip of wine enjoying his friends company.

"I do Janny, one of my mum's favourite songs, Doris Day sang it."

Janet had a sweet sounding folksy voice. They all did Michael thought. Pretty well all the girls in the group were not only musically talented but had sweet sounding voices. Well except for Mags who didn't seem to have a lot of interest in music.

He was going to miss their singing.

"So we're all good Pastor...I think we've got all our bases covered. I'll keep you up to date of any goings on...I'll give you a ring once a week."

"Thanks Jeffrey…yes the commune has got a few things happening in the next twelve months."

"Sure has," replied Jeffrey.

"I've decided we'll start with the farmhouse renovation for the girls around February, and then midway through the year probably late July I reckon we'll be ready to start building the new separate admin block beside the school."

"I think I told you we are going to use materials on it to tone in with the look of the schoolhouse, so it all blends into that sense of old worldliness, you know, the charm of another era."

"You're such a romantic babe," Janet chimed in.

"Yes and a creative romantic at that," chirped Jeff as he continued.

"That frees up the current lunchroom and admin at opposite ends of the schoolhouse to be turned into classroom space."

"Yes I like your design of that Jeffrey."

"So the new admin cottage is a reception area, three offices, and a long room along the back for the telephone counselling ministry?" queried Janet.

"Yes and it's a counselling room at night only and a lunchroom for the school staff during the day."

"Should work well Jeff…you're a genius."

"Yes…hopefully Michael, and Danny boy is going to put in all the wiring for the phones…two lines in and a further four extensions."

"Hey Michael," Jeff continued, "I meant to tell you, you'll love this."

"I was shooting the breeze with Morty the other afternoon. He was up at the school for the PTA meeting and I happened to mention about the telephone counselling services we were starting up."

"And he said have you got any business type cards about it cobber?"

"And I said, no, not really cobber, why?"

"He calls me cobber…I call him cobber back…it's fun."

Michael grinned.

"And he said well mate after about ten o'clock on Friday and Saturday nights Morty's gets quite a few patrons in who are emotionally out there type of people, or as I call them, yobbos with probbos…ya know wanting to cry on my shoulder…looking for some paternal advice."

"And I was thinkin', rather than just saying bugger off and turfing them out, I could be charitable, I could give them your card and they could phone you for help."

Michael laughed, "that's Morty."

"But if he's serious it's not a bad thought…you know to advertise the service."

"I like Morty. Hey Michael I think it was a great idea putting Jenny Purcell in charge of the telephone counselling team …she so loves to help people."

"She does Janny."

Jeff took a sip of wine.

"Jack Wainwright is loaning us a couple of his boys gratis to work a few days a week on it for a few weeks. I figure that, plus with a couple of working bees all hands on deck, we should see our new admin block up and running after about eight weeks, which will make it around mid October at the latest ready to go."

"And Michael go with me on this. When it's almost finished I'll casually point out to Sloan which office is slightly bigger than the others. He will choose it for himself, his ego will make sure of that, but it's all good. I've arranged on the plan for the bigger office to face the hot afternoon western sun."

"Don't want him spending every afternoon in there having tea and tickle sessions."

"Jeffrey, stop it," interjected Janny, "that's naughty."

Michael grinned. Even though it came across as a joke he knew that Jeffrey was serious.

He changed the subject.

"So…and you're alright Jeffrey doing the radio show for me…keep it simple you know…short punchy messages intermingled with good music…and it doesn't have to be all church hymns…other secular music preferably something with a message though can be included."

"I know I was criticized by a few of the die-hard Pentecostals for using Cat Stevens song Morning Has Broken as my opening theme because of his leaning towards the Muslim religion, but the youngies like it…goodness it's number one on the hit parade charts…it's a beautiful song…it's a song of praise for every new day."

"You're right Michael," continued Jeffrey.

"It's modern very current and has a relevant spiritual message. His religious brand is unimportant, it's his message that counts."

"And another song I was thinking of using…you'd know it Michael… came out a few years ago…a good message to it…Barry McGuire's Eve of Destruction."

"Ah yes…bring back my Woodstock days."

"I love that song babe," chimed in Janet.

"So you're all good with that mate?" Michael asked.

"Yep I'm all good with that," replied Jeff, "and Danny boy has offered to do the controls and manage the turntable for me so it's all good."

"Thanks Jeffrey…I appreciate that."

Jeffrey continued.

"Once we start work on renovating the old farmhouse for the girls centre, it shouldn't take long, with four building contractors in the fellowship now and we've got these weekend working bees down to a fine art…well I reckon…about four or five weeks and we can knock it over."

"And thank you Michael for giving me the girls farmhouse ministry…I can't wait to get started on a new challenge."

"Hey you're welcome Janny…I think you'll do a great job."

It would be mid January 1972 when Michael conducted his final Sunday service in the downtown auditorium before his departure, and although he was not leaving on a permanent basis there was enough emotion in the auditorium on that night for anyone to believe that he was. Some firm friendships had been forged and many allegiances struck up over the two years of the evolution of the commune.

New Year's Eve had been spent with Kelly, Judy, Archie, Archie's brother Peter, Jeffrey and Janet, and Danny and Zelda at the local Returned Serviceman's Club. It was Kelly who suggested they do this, to give the group some farewell time together with Michael. Margie was spending New Year with her parents and sister Francis back home in Gratton.

The club's New Year's Eve party, apart from the fireworks in the park, was Lighthouse Bay's main New Year's Eve party venue. It had become traditional for Archie's parents Aurelia and Makis to book a table for her family for a night of partying and dancing. Makis had long since lost his enthusiasm for tripping the light fantastic. He preferred the traditional Greek New Year activity of playing cards or rolling dice, but would go along albeit reluctantly.

Aware that Aurelia and Makis would be attending the same venue, Kelly had through a friend who worked at the RSL secured a booking for a table of eight situated on the opposite side of the room from where Archie's parents would be. She knew this would give Archie more freedom to relax.

"Heads up guys…here's the deal," announced Kelly as they took their seats at the table.

"You are all tonight allocated a specific forty five minutes or round about of what we will call snog duty watch."

"What's snog duty watch?" queried Zelda.

"Okay for those of you poor deprived souls uninitiated in the pastime of snogging let me explain…and listen carefully," continued Kelly.

"Snogging in layman or laywoman's terms is the word used when a couple, a male and female, start to get a little amorous with each other."

"Now before I continue, does anyone of you loved starved people have trouble understanding the word amorous?"

"No…okay…I shall continue."

"During your forty five minutes on duty you are to be alert if at any time during those forty five minutes Arch and young Mikey fall into a snogging position."

"If you observe this to be happening you are to immediately cast your gaze across to the far side of the room, the corner table, visible through the crowd only by standing up, and check that Archie's parents are both firmly seated in their chairs."

"Now we know her dad being Greek would rather be playing cards than doing a twinkle toes on the dance floor so it is highly unlikely that he will be standing."

"However…and I do stress…however…we must be open to all possibilities that at some stage of the night he or Aurelia might want to stretch their legs…and wander over to us."

"If they appear to be heading over this way you will call out the words…snog alert…snog alert, that's snog not smog. Don't say smog as you will get all the trawler fisherman in close proximity agitated, and Arch you and cutie pie here at the call will immediately cease and desist your snogging."

"Got it…okay…here's the roster."

"Danny boy you're on first."

Everyone laughed.

During the night as Kelly had predicted Archie had found it slightly difficult to relax totally with Michael, her parents being seated in the same room. Archie had told her mother that she would be there with a few friends, not on a specific date. She was slightly more relieved when she saw her mother taking photos of her and Michael on the dance floor during the night.

"Mum seems okay," Archie whispered in Michael's ear as they slow danced to the D.J. playing the song MacArthur Park.

"I just saw her taking a photo of us."

"Maybe she is just gathering evidence Arch, think about that."

"Yeah right," Archie laughed, "hadn't thought of that."

"Michael don't be naughty…I am hoping she is happy I am having a good time."

"Are you having a good time Michael?"

"I am."

"I always have a good time when I'm with you."

Archie pressed her cheek against Michael's and softly sang in his ear; MacArthur Park is melting in the dark, all the sweet green icing flowing down.

"It's funny Michael isn't it how most people either love that song or hate it."

"Yes…you're right. I think that those who don't like it probably get frustrated because they don't understand what it means."

"They're strange but kind of haunting words Michael aren't they?"

"I wonder what Jimmy Webb meant when he wrote them?"

"I have heard a variety of theories but I can tell you another one which sounds pretty feasible," Michael returned.

"Sure."

"That album of his songs sung by Richard Harris which you gave me last Christmas had a pamphlet in it that told a little about each song and how Jimmy Webb came to write them."

"Did it really?"

"Yes."

"Cool."

"With the song MacArthur Park it said that when Jimmy Webb lived in Los Angeles he was in love with a girl and quite regularly they used to go for walks in MacArthur Park. They had been going steady for a couple of years and one day as they are seated on a park bench in the spur of the moment she proposed to him."

"He was unsure whether he wanted to take that serious step into marriage so he didn't say yes which to her meant no. So thinking he might not want a long term future with her she started going out with someone else who was keen on her and seemed more stable, and eventually she married him."

"So MacArthur Park is where he lost her?" queried Archie.

"Apparently."

"After they had broken up he often goes back to MacArthur Park and sits on the same bench where they had sat together and thinks of what he's lost with thoughts of regret."

"MacArthur Park is where he lost his true love."

"The words of the song speak of how he watches the old men playing checkers by the trees as they had done together so many times."

"And the cake melting away is their wedding cake, which symbolizes a life together that they would never have: the wedding cake of life that he would never get to taste with her and never have that recipe or chance again."

"So I suppose that's why there is a sort of hidden sadness in the words and tune," Archie whispered.

"Yes I guess so…anyway that's what the pamphlet said…I presume it's true."

Archie held Michael close.

"Sad Michael…sad."

"I suppose not all fairy tales have a happy ending."

"I suppose not my precious."

Archie fitted her face into the curve of his shoulder and pressed her body against his, filling her lungs with the scent of him and softly whispered, "it's que sera sera Michael."

"Whatever will be will be Archie."

"Happy New Year Michael."

"Happy New Year Archie."

The month of January went quickly. Archie had spent the last few weeks of January preparing for the new school year, and Michael had spent time tidying up loose ends at his workplace and handing over the reins to his assistant who would be his twelve-month management replacement at the Co-Op.

The eldership had met and decided to give the responsibility for oversight of the church and related activities in Michael's absence to the Reverend Garret Sloan, much to the disdain of Jeffrey Gibbons, whilst Archie would have oversight over the school, referring any really difficult situations to Sloan for guidance.

Based on the admonition given to Michael by the Reverend William Hawkesbury to watch Garret Sloan, Jeffrey and Michael had made an arrangement to catch up on things during Michael's once a month sleepover at the Gibbons' home. But should anything arise relating to Garret Sloan that was of serious concern to Jeffrey, in reality or just intuitively, Jeffrey should immediately phone Michael and share it with him.

It would be on the first Saturday in February that Michael stood on his balcony for what he suspected would probably be the last time and there were mixed emotions. A sort of happiness for all that had happened there but accompanied with a tinge of sadness, as he knew his time in this apartment was over. It has been a wonderful two years he thought.

The day was starting to wind down, it was mid afternoon and some trawlers eager for an early catch had already commenced their ritual chug up the river, with the sound of the ships horns taking Michael's mind into a brief moment of reflection.

He thought about everything that had happened in this his home over the previous two years, but especially his time in it with Archie: his coffee date at the Plaka Café in the morning, followed by that event filled first paddleboat ride in the afternoon and the wonderful alone time they had together that first evening.

Their walk in the rain back to his apartment after the ride, the cosiness of the fire, the comfortable and relaxed conversation over a wine as they got to know each other, and the way she felt as he held her in a goodnight embrace.

He thought about their group gatherings, the music, the laughter and the fun and adventure spent in a conversational exploration of life with these his newly found like minded friends, and how the idea of the commune was birthed on this balcony.

Michael considered himself an amateur poet of sorts and over the years in moments of melancholy he had put his poetic pen to work, sometimes successfully and sometimes quite unsuccessfully. As he thought about all the good things that had happened in this apartment his mind flitted to the last line from the first poem of love he had written on a Christmas Day many years ago and he was aware that it applied so very much to this time right now. "For everything that passes…something beautiful remains."

He thought of his slow dance to the song MacArthur Park with Archie on New Year's Eve and how this apartment and the love, bonds of friendship and new adventure that it brought was surely the beautiful cake with all its sweet green icing: a cake representing a time now passed and a unique recipe for peace and contentment, the like of which he might never experience again.

But it was time to go. Michael slowly walked to his car and tossed the last of his personal belongings into the boot. He came back inside the apartment for one last long look around this home he had come to love. He knew he was stalling; it really was time to go.

Michael closed the door behind him, double-checked to ensure it was locked, paused for a moment, then drove to Patty Patel's Real Estate office, dropped the keys off, and slowly set his course for the city, quietly thinking in the moment…que sera sera.

66 *"Michael, Garret Sloan has got no moral compass, we need to accept that, and in our acceptance acknowledge that he has got to be stopped and he will be stopped."*

Reverend Terry Channing

The Ordination

FOURTEEN

"Good Morning Michael, God bless you," came the warm greeting from behind as Michael quietly browsed the books in the Christian City Church bookstore on his first Sunday morning back in the city. He turned around slightly startled by the loud cheery voice seemingly coming out of nowhere. It was the Reverend Terry Channing. He shook Michael's hand.

"Welcome back to the big smoke."

"Settled in okay?"

"Yes I have thanks Terry."

"I've got a small apartment quite close to here, and it's only about an hour's drive to work up the coast each day."

"Yes," returned Terry, "I heard about your move through George Purcell actually."

"Right."

"Yes he gave our church treasurer Tom Parish a ring the other day, something to do with the upcoming end of year financial returns, your work being a registered charity. Tom said George had mentioned about your move and what was happening down there."

"Michael, if you don't mind me asking, how do you feel about Garret Sloan looking after church business in your absence?"

"Well it was an eldership decision not mine personally Terry." "Let's just say a couple of the elders had some apprehension."

"Would you be one of them Michael?"

"Yes myself and Jeffrey Gibbons."

"But Terry purely based on a conversation I had with Bill Hawkesbury."

"Hmm Jeffrey…yes I like Jeffrey. He seems a straight shooter," replied Terry whilst pausing as if in thought as to how he should phrase the discussion further, since they were both standing in a public place.

"Yes he is Terry…he is pretty intuitive about things and people."

"And what caused your apprehension might I ask?"

"Terry the jury's out on the full reason why, I don't know, there's just something about him. I'm not sure, but I know Jeffrey doesn't totally trust his motives in this sudden interest he has in the commune and I trust Jeffrey."

"You know Terry, Sloan's certainly not a person who you could imagine would embrace any kind of hippie lifestyle or be an advocate of a new way of educating children or for that matter any of the overall objectives of the commune apart from the church."

"He seems to be more focussed on how big a church could be built, you know, the numbers."

"Sure…I understand," replied Terry, "in this Charismatic movement there's a lot of Pastors coming out of the woodwork with that kind of ego driven agenda."

"To some it's no longer about a passion for saving souls as they espouse, it's just the agenda they push to fill more seats and build the church coffers and their own personal financial standing."

"There's a lot of questionable activity like that happening in the Charismatic Movement in the States. Mega churches popping up everywhere."

"So…Bill Hawkesbury passed my brief message on to you about Sloan."

"He did…but I wasn't aware it was from you Terry."

"Well it was from both Bill and I actually. We both agreed that you needed to be alerted about Sloan, more so now since we heard you were being transferred for twelve months."

"Just a quick question Michael," Terry continued.

"What do you think about Unwin Nicholls?"

"He seems a pretty good guy."

"Hmm…right," Terry paused.

"Bill tells me he's pretty focussed, almost over focussed you could say on end time theories, you know the so called doomsday stuff. He apparently asks Bill a lot of questions when Bill goes down there to preach."

"Right," replied Michael. "I am aware he has an interesting library in his office and some sustainable living lifestyle habits, but apart from that I don't know anything."

"Right," Terry paused, "right."

"You know he and Sloan go back a long time. At least five or six years or so?"

"No I wasn't aware."

"Oh yes. Over the years when Sloan would come back to the office here after one of his crusades he would always mention that his good friend, as he calls him, Dr Unwin Nicholls takes him out to dinner every time he is in Springfield."

"I got curious so I told my secretary who is seated alongside him in the office to casually ask the question when the subject came up again as to how long he had known Dr Nicholls."

"She did and he said that he first met him around 1964 when Dr Nicholls got saved at one of his tent meetings."

"Interesting," Terry paused thoughtfully again, "interesting."

Terry glanced at his watch.

"Oh Michael, and one other thing, how well do you know the Morrison family?"

"You mean Dr Margie Morrison?"

"Well I mean the family in general. You know her parents Jim and Thelma too?"

"It's just that I had a call from a friend who pastors a charismatic church in Gratton, you know a couple of hours south of you."

"Right."

"The Morrison family used to attend his church before they moved to Springfield…well I think one of the daughters who is studying still attends but is intending to move to Springfield when she graduates."

"He mentioned that a few older couples in his church, retired couples, had approached him for advice."

"They are apparently being influenced by the Morrison family to sell up and move to Springfield. Jim Morrison is apparently telling them that your church in Springfield is going to be the hub for the Charismatic Movement in the district and the best place to be to see God's unfolding work in the state."

"They're using the term for your church…a spiritual lighthouse."

"Right," replied Michael, "very original."

"Yes I do remember Terry that when I first met Margie at a Carols by Candlelight she mentioned her parents were moving up and her sister Francis was still living in their house in Gratton and would stay there until she graduated. So I believe she's moving to Springfield pretty soon, probably as soon as they sell the family home. She graduated this year, just finished."

"Not sure what this lighthouse stuff is all about."

"Right Michael…right."

"Well anyway Gary the pastor down there was a bit concerned about people in his church being influenced by Jim Morrison to pack up and move to Springfield. The old numbers game I suppose."

"He also mentioned that when Sloan is in town in Gratton doing his crusades he always stays with the Morrisons. They are very close. The Morrison family is die-hard Pentecostal of Sloan's vintage."

Terry paused again obviously thinking about this.

"Anyway," he continued, "just thought I'd ask you. I told Gary I would. Apparently Sloan still stays at their house when he is in town even though the parents are in Springfield."

"Gary thinks that Margie and Francis are pretty close to him too."

"Interesting you say that," replied Michael, "Margie does get very defensive of Garret Sloan whenever Jeffrey Gibbons raises the question of his credibility. Even if just in a joke."

Terry looked thoughtful.

"Right Michael…right."

Terry paused for a moment in thought and then glanced again at his watch.

"Michael I've got to go. I've got to go to our pre-service prayer room with my pastors. You are welcome to attend if you want or keep browsing…whatever you like."

"You know I'd like to continue this conversation. There are a few things you need to know. How about you and I catch up sometime during the week, you know after your workday finishes. Or we could make it next Saturday morning if it suits?"

"Saturday morning would suit me better Terry. My week days can sometimes drag out into evenings."

"Okay…so say 10 am next Saturday here."

"Suits me fine."

"Great…the bookshop will be open, so just ask and they'll show you to my office."

"Look forward to a chat."

"Bless you Michael." Terry shook hands with him and left.

Michael continued browsing for a few more minutes then paused at the notice board and stand near the exit door. It contained pamphlets about various upcoming church activities. This looks interesting he thought, March 17th a series of mid-week meetings on the Principles of Discipleship and Shepherding from visiting American church leader the Reverend Juan Ortega.

He picked up one of the pamphlets from the stand and headed towards the main auditorium for the church service, passing William Hawkesbury on his way. They shook hands as they passed.

"Michael…God bless you brother…gotta keep going…off to the prayer room."

"Good to see you Michael…and I'll catch up with you next Saturday at your meeting with Terry…I just passed him, he said we were getting together…gotta rush."

⸻ ∞ ⸻

The following week passed swiftly as Michael settled into his new work routine. It was an hour's drive each way from the city to the Northern District Co-Op. The highway was always extremely busy with commuters who lived at the coast but worked in the city or vice versa. Michael missed the simplicity of his Springfield life and certainly the leisurely fifteen minute drive to his office in downtown Springfield from his apartment in Lighthouse Bay. Saturday morning seemed to come around very quickly.

"Good Morning Terry, Bill, good to see you again."

"Morning Michael…you know Bill of course…and this is my secretary Joyce…she's going to take some notes on what we discuss…please take a seat."

Terry Channing's office was both neat and professionally laid out. In fact Michael thought, everything he had observed about Terry over the last few years, his dress, his precise manner of speech, his conversation no matter how short, his preaching style, everything about Terry Channing came across as professional.

Exuding self-confidence but not in an arrogant way, previously a highly successful businessman having retired as a CEO in the business world of insurance at 65 years of age, it was obvious to Michael that Terry Channing was not in the church for what he could get out of it but rather for what he could give to it.

"Michael I thought it was wise to get together with you as quickly as possible to discuss a few things about the work in Springfield and to pledge my assistance to you should you need it anytime in the future."

"I've included Bill in this discussion as I know you and Bill are good friends and also due to the nature of a couple of things I want to discuss; it's important that you and I have a witness to this conversation."

"And Michael feel free to ask any questions as we talk."

"Okay…let's pray first for wisdom and guidance."

"Right…down to business."

"Firstly Michael I must ask you…are you interested in my personal spiritual oversight of your ministry and the work the commune is doing in Springfield?"

"Not oversight in any authoritarian way but my being available to assist you should you be required to deal with any situation that causes you a bit of uncertainty."

"Of course Terry, I trust you and Bill, and as you know I am pretty new to all this church business. I'm really learning as I go. So any guidance no matter how small would certainly be welcome."

"That's good," replied Terry, "we needed to get that sorted first."

"Michael the reason I've got Bill sitting in on this is so that we are all on the same page. If at anytime something serious comes up regarding your commune and I am overseas, as I do a bit of travel preaching and teaching, then Bill can be your substitute point of contact."

"Michael this church business can at times get a little tricky when it comes to making serious decisions or should I say decisions about serious matters, mostly because of the amount of over inflated egos that get involved in leadership positions. You may have discovered this already. So it will be handy for you not only being able to bounce things off myself and Bill but it also gives you a point of deflection."

"What do you mean deflection Terry?"

"Well Michael most church leaders particularly in the early stages of their ministry fail to understand that their congregations are a conglomeration of walking talking egos, each one at varying levels of intensity. It's exactly the same at the leadership levels in big business. So in some ways we have to use business principles to manage church business. We certainly need to have good people skills and I sense you've got them."

"Thanks."

"Michael people have strong viewpoints and opinions that are powered by strong egos that at times tend to set God aside whilst they promulgate their own personal needs. When you combine this with the strong individual allegiances to particular leaders that people develop in a group environment, things can sometimes get messy when the man at the top has to make a decision that impacts on those ties to a certain leader as they see it in a detrimental way."

"I call it the misguided loyalty factor."

"It happens in every church, it happens in this church."

"I have four pastors and each one of those pastors have followers you might call them, and some of those followers actually accept their every opinion and believe and defend their pastor's every word, right or wrong."

"So if I make a decision that I believe is in the best interests of our church and any one of those leaders vocalizes his disagreement of my decision to his followers, those people with strong allegiances will take it upon themselves to murmur opposition to my decision."

"The Book of Jude, you'll recall Jude was the half brother of Jesus, tells us to be aware of murmurers in the church, complainers, walking after their own lusts and desires because of admiration for a particular person."

"So Michael, back to your question."

"What do I mean by a point of deflection?"

"As your church grows and leadership allegiances form, if you find yourself in a situation after consulting me that you have to make a serious decision that will impact on the egos of some, then use me to deflect their opposition and unreasonable murmurings. Deflect their opposition from yourself by telling them you discussed it with me."

Terry laughed, "sort of like do you remember as kids when we got into trouble with our folks we would point to a fellow sibling and say, 'he started it', well this type of deflection is the adult version."

"You simply say that you discussed it with Terry Channing and God, which if it is something serious no doubt you have, and tell them you were acting on the decision that was reached between the three of you."

"You had a sort of spiritual board meeting with God as the chairperson, you know what I mean."

"It tends to diffuse things very quickly."

"It's like when I was in business if some of the supervisors vocally disagreed with a decision made by my General Manager, and started murmuring, and my GM said well look guys I discussed this with our CEO Terry Channing and this is the decision that was reached, then that short statement has a way of diffusing things quickly."

"You know what I mean," he grinned, "to use business jargon…they tend to pull their heads in pretty quickly."

"But of course I'm only talking about big serious decisions that you know will most likely impact on everyone in your organization. I'm not talking about day to day decisions in the running of things."

"How do you feel about that?"

"No problem with that Terry…that sounds fine with me."

"Good, well we are going to talk about some pretty personal things so I remind us all of the need for complete confidentiality about everything."

"Let's start with Garret Sloan and I'll be blunt."

"Garret Sloan is a functioning member of this church, involved in the administrative side and as a part time preacher and crusade evangelist. We pay him a stipend for his time here and the rest of his salary is funded from his crusade offerings."

"Sloan was put here on three years probation by the Assemblies of God church board for what is described in his file as several unsubstantiated but serious instances of unacceptable behaviour in his involvement in three different churches between 1960 and 1965."

"I believe the subject matter of the allegations and I must stress they are allegations only, which he has continuously denied, were number one sexual, and number two about putting extreme pressure on people for financial donations, and I mean extreme."

"Sloan's defence was that the financial allegations came from those who were disgruntled with his leadership and the allocation of funds to his pet church projects, and that the sexual allegations came from wanton women who made advances to him which he rejected so they reacted against him."

"In his discussion with me he even tried to baffle me with bible verse. He referred to the women involved as the same as mentioned in the Book of Timothy where Timothy describes the presence in the church of weak women, burdened with sin, and led astray by various passions. A total misinterpretation of the word or as we would say in business a complete snow job."

"Timothy was focussing on the behaviour of the men who are themselves possessed by a deviant spirit who give in to their lusts and actually enter the homes of these morally weak women."

"So anyway thus far it's turned out to be a she said he said, and a he said she said. But for the sake of their own credibility the church board had to be seen to be doing something."

"It was a condition of Sloan being allowed to keep his licence to preach under the AOG auspices that he was put here, you'd call it a first warning in the business world. If you put it in law and order terms Sloan is the parolee and I am the probation officer."

"His probation finishes here on June 1st this year."

"Sloan has continually denied the allegations, but my gut feel about these incidents and in reading the testimony of those involved has convinced me he's guilty."

Terry's face showed an expression of seriousness, as did his voice tone.

"I personally believe that sometimes the AOG leadership go to water on things like this, you know frightened of getting sued. And look Michael it's not just the Pentecostal church that we see caught up in this type of stuff, it's been happening in the Catholic and other churches for centuries, not just with women but with children too I might say."

"So many lives and relationships getting forever damaged by these sick individuals and I use that term lightly. I mean some people carry the scars of these incidents with them for decades and decades, some until they die. All of church leadership needs to take a hard line on incidents like this and cut these ministers and priests loose."

"You know Bill I've said to you many times that a day is coming when God will move on this cancer in many churches and these people will be called to atone for their sins."

"But in the meantime let's just focus on our day of atonement for Garret Sloan."

"Michael in doing the Superintendent a favour and becoming Sloan's parole officer I have allowed him to continue with his travelling crusades and given him some involvement in our own church ministry activities. Why only some…because Michael frankly I don't trust allowing him to get too close to individuals in this congregation and I am not yet convinced that he is a reformed character."

"I personally feel the church hierarchy is just shifting a problem but as I said I'm doing a friend a favour. I think they are worried that Sloan would sue them if they took away his licence. Trust me he can be that arrogant. I've seen it many times in conversations we've had. That arrogant Spirit in him can't help itself and rises up and explodes when I push the right buttons."

"Michael, Garret Sloan has got no moral compass, we need to accept that and in our acceptance acknowledge that he has got to be stopped and he will be stopped. The advantage we have though is that righteousness is on our side and the righteous Spirit within us frightens the unrighteous Spirit in him. I can see it in his eyes and hear it in his voice when we speak together. He knows that the Spirit of Goodness will always triumph over The Spirit of Evil."

"Bill wasn't it the Apostle Paul who told us in The Book of Romans not to offer any part of ourselves to sin but every part of ourselves as instruments of righteousness?"

"That's right Terry…in the Book of Romans…we are to be weapons of righteousness…the word weapons indicates we are in a war."

"Righteous behaviour will always triumph over sinful behaviour Michael. Sloan's day of atonement is coming at him like a freight train."

"My concern though is this," Terry continued.

"This Charismatic Movement is exploding and independent Pentecostal churches are springing up everywhere. Now a lot of the long time tent preachers are looking for a church of their own as their tent crusade numbers drop. When June 1st comes, when his probation is up, Sloan will see that as an avenue of escape for him from the AOG hierarchy and in particular from me, and look to set up his own church."

"There are going to be so many independent Pentecostal churches springing up in this Charismatic Movement that their leaders won't need a licence from the AOG for legitimacy. The sheer weight of numbers will make them look like a church brand in their own right."

"And my gut feel is that he has his eye on you and the work that you and your people have established in Springfield."

"Interesting you say that Terry."

"Why's that Michael?"

"Well last month the eldership approved a series of applications to build homes on the property and two of them were from Sloan and his minder Thorpey. The applications for building will be approved by Council around end of March. So if they both start building straight away they should be finished around end of June, or early July."

"Bingo Michael...bingo...you see what I said to you yesterday Bill... you've got to keep one step ahead of this bloke."

"Michael I say this because it needs to be said. We've got to get this bloke before he causes irreparable emotional and spiritual damage to any more people...and we will."

"You see Michael it's not just that a predator's targets feel disappointed and damaged in themselves in these type of situations, they also usually end up feeling disappointed in the things of God and that's the sad thing."

"A lot of them end up giving up on their faith...and we can't have that."

Terry paused.

"Okay...that's Sloan."

"Now...let's talk about Thorpey."

"Thorpey is one of those followers I was talking about who think that their leader can do no wrong. But Thorpey is a little bit different. Sure he's ego driven but not misguided. He has his own leadership agenda. Thorpey and his wife have followed Sloan and Bettina from church to church following the revelation of each scandal. Michael they are both what is commonly referred to as enablers…you know what an enabler is?"

"Sure…well I'm pretty sure I know what you mean…I'm thinking that it is used mostly in reference to a marriage relationship but can be used with regards to any kind of partnership. Isn't it when one partner condones or turns a blind eye to the bad behaviour in another because it suits them personally to do so…but in condoning it this enables the person to continue behaving badly?"

"Couldn't have said it better myself Michael."

"Michael there is a saying that an enabler by their behaviour feeds the wolf inside another and strengthens it to go out hunting again."

"A good friend of mine the Reverend David Wilkinson who wrote the book The Cross and The Switchblade, don't know whether you've read it Michael, once preached this when I was visiting his church in Times Square in New York."

Michael quickly interjected, "yes I have actually read it Terry…a friend loaned it to me when I first moved to Springfield."

"Right…well that person who loaned it to you was a good friend, because there are some important spiritual life principles in it."

"Anyway in his sermon he told the story of a very old Cherokee Indian, probably about Bill's age," they all laughed, "and this Indian was talking to his young grandson."

"The grandfather tells the grandson that there is a battle raging between two spirits inside all of us. One is called the Spirit of Evil, containing you know thoughts and emotions fueled by the devil's agents: things like anger, hatred, jealously, greed, lust, resentment, inferiority and lies, things that hurt and divide people's relationships."

"The other spirit in the battle is called the Spirit of Goodness whose spiritual agents are things like love, joy, peace, hope, humility, kindness, compassion, empathy and truth."

"So this young boy thinks for a moment and then asks the question, well Grandfather which spirit in us wins the battle… Evil or Goodness?"

"And the old Indian named Bill," Terry grinned, "puts his hand on his grandson's shoulder and replies."

"The one you feed Grandson, the one you feed."

"It's a great illustration of how the warfare in the spiritual world works Terry," commented Bill.

"It is Bill."

"An enabler is someone who by giving acquiescence or condoning the bad behaviour of someone else actually feeds the spirit inside of that person and strengthens it to carry on doing what it is doing."

"I have personally sat with Bettina and she totally supports Garret's pleas of innocence and actually turns on those who would accuse him, including me. She tells others that I have got it in for Garret. You see an enabler like Bettina, because of her own needs, convinces herself that the only option she has is to support her spouse to avoid conflict or even a divorce. Bettina comes from a strict church upbringing. So to end the relationship and get divorced would be anathema to her."

"So she supports him, covers for him, lies for him, blames others for him, pretty sick way to lead a Christian life," commented Michael.

"She does Michael, and it is, but unfortunately a lot of those die-hard Pentecostals still live under the Law of Sin and Death. They don't under-stand the Atonement."

"So in behaving this way she feeds the appetite of the wolf in Garret enabling him and freeing him in his thinking to go out and hunt some more. These things never have a good ending."

"And Thorpey, you were saying?" queried Michael.

"Thorpey," Bill laughed, "might I comment Terry."

Terry leaned forward, nodded, and gestured to Bill to go ahead.

"Michael I've had many conversations with Thorpey between services. He seems to always want to suss me out. I think he likes being seen talking to the so called elder statesman because he doesn't relate particularly well to anyone else."

Bill laughed again.

"Simply said Michael, Thorpey is purely an ego driven individual with an over inflated sense of his own abilities who thinks he has hooked himself to a star. He wants to be a Pastor and have his own church and I believe he figures Sloan is his best avenue for achieving this."

"In doing this he will always turn a blind eye to Sloan's indiscretions. That's why he has followed him from church to church."

"He's another enabler in Sloan's life."

"You're right Bill…very very true," commented Terry.

"So with Thorpey Michael as I said about Sloan…watch him."

"If he gets wind that we are looking at Sloan he will turn on you like there is no tomorrow."

Terry glanced at his watch.

"So that's about it Michael. I know we've taken up a bit of your time but I think it was worth it."

"Any questions from your side?" continued Terry.

"No Terry, all good, and thanks for sharing all that with me. As I said Jeffrey and I have had our suspicions so what you've shared firms up in my mind that the arrangement Jeff and I have made for him to keep an eye on things is valid."

"Absolutely Michael, and let Jeffrey know not only to be on the lookout for suspicious incidents but also for little allegiances that may spring up. You know things like small select groups of people meeting for regular prayer groups in their homes on a regular basis. This is how a lot of breakaway factions start off."

Terry paused in thought.

"You know it's interesting Michael how no one down there seems to know of the close relationship between Dr Nicholls and Sloan…interesting."

"Yes" commented Michael, "but probably more interesting Terry is why Unwin would want to keep it a secret."

"You're right Michael…you're right…very intuitive."

Terry stood up obviously to finish the meeting.

"Michael thanks for coming in…I'm pleased we've had this chance to talk."

"Thanks Terry…Bill…so am I."

"Michael, Bill and I have discussed it and we'd like to pray a prayer of ordination over you before you go. You know you've passed all the exams, done the study, and are now doing the work of a pastor but have not been officially ordained for the role. It's a biblical principle from the Book of Acts that we lay hands on anointed people and send them forth officially."

"It is a sort of transference of spiritual authority and the wisdom of the Holy Spirit from us to you…God's commission you could call it."

"All good with that?"

"Sure."

The three gathered in a circle hands on each other's shoulders as both Terry and Bill prayed for Michael alternately.

"Terry I have a prophetic word for Michael?"

"Go ahead Bill."

"Michael it is the Lord that shall raise up men, it is the Lord who has raised you up. For it is the Lord who raises up and who putteth down, not man. Know assuredly that the hand of thy God shall be upon you for good as you walk before him in humility and in wisdom, as you walk before him in righteousness and holiness, for he desires that you might stand before him and lead these people. Because you have not sought this your God has raised you up and elevated you that you might fulfill that which is his Divine purpose."

"Amen," commented Terry, "thanks Bill."

Bill hugged Michael.

"Congratulations Pastor Michael."

"Thanks Bill."

Terry continued.

"Michael just one more thing I'd like you not to discuss today with Jeffrey Gibbons. I certainly trust Jeffrey but I think the less people that know about our discussion and arrangements the better. I don't want Sloan to in any way get wind of it. In his normal arrogant way he'd be thinking he is about to break free from my control this June and I don't want to disappoint him."

"Not a problem Terry."

"Michael I know all this could be seen as a bit clandestine," commented Bill as they walked out of the office, "but it's our responsibility as shepherds of the flock to be alert if wolves have entered the paddock, and to certainly keep any person that is seen as predatorial away from them. And if that can't be done physically then we've got to trap the wolf."

"The wolf is one of the most cunning animals alive Michael and if it's not separated from the flock entirely it will find a way of meeting its own selfish needs through the flock."

"Good analogy Bill...I understand fully, thanks."

Discipleship and the strict principle of shepherding was a teaching in the church, predominately the Pentecostal church, that during the seventies would quickly expand and over the years sweep the entire globe. Loosely named the discipleship movement, it involved individual church congregation numbers being broken down into small groups called cells: a cell being a group of about ten people. Each cell would have a leader appointed to their group who was known as their shepherd.

It was carried out purely on a voluntary basis, but because of the hype that came with it most original and long-term members of local congregations would eventually succumb to getting involved in a cell group. For some people, particularly spiritually ambitious males, becoming a cell group leader was also seen as a stepping-stone to having some sort of future pastoral role in a church: almost like a pastoral apprenticeship.

Heading up all the cells in a church would be the resident Pastor of the church. He would be known as the Chief Shepherd. Each shepherd was responsible to the Chief Shepherd for the spiritual and emotional well being including the lifestyle direction for all members of his or her cell.

Whilst some historians of religion would years later describe it as being founded with the best intentions, others would describe it as being false teaching, not biblically based, and having come out of poorer communities in Latin America, hence not being suited culturally to the wider and broader worldwide community of believers.

It would be in mid March 1972 when the Reverend Juan Ortega arrived at the Christian City Church for a three night series of preaching meetings on the subject of Discipleship, Shepherding, and the functional role of what was known as the Cell Group in the church's organizational structure.

If you were in a church that practised these teachings and a member of one of their cell groups, you were one or the other, either a shepherd or a sheep. The relationships were formally and theologically described as covenant relationships. All church shepherds were in submission, as it was called, to the senior pastor of the church who was known as the Chief Shepherd.

Down through each cell group from the shepherd to each individual sheep came this authoritarian oversight, of course purported to naturally be for the sheep's spiritual growth and benefit, and up through the pyramid in return came the financial gifts and tithes, a donation to the church of ten percent of the sheep's net income. It was the perfect scenario to keep control of the masses and fund the financial needs and spiritual ambitions of the shepherds. The whole system was open to abuse.

It would not be until the early eighties after a continuous ongoing discovery of abuse that the Christian Ministry Group who introduced the concept disbanded, with Bob Manfred one of the original founders publicly admitting that he was in error in introducing this system into the church.

He publicly repented, asked for forgiveness and apologized for his role in bringing this deceptive teaching into the church. Teaching that saw so many people put the word of their shepherd before the intuitive voice of God, and experience the hurt caused by some shepherd's misuse of authority. Families being split up, relationships destroyed, sexual misconduct, financial mismanagement, and lives turned upside down. Manfred would in his apology describe the discipleship movement as perverse and unbiblical obedience to church leaders.

That was later, but the year now was 1972.

Terry saw it as a bit of a coup that through his contacts in the United States the Christian City Church had secured the only teaching sessions of Juan Ortega occurring in the state and an influx of Pentecostal ministers from near and far to the meetings was expected. Terry and his team of organizers were not disappointed. The first night of the meetings saw a capacity crowd of around 800 to 1000 people squeeze into the auditorium in eager anticipation of what they were going to hear from Juan Ortega.

It would be around five minutes after the start of the worship session that Michael, seated on the far side of the room, glanced towards the entrance and observed Garret Sloan and Unwin Nicholls quietly slip into two of the excess seats that had just been put out at the rear of the auditorium.

The time had now arrived when Garret Sloan knew he would finally be able to legitimately appropriate and implement the teaching that he had first embraced on that secret trip to the church of Oliver Robards in February 1970. For Garret Sloan the shepherding movement was about to become his new ideology.

"But I tell ya mate…I was curious, as curious as a cobra in a chookhouse."

Morty Mortensen

The Recall

FIFTEEN

Perhaps because of the busyness of Michael's work schedule and his monthly weekend trip back to Springfield the first six months of his temporary transfer seemed to pass quickly. Michael had adopted a strict routine for these visits, and during his three-day stopover with the Gibbons the bonds of trust, friendship and affection had grown stronger and stronger.

It would be during the four hour drive down that Michael would continually question in his mind whether keeping his discussion with Terry Channing secret from Jeffrey Gibbons was the wisest thing to do. After all he reasoned, the subject matter of the discussion directly related to Jeffrey and the arrangement they both had established with regards to keeping an eye on Sloan's activities.

But there was also concern about this secrecy from a personal point of view. Michael was aware from his own life experience that keeping secrets from a trusted friend that involved them did not bode well for ongoing successful relationships, particularly if at some stage in the future the person becomes aware that certain things were being withheld. Trust can be broken.

Whilst Michael always enjoyed his visits to the commune and the eldership updates, it was two other things he looked forward to most of all on his monthly visit to Springfield: hot chocolate and a conversational catch up with Jeff and Janet on the verandah of their cottage, and spending time with his beloved Archie on the Saturday afternoon and evening.

The Friday night talks with Jeffrey and Janet were really a pre-emptive brief on the subject matter that would be discussed at the Saturday morning eldership update, but to Michael it was far more personal. Not only could the progress on particular projects be discussed, but also the spiritual progress and involvement in the work of particular personalities.

It would be on his drive down to Springfield during the last weekend in July that Michael decided to fill Jeffrey in on the meeting that had occurred in February with Terry Channing and Bill Hawkesbury. Jeffrey needed to know that his suspicions were pretty well correct. He would do it during the part of their conversation that became a regular item on their catch up agenda…the activities of Garret Sloan.

The progress with the project over the first half of 1972 had been significant. Over the seven months the congregational numbers had increased to an average Sunday night meeting of around five hundred people. School enrolments had increased to around sixty students with plans in progress for the inclusion of a high school curriculum. It would be ready to go by November, which would enable a smooth transition for those primary school children who were approaching secondary school level.

The Christian City Church and the Springfield Christian Church had overwhelmingly embraced the teachings of Juan Ortega on discipleship and shepherding. In the commune twelve cell groups had already been set up by the eldership and had commenced conducting their weekly home group meetings. But there was one important point of difference in the structural implementation of the shepherding programme in each church.

Terry Channing in his wisdom had made it a purely voluntary choice for members of his congregation to join a cell group, whilst under Garret Sloan's influence the Springfield Church eldership had incorporated it into the salvation experience of all new arrivals into the fellowship. A newcomer would come to the church, be saved, and immediately be pressured into a cell group. It was an effective way for Sloan to begin controlling the masses.

The rambling farmhouse tucked away in the lower corner of the property had been renovated over a two month period by Jack Wainwright, the builder friend of Unwin Nicholls, who had been heavily involved in the restoration of the downtown auditorium. It was officially named Magdelene House, a home for growth and change, and provided accommodation for ten girls at a time. Janet Gibbons was appointed the house supervisor with Zelda Westwood as her assistant and both Jenny Purcell and Janet had lovingly put a curriculum together for teaching and training the girls.

The training in itself was fun, biblically based, but designed to bring some sort of disciplined normality into the voluntary participants lives. All 'would be' participants who applied to enter the house were chosen on the basis that their lives demonstrated that they were anything but disciplined and normal, and seriously wanted to get their lives back on track. It was like you needed an off the rails resume to get selected for the position.

The programme provided a two-month in house residential stay with the only contribution financially from participants being for food. The course enabled the girls to develop their spiritual life, their daily disciplines, and be skilled up in areas such as cooking, craftwork, job seeking, resume preparation skills, and personal financial management and budgeting. It also helped them to develop conversational skills that produced a more socially acceptable social behaviour.

"Hey Michael, guess what?" came the voice from the Gibbons' kitchen as Janet prepared three cups of hot chocolate to ward away the coldness of the winter night.

"I give in Janny...I can't think of anything...what?"

"You know that little cubby hole beside the auditorium that opens up onto the outside footpath?"

"Yes I do...it was the kiosk for the original picture theatre but was too small to do anything with when we renovated the building so we just left it for storage."

"Yes," continued Janet, "well Morty's opened it as a takeaway coffee, tea and milkshake kiosk."

"Oh yes…and they sell Greek cookies to go with your drink."

"Seriously?"

"Yes…serious."

"Only two small tables with chairs on the footpath so it's really a takeaway kiosk…like a little milk bar."

"He's named it The Triple C Cafe."

"He reckons the three c's stand for coffee, cookies, and charisma, which is him."

"Don't you love him?"

Michael laughed out loud, "I love it."

"Morty reckons these takeaway drink places are going to be a big thing in the future," Janet continued, "he said he read it in a magazine. He said we're going to go the way of the United States with lots more people taking up coffee drinking. He's a trend setter our Morty."

"He's trialling it at this stage, only opened it three weeks ago. He told everyone the mayor wanted to come and open it but couldn't as he had to go to a funeral."

"Yeah right," quipped Jeffrey.

"And he only opens on Saturday morning, Saturday night after the movies finish, and of course on Sunday morning and night after the church services," continued Janet.

"He has Kelly looking after it on the Saturday mornings and Saturday nights and he looks after it on Sunday nights. I think that's because it gives him a legitimate chance to get up and go outside if the preaching is going for too long."

Jeffrey laughed, "exactly."

"Morty can't sit still for too long."

"He gets his cookies supplied wholesale from The Plaka Café. Archie's mum loves him. They are Koularakia cookies. It's a hard word to pronounce so Morty calls them his Kookaburra cookies."

"Sounds great."

"What do you reckon Jeffrey, you up for a Kookaburra cookie after the eldership catch up tomorrow?"

"I'm in Michael."

It would be when the eldership meeting at the Evelyn Auditorium had finally finished and after the other elders had dispersed that Michael and Jeffrey had stayed behind to catch up on things discussed at the meeting over a coffee.

"Okay young Jeffrey…time for a coffee, a Kookaburra cookie and a chat with Kelly?"

"You betcha."

Michael and Jeffrey walked around the auditorium making sure all the exit doors were secure.

"Interesting meeting," Michael commented as they secured the front door.

"So Sloan looks like he will be the first to move in to his house on the property," Michael commented as they twice checked that the door was locked and walked over to the kiosk.

"Yeah…looks like it…although I was down there late the other afternoon picking up Janny from the girls' house and I wandered down to have a look…builders had gone home. I reckon Thorpey won't be too far behind him…looks like they are neck in neck… they're using the same builder."

Jeffrey raised his hand and lowered it patting himself on the back.

"From my extensive construction experience I reckon the quality of his work is good."

"It's Jack Wainwright."

"His wife is very involved in church stuff and is in a cell group, but not Jack."

"Although I see him occasionally at the Sunday night service. He usually comes when Unwin is on the preaching roster."

"Right."

"Jeffrey run that off me again re the decision to bring Thorpey in as part of the eldership?"

"Well apparently Don Morcum had been thinking about stepping down for a while…I think his work at the law firm keeps him busy… and he originally got involved in the whole commune thing because of his passion for getting a Bible based school going. He's not really into church management, just came in at the start to help us get the eldership up and running."

"He apparently still does a lot of work for the Anglicans in town. He's a member of the church. So I think he's a bit stretched time wise. Either that or he sees it as a conflict of religious interest."

"Anyway Sloan suggested Thorpey replace him, Unwin and George went along with it…so it happened."

"Right."

Michael and Jeffrey both turned and walked towards the kiosk.

"Cobbers," came the sound of a familiar voice.

"Mickey me ole pastoral pal…and not forgettin' you Gibbo me ole chippie cobber…how are yuh?"

"Good Morty…good."

"What …no Kelly on deck today," queried Jeff.

"No mate…she chucked a sickie…well not really…she had to take the morning off…said it was personal…so I'm slummin' it cobber…all on my Jack Malone."

"Anyway I'm glad I am on cause there's somethin' I needed to talk to you about."

"Bung Lung is getting ready for the lunch crowd at Morty's and I'll be back there as quick as a robber's dog to help after I finish here, before he gets his Chinese noodles in a knot. He gets really agro if it gets busy and he's by himself."

"So…what's your poison today…coffee and cookie for two…at mate's rates?"

"Yes thanks Morty."

Morty busied himself while Michael and Jeffrey sat down at the small brightly coloured café table, both enjoying the warmth of the winter sunshine on their faces and the crispness in the air.

"Be interesting to see what it is he wants to discuss with us later," Michael commented, "speaking of that here he comes now."

Morty placed the two coffees on the table.

"There ya go cobbers."

"Back in a flash with ya cookies."

Morty returned with two oversized cookies and with the words "enjoy cobbers" placed them on the table, pulled a chair over from the other table setting and proceeded to join them in conversation.

"Now boys I need to ask you a question."

"There's sometin' that's been bugging the bullshit out of me for a few weeks and I've been waiting for you to come down to talk to you about it Mickey."

"I was gunna ask the Professor, you know, the Doc, but a little voice said to me, no, wait for Mickey."

"Cause it concerns someone that the Doc has been getting very close to in the last few months…ya know…their both in my restaurant lunching together a lot…ya know…almost like what do they call them… Chinese twins."

"Siamese twins," quipped Jeffrey.

"Yeah right Siamese…clever dick," came Morty's reply.

"Anyway that little voice said wait for Mickey."

"And also I had just found out that the small office at the top of the stairs, ya know beside the professor's clinic door, the sign says G.S. Enterprises Pty. Ltd., well Patty told me that it was available for rent around February next year."

"So I says what, is the tenant moving out?"

Jeffrey grinned.

"Yeahhh…chippie…I know…dumb question…I was a bit tired…late shift…if it's for rent he must be moving out…I know."

"And Patty says yes…he's getting a new office up at the commune."

"And I says who is he oh maestro of real estate?"

"And Patty says…G.S. Enterprises, Garret Sloan Enterprises."

"Mate it's apparently been his office for the last couple of years…right besides the Docs…no one told the Mortmeister."

Michael frowned and turned to Jeffrey.

"I remember you saying at the Carols night you had heard a rumour that Sloan had rented an office downtown. You called it his counting house where the king counts his cash…or something like that."

"Yeah…but I didn't know it was right beside Unwin's."

Morty continued.

"So mate the old Mortmeister starts to put two and two together."

"You know…Sloan…regular lunches with the doc."

"And not only that for the last few months he has been having regular coffee with Mrs Doc."

"Who…you mean Unwin's wife?"

"Nooo cobber…Mrs Doc…the Magsmeister."

"You mean Margie Morrison?"

"Right cobber…you're gettin' with the programme now."

Morty glanced sideways from left to right and lowered his voice.

"Boys I don't want to start a wrong rumour…but I tell you what cobbers," Morty winked and clicked his mouth twice, "pretty cosy over coffee them two…pretty cosy."

"Anyways so when I thought I'd talk to the doc about what had been bugging me that little voice said to me, "no wait till ya see Mickey."

"Ya know…that little voice you preach about a lot. Ya know…ignition."

"You mean…intuition," quipped Jeffrey grinning.

"Yea…whatever chippie…ya know that voice in your head."

"Sure Morty…I know what you mean," interjected Michael sensing that Morty was a little embarrassed with Jeff correcting him.

"Okay…well here's the drum."

"This is where it gets flammin' interesting."

"Cobber ya know we live in God's country, like here in this district. Lots of sunshine…a shit load of rain…ya know everything's green… plenty of water."

"Not like when I was cooking out on the station which had shit loads of sunshine and as for rain, well mate I'd pee more in a bucket in one day out there than the rain we'd get in six months…very dry cobber… ya know."

"Sure…I get you Morty."

"Okay…well here's the deal…I think there's sometin' shooftie goin' on up at the commune."

"Right," replied Michael, slightly puzzled about what was going to come next.

"Look cobbers it happened around early June…and its kinda bugged me since then."

"I was up at the girls' farmhouse on the Tuesday night."

"Ya know I don't open Morty's on Tuesday nights…it's my night off."

"Well anyway…your missus young Jeffrey had asked me would I come up and do a sort of basic cooking class with the girls…ya know how to boil an egg stuff."

"By the way chippie your missus is a bonza sheila mate…she's doin' a great job with those girls…hang onto her."

"So anyways we had a great time…ya know lots of laughs…I told em a few stories."

"Well I finished about 8.30 cause the girls have a 9.30 curfew, gotta get their beauty sleep."

Morty leaned forward, looked around as if to make sure no one else was listening in, and continued.

"Anyways I'm hot to trot…ya know feelin' good…it was a good night…and it's good to try and help those sheilas learn how to cook… and as I gets in my car I sees some lights like headlights…right down the back of the property where a couple of the houses are goin' up."

"So I says to myself…Mortmeister…as a responsible head of the PTA you need to go and see what's goin' on."

"I thought some galah might av been knocking stuff off from the building site."

Jeffrey and Michael glanced at each other and grinned.

"So I thinks just walk down Morty me ole mate, don't drive as you might not want whoever's there to see you…ya know I don't want to get a repo for being a snoop…but I tell ya mate I was curious, as curious as a cobra in a chookhouse."

"So I gets out of my car…ya know…it was dark but still pretty visible…I mean I could see them but they couldn't see me…and this is what I was talking about with the rain."

"There's this big truck there unloading two friggin' huge tanks…ya know…for water storage…mate…friggin' huge they were…not the normal house size."

"And they had this sorta crane thing on the truck that was lowering them onto the slabs of the two house sites in the corner through the open side…ya know…three of the sides have already been bricked up to floor level."

"And I thinks…why does anyone in this area with town supply of water and all the rain we get here need these friggin' huge tanks to store water."

"And I thought…Meister there's somethin' shooftie goin' on here… someone's pullin' a shooftie."

"And mate guess who was directing the show?"

"I give in," quipped Jeffrey.

"Tommy the torpedo head mate…you know ole bullet brain."

"You mean Thorpey?"

"Yeah mate …the Thorpmeister himself."

"Annnd…Jacko the builder…you know Unwin's mate…the guy that built his house. He's done some work for me too at Morty's, Unwin recommended him."

"Yeah…so Torpedo and Jacko are directing tank traffic."

"So I says to myself I'm out of here like a robber's dog and I sneaks back up to me car and heads home to have a cuppa with the missus."

"So I sits down and she says how did the class go love?"

"And I says the class was bonza but somethin' funny happened after… and she says, what darls?"

"And I says…love…two houses, ya know, Sloans and Thorpeys at the property was getting a delivery of two friggin' huge water tanks. I mean it's at night for a start and why would they even need such friggin' huge tanks?"

"And I tell ya wot cobbers…she's good the missus."

"She said…well darls perhaps the delivery truck was one of those long haul drivers from interstate…ya know…on a schedule…had to unload and get back on the road…like we saw with the supply deliveries out on the station."

"I said right luv…yeah…didn't think of that."

"And then she comes out with the cracker mate."

"She says…orrrr…and I says …orrrr what?"

"And she says…orrrr darls perhaps the owners of the houses didn't want anyone to see what was being delivered."

"Eh…what a cracker…I reckon she nailed it mate."

"Sometin' shooftie was goin' on."

"So I said luv why would they want tanks that big?"

"Pretty obvious darls…they must be expecting some time in the future to be a bit short on water…that's what the people out west do…everyone has a house tank even if the you're tapped into the town supply."

"Perhaps those preaching people know sometin' that we don't know luv."

"So anyway cobbers I tossed and turned a bit that night…couldn't sleep it was buggin' me…so I gets up early…well early for a restaurateur like me…it was around 7."

"See I thought I'd take the ute up to the property…pretend I was picking up some veggies for Morty's…and cruise past and have another look…not that I'm a snoop."

"Anyways cobbers…ya not gonna believe this…when I goes past I sees a team of Jacko's brickies just finishing off bricking up the last side of each wall on the slab."

"Mate you think I was up early…they must have been up at the sparrows fart…they had pretty well completely finished."

"And the big friggin' tanks mate were tucked away like a dead dingo in a ditch…hidden cobber…nowhere to be seen."

"I reckon the missus was right mate…old torpedo head didn't want anything to be seen."

Michael looked at Jeffrey.

"Hmm…that's interesting…thanks Morty…hey thanks for letting us know…and do me a favour mate if you would…keep this to yourself."

"Okay…anyways I'll keep goin'…just give us a cooee if you want more coffee…I feel better now I've got that off my chest."

"Yes…thanks Morty."

Michael turned to Jeffrey.

"So the two building sites would be Sloan's and Thorpey's?"

"That's right."

"Interesting."

"It is."

"Jeff from a builder's opinion how long before both houses are finished?"

"I reckon about another three weeks and they will move in…so looking around mid-August."

Michael and Jeffrey stood up to go.

Jeffrey walked up to pay the bill and Michael called out.

"Morty my man, gotta go, things to do, people to see, you know. Thanks for the coffee mate and thanks for the talk…you did well."

Jeffrey handed Morty the money.

"Yeah…keep on keeping on mate…I thought I was the Sherlock Super Slueth but you've outdone me," quipped Jeffrey.

Morty laughed as he walked down and started removing the coffee cups and plates.

"Onya boys…well I do feel better that I've got that off my chest…see ya at the service tomorrow."

Michael and Jeffrey walked slowly around the corner to their cars, heads down, and both deep in thought.

"What's that scripture in Corinthians Jeffrey about God choosing the things that the world finds foolish to shame the wise?"

"He's a good man our Morty."

Jeffrey turned to Michael.

"You thinking what I'm thinking Michael?"

"If it's end times stuff…you know storing up water…the current doomsday teaching…then yes I am thinking what you're thinking."

"Exactly."

"I mean from what I have seen Unwin and his end times book collection and his sustainable living set up and now this with the hidden water tanks…mate something's crook in Tallarook."

"Not forgetting Unwin has this huge water tank on his property…but at least his isn't hidden."

"Could that be because he has a lowest house," Jeffrey grinned.

Michael laughed.

"Good thinking Sherlock…silly me."

"What do you want to do?"

"At this stage Jeffrey…nothing…absolutely nothing."

"Let's lock it away Jeffrey."

"You don't want to bring it up with the eldership?"

"Shisenhowser no Sherlock…we do that and we could be outgunned."

"Matter of fact now with Thorpey on the eldership we'd get snowed, and I don't want to alert Sloan that we are curious about things."

"You know…look at the eldership…from what Morty says about Unwin and Sloan lunching each week together and of course Don Morcum being good mates with Unwin. And I'm not sure where Georgey sits. I mean I'm pretty sure he's one of the good guys but he's building a house just across from Thorpey, and of course now with Thorpey on the eldership we know he'll back Garret."

"So with all that going on I would say that there is a definite possibility we could be outgunned if we raise the subject, and then they would really go to ground."

"For the moment we'll just lock it away…just lock it away Jeffrey."

"Hey listen also…I'm heading off to see Archie and we are going to a movie tonight but I'll be back at your place at around 10.30…she's got a big day tomorrow."

"All the littlies from Primary are putting on a Fruit of The Spirit play after the morning service."

"If you're still up around 10.30 there's something I need to share with you about a meeting I had with Terry Channing and old Bill."

"Sure…no problem…yeah we'll be up…sounds interesting."

"It is my friend…indeed it is."

"How are the cell group home meetings going?" Michael queried Jeffrey as they sat sipping hot chocolate and listening to the sounds of the crickets and the odd owl on the Gibbons' verandah on a balmy night in late August.

"Yeah good Michael good…Sloan is real keen on them…but yes they seem to be going okay."

"He doesn't like the voluntary basis of being in one though. He's pushing so that every new convert that joins the church is automatically slotted into a cell group with a shepherd over them."

"And he's talking about introducing a system where the weekly tithes are collected by the cell group leader at the home meeting so that the collection on Sunday becomes a sort of over and above offering."

"He's figuring that in a small group no one has an opportunity to evade giving their tithe."

Michael grimaced.

"Oh I don't like that Jeffrey...I don't like that at all...that's Old Testament stuff...The Law...the Old Covenant...fraught with danger."

"Too many pastors are using that seed faith teaching to raise funds."

"I know...I didn't go for it...but was howled down by the others at the eldership meeting...they said we needed the finances to grow the work."

"How many people in cell groups now?"

"About one hundred and fifty I think it is now. That's another interesting thing...well in part a funny thing. Sloan has Thorpey count the number of people at each service and give it to him."

"He's really playing the numbers game isn't he Jeffrey?"

"Yes but don't think it's too effective though."

"Why's that?"

"Inaccurate feedback."

"Thorpey has trouble when he runs out of fingers."

Michael laughed.

"And you'll love this...I've seen it happen a couple of times."

"Thorpey usually does the count towards the end of the service just before the altar call and it's the same time that Morty gets up to go to his kiosk to get ready for the coffee rush."

"So Morty who's sitting up the back sidles up to Thorpey who is totally focussed on not losing count and having to start again and nudges him and asks what number are you up to cobber?"

"And Thorpey stutters and splutters and loses count...love it."

Janet and Michael laughed.

"Jeffrey how was each person selected for a particular cell group originally?"

"Michael you call me super sleuth…you're asking a lot of probing questions tonight."

"Just catching up on things my friend."

"Archie mentioned to me last night that she had recently changed her cell group leader."

"Yeah you're right…I'll tell you about that."

"Um with the original selection of who was put in which group, it was all white boarded at the eldership meeting."

"Or should I say Garret white boarded it."

"Sloan had preached about discipleship at the Sunday services, and once those interested had put their name down on a notice on the notice board at the auditorium Sloan took the list and whiteboarded them into cell group leaders and the names in each group."

"He had it finished before the eldership meeting started, to save time he said. So all he did was read out the names on each group and basically everyone of the elders gave them the tick."

"Wow," Michael replied, "how covenient."

"What do you mean Michael?" queried Janet.

"I mean that Sloan got to choose who he wanted in each group."

"I see what you mean Michael," Jeff replied, "and I didn't see it at the time. But after you shared with me about your meeting with Terry and Bill when you were down last month it did start to bother me."

"Yes and sometimes you see some personality clashes too," Janet commented.

"Like with Prissie."

"Yes," replied Michael, "that's why I asked about the cell groups… Archie's mentioned that she had changed groups…she said she swapped with Prissie."

"No big deal," replied Jeff.

"Prissie came to see Janet and me the other week. She was having some sort of personality clash with her cell group leader's wife and wanted to change groups."

"She didn't say much about it just that she wasn't getting on with his wife. She felt she was ignoring her and making her feel not welcome in the group."

"Not sure how true that was but anyway I mentioned it to my group... you know looking for a volunteer to switch with her and Archie volunteered...she thought everyone should switch around at times...you know to get to know other people."

"So the eldership didn't have a problem with the switch?" queried Michael.

"No not at all...Sloan was all for it...it all worked out okay...so Prissie's in our group now."

"Thanks Jeffrey...thanks for looking after her."

⚬

It would be a Thursday afternoon in late November when Michael's office phone rang.

"Michael it's Prissie...I'm sorry to bother you at your work. I got your phone number from Janet. I said I needed to talk to you. Is that okay?"

"Sure Prissie sure...no problem at all...what can I do for you...is everything okay?"

"Well no Michael it isn't...I really need to talk to you in person. Michael...some things have been going on between myself and my cell group leader...it's not right...my secret pal from the Women's Guild Jenny has indicated I need to talk to you about it...can I come and see you?"

"I'll drive up to the city."

Michael sensed urgency in Prissie's tone.

"Sure...no problem...what about this Saturday...does that suit you?"

"Saturday would be good."

"Okay make it around 11.30."

"Do you know where the Christian City Church is?"

"Yes I do I've been there before."

"Okay well come there. Terry Channing lets me use an office there when I need it for church business."

"Just come to the bookshop and they'll point you in the right direction. Is that okay?"

"That's great Michael…thankyou."

"Okay Prissie…drive safe and we'll see you at 11.30 on Saturday."

Michael leaned back in his chair hands locked behind his head thinking about the brief conversation with Prissie and wondering what her problem was. She seemed a little nervous and distressed he thought.

The intercom system on his phone buzzed.

"Mr Winton I have another caller on line 2 for you."

"Okay thanks…did they say who it was?"

"No he didn't…but it's a male and he had a really abrupt sounding voice with a real gravelly tone if that helps."

Michael picked up the phone.

"Patty my friend…how are you?"

"Mikey," came the gravelly reply, "how did you know it was me?"

"Moving in the spirit Patty…moving in the spirit…what can I do for you?"

"Yeah…right."

"Mate I just thought I'd give you a buzz and let you know that the couple who leased your apartment after you left have just bought a home from me."

"That's great Patty…and?"

"Well cobber it settles just before Christmas."

"Are you still moving back down here in January?"

"Yes I am."

"Well mate if you like I can let them out of their lease a month early and hold the apartment for you if you haven't made any other rental plans."

Michael could not believe his ears at what he heard.

"Patty you are an absolute champion yes yes…thankyou…that would be great…I really owe you."

"It's not a problem Pastor…thought you might like that…and mate since you feel you owe me I'll give you a call if I get stuck and need any favours from God."

Michael chuckled, "yes right…I'm good at that."

"Okay…gotta go…I'll have the lease papers drawn up and get you to sign them when you are down next."

"Thanks Patty…once again thanks."

"And Mikey as a bonus I spoke to the owners and they are going to give it a paint job on the inside to spruce it up for you after the tenants move out."

"So it will have a week to air before you move in."

"That's great Patty thanks."

"No problem…see ya Mikey."

Michael leaned back in his chair and thought about his first meeting with Patty on that Saturday morning at the trailer park and Patty's subsequent help in getting Prissie a place to stay and a job at the boutique when she had moved down to Springfield after her marriage breakup. And now this call he thought. Maybe I underestimated you Patty my man he thought. I'm starting to think you are definitely one of the good guys.

66 *"Mistakes can become lifelong regrets if we hold on to them or lifetime lessons if we let them go. It's our choice."*

Michael Winton

Secrets In The Sisterhood
Capricia Rossi

SIXTEEN

P rissie entered Michael's office on that Saturday morning and after being warmly greeted with a hug she sat down.

"Michael I've carried this guilt with me for too long she said. I'm tired of it. I want this thing to end. I hope you can help me to make it so."

Channing was right Michael thought, some people will hold on to the hurt caused by a sexual predator for months, for years, and in some cases for decades.

The beginning of the Sisterhood as it would come to be called, almost commenced by accident. It was during a picnic lunch break at a week-end working bee at the commune in Feruary1971 as Marie Nicholls and Jenny Purcell sat in the shade of the huge fig tree sheltering the southern end of the newly restored schoolhouse, that the subject of the formation of a Women's Guild came up.

Women's Guild groups had played an important role in most denominational churches over the centuries, particularly in the Anglican, Baptist and Presbyterian ones. The members paid regular dues, had birthday collections, and got involved in charitable events where the proceeds would be donated to any missions the church was supporting.

Marie's family history was Anglican or Church of England as it was called and Jenny's church history was Presbyterian. Both had memories of their own mothers, on the last Wednesday morning of each month, dressed up, hats on, diary in one hand and a plate of small cakes or sandwiches in the other heading off to their local church Women's Guild meeting.

Their monthly meeting would include birthday songs for those having a birthday that month, a devotional time led by one of the members on a rotational basis, and a review of past and future charitable activities, concluding with refreshments.

A long-standing tradition of the Guild was to have what was known as a secret pal. At the beginning of each year members would anonymously draw their secret pal's name out of a hat for the following year. During the year unsigned cards of blessing could be sent off to your secret pal and then at the Christmas luncheon at the end of the year you would bring a gift and present it to your pal to reveal who you were.

It would be during a lunch meeting at Morty's Restaurant the week following the working bee that the plan for the formation of the women's group would be worked through and subsequently formalized. Along with Marie and Jenny there would be five others invited to be initial members.

They would be five women who it was felt could add a good mix of personality and acumen to the group. Naturally all had to be attendees of the commune's church fellowship and preferably have their children, if they had any, attending the primary school. After much thought and discussion they reached a decision.

They selected Capricia, known as Prissie, a thirty six year old Italian mother of two young girls, a former model, stunningly beautiful, and now the manager of a boutique women's clothing store on the tourist strip at Lighthouse Bay. One of her two little girls was of school age and attending the community school.

There was Colleen Jones, the red haired confident mother of two who was the manager of a Christian bookstore in town who had two children attending the school and Judy the wife of Patty Patel the realtor, with one child attending the school.

Lastly they chose Bettina Sloan and Cherie Goldway. They chose Bettina, the wife of Garret Sloan, because she was spending a lot more time in the area due to the involvement of her husband in the spiritual activities of the commune and Bettina's good friend Cherie who travelled a lot with her, and whose presence they thought would help Bettina feel more comfortable in their monthly get togethers when they were in town.

To Marie and Jenny however they had selected a good mix of normalcy: Godly women, mothers interested in the school and the ongoing work of the commune, and a selection of women who they felt were dedicated in spiritual matters, intelligent, honest and open, and likely to make a positive contribution to the group. It would be around mid march 1971 that they held their first meeting.

———◇◇◇———

May 1994.

Prissie had woken up troubled. She was part sad and part angry. It was May 5th 1994, it was her birthday, and she had just turned sixty years of age. However once again, as had occurred on every one of her birthdays for the last twenty years, Prissie really didn't feel like getting up, and certainly didn't feel like celebrating.

She lay on her bed in her small cottage at Lighthouse Bay, staring at the ceiling. She knew she would have to get up soon, go with the flow, and act excited about the day, particularly when her two grown up daughters would make the obligatory phone call to congratulate her on her 60th. But for Prissie May 5th was not just a birthday anniversary but also an anniversary of a different kind, a devastatingly emotionally different kind. It was the day she had received the phone call from Janet Gibbons.

As she lay thinking in the silence of the morning, the same singular question was once again racing through her mind as it had done so every year before.

"Who was that foolish girl at the time, and why did she allow those terrible things to happen?"

In her growing years both her mother and father had taught her the importance of making right choices, and an understanding of the difference between right and wrong. As a teenager her mother had instilled in her the virtues of purity and of faithfulness and honesty in relationships. Why she wondered had she blocked out all that her parents had said and given in to lust without a second thought?

She was both angry and sad.

She was angry with her brother Luca, Luca Rossi, and she knew she shouldn't be. After all he was only looking after her best interests when he phoned Michael Winton on her behalf. But she had wrongly reasoned that if Luca hadn't contacted Michael then she wouldn't have ended up in Springfield and those incidents wouldn't have happened.

She was sad for Michael Winton. After all, these events in Springfield had perhaps in some way changed the course of his life forever too. She wasn't sure that this was true, but it made her sad to think it might be as he had been nothing but kind and loving to her, expecting nothing in return.

It had been her brother Luca who had brought him into the situation when he phoned Michael, his old bible school buddy from up north, and asked for his help regarding his sister. Prissie had phoned her brother that morning. She had felt that there was no one else she could turn to. She had always been close to her brother, him being her older and wiser sibling as she put it. After all he was a junior pastor in a large church so he would know all about troubled relationships and advise her on what she should do.

It was October 1970 and Prissie was going through a time of heartbreak and desperate feelings of loss and loneliness. Her world, the world she had felt so safe and secure in for the last seven years, had in the previous few months progressively fallen apart and she just didn't know what to do.

To the observer Capricia appeared to have it all. The family was renting a lovely home in a leafy suburb in the city. Both her and her husband had nice cars, her handsome lawyer husband Tom had a well paying job, and they had two beautiful young girls aged five and two. A strikingly attractive brunette model Prissie had over time through hard work snared a lucrative contract modelling lingerie with a major underwear manufacturer.

But Prissie had, on her husband's request, set aside her personal dreams and given up her catwalk career to raise a family and support him in his vocation. She loved Tom, she loved him more than anything and would have done anything for him and did.

Tom was what was commonly known as a control freak. When Tom had told her to give up her modelling career and stay home she did. When Tom had told her she needed to have breast implants so that she could wear low cut dresses to the many work social functions they attended she went ahead and had the operation.

But it didn't go as well as expected and over the years she had come to literally hate her breasts. When she looked in the mirror she felt scared and embarrassed. Scared that she now had this chemical substance called silicon in her body and embarrassed as she thought her breasts just didn't look natural. Shaped like two oversized tennis balls with both pointing outwards and giving no appearance of cleavage, she felt it surely looked obvious to others that they were false.

When Tom insisted on her wearing low cut dresses to social functions she would feel uncomfortable for most of the evening, particularly when she was being introduced to someone. She wondered if they knew and was worried that perhaps they might be laughing behind her back.

Sure Prissie had felt the distance growing and tension arising more frequently between her husband and herself since the birth of their second child, but had dismissed it as being a phase that all young families go through. He was working late nights; she was raising the girls almost as if she was a single parent. Of course they would both be tired and their sex life would suffer as things got tense. That was a normal part of marriage wasn't it she reasoned.

For Prissie it was easy to justify that kind of thinking to lessen the stress, even as Tom spent more and more late nights at the office and went on business trips more frequently. Easy to justify until he came home early one afternoon and told her that he was leaving that night, moving interstate and wanted a divorce, that he was involved with another woman.

In that moment Prissie's storybook life completely crumbled and her world just fell apart. It would be the next morning, pale and drawn after a long sleepless night that she made the phone call to her brother Luca.

Prissie was surprised when she received the call from Michael Winton late that same night. She remembered that after introducing himself as a good friend of Luca he had asked her were the children in bed and could she talk freely. She remembered thinking how calming Michael was as he softly spoke. That the sound of his voice and the tone of his conversation, so in control and so composed, had made her feel that perhaps things would work out okay. He had given her hope.

It was arranged for Michael to come and see her the next day after lunch as he would be in the city for a work meeting and would have the afternoon free.

Michael visited that afternoon and spent two hours with Prissie. To him she looked fragile. Since her normal skin tone was a natural milky white type the darkness under her eyes from lack of sleep was even more pronounced. He was touched that she appeared to have dressed up both herself and her two little girls for their meeting. She in a simple but stunning knee length black dress accompanied by a single string pearl necklace and full makeup, with her girls in their pretty dresses with hair braided and ribboned.

He was gripped not only by her gentleness and honesty in sharing the events that had passed, but moved deeply by the obvious devastating heartbreak she was feeling and her fear of the future for both herself and the two little girls. No job, no income, no home to call her own and a husband who had taken a work transfer interstate along with his girlfriend. The marriage was over and Michael sensed that for Prissie her world was over.

He likened her in his mind to a bird with a broken wing, that was the only way he could explain it to himself later: unable to help herself, not knowing who to turn to. He knew in that moment for the emotional well being of Prissie and her girls he had to help her take charge of her life and guide her through and past this devastation. It was with this mindset over the next few weeks that Michael set about organizing things to help her.

He spoke to the owner of the property she was renting, arranged to have her lease terminated without penalty, secured her bond, and bundled up the family and their belongings in a move to Springfield. With the help of Patty Patel, he secured accommodation for the family at a reasonable rental price, a job for Prissie at a ladieswear store in Lighthouse Bay and enrolled her oldest child in their primary school at the commune.

Now here it was twenty years later and she was lying on her bed not wanting to get up. This would be the same ritual for Prissie as it had been for every one of her birthdays since she was forty years of age. She would have trouble sleeping the night before, awaken early, lie flat on her back on her bed, and continuously mull over in her mind the events in 1972 that had caused her to be involved in what she felt later were the most regrettable incidents in her life.

It had been late afternoon around 5 p.m. on her birthday on that day in May 1973. Prissie had spent the day celebrating her birthday with friends and was with her two young daughters when the phone rang. The serious voice on the other end of the line was that of her new cell group leader Jeff Gibbons' partner, Janet.

Capricia had been moved into the Gibbons' cell group some eight months earlier after explaining to Jeffrey that she did not feel comfortable in her existing group. She did not at the time truthfully explain why she felt uncomfortable, that would be discovered later.

Janet advised her that a meeting had been called for 7 p.m. sharp that night for all members of the community's discipleship cell groups at the downtown auditorium. There was no explanation as to what the meeting was about, only to say that the Reverend Terry Channing from the Christian City Church was calling the meeting, Pastor Michael Winton would be there, and that it was very important that as many people as possible attend.

But Prissie didn't have to ask why. She knew. She knew that it would be in reference to a meeting that had occurred between her and Michael Winton late November 1972 at the Christian City Church just before Michael had returned to Springfield.

The meeting with Michael had been prompted by messages she had received the previous two months from her current secret pal in the Women's Guild or the Sisterhood as they called it. She was later to find out it was Jenny Purcell.

Jenny Purcell was a beautiful Christian soul who believed totally in what were known as the Gifts of The Spirit that were given to the church to edify and to build people up. In church services she would focus on the Gift of Prophecy and in any one on one relationship she was always alert for Words of Knowledge or Words of Wisdom. These were intuitive messages from God, given to her to be shared with someone else for their benefit.

For some months Jenny had felt she was receiving messages to be passed on to her secret pal Prissie encouraging her to face up to something sinful in her life and to deal with it sooner rather than later. She did so in written note form simply signed 'your secret pal.' Capricia had heeded these messages after some time and approached Michael with her problem. She believed in the moment of that phone call from Janet Gibbons on her birthday in 1973 that this was the culmination of her talk with Michael and she felt a little sick in the stomach.

Prissie had only been settled in the district for a couple of months and was still hurting inside from her marriage breakup, but was comforted in the knowledge that not only did she have her friends in the Sisterhood to share with but that Michael himself had given her unlimited counselling time for any difficulties she might be experiencing as she put her life back together. He was always available.

But eventually the demands of a growing commune reduced the unlimited access that Prissie had to Michael's time for counsel, so in June 1972 when the concept of shepherding, discipleship, and functional cell groups was brought into the organizational structure of the congregation, it was embraced whole heartedly and enthusiastically by Capricia.

In being part of these home meetings with a functional group of no more than ten people Prissie found that her access to private counselling sessions and spiritual guidance from her cell group leader was everything she needed. Prissie now had the emotional and spiritual safety net in life she felt she had been looking for.

She liked her cell group leader or her shepherd as he was titled in the structure, and valued what she saw as God speaking to her through him. Because of this she felt comfortable in seeking private prayer counselling from him. Her first prayer counselling discussion came and went and Prissie had thought that it had gone well. She felt in her shepherd someone who was genuinely interested in her emotional healing and felt comfortable in sharing her private feelings with him.

He had a gentle approach she had thought as he sat on her lounge room sofa beside her talking, before he had prayed about specific things. She felt relaxed that he seemed comfortable with the occasional interruption from her children coming in and out of the room during the session.

Even when he questioned whether she might be feeling the need for love and intimacy in light of her two year separation from her husband, she remembered that he had worded his question in such a casual way that she felt not the slightest cause for concern as she revealed to him that yes she was feeling a little starved for love and affection. He had justified his sometimes deeply personal probing saying that he needed to be specific when he prayed, to pinpoint things. God does not like vagueness he would say.

She felt relieved when he questioned her about the controlling aspects of her husband's behaviour, that she was finally able to admit to someone that she had never really wanted to give up her career and had certainly never wanted to have breast implants, but had done so to keep the peace.

She felt no concern that when as he finished the session he had suggested she might need a few more: rather she welcomed it. She felt no unease when he indicated that it probably would be better to have their session a little later at night, as the children would be tucked away in bed. She liked the fact that he hugged her physically and pressed in close as he said goodnight and that he paused in the moment to hold her. She felt safe.

Some two months after the first two counselling sessions her cell group leader suggested that he should pop in occasionally to pray with her and check up on her progress. Dr Shepherd home visits as he jokingly called it.

Because of his busy work schedule, as he put it, the visits would occur at night and to try and narrow it down for her it was agreed that it would be around 8 or 9 o'clock Thursday or Friday night and he would arrive unannounced. Rather than wake the children up by knocking on the front door it was arranged that he tap on the side window of the lounge room or alternatively, depending on the time, the adjoining window of her bedroom. She could then unlock the front door and he could pop in for a cup of tea and a chat and some prayer for her on his way home from work.

Capricia in her needy emotional state, in her naïve adult innocence, and in having a submissive personality borne out of years living with a controlling husband, accepted this as a comfortable arrangement as her shepherd knew she would. He knew her vulnerabilities. The Spirit of Lust, The Spirit of Manipulation and its companion The Spirit of Control were beginning to initiate the events that were to follow.

As she lay on her bed thinking on this her sixtieth birthday she remembered how scared she had felt when she contacted Michael Winton by phone and arranged to see him in his office in the city.

"Michael…some things are going on between myself and my cell group leader…it's not right…my secret pal from the Women's Guild has indicated I need to talk to you about it…can I come and see you?" That was all that was said and Michael arranged the time for their meeting.

She remembered that it seemed like an eternity of time to drive from her home in Lighthouse Bay to Michael's office in the city. Her head had been spinning trying to remember the sequence of events. When things had started, how long they continued for, and when they had finished. What questions was he going to ask her?

She felt desperately embarrassed but knew that if she had to confess these things to anyone that Michael Winton would be the kindest and non-judgmental. Or at least she hoped he would.

Did it start one month after the first cell group meeting or was it two? Did it go on for two months or was it three? She was having no trouble remembering the actual occurrences, but she was still having trouble with the times in her mind as she nervously entered Michael's office. She was feeling scared in the moment but Michael quickly put her at ease.

He was his usual warm, loving and understanding self as he sat quietly listening to Prissie talk, after initiating the conversation and only occasionally interrupted asking questions to clarify times and dates more than anything else. She remembered him not giving any appearance in his mannerisms of shock or surprise as she shared the intimate details of the incidents with him.

The secret lover type arrangement she had with her shepherd with him tapping on her bedroom window late at night to gain entry and the initial holding and cuddling for long periods of time on the couch after the prayer sessions. The evening he had suggested she put on one of her negligees, part of a collection she had kept from her modelling days and lie face down on her bed for him to give her a neck massage as she looked tense, and how it had ended up being a neck to toe massage. A massage that she realized later after the visits had ended he was using as a relaxing technique and a pathway to getting her aroused.

The more she spoke to Michael about what had occurred and felt his non-judgmental attitude the more comfortable Prissie felt in telling him everything, for there were many more serious things to come. Michael's way of counselling was different to her cell group leader. She remembered he was exactly the same when she had spent time with him shortly after her marriage breakup. He was always very professional. He would sit opposite her in his chair, never beside her as her shepherd had done on the couch.

Michael would stare intently at her sometimes raising his closed right hand to rest his chin on, whilst his index finger would be extended upwards towards his nose as he leaned back into his chair. He would occasionally give a slow tap across his lips with it as if he was in deep thought trying to discern something.

She had wondered when over time she had come to understand spiritual things better, whether he was trying to ascertain the truthfulness of what was being shared or was he listening to his intuitive voice for a message from God. Perhaps both she had thought.

She would remember that as she shared the incident regarding the Spirit of Sadness and the Spirit of Regret that he showed no expression of surprise, but rather nodded his head as if in agreement. She thought that perhaps he had heard things like this happening before and so he would not be shocked. And in a selfish way she hoped he had. Prissie had been working up to this incident, keeping it to one of the last. It had happened on her shepherd's fourth visit a fortnight after he had given her the massage.

It was 10 o'clock at night when she heard the familiar tap on the window and opened the door to let him in. She had been in her tracksuit relaxing on the couch watching television and quickly jumped up to answer the door. Prissie had been looking forward to him calling on her again. She was enjoying getting this personal attention from her cell group leader. But not only that, she had been getting lonely over the previous few weeks for some sort of male company and this in a way fulfilled that need.

He had not long commenced the counselling session when he told her that God was impressing on him that she was possessed by a Spirit of Sadness and a Spirit of Regret from dwelling too long on regretful things in her marriage and that she needed to be released from these spirits. That she needed to be delivered from these demons that possessed her and were tormenting her, otherwise she would never find peace in her life.

Prissie shared with Michael that he had prefaced the deliverance session saying that there had to be a direct focus in prayer on that which was causing her most regret. He told her he believed it was the way in which she had been forced by her husband into having breast implants and the disgust, embarrassment and regret she felt. Prissie trusted him, she was gullible, she was alone with a man she felt cared about her; but as she realized later she was the perfect candidate for his perverted practices.

He suggested that she remove her tracksuit top, take off her bra and expose the breast implants that she had been forced by her husband to have that she regretted so much. She felt embarrassed but she did as asked because she trusted him. He was like a doctor to her in a way she explained.

He suggested they then move to the bedroom, both stand in front of a full-length mirror with him behind her, and for she to hold her breasts while he put his hands on top of hers and prayed. She was told to stare at her breasts whilst he led her in a prayer to verbally renounce the devil in them and that he would then cast the demons out.

After the praying and the supposed casting out had finished he had gently turned her around to hold her. They had stood there for some minutes with Prissie clothed only in her tracksuit pants quietly sobbing. She remembered that as he had held her he had rubbed her naked back in a sort of patting movement, put his lips against her ear and whispered, "that's right Prissie, let it all out, let it all out, you're having a release, God is healing you."

As she shared this Michael paused in the moment and his thoughts flashed back to a meeting he had been involved in with the Reverend Terry Channing some nine months earlier in Channing's office. He remembered Terry's final words to him as the meeting concluded, "and whatever anyone shares with you in any one on one conversation Michael, get as much information as possible, and get them to write it down and sign and date it."

Prissie was slightly taken aback by Michael's next question but answered it immediately accepting that he knew what he was doing and for some reason he needed to ask that question.

"I know this is personal but I need to ask it Prissie."

"Did he have an erection when he was praying with you and then afterwards when he was hugging you?"

Prissie felt herself flushed by the question. It had been something she had tried to wipe from her mind, but she answered honestly.

"Yes he did Michael. I didn't think about it at the time but did later. Yes he did."

"And do you remember if it felt like he was deliberately pressing it against you like full body contact, or even slightly rubbing it against you?"

Prissie paused and with tears welling up in her eyes replied.

"Yes it did Michael…yes he was pressing it against me and moving slightly."

"Thank you Prissie…I appreciate your honesty."

"Prissie another question. You mentioned that after prayer on the couch he would cuddle you for quite a while. Was there any type of sexual penetration involved in these cuddling sessions on the couch?"

"You mean did we have intercourse?"

"Yes...or touch your private parts in any way...anything else involving physical contact?"

"Yes there were...a couple of times...I was going to get to that."

"What happened Prissie?"

"Michael this is so hard to talk about."

"I know but we need the whole truth."

"Right...well yes...it was on about his fifth counselling visit I think."

"Around what date would that have been...you know...around what time of the month?"

"It was about mid August I think."

"Okay can you tell me exactly what happened?"

"Well it was after a counselling session and I was a bit emotional and sort of physically shaking and he was cuddling me and all of a sudden we started kissing...and then it happened."

"What happened?"

"Michael I'm so sorry...it all happened so quickly. We were both getting aroused, well I know I was, and he whispered that I had just had a spiritual release but I needed a physical and emotional one too."

"And before I knew it he had taken my hand and was rubbing it against his...you know...and I could feel his erection through his trousers...and then he slipped his other hand up my dress and into my panties and started masturbating me...it all happened so quickly...I'm so ashamed Michael."

Prissie started to sob and Michael handed her a tissue.

"Okay what happened then?"

"Well when we had finished he said we had better pray and ask for forgiveness for any lust that had entered our hearts and so he prayed."

"It was a pretty quick prayer and then he left straight away."

"And Prissie how many times did this sort of thing happen?"

"It happened again about two weeks later...about three or four times all up I guess."

"And there was definitely no intercourse involved?"

"No Michael."

"But a few times I also masturbated him and gave him oral sex."

"I'm sorry Michael."

Michael sensed that Prissie was feeling drained by the conversation. She looked pale and drawn.

"Okay that will do us…we'll have a short prayer asking for forgiveness for all that happened and for God's peace in your life and then we'll finish up."

They prayed together and Michael turned to Prissie.

"Remember Prissie that the Bible says when we are forgiven by God, which you are now, our sins are cast into the sea of God's forgetfulness to be remembered against us no more."

"In your case God no longer remembers that these things happened because there is genuine repentance."

"He does remember it against your shepherd but not against you. So if God does not remember it against you, then you have no right to remember it against yourself."

"In other words no ongoing guilt okay."

"A wise minister once told me that a false sense of guilt will cause people to hang onto the memory of regretful incidents like these for decades. Don't let that be you."

"Mistakes can become lifelong regrets if we hold on to them or lifetime lessons if we let them go. It's our choice."

"Yes thank you Michael."

He stood up hugged her and placed a foolscap block of paper on the coffee table beside her.

"I'll get you a cup of tea and I'd like you to write down everything that occurred between you and him, dates and times if possible, including the date he first visited and the date he last visited as best you can remember them."

"Michael there were other things like a fetish he had for me brushing his hair as he lay with his head on my lap, he used to get an erection then, and the see through lingerie modelling session that he asked me to do."

"You want me to include those things?"

"Yes I do Prissie, everything."

"Write all those things down in addition to what you have shared with me."

"Remember I want you to write down everything that you can remember. I want as much information as possible. And could you please date it and sign it at the bottom and print your name under it."

"Sure Michael sure...and I'm sorry Michael, I really am."

"I know you are Prissie and I appreciate you coming forward about this."

Michael had left the room, returned with a cup of tea, and then given her time to write up what he had asked. Prissie wrote up three foolscap pages, left his office and handed it to Michael who was talking to someone in the reception area. She hugged him, thanked him and left.

It was 7 a.m. on this her sixtieth birthday. Prissie had once again completed her compulsive birthday reverie and was still lying on her bed almost drifting off through mental tiredness when the phone rang and startled her. She moved quickly from her bed and hurried to the kitchen to answer it, and was greeted by the cheery singing voice of her oldest daughter Lindy.

"Happy Birthday to you...happy birthday to you...happy sixtieth birthday dearest mummy...happy birthday to you."

"Thank you sweetheart...thank you."

"Mama the girls and I just wanted to tell you we love you and that you're the best mum in the world."

Prissie could hear her two little granddaughters in the background calling out Happy Birthday Gramma.

"We want your sixtieth birthday to be the first of dozens more of the best birthdays of your life."

"Make them all a wonderful celebration mama, as we will."

"Now that's a good start to my day," Capricia replied, "thank you baby, thank you."

"I will sweetheart…I will…I promise you I will."

Prissie finished her phone call and stood quietly in her kitchen waiting for the jug to boil for her first morning coffee. She was reminded in her mind of the final words that Michael had said to her after praying for her in that counselling session some twenty years before. She thought about them once again as she poured her coffee and sat down on the lounge.

"Prissie…mistakes can become lifelong regrets if we hold on to them or lifetime lessons if we let them go. It's our choice."

She knew he was right, she had been holding on to certain things for far too long. She thought about the words her daughter had just said, the happy voices of her grandchildren, and the promise she had just made in return, and knew in her mind from that day forward her birthdays would never be the same depressing time again. It was time to let go and she did.

She knew in that moment that all regret had gone through a metamorphosis. She had turned the mistakes of so many years before into a present day lesson. She had finally cast her past into the sea of God's forgetfulness to be remembered against her no more.

> "Don't know…all Georgie said was that Davo had come to his house absolutely fuming…wanted out in a week…said he was moving down to Gratton… called Sloan the great deceiver, the false prophet, and said the only thing Sloan didn't have was a 666 stamped on his forehead."

Jeffrey Gibbons

The Return

SEVENTEEN

It would be the Saturday following Michael's visit from Prissie that saw him walk, folder under arm, into the Christian City Church auditorium and head up the stairs to Terry Channing's office. He was sure that Terry would be there, as it was well known that Terry spent most of the time including his weekends attending to church business, and apart from that Michael for some reason really didn't feel like making a formal appointment.

"Knock knock…busy?"

Terry looked up from the bible concordance he was examining on his desk.

"Michael…no…well not for you…come in brother."

He stood up and extended his hand.

"Good to see you Michael…God bless you…how's your week been?"

"Take a seat," he gestured.

Michael sat down in the leather recliner chair opposite Terry's desk after placing his folder on the corner of the coffee table.

"It's been good Terry…good…sorry to barge in unannounced…but I needed to talk to you about something."

"It's not a problem at all Michael…I was just adding the finishing touches to my message for tomorrow…what can I help you with?"

"Would you like a coffee for a start?"

"No I'm all good Terry but you go ahead."

"Thanks I will…the eyes have been getting a bit weary looking up scriptures."

"So," Terry continued as he proceeded to make his coffee, "how can I be of service to you?"

Michael leaned forward and picked up his folder.

"Terry I had a visit, well actually a pre-arranged appointment with a lady from our church in Springfield here last week…and by the way thanks for letting me use the spare office downstairs for church business."

Terry seated himself in the recliner chair opposite Michael placing his mug of coffee on the table.

"No problem at all…go ahead."

"Her name is Capricia Rossi…but she's known as Prissie."

"Anyway she sounded a bit distressed when she phoned me on the Thursday asking to come and see me, so I fitted her in on the Saturday."

"To cut a long story short the background to this is that I have a good friend at the AOG in Citiville…Luca Rossi…he's a pastor there."

"That's right I know Luca…an Italian bloke…very warm…I met him when I was preaching up there," commented Terry.

"Yes well Luca is Prissie's brother. He contacted me in October 1970 when Prissie's husband walked out on her, left her for another woman, and asked me if I would go and see her, you know to give her some counsel."

"Well I did and she eventually moved to Springfield with her two little girls. We got her a job and accommodation. She now manages a boutique clothing store in Lighthouse Bay."

"That's good Michael…good."

"Okay…the reason she wanted to see me."

"Guilt."

"Guilt from what Michael?"

"Guilt from having had a sexual relationship with her cell group leader…her married cell group leader."

"Right."

One of the things that impressed Michael most about Terry Channing was his calm professionalism. No sign of shock after what he had said, just a one word reply, right.

"I presume she isn't now…I mean it's stopped," Terry queried, "it's not an ongoing affair?"

"Yes it has stopped…it lasted for about two and a half months until she asked Jeffrey Gibbons if she could be moved to another cell group… she didn't tell him why…she just said that she wasn't getting on with her cell group leader's wife."

"Having sexual relations with a woman's husband does that," Terry smiled, "I can guarantee she didn't get on with the wife, and that would be why."

"Women can sense things like that, you know if something's going on. I call it God's inbuilt radar to protect the sanctity of marriage."

"Was she truly repentant Michael do you think or just looking to clear her conscience?"

"Yes Terry she was truly repentant and I prayed with her about it. She's a good lady deep down…just lost it I guess…and of course manip-ulated very cleverly by her cell group leader."

"Okay…good."

Terry paused for a moment chin resting on his hand and moved his head from side to side.

"You know Michael I've been kind of waiting for the first one of these to happen."

"What do you mean?" Michael queried.

"Well we had Bob Manfred here as you know the other week…sort of a follow up visit after Juan Ortega…and I said to Bob the only thing I was worried about with this shepherding movement, this discipleship teaching, was the potential for the abuse of power."

"I said you have these young men, the wannabe pastors, getting their first taste of pastoral responsibility with a small group, almost like a mini church. Then the ego starts to get involved."

"You know females come to them for counselling and they get a taste of the influence they have and the control they can exert. I mean here they are getting attention from females who are sharing some pretty personal things with them, things they perhaps wouldn't share with their own husbands. It's pretty intimate conversation."

"They are completely exposing their vulnerabilities, and of course for a potential predator, that dare I say is manna from heaven."

"I told Manfred this could be expected…he didn't seem to be too concerned though…and now…here we have it."

"Right…well anyway," Michael continued, "I spoke with Prissie for about an hour and had her write down everything, you know times and dates, the whole works, and sign and date her admissions."

Michael leaned forward and passed the folder to Terry.

"It's all in here if you want to read it?"

"Good Michael…good."

Terry took the folder, "yes I had better read it Michael."

"So who is this young cell group leader…do I know him?"

"Yes you do Terry," Michael paused and stared across at Terry, "you know him very very well, and he's not that young."

Terry's face assumed a stunned expression.

"You're kidding…it's not?"

"It is Terry…it is."

"Sloan."

"Whew Michael…now I really do want to read this."

Terry had an expression of surprise on his face and at the same time he looked relieved.

"Wow…wasn't expecting this when you walked in."

"Amazing Michael isn't it. How long has he been off my leash now, about six months?"

"Didn't take him long did it?"

"Well perhaps with this we've got him."

Michael continued.

"Terry we've got him on this but I want more."

"What do you mean?"

"Well think about it…Sloan has in a way been off your leash on a part time basis for a lot longer than you think."

"How do you mean?"

"Well he's been on the road in that district for at least three years whilst under your authority and has been doing tent preaching in that region for the last what six to eight years."

"Sure."

"Well you can't tell me that there's isn't a lot more dirty laundry in the crusade basket than this."

"He hasn't just taken a lust break from when he came under your authority, been a good boy all that time and just now started up again. I can't see that."

"He's a wolf Terry…he's just got more cunning to avoid detection."

"This would surely not have been his first little slip up. I mean the man's obviously got deep demonic problems."

"I guarantee if I dig deep enough I'll find more."

Terry thought for a moment.

"You're right Michael…you're probably right."

"Terry it was you who said that last time he got off any accusations it was on a technicality…the old she said he said stuff you called it."

"That's right I did."

"Well then this time we need to get a sufficient quantity of dirt to totally bury him…it's the only way to finish this…it's got to end now before he destroys any more lives."

Terry paused while he gathered his thoughts.

"You're right Michael…you're right…so how do you think we should handle it?"

"Well I've had a bit of time to think about it during the week as I've been driving."

"For the moment I don't think we should do anything…just sit on this," Michael pointed to the folder.

"It's not going anywhere and will still be there for us when we decide to move on him…but I want to gather more information that he can't bluff and bluster his way out of. As you said he tends to be quite arrogant."

"I'm due to start back down there at the end of next month. I've arranged with my boss that I take a backload of annual leave so I'll be able to settle back in to the fellowship full time for about four months. This will give me time to dig around."

"Good…good."

"So that's first."

"The other thing is, I was talking to Jeffrey the other day. He said Sloan is starting up some sort of travelling healing ministry team to minister to churches both here and overseas."

"That sounds like Sloan," Terry commented, "always trying to raise his own global profile."

Michael continued.

"Right… well he's getting Unwin Nicholls to head it up with him. Apparently Unwin believes he has his own healing gift and I would think Sloan sees some credibility coming out of the fact that his ministry team has a doctor on it that believes in the gift of healing."

"I believe Margaret Morrison is involved too."

"Yes…well he does love being around people with titles," returned Terry.

"Well I've been told by Jeffrey that Sloan is planning an overseas trip with the team late January for a couple of weeks to South Africa to visit a couple of churches the Women's Guild has been supporting with missionary offerings."

"They're going in January before the new school year starts."

"Who's he taking with him?" enquired Terry.

"At this stage Jeffrey said it's Sloan and Thorpey and their wives, and Dr Nicholls and Archie Vernados."

"The eldership have apparently approved the church to fund Sloan, his wife and Archie, and the rest are paying for the airfares themselves.

But they will probably get reimbursed with the love offerings from the churches over there."

"Right…so why would he be taking Archie…she hasn't mentioned it to you?" Terry queried, "I know you both are close."

"Yes we are close and not sure why she hasn't mentioned it…she probably will when I go down at the end of the month."

Terry maintained his concerned look.

"It's just that I'm not in favour of pastors taking single girls on mission trips. It's not a good look. You know Michael, you're in business, it's like the boss taking his secretary on a business trip."

"Sure Terry…but I presume he's taking her because of her work with children…and of course she's very musically talented…and she's in his cell group now…she went into his cell group when Prissie came out. And of course she and Bettina are both members of the Sisterhood that have been supporting these churches as part of their charity work."

Terry's face showed an expression of more concern but he said nothing.

"So anyway with Sloan and Thorpey out of the picture for a couple of weeks it will give me a chance to have a good snoop around."

"Are you happy with that Terry?"

"It means it might take a few months but we'll get him. Righteousness will eventually triumph over evil. We'll get him."

"You're right Michael…we'll get him," returned Terry with an increasingly confident tone in his voice, "yes I'm happy with that."

He paused for a moment.

"Do you have any thoughts about where you would start?"

"Terry you've heard of that saying just follow the money trail."

"Well with the help of Jeffrey Gibbons I am thinking I will follow the relationship trail…you know…which females Sloan seems to be close to… and at the same time which females Sloan's wife won't get close to or just openly dislikes. Sometimes the wife's attitude in relation to certain women is a dead giveaway that they think something is going on. They notice any woman who gets more attention from their husband than others."

"According to Prissie she thinks Bettina was suspicious of her which was why Bettina snubbed her at the home meetings."

"Let's see if Bettina can help us bag a wolf."

"If anybody can flush information out it will be Jeffrey once I let him off the leash."

"He and Janet are good people and once I let him into our confidence if there is more to discover he will discover it. He takes his nickname super sleuth very seriously."

Terry chuckled.

"Yes…right."

Michael stood up to leave.

"I won't take up any more of your time, I'll keep you updated."

"Okay Michael, well thanks, and good work. I feel relieved we are finally getting somewhere with this."

"Can I hang on to this folder and give it back to you at the service tomorrow?"

"Sure Terry…sure…keep it actually, I've got the originals."

Michael shook Terry's hand.

"Thanks for your support Terry."

"No…thank you Michael."

Terry watched Michael turn and leave the room.

He's a good man Terry thought to himself, a good man.

The year of Michael's absence, to him had passed quickly and much had been done in terms of the work in Springfield, much had happened and many developments had taken place. The homes of those who had decided to take up residence on the property were completed which saw the Sloans, the Goldways, the Purcells and the Rogersons take up residence at the end of August. The property was starting to get a sort of commune look and feel about it.

The training centre for girls at the farmhouse continued to power ahead with significant life changing successes. Having Zelda on the training team at the farmhouse was of great benefit since she related very well to the girls who had mostly come out of a nomadic hippie type lifestyle like herself. Then there was an added benefit to the participants also. Most of the girls who were part of the initial intake came away fully competent in the art of belly dancing.

Francis Morrison had joined the rest of her family in Springfield and started up her own medical practice with her sister Margie. Her brother Ron had settled in to the teaching environment in the school and had made the choice to continue in this vocation.

The new administration building having been completed had a small unofficial opening in late November, and Jeffrey being true to his word had engineered it so that Sloan selected the larger of the three offices for himself, which co-incidentally faced the western sun each afternoon. The telephone-counselling ministry had been set up by Jenny Purcell and was fully functioning with no shortage of volunteers wishing to be trained and involved.

Michael had been very busy tidying up the loose ends of his twelve-month work project up north, which meant he worked through Christmas and did not get any time in Springfield in December, but was excitedly anticipating his return to Springfield the first week in January. It would be on the Boxing Day after his Christmas Day walk along the beach that Michael decided to give Terry Channing a ring at home.

"Terry…Hi…Michael…how are you?"

"Sorry to interrupt your weekend."

"Not at all Michael…not at all."

"God bless you…what can I do for you?"

"Merry Christmas Day for yesterday."

"And to you too Michael."

"Terry just a quick call."

"As you know I am heading back to Springfield in a couple of weeks but wanted to get together with you and Bill to go over a few other developments that have occurred in the last six months. I think it's important to keep you in the loop…you know…the deflection process you mentioned."

"No problem at all Michael…Boxing Day today…what about tomorrow in my office…say 9 a.m…suit you?"

"It does Terry thanks."

"Okay Michael…see you then…look forward to it…bless you."

Many uneasy thoughts had begun to cross Michael's mind as to what might be going on in the commune with regards to the real intentions of some of the leaders. He had spent a reflective Christmas Day pondering these things. Whilst he was determined not to go over the top in his ruminating, he had begun to think that this could turn out to be a lot more than one sexual dalliance and that other serious things were going on.

It was now not just about a follow up on Sloan's deviant activity as disclosed by Prissie. It was evolving into things that appeared to be making the situation even far more serious, potentially dangerous. Alarm bells were ringing in his mind as Michael spent a few hours on Christmas morning having his obligatory walk along the beach of a tiny seaside village a half hour drive from the city.

He was disturbed about the direction the cell groups were being pushed by Sloan in turning them into little authoritarian type groups collecting tithes for the financial benefit of the work.

He was also starting to hear rumours from some of the young single adults in the church that certain cell group leaders were giving their group members advice bordering on non-negotiable instruction: advice on who they should date, whether they should marry someone or not, advice on where they should live, and even getting involved in the personal financial budgeting of members.

Even more concerning was when Danny had approached Michael after a church service in late November to tell him that a young woman in the church had been counselled by her cell group leader that it was highly unlikely she would ever marry. The shepherd had told the girl that God had impressed on him that she was being called to live a life of celibacy as part of the Bride of Christ.

It had been a busy time after the service, people were interrupting their conversation and Michael had failed to ask Danny who the young woman was. He made a mental note as he walked along the beach to revisit this with Danny. Note to self he thought, catch up with Danny boy and find out who the people were involved in this piece of heretical nonsense.

He suspected that the leaders doing things like this were learning this kind of controlling attitude from Sloan. It was consistent with Sloan's control agenda, but Michael knew he had to be sure before he acted. Pure rumour was not sufficient evidence to challenge Sloan on it.

Jeffrey had advised Michael that Sloan in his sermons was preaching more and more on the theme of seed faith or the prosperity doctrine: the threatening, almost blackmail type of fund raising tool being used by the large Charismatic churches in the United States. The preacher would preach that if you wanted to be financially successful, or if you wanted a specific healing, then the way to these blessings from God was to give financially to the church and that the more you gave the more blessed you would be.

Then there was the close association that had developed between Sloan and Unwin and between Sloan and Margie Morrison, and the feedback given by Terry Channing that Sloan and Unwin were friends from way back, with Unwin seemingly hiding this long association that they had together from all those around him.

There were the many times he had visited Unwin at his clinic and not once had Unwin mentioned that G.S. Enterprises, the tenant next door to his clinic, was actually the Springfield office of Garret Sloan prior to his moving into the commune.

There was this fascination that Unwin seemed to have for end time theories and the fact that he had set himself up totally for self-sustainability should the times get tough, as some of the doomsday theorists of the day were proclaiming. The doomsday writers were speaking of an impending drought and a worldwide famine coming upon the earth prior to the return of Christ. Unwin appeared to be embracing this teaching.

Michael recalled his conversation with Morty regarding the huge water tanks being placed underneath the homes of Thorpey and Sloan and the secrecy surrounding their installation. His mind started to have thoughts of a subterranean doomsday cult working quietly and secretly behind the scenes in the day-to-day operation of the commune.

He laughingly questioned in his mind as he walked along the beach whether paranoia was setting in but he knew it wasn't. He knew the original involvement of he and his group of friends in establishing the commune was honorable, but after his conversation with Morty about Margie's cosiness with Sloan, Michael was starting to have second thoughts about the truthfulness of her alignment with the group's intentions.

Maybe she too had pursued her own agenda all along. After all it was she who had initiated Michael's meeting with Unwin about the property they eventually purchased for the commune. What was the real motive behind the connection between Sloan, Unwin, and Margie?

What else is there I need to discuss with Bill and Terry tomorrow Michael thought as he turned around and commenced the walk back to his car? There were probably a lot more things. Time to get home and start writing a list for tomorrow's meeting.

⸺⸺ ∞ ⸺⸺

"Merry Christmas Pastor Michael for yesterday," came the cheery voice on the phone line as Michael sat pen in hand writing up his list.

It was Janny.

"Just wanted to do that before Jeffrey got on the line."

"Thank you Janny…and Merry Christmas to you."

"Bless you Michael…here's Jeffrey."

"Ditto for Christmas and a happy Boxing Day to you brother."

"And to you Jeffrey."

"Mate just thought I'd give you a quick call on a couple of things that came up last week."

"Sure Jeff."

"You mentioned that you would probably see Terry this coming week to update him before you came down."

"I am. Just doing a list of items to update him on now…I'm writing a list and checking it twice…going to discuss who's naughty and nice."

Jeffrey laughed.

"Okay Santa's helper…well here's a couple of things you can add."

"Remember you told me that in your meeting with Terry he had said to be on the lookout for sort of breakaway groups meeting together, you know like prayer groups that are not part of the normal."

"Yes I do."

"Well Danny boy mentioned to me last week that Sloan has a prayer meeting twice a week down at his home on Wednesdays and Fridays around 7 a.m. He said that when he heard about it he thought he would go along, and mentioned his intention to Ron Morrison. He said that Ron had fobbed him off. You know given him a subtle brush off, basically indicating that it was by invitation only."

"You're kidding."

"No mate dinkum."

"So old super sleuth thought, I might loiter around the Admin block around 6.45 a.m. on the day in question, you know with my tool belt on, like a tradie looking for a task, and have a gander at who goes to the prayer group."

"So I'm standing there tapping an imaginary nail into the office wall and who should drive the old Volvo past and pull up outside Sloan's house but Dr Unwin Nicholls. Next came doctors on wheels, a car carrying Mags and Francis. Then old Thorpey wanders across to

Sloan's house wiping the sleep from his eyes."

"And then who should hurry past but Ron heading down towards the house, carrying a clipboard might I add, perhaps as a type of camouflage? You know, well, I'm off to a school meeting."

"But here's the rub."

"I was just about to head off thinking my mission was accomplished and guess who drives past in his ute, pulls up outside Sloan's house and goes in?"

"I give in, who?"

"It was Jacko Wainwright."

"You're kidding…he is hardly ever at a church service. Why would he be going to a prayer meeting? I mean I know his wife is at every Sunday service, but not Jacko."

"You're right Michael…but you know what he is…he's a very close friend of Unwin Nicholls."

"You're right Jeffrey he is…he built Unwin's house."

"And Sloan's and Thorpeys."

"Yes…that's interesting."

"Anyway, I've named them the secret seven."

Michael chuckled.

"I used to love the Secret Seven adventure series by Enid Blyton when I was a youngster. They used to have them in the school library."

"Yeah mate…me too," quipped Jeff, "she was a pom like me, you couldn't help but like her. I liked her Noddy books too, remember Noddy and Bullwinkle?"

"I do…I do…loved Noddy and Bullwinkle."

"Anyway not sure whether I'm going to like this secret seven in the same way."

"So you've got that?"

"Yes thanks Jeffrey…got that…I've written it down."

Jeff continued.

"The other thing is that Sloan has started to do a lot more counselling in his office down at his house."

"Well Jeffrey you did give him an office facing the western sun."

"Yeah I know…blame me…but these counselling sessions are in the morning mate, sun's in the east then," continued Jeffrey, "and it is always one of the female staff or other females going down to his house…never any males."

"How do you know that?"

"Danny boy told me mate…Danny boy…he works there three days a week as a teacher's aide."

"Okay…so what are you saying?"

"Well the other day one of the girls passed me as she was walking back up to the schoolhouse and the look on her face…you know the red eyes…she had really been crying."

"Who was it?"

"Well I'm sorry mate but it was Archie."

"And I went to ask her was she okay but she brushed me off because Sloan was only about twenty paces behind her walking up to the schoolhouse too."

"So Sloan…I reckon he picked up on the fact that I was curious, he would have seen me approach Archie, because he walked out of his way to go past me and as he did he said, great day Jeffrey, the Lord is really starting to do some wonderful work in our school staff's lives."

"Something not quite right there, Jeffrey."

"Yes I agree, and one more thing and this could be really interesting. It's unfolding even as I speak. I think I will have to get paid a detective allowance as part of my package, it's been a big week."

"Jeffrey I've told you before, you don't have a package."

"Yeah right…I forgot."

"So what's this thing that's unfolding as we speak?"

"Okay, I got a phone call from Georgie Porgie this morning…George Purcell."

"Sloan has called an urgent eldership meeting for tomorrow night to discuss…get this…Dave and Thelma Rogerson are moving off the property and Dave wants the church to buy his house and pay him for all expenses occurred."

Michael sat for a moment stunned…trying to absorb what he had just heard.

"But Davo and Thelly only moved in what…only about four months ago…what's going on?"

"Don't know…Georgie said that Davo had come to his house absolutely fuming and wanted out in a week."

"Davo said he was moving back to Gratton…called Sloan the great deceiver and a false prophet…and said the only thing Sloan didn't have was a 666 stamped on his forehead."

"Apparently when George asked him to come inside to talk and tried to calm him down Davo went off again…said to George that if he wanted to talk to anybody go and talk to Beelzebub your neighbour over there and had pointed to Sloan's house."

Jeffrey was laughing as he explained it.

"I know it's not funny mate but I tell you…as Patty would say…you wouldn't be dead for quids would you?"

Michael chuckled.

"Wow…so he called Sloan Beelzebub…aka the devil."

"He certainly did Pastor…he certainly did."

"So what did George do?"

"Told me he couldn't do anything…he just couldn't calm Davo down. So he told him that he would talk to the eldership and get back to him. He was hoping I think that when Davo calmed down and got a bit more rational he would be prepared to talk through whatever was bugging him."

"Sounds like a pretty big bug Jeffrey to come on that strong. I mean Dave and Thelma are a really lovely quiet couple…and I know they loved the thought of living out their retirement on the property."

"Something's gone dramatically wrong."

"Yeah you're right Michael…and get this."

"After George had said he would talk to the eldership and get back to him Davo had stormed off. Then he stopped, turned around and yelled that if he didn't get a buyout, and all the money he had spent on the house back, he hoped the church would enjoy reading about itself in the local rag."

"Whew…something's crook in Tallarook," Michael replied.

Jeffrey continued.

"Anyway to cut a long story short until the next instalment George phoned Garret to tell him about Davo's visit. Garret's version of events was that Davo has got his knickers in a knot about some of his preaching and accused him of heresy. So according to the gospel of Saint Sloan he said that he got a bit riled about being called a heretic and told Dave that if he didn't like being here he was better off out."

"That right."

"No not really sure…probably not…but that's what Sloan said transpired."

"So then Sloan apparently told George to call an urgent eldership meeting for tomorrow night and they would sort it out…and that he had a couple of ideas."

"To be continued Pastor Michael."

"I will advise you of the outcome of the eldership meeting."

"Okay thanks."

"So Jeffrey, Dave had said he was going to move to Gratton?"

"Yes he did."

"Okay let me know how it goes…but I can tell you one thing Jeffrey my brother."

"What's that?"

"If Sloan does a snow job on this and particularly if he comes up with a way to pay Dave and Thelma out and Davo is gone before I return… then you and I will be taking a little trip my first day back."

"Right," replied Jeffrey, "and where might that be to Pastor?"

"To the new home of Dave and Thelma Rogerson in Gratton Jeffrey, for a cup of tea and a long talk."

"Oh and Jeffrey one more thing I need for my meeting with Terry tomorrow."

"Sure."

"Last time I was down Danny boy started to tell me a story about one of the cell group leaders who had told one of the female members of their cell something about that she was destined to live a life of celibacy as she was to be part of the Bride of Christ."

"I think that's what he said. We got interrupted and I drove back after the service and didn't get to ask him who the people were."

"Do you know who they were?"

"Of course…I'm sorry Michael I would have told you…I thought Danny had."

"It was Sloan Michael…Sloan was the cell group leader…and it was Archie who he told this to."

Michael breathed in and out deeply and sighed.

"Okay thanks for that update Jeffrey…I had better let you go, this phone call is costing you."

⸿

"Hi Janny…it's Michael…is Jeffrey there please?"

"Hey Pastor Michael, yes he is, when are you back, tomorrow?"

"Yes I am Janny but I don't want anyone to know. That's why I want to talk to Jeff. To see if he's free for a drive down to Gratton."

"I'm sure he is Michael…if he has got any jobs on he can stall them for a day…I'll put him on."

"Michael I have a bit of additional news," was Jeff's first sentence as he picked up the phone.

"And yes Janny just mentioned re Gratton tomorrow…no problem… call me when you arrive."

"Mate things just keep getting weirder and weirder."

"As I mentioned to you yesterday Mags moved into Davo's house last weekend."

"Right."

"Well I'm up at the school yesterday...you know...getting a few things done before the kiddies get back. I pulled up at the office and there are two brand new, yes brand new, British racing green coloured Holden Commodores parked out the front of the admin office...mate they were sparkling new."

"So I got a bit curious and headed into the office."

"Not many people around being the holidays but Bettina was on duty at reception and Sloan was chilling out in his office, you know leaning back in his chair hands behind his head shooting the breeze, with Mags sitting on the other side of the desk."

"The office door was open for a change by the way."

"So I goes to the reception and said to Bettina, just letting you know I'm here doing a couple of jobs in the classrooms, if anything else needs doing let me know."

"Well Sloan sees me at reception and calls me in waving, Jeffrey Jeffrey, come and hear about the blessing of God to Bett, which is what he calls Bettina as you know."

"So I went into his office said hello to Mags and this is what Sloan said... are you ready for it?"

"I am mate tell me."

"Okay Pastor I'll try and say it the same way Sloan did."

"He said Jeffrey Jeffrey isn't God a wonderful God...Dr Morrison has just given a gift to Bett, because of her tireless service to the work, a brand new car...isn't that wonderful?"

"Mate I was stunned I mean knowing that there is no undying friendship between the two."

"I mean you spend a day in that office and the most frequent sentence you will hear Bettina say when she answers the phone is, "I'm sorry Margie, Garret's tied up at the moment.""

"And then Sloan went on to say."

"Yes Margie had to get a new car for the surgery home visits and they were clearing the remaining stock in that colour green so she got a tre-mendous deal, and then the Lord impressed on her to get one for Bett for all the hard work she does. It's truly wonderful."

Michael grinned over the phone line.

"And what did you say Jeffrey?"

"Michael I just wanted to get the you know what out of there. So I mumbled something pious like that's wonderful, enjoy Bettina, better get these jobs done, and as Morty would say I took off like a robber's dog, might I say before I got physically ill."

"Can you believe that…what do you reckon that is all about?"

"Two identical green cars she bought and gave one to Bettina."

"What is that all about?"

"Jeffrey heaven only knows but I think I might also."

"You do?"

"Yes but I'll talk to you about it tomorrow."

"See you around 11 a.m. mate."

It was a pleasant day for a drive to Gratton with the sun shining brightly in a perfect blue sky.

"Shame we're not two months earlier Jeff…would have seen all the Jacarandas resplendent with their purple flowers…is purple the colour?"

"More of a blue-purple I think."

"You're right though. Janny and I drove down to Gratton last year in early November for the Jacaranda festival and it was absolutely beauti-ful. Street after street lined with these trees fully in bloom. They had a parade too, you know all these beautifully decorated floats."

"What do they call Gratton…Jacaranda City?"

"They do Jeffrey…they do."

"Hey Michael speaking of beautiful things I've got a good story to tell you about our friend Danny the Dreamer."

"Right."

"Well he came over to see me early the other morning and said that he had a dream that troubled him. He was really looking for advice as to what to do."

"Anyway he described the dream to me and it concerned Garret Sloan. In the dream he said that Sloan had appeared to him as a powerful image standing at the end of his bed and in a moment had twirled around and changed into diabolous himself, the great deceiver, the father of lies, the devil disguised as a shepherd."

"He asked me what he should do…and I half jokingly said…go and tell him Danny boy," Jeffrey paused and laughed, "not thinking he would just go and do that without any more consideration."

"So he did…he went to see Sloan and told him."

"Really."

"What did Sloan do?"

"Danny boy said he went pale and then basically went into offensive mode…you know…sprouting off about him being Danny's shepherd and that Danny needed to take notice of him and that the dream was just the devil trying to deceive Danny."

"So how did Danny take that?"

"Mate I reckon Sloan confused him a bit in the moment but then again Sloan is good at that…you know…getting on the offensive and acting all spiritual to get the upper hand."

"Well you know what I think Jeffrey?"

"I think Danny really truly could have a gift there, that's what I think."

"There are two people now who think Sloan is of the devil…Davo and Danny."

"Yeah…I think you're right."

Michael continued.

"So tell me again the eldership meeting was over in fifteen minutes?"

"Sure was…Garret told the story that Dave had approached him, to tell him that he disagreed with Sloan's preaching on tithes and this drift over to preaching on the latter days from Revelation."

"Then when Garret said to him why don't you stay home when I preach, or something like that, well mate it was a red rag to a bull according to Sloan. An argument ensued and Dave said he was leaving the church."

"Jeffrey if I wasn't driving I'd raise both hands and give a slow clap…I mean…something's not right there."

"I know, I know" replied Jeff, "the problem was that Dave refused to talk to the eldership…he just wanted out and quickly."

"So whatever Garret said could not be disputed," replied Michael.

"Right…and I also think Unwin wanted it to disappear. He didn't want any bad publicity that might reflect on him personally or professionally."

"So then let me get this right."

"The day after Boxing Day Garret talks to Margie Morrison about the commune needing to find a buyer quickly to pay Dave and Thelma out and Margie immediately offers to buy the house."

"This is the same Margie Morrison that just bought a car for Bettina."

"That's about it Michael."

"Davo moves out and Mags moves in…I think she is moving in this weekend actually. Once Dave got his money he just wasn't hanging around. Up drove the removalist truck and he was gone."

Michael shook his head from left to right.

"Speaking of Mags Michael, what were your thoughts about her gift to Bettina of the green Commodore…you said you think you know?"

"Jeffrey those two are trying to take us all for mugs."

"You mean Garret and Bettina?"

"No I mean Sloan and Mags."

"Think about this…which house is the most obvious in terms of visibility on the property from the school and from the road that goes down to the school?"

"Well it's Davo's house or should I say Margie's now…it's full view out in the open about 100 metres from the road and the school."

"That's right and it's low set ranch style with two big lock up garages and that circular driveway out the front where visitors park their cars."

"Right…so."

"Jeffrey if you were driving down the road to the school say 9 or 10 o'clock at night or anytime for that matter and you glanced across and down to that house and you saw a green Commodore parked out the front, whose car would you think it was?"

"Well I'd probably just think Mags is home."

"Exactly…anyone would…Margie's house, Margie's car."

"Oh…I get you."

"Keep an eye on things and see who spends the most time driving around in Bettina's new green car."

"I guarantee in a very short time it will be Garret."

"And that allows Garret to visit Mags anytime, park his car out the front while hers is in the lock up garage, and anybody who sees the car out the front will just expect it to be Margie's."

"Jeffrey as I just said they both think we are all a pack of mugs."

Michael glanced at Jeffrey.

"Mate did you study Shakespeare's Hamlet at high school?"

"No we had Macbeth."

"You?"

"Yes we had Hamlet."

"I have a favourite line in the play…it's funny how it's stuck with me over the years."

"What's that?"

"It was when an officer of the palace guard sees the ghost of the dead king walking over the palace and in describing what he had seen as wrong or not quite right he says, something is rotten in the state of Denmark."

"Jeffrey…that story from Sloan re Davo and the one about the green car…I think something is rotten in the state of Denmark."

"Yeah I think you're right."

"Or as you say Michael, in the Aussie vernacular, something's crook in Tallarook."

"Let's see what Davo has to say Jeff now that he's got his money and hope-fully calmed down…and you got on pretty well with him didn't you?"

"Yes I did…he's a retired builder…it was me who actually invited him to visit the church in the first place."

"Hmm," replied Michael, "well let's hope he doesn't hold that against you."

"Look before we get there I had better update you on a meeting I had with Prissie a few weeks ago."

"Yes she said she was going up to the city for the day and was going to pop in and see you."

"Yes she did…and you need to hear this."

⌘

"Well thanks for a lovely date today Pastor," Jeffrey quipped as Michael dropped him home at 6 p.m. that evening.

"It's been a…how could we describe it…an eye opener."

"Wanna come in, Janny will make you a chocolate?"

"Thanks but no thanks mate I'll keep going."

"Got to get back to my newly painted apartment and get my bags unpacked and I need to have a think about where we go from here…there are a lot of things to work through."

"Not wrong Michael."

"Mate are you and Janny free to come around tomorrow night. I think we need to sit down and just nut everything out and work out where to from here?"

"Not a problem for us …what about around 6 ish?"

"Sounds good Jeffrey…I'll see you then…and thanks for your work today mate…you have a way with words…you did good with Dave…and we got what we wanted…just have to figure out now what to do with it."

"No problem…nite…see you tomorrow night."

"And don't worry about food Pastor…I'm sure you haven't had time to pick up any groceries…we'll bring some leftovers."

"Thanks mate…that's great."

"Michael do you remember last year, no, the year before last at the Springfield Show when Dan and Zelda put on that puppet show for the kids in the tent?" queried Jeffrey.

"I do…they were good."

"More lasagna Michael?"

"No I'm good Janny…thank you…that was beautiful…very kind of you. I'll pick up some groceries tomorrow."

"My pleasure."

"Sorry babe for interrupting you."

"No that's okay," continued Jeff, "I was going to say I'm starting to feel like we may have been like those puppets at the show for the last few years…someone else has been pulling our strings…do you know what I mean?"

"Well sort of," replied Michael, "but I think all of us went into this commune thing with the best intentions. It's just that it appears some others have come in with a different agenda…more self-interested than ours and are attempting to hijack it."

"Yeah…right."

Michael continued.

"I mean what if this is really a game in Lila…you know the Divine Playground."

"What if Divinity's intention was what we have actually brought to pass…a fellowship of believers…connected…loving each other…looking after each other…working together…giving selflessly…a school for those parents who want their children to know God…you know a lot of good things have come out of this."

"So where are you going Michael?"

"I mean…this commune…really good things have been created in

God's name with all our efforts...we have all been vehicles for God's creative work."

"Well if we are co-operating with the creative forces of the universe... you know Goodness...who does that subsequently invite into the picture?"

"I mean we all believe in the supernatural and that life on earth, it's first and foremost God's creative will being translated here on this earth don't we?"

"Sure."

"So who would be getting the nasties about that?"

"You mean satanic forces Michael?" enquired Janet.

"Exactly...it's a game remember...a spiritual warfare game."

"And if the forces of goodness have worked through us to create something beautiful and connected and still growing, then satanic forces, the deceiver, will come in to try to disconnect and destroy it."

"Good things on earth, Divinity's will, are all brought about by people and similarly bad things, you could say Lucifer's will, are brought about by people also. We are all vehicles of expression for either goodness or evil in everything we say and everything we do...there's no in between...you can't be half good or half bad in anything in life...it's absolute."

"And the other thing is that even though we feel that what is coming out right now is horrific...you know I've always been a firm believer that God's timing is never wrong."

"So rather than us looking at ourselves as puppets, how about we take on the role of puppet master and work out a play with God's guidance that brings a righteous conclusion to this."

"When I was a young boy once a month I had to deliver a fruit cake to a church friend of my mother, Nell Stanton. And one time after I had delivered the cake she gave me a small New Testament book. And she had hand written on the inside front cover...trust in the Lord with all your heart, lean not to your own understanding, in all your ways acknowledge him, and he will direct your paths."

"So really that's all we have to do…believe that our paths are being directed by a spiritual force magnificently more powerful than the forces directing Sloan…and things will work out. Hopefully it will be with minimal collateral damage on the commune or us. But of course there will be some. There are always casualties in a war."

"But the thought of that can't deter us…we must act…evil prospers when good men do nothing."

"Michael."

"Yes Janny."

"I like Dr Nicholls."

"So do I Janny."

"Well do you think he is aware of what Sloan is up to with the sex thing? Jeffrey told me about what happened with Prissie and now the Dave and Thelma thing…it's awful. It makes me feel sick in the stomach."

"So do you think Dr Nicholls knows?"

"Couldn't say one hundred percent for sure…gut feel probably not… but Unwin could turn out to be an enabler…which is almost as bad as someone who knows."

Janny began clearing the table.

"What's an enabler Michael?"

"Someone who either knows that some sin is being committed or suspects it but doesn't do anything about it because it might interfere with their own agenda."

"So they are actually condoning it?"

"They are."

"Bettina, Thorpey and Cherie…I would guarantee they are enablers from what Terry Channing shared…Unwin…wait and see."

"Okay well how about you two boys continue your battle plan on the balcony…it's a beautiful night out there…and I'll tidy up inside here and bring you guys out some coffee soon."

⸺⧈⸺

"I bags the squatter's chair," Jeffrey said moving quickly to the balcony door.

Michael sat down beside Jeffrey.

"My pleasure to give you permission to sit there."

"So Jeffrey have you said much to Janny about our visit with Dave and Thelma?"

"Yes mate I told her everything…she's my girl…we have no secrets."

"How did she take it?"

"Like a bomb hit her."

"I told her about Prissie first and then the Dave and Thelma thing."

"We were up until after midnight."

"But then she said something that really made me think."

"What was that?"

"Well it lines up with what you just said in there about God's timing never being wrong."

"She said babe…isn't it amazing that if Dave hadn't decided to return the borrowed shovel to Sloan's house at that particular time we might not be having this conversation now."

Jeffrey continued.

"I mean poor old Dave doing the right thing returning the shovel to Garret's garage and catches the Mickey Mantle of ministry hitting a home run with his medical mistress."

Michael laughed out loud, "you have a very poetic way with words Jeffrey."

"But you've gotta laugh haven't you?"

"Yeah…otherwise you'd cry," Jeff continued.

Jeffrey chuckled.

"I mean Pastor think of how Morty would tell this story."

"Well cobbers," he would say, "bit of bad luck for Sloany…gettin' caught out…he would probably have only been on the plate for no more than three minutes…then again that's all the time he probably needs to hit a home run."

Jeffrey and Michael started to crack up. They knew it was a stress reliever. They were both seeing the funny side of it now in addition to the seriousness. Janny came through the door with the tray of coffees.

"Good to see you guys laughing…it's a good stress reliever…and boy don't we all need that?"

"So…come on…share the joke?"

"No nothing for a lady's ears Janny…your dear Jeffrey was just doing an impersonation of Morty."

"Okay then if that's the case you are probably right…not for a lady's ears."

"Michael I'll leave you two to it…but just one question or no maybe two."

"Sure Janny."

"I'm still a bit shocked by all of this…and so very disappointed in Mags."

"I'm sure you are."

"Okay first question…do you think Prissie and Mags are both complicit in what happened…you know in there with their eyes wide open or were they just conned by Sloan?"

"No and yes."

"What do you mean?"

"I mean Prissie no and Mags yes."

"Why Mags yes?"

"Because according to the statement we have from Dave, when Dave confronted them both and threatened to take what he had witnessed to the eldership, he said Mags turned to him as she buttoned herself up, and I think the word used was arrogant Jeffrey wasn't it?"

"Yes it was."

"They turned to Dave and very arrogantly said go ahead old man no one will believe you."

"That's what sent him off…not just what he saw but the arrogance of the two in thinking they were untouchable."

"Oh Michael…that's so sad…we never really knew her did we?"

"No I guess we didn't Janny…the hidden things of the heart."

"Did you say you had a second question?" continued Michael.

"Oh yes…do you think there's more to uncover…I mean more women he's been involved with?"

"Yes I absolutely do Janny…sadly…and that's what Jeffrey and I are going to find out."

"We'll probably never find out the full extent but we'll definitely find some."

"I think he's a demonically controlled sexual predator."

"Okay…right…well I've brought my book…so I'll leave you guys to it…I'm so angry at him."

"I know Janny…thanks for the coffee."

"Oh just one question Janny before you go in…you work a bit up at reception don't you…when Bettina and Cherie are on?"

"Yes I do…I do filing for the school and Bettina and Cherie are most days there, glued to the reception desk like they personally own the place."

"Okay tell me this."

"People come to reception throughout the day and ask is Garret in I would presume…you know wanting to see him."

"All the time."

"Tell me this."

"Are you aware of any female visitors that come looking for Garret and sort of get the cold shoulder from Bettina. You know her voice tone or comments to Cherie after they have gone that definitely indicates she has a problem with them?"

"Absolutely."

"You mean there absolutely are," Michael replied, surprised by Janny's quick answer.

"Yes there are three or four."

"Who are they?" enquired Michael.

"Okay…let's see."

"In order of degree of dislike she obviously has big issues with Colleen

Jones…from the Emmanuel Bookstore…she'd be top of the Bettina dislike list."

"Really?"

"Yes…Colleen is always popping in with samples of new books for the bookstore."

"Bettina really gives her the short shift…you know."

"I'm sorry Colleen …Garret's very busy right now."

"Next she definitely has issues with Mags…well I guess we now know why."

"And just lately she seems to be having issues with Archie…not sure why."

"Lastly there's that darkish skinned girl…not sure what nationality she is but she talks with a sort of Jamaican accent…like you hear on those Bob Marley songs."

"She's only new to the church…I think her name is something like Charmaine…not sure."

"Okay…thanks Janny…enjoy your book…we won't be long."

"Now there's an interesting coincidence young Jeffrey."

"What's that?"

"Tell me my learned friend," continued Michael, "Colleen Jones and Margie Morrison what do they both have in common?"

"Certainly not their hair colour…one's brunette and the other is a redhead…one's curly and one's straight."

"I don't know…enlighten me Pastor Michael…what do they both have in common?"

"Jeffrey the houses of both women were Sloan's primary accommodation when he visited their towns on his crusades over the years."

"Colleen in Springfield and the Morrison home in Gratton."

"It was you my super sleuth friend who found that out."

"Crikey…so I did…I'd forgotten."

—∞∞∞—

Jeffrey took a sip of his coffee and turned to Michael.

"This is not looking good mate is it?"

"No it's not Jeffrey…but we press on."

"When did you say the ministry team fly out to South Africa… Saturday was it?"

"Yes Michael."

"The admin office has the spare keys to all houses on the property doesn't it?"

"Yes we have a set of keys for all houses."

"Okay…Monday when it's all clear you and I are going to go for a look…we'll try to do it when no one is around…but you can always use the excuse you are looking at maintenance issues."

"Okay…what are we looking for Pastor?"

"Well to put it in Morty's language…a big friggin' tank…and any other doomsday paraphernalia."

"Done."

"Now young Jeffrey…let's talk about the four names Janny gave us… and what we do with them."

"Oh and one other thing…the three women involved in the secret seven prayer group meetings."

"Yes…Mags…Archie…and Mags' sister Francis."

"That's right."

"How well do you know Francis Jeff?"

"Actually getting to know her quite well…she's come into my cell group."

"What's she like…since I've been away for twelve months I can't say I really know her?"

Jeff continued.

"Well for a start she's totally different from her sister…you know how Margie can be quite, I was going to say confident, but perhaps now after what Dave has told us we could change that to arrogant…well Francis is totally different."

"You know if ever I used to joke about Sloan how Mags would always defend him?"

"Well with Francis…totally different…something there…don't know what it is…almost as if she dislikes him."

"And apart from that she seems just a genuinely nice person…a bit naïve and young for her age but that could be because she's spent the last six years with her head buried in medical books."

"Okay…thanks…let's add Francis to our list of three names to talk about."

"Mate you don't think Sloan would be having it on with both sisters do you?"

"Not sure what I think Jeffrey…but if you look at motive and opportunity…well we all know Sloan's motive is to get people under his control and he is using sex to do it with the females."

"My gut feel is that in some ways he thinks if he can control the women the men will follow."

"In terms of opportunity hasn't Francis been alone in the Morrison house in Gratton for twelve months after the family moved up here?"

"Yes she has."

"Well there's an opportunity for Sloan."

"True."

"Terry Channing mentioned that Gary the AOG pastor down there said that Sloan only stays at the Morrison's house when in town. The house all to himself…just he and Francis…mate I wouldn't put anything past Sloan."

"You know Michael when this all breaks the whole work could implode…I mean Sloan has built up a following these last couple of years."

"Yes it may…the degree of collateral damage will depend on how well we manage it through."

"But Jeffrey we didn't come into this for the glory factor, we came in for the goodness factor."

"I like that Michael…and it's true."

"So if it implodes…que sera sera…it implodes…hopefully it won't."

"But one thing is sure…people will take sides…some will get angry, open themselves up to the spirit of deception and defend him to the last."

"As I've said before people have their own agenda…and it doesn't necessarily have to be a big agenda. Some people will just be angry at us for exposing this and disrupting their little cocooned lives."

"As I always say people convinced against their will are of the same opinion still."

"I mean think back on all the times Mags in conversation with you Jeffrey defended Sloan to the hilt, and all that time he's hitting home runs with her on Saturday mornings and she's praying with him for other people's sins on altar calls on Sunday nights."

"Yeah your right Michael."

"Look I've talked this through with Terry…unfortunately there will be collateral damage…I may be part of it…but Sloan's a bad dude… he's a wolf in sheep's clothing…and he has to be stopped."

"As I say all the time…evil triumphs when good men do nothing."

"It's a spiritual warfare in the heavenlies translating to a warfare between the good guys and the bad guys here on earth."

"We are all called to righteousness…to do the right thing."

"You with me?"

"Of course Michael…both Janny and I are."

Jeffrey paused for a moment and appeared to be gathering his thoughts.

"Michael I know you might be avoiding this thought, I know I am, but we probably need to discuss it as a separate component, how do we handle the Archie side of this?"

"No I have thought about it…long and hard."

"Okay…this is how I see it."

"Naturally I'm thinking that the overall process will follow similar to the way it did with Prissie, in that we will arrange for a sit down session with Colleen and with Francis and anybody else we find to get full written statements of any wrongdoing."

"No good talking to Mags…if she's adopting the arrogant attitude that Davo said she did, she is going to give us nothing, and certainly not going to give Sloan up if this has been a long term relationship and ongoing, which I'm starting to think it might be."

"She's got a title you know, doctor. She's more valuable to him than Prissie. Prissie was probably just one of Sloan's little dalliances on the side and there's probably a lot more around but we would be lucky to find them."

"No doubt Sloan and Mags have already compared notes as to how they will handle it if I raise the subject now that I am back. No disrespect to the eldership but Sloan will be feeling cocky thinking he's successfully snowed the eldership and now be waiting to see my reaction."

"So with Margie, no interview, we'll go with the written statement Davo gave us which includes her anyway."

"Now I think we need two more written statements signed and dated from two other women that Sloan has had sexual relations with and I'm thinking start with Colleen and Francis."

"Remember that Terry does not want for it to end up this time being a she said he said argument."

"I'm not copping out with Archie but I'm saying not me but you interview her last. But she will definitely be interviewed."

"Jeffrey with what I'm seeing I don't have a good feel about Archie's involvement, they've been in each others pockets these last twelve months, and I have resigned myself to the fact that if she is or has been involved with Sloan then the beautiful relationship we had will be part of the collateral damage."

"I know that…I've resigned myself to the fact."

"The only thing I'm wanting to save is her job in the school, it would break her heart to lose it, all because of that wolf doing what he does."

"I guess what I'm saying if you are agreeable Jeffrey is that we go with Colleen and Francis and if it works we get their written statements and then you interview Archie straight after that, but we don't put her interview in writing. Just see if she's willing to come clean if there is anything."

"I think I owe her that."

"Are you comfortable with that Jeffrey?"

Jeffrey's voice lowered and he spoke gently.

"Of course I am mate…of course I am."

"Okay thanks…now how about I'll get us another coffee and we'll talk a bit further on how and when we are going to end this."

66 *"We're thinking Terry that there is a subterranean doomsday cult operating in the commune buying guns and storing food and that the secret seven prayer group that I told you about are the members at this stage…or at least some of them."*

Michael Winton

To Trap A Wolf

EIGHTEEN

It would be around 8 p.m. on the last Friday of the month of March 1973 that Michael picked up the phone at Jeffrey and Janet's house to make the call to Terry Channing.

"Michael…bless you…how did you go…get everything tidied up?"

"Yes Terry all completed today as I mentioned we would in our conversation at the start of the week."

"Jeffrey and I are thinking of driving up tomorrow and going through the paperwork with you."

"Sounds good Michael…how does 11 a.m. suit you…means you don't have to rush?"

"Sounds good Terry…bless you…see you at 11 tomorrow."

Michael turned to Jeffrey and Janet who were standing slightly nervously beside him.

"We're in Jeffrey…this is it mate…showtime."

It had been an eventful six weeks since Michael's return to the commune with much catching up to do. There were many secret missions and secret meetings for Jeffrey and Michael to complete as they tried to make sense of this seeming madness that had engulfed parts of the commune. There was an urgency in their hearts and minds to try and wrap up their investigation as quickly and as quietly as possible, whilst at the same time keeping an absolute lid on what they were doing so as not to give anything away.

Sloan's reaction should he find out was considered to be unpredictable and it was recognized by both Michael and Jeffrey that this cloud of arrogance that hung over his personality would cause him to move into survival mode should he detect any challenge to his position.

However things had eventually all come together.

"Good Morning Terry...Bill...bless you," came Michael's cheery greeting as he entered Terry Channing's office with Jeffrey.

"Good Morning Michael...good morning Jeffrey," came the responses from Terry and Bill in return.

"Take a seat guys while I make us all a coffee...I'm sure it's been a tiring drive, well a tiring week probably."

"Thanks Terry."

Michael placed the four folders on the edge of the coffee table and he and Jeffrey flopped back into their seats.

Bill patted Michael on the shoulder.

"Terry and I appreciate what you and Jeffrey have done these last few months my brother. Terry has been keeping me up to date with the conversations you and he have been having. You've both stayed the course and done what is right...well done."

"Thanks Bill."

Terry placed the tray with the coffee mugs, milk and sugar on the table.

"Help yourself guys when you're ready."

"Thanks Terry," replied Jeffrey slightly in awe of his surroundings, "I'll do yours Michael if you want to start."

"Yes Michael, go ahead."

Michael reached for the folders and handed them out.

"Okay I've done copies of the documentation for all of you in case you want to refer to them as we speak. I still have all the originals. I was thinking Terry that I will just give you a broad outline of what we found...the detail is in each of the signed admissions."

"With the doomsday cult stuff I've just done a summary of what

Jeffrey and I discovered with a couple of photos."

Terry and Bill both opened their folders.

"Good work Michael…good work, can you start with what you found at Sloan's house? After talking to you on the phone I was slightly blown away. I was expecting you to find stuff re his sexual liaisons but I never expected this…you said guns and food stored up."

"Yes Terry…Sloan has an office at the front of his house, just inside the door. It is where he does most of his female counselling. Although I understand he uses the soft sofa in the lounge room when Bettina is unlikely to come down the hill and pop in."

"It was Jeffrey who actually discovered this in his office. You were checking for termites weren't you Jeffrey?" Michael grinned.

"Borers actually Michael," returned Jeffrey slightly nervously.

"There was a sizeable trapdoor covered with a mat in his office leading to a sectioned off area under his house. You remember I told you about Morty's story regarding the water storage tanks."

"Yes I do."

"The trapdoor hole had steps leading down to under the house. Jeffrey and I climbed down and lo and behold Morty was right: one of the biggest rainwater tanks I have ever seen."

"And the other stuff?"

"Food Terry food…cartons and cartons of canned food…you know the type with about seven years life on it…sitting on purpose built racks on one of the walls and right beside that a wooden storage box which when we opened it we found six rifles of the 303 kind and enough ammo to start a small war."

Bill shook his head sideways, "or enough ammo to defend the food and water supply…it's almost unbelievable…the man is mad."

"And dangerous Bill," Michael replied, "that's doomsday cult stuff, or what do they call them…doomsday preppers."

Terry had opened his folder and was looking at the photos.

"This is good Michael…and Jeffrey…good."

"We're thinking Terry that there is a subterranean doomsday cult operating in the commune buying guns and storing food and that the secret seven prayer group that I told you about are the members at this stage…or at least some of them. Who knows who else he might have involved, he has a lot of impressionable followers."

"Dear God," replied Bill, "and I've probably been feeding them when I come down and preach from the Book of Revelation on the Apocalypse."

"No Bill…not at all…you haven't been preaching on storing up food and water and buying guns…this is demonic…I personally believe Sloan has a Spirit of Deception operating in his life as well as a Spirit of Control," continued Michael.

"As well as a dozen or so others," Jeff chimed in.

Terry chuckled, "I think you're right Jeffrey."

"So with the house well that's all and everything's in the folder," commented Terry.

"Yes it is Terry. It's a house of dirty tricks and we are presuming we would find the same at Thorpey's but couldn't get in as he has someone house sitting…but we know from Morty that he has the same water tank installed as Sloan."

"It's actually the same size as the one Unwin has at his property only his is visible, above ground. Jack Wainwright who is a builder friend of Unwin installed all three tanks. He built all three houses too and we believe he is a member of the cult."

"Now a brief summary of what we discovered about Garret's sexual activity Terry which I believe is well and truly enough to nail him. I'll give it to you in compressed form, if you want the longer x rated version it's all in the written, dated and signed admissions in your folder."

Terry grinned. He liked Michael's sort of casualness and at the same time determination in what was unfolding.

"Can see you've worked in business Michael."

"To summarize it all Terry, Sloan has been having sexual relations with at least four people that we know of and in my opinion there would be a lot more over the years…and as I said I'll give a brief explanation about each one."

"By the way these four are all within the same time frames so it's not that Garret has an affair, finishes it and moves on to the next one. He's not that chivalrous. These incidents were all occurring pretty much simultaneously. The man is a predator of the highest degree."

"I mean whilst he was probably wrapped in an intimate embrace professing his soul mate love for Margie Morrison, he was the next night or maybe even the same night tapping on the window at Capricia Rossi's house seeking some sort of sexual gratification."

"Or if not at Prissie's place he was in Gratton staying overnight alone with Francis Morrison having mutual masturbation sessions with her, and as you know Terry, Francis is Margie's sister."

"He's a weak man Terry…a weak man."

"You sound righteously angry Michael," commented Bill.

"I am Bill…I am. This man is on a self-satisfying mission that will destroy lives. I think the way you put it Terry was that lives are destroyed for decades."

"I did Michael…I did…and it's true…I've seen it before…people carry the guilt and shame for decades."

Michael leaned forward.

"Okay if we work through one by one…and as I said I'll give you the brief version…the detail is in the folder."

"Margie Morrison we did not interview, however reference to her is made in Dave Rogerson's statement."

He turned to Bill.

"Bill I think you know Dave…he lived on the property?"

"I do Michael…I stayed at his house once before I started staying with you…he seems a gentlemanly type of chap."

"He is Bill…a lovely man."

"Margie was caught in a sexually compromised position with Sloan in his garage by Dave Rogerson. She later conspired with Sloan for her to purchase Dave's property from him for them both to get Dave out of the way off the property as quickly as possible."

"When Dave confronted them after he had caught them in the act and threatened to go to the eldership he had been arrogantly told, go ahead, no one will believe you."

"I have also put in some detail about Margie buying Sloan a car identical in make and colour to hers so that he could visit her at her house on the property at night and park out the front without raising any suspicion."

"She and Sloan are now neighbours, very cosy."

Terry shook his head.

"We did not interview Margie Terry because we believe since the incident with Dave Rogerson she would have dug in with Garret and to talk to her would have given the game away to Garret."

Terry nodded.

"Very wise Michael and Jeffrey…very wise."

"Okay the next one."

"Capricia Rossi."

"I have already discussed her with you Terry but have included a copy again of her admissions in the folder, in particular for you to read Bill. It is a terrible story of manipulation and deception. He took sexual advantage of this mother of two's emotional vulnerabilities that he first learned about on an altar call and then subsequently explored in more detail with her as her cell group leader."

"I believe when he set up the cell groups he deliberately chose her for his group, because knowing about her past he knew her emotional history, needs and susceptibilities."

Terry shook his head sideways.

"It's interesting you say that Michael, I've seen that before. Sometimes with predators like this the altar calls become their hunting grounds. Either the altar calls or counselling sessions."

"Next we have Colleen Jones."

"Colleen Jones is the manager of the Emmanuel Christian Bookshop in Springfield."

"She had a sexual relationship with Sloan over a period of time, at least two years perhaps more. The liaisons occurred when she and her husband provided accommodation to Sloan during his crusade visits to Springfield. Most times when he stayed at their house Bettina was not with him which gave him free rein."

"The activity between them was the whole sexual smorgasbord and occurred when Colleen's husband was at work."

"We believe her husband may have been suspicious of her and Sloan which we think destroyed any hope of him having a salvation experience when he occasionally attended a church service."

"He is known and talked about by most as the one who never goes forward on an altar call…perhaps we now know why."

"Details…dates…times…are included in her signed statement."

"According to Colleen shortly after Sloan and Bettina moved permanently to Springfield she approached him in his office to pressure him for more out of the relationship. In some demonically deceived and crazed way I think she thought Sloan loved her, that she loved him, and that eventually he would leave Bettina and live happily ever after with her."

"Well you're actually right Michael," commented Terry, "I've seen this before and I'm sure Bill has."

"Once the Spirit of Lust gets a hold on someone they will not only convince themselves of things that no sane rational mind would but they also start doing things that no sane rational person would."

"They believe they have this God given unbreakable bond with the person."

"These spiritual forces are powerful. And once they open themselves up to one of them, others will also flood in. They hunt in packs."

"I'd say Colleen has opened herself up to a Spirit of Lust, then a Spirit of Adultery has come in, then a Spirit of Deception and finally a Spirit of Control where she actually believes she can dictate to Sloan the terms of her relationship with him."

"You agree Bill?"

"Yes…you're spot on Terry…what started out as a lustful obsession has turned into a lustful possession…she's possessed alright."

"Sorry Michael…you were saying."

"When Colleen put pressure on Sloan in his office his reply was that since he now lived in town, if she wanted him to continue the relationship then she would have to be more discreet than she was being, and certainly not put any pressure on him for anything more than casual sex. Otherwise it would be over."

"He's a real charmer," commented Bill.

"He was still prepared to do it right under Bettina's nose but only if Colleen didn't pop into the office to see him as much or pressure him for more out of the relationship."

"That's right Bill."

"Okay…Margie…Capricia…and Colleen…that's it from me."

Michael turned to Jeffrey.

"Jeffrey I might get you to give a brief overview of Sloan's relationship with Francis thanks, since you interviewed her."

"Sure Michael…sure."

Jeffrey looked at his folder notes and paused for a moment and took a deep breath.

"Bit different from your day job just working on the old building site Jeffrey?"

"It is Bill…it certainly is."

"Go ahead brother."

"Okay Sloan stays overnight in Gratton at the Morrison's house when he is in town. The family has been long time supporters of Sloan and recently moved to Springfield. Francis has been alone in the house completing her medical studies these last twelve months."

"She readily admitted her sexual liaisons with Sloan and seems to hate him for conning her. She was all too ready to give him up. The first time they had sexual relations it happened this way. He certainly has some different lines this bloke."

"They were both seated on the couch after dinner watching television and Garret had suggested they both hop into their pyjamas to get comfortable."

"Whilst seated on the lounge beside her, both in their pyjamas, Sloan started to talk about the importance of her as a doctor understanding sexual things, you know, how the male female bodies work. He indicated to her that he felt she was a little naïve in those matters."

Jeffrey shook his head and stopped talking for a moment.

"I mean can you believe this bloke?"

"Anyway Sloan then decided he would teach her all about these sexual matters in which she was naïve. Sloan decides that he will teach Francis all about the ancient art of mutual masturbation and oral sex. Practical experiments followed after the theory had been successfully completed."

Bill grinned at Jeffrey's choice of phraseology.

"Guys I won't go into any more detail, it is all in her admissions including explicit comments about the state of Sloan's appendage at the time. The sex education course continued whenever the opportunity arose."

"And oh yes…here's the sick part…Sloan would always lead them both in a prayer of repentance after he ejaculated for forgiveness for their lustful behaviour."

"Isn't he a gem?"

"Francis also recalled the time when they were at the property for a working bee that Sloan had taken her into his office in the new admin block, shut the door and closed the blinds."

"He had then proceeded to discuss with her, whilst fondling her breasts, the fact that she needed to wear a better fitting bra size, as she was drawing attention to herself with her large breasts which tended to move about too much in the current bra size she was wearing…so he said."

"Did I mention that he was fondling her breasts as he was giving her this lecture on underwear etiquette?"

Bill grinned.

"I mean can you believe this guy?" Jeff continued.

"Unfortunately I can believe it…Sloan's a liar and a predator."

"But you know what our greatest challenge will be," continued Terry, "not getting rid of him, that is a foregone conclusion. Our problem will be in convincing others the rightness of our actions whilst not being able to give them names and dates. Because a lot of people won't admit that Sloan is capable of this. It won't suit their agenda."

"But look, well done men…I presume that's all there is…and by the way it's well and truly enough."

"There is one more thing Terry that Jeff and I are wondering about. It's whether or not Sloan might be grooming Archie or even if it's possible something has already happened."

"Goodness no," replied Terry with a hint of exasperation in his voice, "but I guess you knew when we spoke the other day Michael that I was concerned about this South Africa trip."

"I did Terry…and other things have happened with him telling her that she won't marry because she has been selected to be a part of the pure Bride of Christ."

"A lot of heretical nonsense but we believe he may have sucked her in."

"I know that must be very difficult for you Michael, considering how close you and her are," commented Bill.

"Yes it is Bill…but we've got to do what we've got to do."

"Anyway Jeff is going to have a talk to her at the time of Garret's exit to see if anything has been going on and whether she needs some counsel of sort. But there is no intention to get any written admission."

"She has done a wonderful job with the children at the school. I would hate to see that ruined which it would be if the parents got any wind of a one off lapse in moral judgment."

"Are you comfortable with that Terry?"

"I am Michael…I am…you're a good man Michael Winton."

"Thanks Terry."

"I think we've got enough with all this to act anyway Terry…your thoughts?"

"Yes we have Michael…more than enough."

"I might just spend a few moments in finishing our meeting to give you and Jeffrey a heads up on how this will play out. Bill knows this… he's seen it before."

"No problem."

Terry stood up, breathed in and breathed out.

"Let's stretch our legs for a moment first eh?"

It was a quiet trip back to Springfield that afternoon for Michael and Jeffrey. Each of them were silently ruminating on what Terry and Bill had explained with regards to how the whole situation at the commune would play out and the potential fall out from it. It was obvious that both of them, Terry and Bill, had been through similar situations in their individual church lifetimes.

Terry had expressed it this way.

"I think the first thing we need to be sure of in our minds, and we are, is that God is on our side. God is always on the side of righteousness and opposed to unrighteousness. We as pastors have been called to live righteous lives."

"The other scripture that keeps coming to me is that God has called us to peace not unrest, and I know that is a firm belief of yours Michael, we have discussed it before."

"We also need to be firm in our hearts and minds that the behaviour of Garret Sloan to both these aspects of a pastor's calling indicates a total unwillingness to abide by these two principles that God has called us to live our lives by."

"To seek to live righteous lives and to pursue peace."

"His life in terms of attitudes and actions is saturated with unrighteous behaviour which has in the past, and is in the present, bringing unrest and a lack of peace into the lives of people he was called to keep safe and to protect as a shepherd would his sheep."

"He is not a shepherd…he is a wolf…a wolf in shepherd's clothes."

"Not only that, I see him confirmed by his actions to be a sexual predator and a spiritual sociopath having no regard for the hurt he is causing people. Rather he is only focussed in his mind on getting his sexual desires fulfilled and in doing so enabling his agenda for power and total control over others to come to pass."

"Okay how will this roll out?"

"Bill and I will take the matter to the General Superintendant of the AOG and advise him of our intentions to dismiss Garret Sloan, not only from his role in your church in Springfield Michael, but from any ministry participation in any other churches under the Assembly of God auspices."

"Will this stop him, no it won't. He will go to ground for a little while and eventually surface again somewhere. They always do if they don't truly repent. The evil stays in their hearts. But our role as shepherds of our own flock is to get this wolf out of our own paddock. That's all we can do."

"The practicalities of how it will happen are these."

"We will do it in a surgical manner. That is the only way to cut out a cancer. It will be swift and decisive giving him no room to wriggle. I will give Michael a ring the night before we are going to act for a rebrief. We will do it in the morning to ensure Sloan is in his office. Michael tells me he is mostly in his office up to 11 a.m. each day."

"Apparently it gets too hot after that," Terry commented, looking across at Jeffrey and smiling.

"I understand that next weekend you guys are having a weekend men's retreat at the Anglican conference centre in Lighthouse Bay with Pastor Richard Amsterdam from Sydney as your guest speaker. At this stage we are looking at dismissing Sloan today week on that

Friday morning prior to your weekend men's camp."

"Richard is a good man and a friend of mine. I will contact him and get him to arrive a day early to be part of the process on the Friday morning."

"Four of us, which is myself, Bill, Richard and a senior minister from the AOG will arrive at Garret's office at around 9 a.m…totally unannounced. We will proceed directly to his office, close the door, interview him, confront him with the evidence, and then subsequently dismiss him."

"There will naturally be some disquiet as to what is going on amongst whatever staff are in the office at the time. I will leave it to you Michael and Jeffrey to settle that through…I do not expect you both to be in Garret's office when we dismiss him…that's our job."

"Remember for Bettina it will be an emotional time."

"She will probably sense when the four men in suits arrive that it is not a courtesy visit…she's been there before…and whilst I feel slightly sorry for her, I also think she has partially contributed to this by continuing to enable her husband in his wrongdoing."

"We will discuss with Garret the financial terms of his dismissal with regards to the church purchasing his house and he will be given four days to vacate. That may seem harsh but it has to be that way. We have got to keep him away from his victims."

"When I say victims I am not referring to Margie Morrison or Colleen Jones…they in fact are both complicit in his actions and we will be telling them that at a chosen time."

"I'm talking about people like Prissie and Francis and maybe even Archie, plus the others we are not aware of."

"I'm suggesting you go ahead with the men's camp over the weekend. I will suggest to Richard that he still attend and try to settle the dissenters down during the men's time together."

"After our interview with Sloan is finished we will leave."

"As I said it will be surgical."

"Bill and I will then head down to Gratton to inform Pastor Gary Nolan of what has occurred. We will return to Springfield late afternoon."

"Michael and Jeffrey as soon as we go will you please phone all your cell group leaders. Advise them to contact all their group members to let them know that there will be a meeting for all at 7 p.m. down at the auditorium that night and to tell each member it's about some serious developments in the church in Springfield, and that it's important they all attend. That's all they need to know at that stage."

"Of course the meeting is open to all church members not just the cell groups, let that be known. I say 7 p.m. because it gives those at work some time to get home. We want as many to attend as possible."

"Michael you, myself, Bill and Richard Amsterdam will be on the platform. You can just introduce the meeting as being called because of serious developments in the commune that they need to be advised of and I will do the rest. It won't take long…people tend to go into a state of shock and wander off home after this type of meeting."

"I will naturally not be naming names as to who was involved apart from Sloan, but will certainly give the reasons for his dismissal being that of multiple incidents of sexual impropriety and gross misconduct."

"Michael and Jeffrey that's all in terms of the dismissal's practical out-working. I am thinking that after the meeting, before Bill and I drive back, that both you and Jeffrey and Bill and I get together somewhere for a quiet coffee and discuss what we each see as the congregation's immediate reaction and the potential fall out."

"We can expect fallout and there will be fallout. It's not a matter of whether there will be fallout it's just a matter of how much."

"To some people this type of thing can be likened to a child finding out their parents are separating…it can be emotionally tearing."

"Some will be thinking and saying that he should be given a second chance, that it was too harsh. Unfortunately they do not know his history in the fact that he was given a second chance and now it's three strikes and you're out. He's a non repentant serial offender."

"That is all confidential and we can't share that with them."

"If there is any person that the loyal supporters of Sloan will go gunning for of course it will be Michael, as he is the one who remains here after Bill and I go home. Michael you and I have already discussed this, the repercussions, but let's revisit it after the people are informed and have headed home on the night, so that we are all on the same expectation page."

"I suggest we four find a quiet place after the meeting finishes on the night for a coffee, some feedback and a regrouping."

"I know just the place," replied Jeffrey, "just around the corner."

Terry smiled, "yes of course…Morty's."

"A man of the people…now there's a man who will probably give us some good feedback…some really good feedback."

"Well that's about it …any questions…are we all comfortable with that?"

"Good."

⸎

Michael turned to Jeffrey in the car.

"I liked your comment at the end when you asked Terry had he spent some time in the army and Terry had laughed and said no."

"But he knew what you meant."

"Well he sounded like a special forces commander in a movie giving his troops battle instructions," replied Jeffrey.

"He did."

"But I also liked Terry's comments after he laughed."

Michael imitated Terry's precise and business like way of speaking.

"Well it is a warfare Jeffrey…it's a spiritual warfare in the heavens being played out here on earth."

"Yes…that was good."

"And what about you Pastor…yeah…nice one."

"What?"

"I wonder how Terry knew that Sloan's office got hot in the afternoon hey."

"I might have told him about your little plan."

"I know you did, that's why he looked at me and smiled."

"Actually he loved the story when I told him, he laughed out loud, and I think he said good on him."

"Well we're almost home Jeffrey…thanks for your support today…we've got a big week ahead of us…but what is…is."

"We certainly have…looking forward to it," yawned Jeffrey.

66 *"But then she would go into sad faced kind of moments when she talked about the things you both would never get to do together. She said nothing can bring back the hour of splendor in the grass of glory in the flower, and something about I guess we'll never see those Black Hills of Dakota together."*

Janet Gibbons

Epilogue
The Atonement

NINETEEN

T horpey was scowling in disbelief. When contacted about the 7 p.m. meeting at Evelyn Auditorium he had been busily engaged as a sales rep for agricultural equipment talking to a client in the township of Gratton some two hours drive from Springfield. He had driven fast and entered the building at 7.05 p.m. to find standing room only at the back of the auditorium and to be greeted by the Reverend Terry Channing's introductory words.

"God loves you and wants what is best for you, and sometimes you will find that it differs from what you think is best for you. But God alone knows what is best for you and what is part of his plan."

"Have you spoken to her since she's been off work Michael?"

"No I haven't Janny."

"I had coffee with her last Saturday at The Plaka. I've been trying to keep in touch you know," commented Janet.

"That's nice."

"I mean I know she wanted the two months off to spend time alone to clear her head…but I know that for us girls sometimes when we're a little mixed up some girl time over coffee can be helpful."

"Hey…I agree Janny…I'm pleased you were able to spend some time with her. I've heard that others have tried to contact her, but well she hasn't taken or returned their calls."

"Except for Kell of course…she's been doing her best to help her through."

"They are good mates Michael aren't they?"

"They're the best of mates."

Jeffrey was thinking out loud.

"It's funny isn't it that it is only after it all blows up that you start to remember things."

"A couple of the girls in my group told me some time ago that when they were on telephone counselling duty at night Sloan would occasionally come into the room, lean over the back of them and start giving them a neck massage. He would say that it's important to come across as relaxed and calm when counselling someone."

"That sounds like him Jeffrey…it was the way he groomed people for what he really wanted…get them used to him touching them…Prissie said that," continued Michael, "the old neck massage."

"Anyway Jeffrey thank you for all the wise counsel you gave Archie during all that happened."

"Hey you're welcome brother…I hope I helped her sort things out in her mind a little."

"I felt sorry for her…she just got caught up in the sticky web of that, what does Morty call him, that rock spider Sloan."

"Hey Michael…this is such a beautiful place and haven't we had such wonderful times here?"

"I'm going to miss all of this."

"Me too dear sister we have had some really wonderful times."

Janny was standing on the balcony of Michael's apartment and it was two months to the day since the dismissal.

"I keep thinking of the Day of Atonement Michael."

"You mean as in us remembering the sacrifice of Christ on the cross?"

"Yes."

"In what way?"

"Well you know Michael when Christ was on the cross when Jesus uttered his final words, it is finished."

"Well this whole thing with the commune now for us guys it's like a day of atonement."

"I mean…we are acknowledging it is finished."

"Well in a way Janny…but in another way it is just a new beginning."

"What do you mean Michael?"

"Well when Jesus said it is finished he wasn't saying I am finished or talking about the fact that he was about to physically die. The Greek for the phrase it is finished is tetelestai, or the verb is teleo, which means to accomplish."

"He was actually saying I have completed the course, completed a particular course of action in a significant event orchestrated by my father."

"When Jesus said it is finished he didn't say I am finished. That would imply that he died defeated and exhausted which he didn't. He cried out 'tetelestai', meaning I successfully completed the work I came to do."

"He was leaving but leaving the church in good hands."

"He was about to hand control over to the Comforter, the Holy Spirit."

"You could say his death had completed the jigsaw in a particular puzzle in Lila…the Divine Playground."

"You know you yourself would use that Greek word, if you were Greek of course, when you reached the peak of Mt. Everest, or turned in the final copy of your dissertation. You'd raise your hands into the air and shout out," Michael lifted his arms, "tetelestai."

"Similar to when I made the final payment on our car," interjected Jeffrey.

Janet laughed.

"But yes Jeffrey…you are right…when you make the final payment on your car."

"The Greek word tetelestai really means that I did exactly what I set out to do…I have accomplished exactly what I set out to accomplish. And in Jesus' case it was to fulfill God's will…to fulfill that of which the prophets had spoken…the cross…the final sacrifice."

"But it wasn't the end of everything…it was the beginning of a whole new world…the ushering in of Pentecost…the arrival of the Holy Spirit…the birth of the church."

"So when you reach the top of Everest it's not the end of everything, it's not time to lay down and die, but time to get up and go, as the beautiful Ian Robinson said. Time to get started again and go back to base camp, time to get on with life. Old things have passed away but all things have become as new."

"Or using what you said Jeffrey about the final car payment."

"When you make your final car payment you don't just park your car in the garage and leave it there. It's not the end of your driving career. You shout tetelestai, and yell out I own you now you little sucker, let's go for a long ride."

"Guys over what, around four years, we accomplished exactly what we set out to do…we stayed the course…that's cause for celebration."

"Jesus stayed the course…he played his part in Lila…that's the true message of the cross."

Janet felt relieved, laughed and raised her wine glass.

"Yes we did, didn't we…we accomplished all we set out to do."

"Okay…a toast with my two favourite people in the whole world…to new beginnings…tetelestai."

"It's been one," Jeffrey paused, "whoops I almost said one hell of a ride, I mean one heaven of a ride."

Michael continued.

"And Janny don't be sad…the work is not finished…the school is not finished…only our involvement in it is finished."

"You're right Michael. I still occasionally get sad though when I think about some things, but I'm happy at other times with the memory of what a wonderful season it was in our lives."

"Hey," she continued obviously trying to talk her sense of sadness through, "didn't you just love our folk song sing-alongs here Michael when Jeffrey would always sing out of tune."

Jeffrey's face lit up in disagreement.

"I did not…I'll have you know I have an incredible sense of musical tone and timing."

"Yeah…like dream on babe," replied Janet.

"You're good at most things including the guitar my beloved, but singing in tune is not one of your best attributes. Remember that wedding reception at the auditorium and we were the third singing duo to get up and perform?"

"Yes…and might I say we smashed it," said Jeffrey tongue in cheek.

"And do you remember how you introduced our singing act Jeffrey?"

Jeff paused and grinned.

"No…not really I don't."

"You said, ladies and gentlemen and children, I hope you've enjoyed the singing acts so far and now it's time for Janny and I to perform the first comedy act of the night."

Michael threw his head back and laughed, "yes I remember that."

"Then I rest my case," replied Janet.

"So when are you heading back Michael…Saturday or Sunday?" queried Jeffrey.

"Well I did say to Terry that I would stay for at least two months to ensure the work had settled. The two months finish this Saturday so I'll give Terry a ring tomorrow and make sure things are on track for my replacement."

"You've resigned from your job…what are you going to do?"

"I'll take a break for a while and then get back into the business world again I guess. One day I might just buy a kombi van, let loose the latent hippie in me, and go on the road. Perhaps do some writing."

"You'd make a good writer Michael," commented Janet, "you have a way with words and explaining things."

"Thanks."

Jeff's tone of voice went a little sombre.

"So who's replacing you in the work here Michael?"

"Apparently it's a pastor who has been looking after the Christian City Church outreach in Fiji. He was originally a pastor at Terry's church until he was sent out to run their outreach work in Suva. But Terry and Bill will continue to support the preaching schedule down here until the new pastor arrives."

"Hey…by the way guys. I had a visit from Jenny Purcell this morning. She gave me a ring on Tuesday and asked if it was okay if she paid a visit on Thursday morning. She found out from the office that I was at home packing. She said she had something for me to take on my future journeys."

Janny smiled.

"That was nice of her Michael wanting to say goodbye personally and give you a gift."

"She's a beautiful person and I'm pleased that George turned out to be one of the good guys and supported you both."

"As a matter of fact I spoke to Jenny myself after it all happened and I think she was feeling a bit disappointed that those involved in this were all members of the Sisterhood, you know the Women's Guild. Obviously George shared with her the names of the women involved."

"She described it as the secrets in the sisterhood that she wished she had picked up on with her Gift of Discernment."

"Hey not true she's not a mind reader," Michael replied, "when you see her tell her not to sell herself short. It was her Gift of Discernment operating with her secret pal Prissie that gave us our first confirmation of what was going on."

"You're right Michael, I'll tell her that."

"Yeah…she did well…she really does take practicing the Gifts of the Spirit seriously doesn't she," commented Jeff.

"So anyway Michael speaking of gifts, what gift did she give you this morning?"

"Well Jeffrey it actually wasn't a gift type gift, it was a gift of a prophetic word."

"Really Michael…what did she say?"

"She said that she received this prophetic word for me as she was praying for the work…so she typed it up…and wanted to bring it over and read it to me."

"Oh isn't she a beautiful soul…can we see it Michael?" gasped Janny.

"Sure I'll get it for you."

Michael went inside returned with a folded piece of paper and handed it to Janet.

She opened it and proceeded to read it out loud.

"Know that I have placed deep within you, a deep anointing, a bountiful supply of love which will radiate from your very centre, to which people will be drawn. Those who are lost and those who are hurting, and those who are bleeding inside will be drawn to you because they will see the love of Christ emanating from you. Know that it will be a never ending supply and that people will be fed from it. Know that your life will radiate richness and my son I say to you today that I have seen the cost in your life and in your faithfulness, and I say to all people I am well pleased with my servant."

"Michael that's just beautiful, isn't it Jeffrey?"

"It is."

Janet folded the piece of paper and handed it back to Michael.

Her voice softened.

"So Michael you finish packing tomorrow and go on Sunday and Archie hopefully comes back to the school on Monday?"

"Yes Janny…interesting timing…not planned that way…but yes that's what it is."

"So you said you haven't spoken to her since the dismissal of Sloan?"

"No I haven't Jeffrey."

"She went on two months leave straight away."

"I guess she needed time to clear her head Michael…you know…her embarrassment with what went on."

"I'm sure she did Janny."

"You know she is grateful to you for keeping her name out of everything that happened. I mean she's hurting, and desperately sorry, but she told me over coffee last Saturday that you kept your promise to her."

"Did I…what promise did she mean?"

"She said that when you both were at the drive in watching that movie Butch Cassidy and The Sundance Kid, and in the part where they were in a shoot out trying to keep someone safe from the bad guys, that you had kissed her on the forehead and hugged her and promised her that you would always keep her safe."

"She remembered that did she?"

"Yes she did."

"Well I suppose I kept her safe from publicity or parental outrage but I didn't keep her safe from Sloan."

"Don't say that Michael. You did all you could do, she made her own choices."

"I think she has spent the last two months going over in her head all the happy times you both had. She talked a lot about what you both had shared together, particularly the fun and the laughter. But then she would go into sad faced kind of moments when she talked about the things you both would never get to do."

"Like she said nothing can bring back the hour of splendour in the grass of glory in the flower, and something about I guess we'll never see those Black Hills of Dakota together."

"I didn't know what she meant…and I didn't ask her…I didn't want to pry…I just wanted to let her pour her heart out."

"She said those things did she Janny?"

"Yes she did Michael."

"She really loves you, you know…it's just sad that that mongrel Sloan, and I use the word lightly, so sad that Sloan messed with her mind with all he did and said."

Janny continued.

"Between Sloan messing with her mind saying she will never get married and her Greek mum messing with her mind saying she will get married but only to a Greek boy…I mean they both screwed her up in a sense."

"The deck was stacked against you two from the start."

"Yes…messing with people's minds was one of Sloan's greatest talents and probably still is," commented Jeffrey, "he did that with Danny too after Danny shared his dream with him."

"If only they knew Michael…if only everyone knew the real truth of what a terrible piece of depraved work he was," sighed Janny.

"I'm still angry at him Michael…well righteously angry as you say it."

"I know Janny but as Terry said there were things that everyone should have been told but we weren't able to tell them. You know his history, and the full extent of what he did in the city over the years as well as down here."

"Has Terry heard what Sloan is up to Michael…it's been two months… has he resurfaced anywhere?" queried Jeffrey.

"Funny you should ask that, when I phoned Terry the other day he was saying that he was in the middle of dictating a type of cease and desist letter to Sloan."

"How so?"

"Well according to Terry there are a lot of breakaway charismatic groups springing up in suburbs all headed up by a lot of wannabe pastors. Anyway there is one that has just sprung up in a suburb on the outskirts of the city with a name, I don't know, something like The Lighthouse."

"Terry said he was checking the church ads and it caught his attention because Sloan used to preach that our Springfield church was a lighthouse to the country. He said he nearly fell out of his chair when he read the name of the guest speaker…it said guest speaker Dr Garret Sloan Global Apostle."

"You're kidding."

"Nope…he's at it again."

"He's apparently been sitting on an honorary doctorate that he received from some non-descript university in the States when he was over there. Terry said it's easy to get one if you make a small donation."

"So obviously Sloan thinks a new title will enhance his reputation," questioned Jeffrey.

Jeff laughed, "what is he…I wonder…perhaps a doctor of dirty tricks."

Michael continued.

"So apparently Terry was getting a cease and desist letter to Sloan with a copy to the pastor of this new church who has obviously given him some sort of refuge. Terry said he was getting the letter typed up and sent but didn't hold out any hope that Sloan would take any notice. He said he had already spoken on the phone to the pastor concerned and that he was just as arrogant as Sloan."

Jeff took a sip of his wine.

"Speaking of Sloan and his cohorts, Michael I was speaking to Morty yesterday and he said that Thorpey had told him he was taking a work transfer next month."

"That's good news…he has been creating a constant undercurrent these last two months. Apart from that he just sits up the back when I am preaching and just glares at me. You can see the hate in his eyes. He's got real problems."

"Well Pastor you did take away his spiritual meal ticket."

"No doubt Jeffrey he will end up supporting Sloan in his new endeavours. You are right though, Sloan is his spiritual meal ticket."

"So enough about Sloan and Thorpey…what about you guys…and has Danny boy and Zelda worked out what they are going to do?"

"Well I spoke to dad the other night, he hasn't been well and wants me to come home and get reinvolved in the family construction business, so that's our intention. If we can sell our place in the next six months we will head back around Christmas. Janny's dad has offered to finance her into her own veterinary clinic so that will be great."

"So yes at the latest we leave around Christmas, at the earliest it will be as soon as our house sells. Patty is hard at it looking for a buyer and is confident he will get one sooner rather than later."

"Yes," replied Michael, "you know I was a bit suspicious about Patty's relationship with Unwin for a while, but he turned out to be one of the good guys."

"And Danny and Zelda?" Michael continued.

"They are looking at heading off when we do and will probably stop over for a little while with us on their way home."

"They're all cool with it?"

"I think they're both looking forward to getting on the move again… that gypsy wanderlust."

Janet had been standing deep in thought during the previous five minutes of Michael and Jeffrey's conversation, staring out to sea. Jeffrey finished his wine and looked at his watch.

"Well it's past eight Janny, work day tomorrow, we'd better go…anyway we'll see you before you go Michael…you're calling in on the way past on Sunday aren't you?"

"Yes I am Jeffrey…it will be around lunchtime."

"Okay we'll have the last supper for lunch."

Michael was grinning from Jeff's comments about the last supper as Janny walked over to him. He stood up to say goodbye and she took his two hands in hers. She looked sad.

"Michael you know how I was saying before that Archie really loves you."

"Sure."

"You know she's thinking that you probably hate her?"

"I guess so…I suppose that's natural for her to be thinking that."

"I was just standing there thinking about all the wonderful things the group used to talk about in our times together here."

"And I remembered one night we got into this big discussion on love…do you remember?"

"I do."

"And you said well you can blame Archie for the confusion because it's all about the Greek language."

"And you and Jeffrey started to talk about the three different kinds of love mentioned in the Bible coming out of three different Greek words...funny how everything seems to be coming back to Greek things tonight."

"Must be a sign."

"Anyway the Greek words you both used were agape for God's love, phileo for brotherly or sisterly love, and eros for erotic love."

"You were taking notes Janny...well done," interjected Jeff.

"No Jeffrey...I'm serious."

"Well after you and Jeffrey debated about that I remember you quoted one of those quotes you had written a long while ago; you said, and it just came to me again as I was looking at the ocean."

"I hope I get it right."

"You said, our lives are fashioned by those who have loved us or those who have refused to love us."

"Did I get it right?"

"Yes you did...formed and fashioned actually."

"Okay...our lives are formed and fashioned by those who have loved us or by those who have refused to love us."

"Michael I guess what I'm talking about is that the subject of love has come up a lot tonight...you know, me telling you that Archie really loves you...Jenny's prophetic word about love that she gave you."

"Archie has got her whole life ahead of her when she comes back to the school on Monday. You know the forming and fashioning of her life ahead as you say."

"Sure."

"Michael I know this is a big ask but I'm asking it anyway."

Janny's eyes started to moisten.

"Archie needs to know that you love her and don't hate her."

"And she needs to know before you go."

"I know it won't change the fact that you are going but I really feel that she needs to know."

"Remember Jenny in her prophecy for you said that you have this bountiful supply of love deep within you. Let Archie know that some of it is for her Michael."

"Will you tell her?"

Janny was starting to well up with emotion in her voice as she continued and Michael knew that what she was asking was coming not from her mind but from a place deep down in her heart out of her concern about Archie.

"I mean you do love her don't you?"

"Yes I guess I do."

"Then will you tell her…tell her…so that when Monday arrives, the first day of the rest of her life, she will walk back into the classroom knowing that you love her and the rest of her life as a teacher or whatever road it takes will be formed and fashioned out of that knowledge… the knowledge that you love her."

"Will you do it?"

Michael looked into Janny's eyes now overflowing with tears.

"I will Janny…I will."

Michael sipped the last of his wine, got up from the squatter's chair and walked inside. He glanced at the wall clock. It was almost 9 p.m. Not too late for a phone call he said out loud as he reached for the phone and dialled the number.

"Hey…it's me…you probably know I am leaving on Sunday."

"I was wondering if you would like to come round on Saturday night, you know, for a long last look at the view from the balcony with me."

"I will throw in a few extras over and above the view."

"I have a nice bottle of red and a great collection of records that you can have a good browse through."

"And I will also throw in a huge list of conversational topics."

"You'd like that."

"Great."

"So I'll see you around 6."

"Sounds good."

"The boats will be chugging up the river around then."

"Okay…cool…see you then."

November 2014.

"A little bit chilly but cosy," Michael uttered out loud as he strolled from the lounge room of his rustic cabin out onto the small verandah that surrounded it on all sides, "chilly but gloriously perfect."

He was staying in this lodge for three nights, a simple log cabin with a fireplace to keep the inside warm, tucked away in a small tree lined grove in the quaint township of Hill City in the state of South Dakota. It was a cabin for two but he was by himself. It was his second visit to this place in the last thirty years. He just wanted to revisit it one more time. He knew it would be his last.

As he stepped out onto the porch that late afternoon the snow was gently falling, beautiful soft fluffy flakes of white brushing past and occasionally touching his face as if giving it a passing kiss while they floated silently to the ground.

Hill City or as it was known in the tourist brochures, the city in the heart of the hills, was the most central and picturesque part of Dakota. It had been a busy few days for Michael with his journey to Deadwood City to the Gold Nugget Saloon, a visit to the gravesites of Wild Bill Hickok and Annie Oakley, a viewing of the sculptures of past presidents at Mt. Rushmore, and a trip to the magnificent mountain sculpture at the Chief Crazy Horse memorial.

Michael glanced upwards at the mountains, line after line of pine-capped hills stretching endlessly to the north and to the south. Rows and rows of tall, dark green pine trees almost black in colour, reaching majestically towards the heavens as if kissing the skies above them. He understood now why the song was titled The Black Hills of Dakota. He stood quietly in the moment reflecting on life.

He thought about the concept of Lila. Was it the fact that God chose people for particular interventions based on their life experience or perhaps did God groom their life experience for involvement in particular interventions in the future. He wasn't sure, but was confident it was one or the other.

He thought about his own life situation in relation to the events that had passed. There was a correlation. He had spent his early years locked into a goodness versus evil understanding of life mostly through movies and books. His experience with the Billy Graham crusade had given him an understanding of the evangelical part of religion and the power over people it gave its proponents.

His childhood involvement in the beautiful theatres of his day had given him a love for these buildings and the stories they told and the stories they kept to themselves. Was it just a coincidence that he had grown up loving the finery of the original picture theatres and then in Springfield he had been involved in restoring one back to its former glory. Or was it really all just part of a game in Lila.

"What if," he thought, "what if life is all about God grooming one's life direction for the specific games in Lila that lie ahead, and what if God chooses your involvement in a particular game in Lila based on your life's grooming."

He paused, rested his arms on the rail along the verandah, thought about the events now forty years past, and wished that he had been able to fulfill her desire, that they together would one day witness this beauty. He remembered her words about the Doris Day song on the night and his reply.

"She makes it sound sooo romantic when she calls it the beautiful

Indian country that is calling her back home. Perhaps we could go there together one day Michael, wouldn't that be great?"

"It would Archie…it would."

Michael wished that she could have been with him now, staring up at what he was seeing, looking up into the hills and seeing the beauty of what the black hills of Dakota meant to so many of the first people of America, the Indians, and also to the first white settlers.

He had settled in his mind long ago the initial doubt he had as to whether or not he had kept Archie safe even though he had carried it with him for the first four years after he had left the commune. For four years he felt in his heart that he had failed her in not keeping her protected from the evil that was around her.

But the slight sense of guilt about not keeping her safe that accompanied him for those years had quickly dissipated in 1978, four years after the dismissal, when the world came to know a little more about the insidious nature of doomsday cults.

It was when a notorious event now commonly known as Jonestown occurred, which saw 918 people, American residents of a religious commune known as the People's Temple Agricultural Project in north-western Guyana, commit mass suicide by ingesting cyanide laced cordial under the instruction from the cult's charismatic leader, the Reverend Jim Jones.

At one stage during his rise to notoriety Jim Jones had shared the church pulpit with a Reverend William M. Branham a close associate of the Reverend Oliver Robards, Sloan's hero. It was at this time Jones realized that faith healing services were a great vehicle for attracting people and their money and concluded that, with the financial resources obtained from the healing meetings he could quickly accomplish his ideological and social goals. Shortly after this he formed his own church, which he named the Peoples Temple Christian Church Full Gospel.

The year of the mass suicide of the 918 members of the People's Temple church was just six years after the launch of Discipleship teaching into the Charismatic churches. One outspoken church historian would years later in reflection come to describe those churches that embraced this discipleship teaching as walking in the future footsteps of Jonestown, only as yet without the kool-aid cordial.

Michael knew that whilst he may not have kept her safe from Sloan himself, he had certainly kept her safe from the ongoing control filled agenda of Sloan, and a potential Jim Jones incident in the making.

He stood there in the moment as the snowflakes fluttered past thinking of the lives that had gone before.

Rose Winton, William Winton, Maggie May and Michael's oldest brother had all passed and taken with them to the next life whatever the answers were to all the questions about his family that had plagued Michael throughout his life. He never did find out the truth of what had subconsciously disturbed him about his father and his older brother for all those years, but at least with their passing the dreams had stopped.

He thought about those people that had crossed his path along his life journey so far, especially during his time in the commune and how he had kept in touch with only a few. But that was all he needed, for the flow on activities of many had been regularly communicated to him in his correspondence with his dear friend in London, Janet Gibbons, who had kept contact with so many ghosts of that time herself.

As for others. Well Terry Channing and William Hawkesbury had both passed to a higher place leaving a legacy of righteousness, love and good works in their individual Christian lifetimes.

Garret Sloan had continued his merciless intent to prosecute his own relevance. He had established a global apostolic ministry group in the main to foster his newly found self-anointing as an apostle. His last days would see him, his body racked with cancer, standing alone in the hall rooms of impoverished communities overseas preaching to a solitary attendee his philosophy of, "well we've all got things in our life we are dealing with."

The spiritual evil within him had finally imploded into his physical life as it always does to its host once its mission is accomplished. The devil uses its host and then destroys them when the host's usefulness expires: and whilst none who knew the real man behind the mask missed him, he was still lauded in his passing by some of the perpetually deceived.

As for others, well Unwin Nicholls went on the road for a while in a healing prayer ministry role then relocated his medical practice to an up market island tourist location. Mags Morrison separated from the clinic she was involved in with her sister and established a medical centre in a suburb on the outskirts of the capital city, which by coincidence was only 1.5 kilometres from the new suburban residence purchased by Garret Sloan after his dismissal from the church in Springfield. She was obviously still one of Garret's groupies.

Jeff and Janet Gibbons were married in an English village, raised a family of beautiful potential construction workers and veterinary surgeons, and had lots of grandchildren. Janet continued to keep in touch with Michael Winton and kept him updated on Archie's life choices.

Kelly Purcell held fast to her faith, found the man of her dreams and lived happily ever after with him and with her children and grandchildren. Her dad George who turned out to be one of the good guys and in the end supported Michael Winton to the fullest pursued his involvement in spiritual things and lived his life loving God and doing God's will as he understood it. His wife Jenny continued after his passing being a gracious and Godly woman whilst blessing many.

And as for Danny and Zelda, well not much was heard from them after they went back home. Some reports said that they could still be on the road having joined some gypsy travelling show where Zelda would dance for the money they'd throw, still bringing joy to many with her bubbly personality and wit. But no one knew for sure.

Some said that Danny had returned to Australia, but others were not certain. Although some photos taken and published of a man dubbed a mystical Melbourne street iconic identity bared a striking resemblance to the young man that Michael knew and loved as his good friend so many years before.

As for Michael Winton, well, it was getting a bit chilly in the late afternoon as his eyes gazed upward to the Black Hills of Dakota: perhaps time to go inside and warm up with a glass of red. He would be leaving this beautiful Indian country early tomorrow and heading back home to his hippie van.

He stepped back from the rail to go inside, but turned around, took one last look at the Black Hills and remembered for a moment Archie's melodic words as she browsed through his record collection of Jimmy Webb songs on that first night: when she had paused and sang the words, this time we almost made the pieces fit…didn't we boy.

In some ways he wished he had stepped out of the car as he watched Archie on the verandah of the schoolhouse back in September 1994, but in other ways he was glad that he hadn't. The road they had both been travelling on had diverged as it reached the wood and they had both been forced to take different paths.

Michael sank into the softness of the fireside couch, glanced at the snowflakes silently falling past the window and thought of her again. He remembered the simple yellow cotton dress that she had worn on their first date and on their last date, the last night they had together. She looked so beautiful. But he knew in his heart that the cake had melted and he would never have that particular recipe again.

But that was then, and now was now, and in that moment as he stared at the snowflakes gently drifting past his window he continued with his toast and lifted his wine glass.

"To my friends, all those pieces in Lila's puzzle so many years back who co-operated with Goodness and completed the picture I say tetelestai…it is finished…mission accomplished…thank you."